THE LEAN LANDS

The Texas Pan American Series

THE LEAN LANDS

(LAS TIERRAS FLACAS)

BY AGUSTÍN YÁÑEZ

TRANSLATED BY ETHEL BRINTON

Illustrated by Alberto Beltrán

UNIVERSITY OF TEXAS PRESS  AUSTIN & LONDON

The Texas Pan American Series is published with the assistance of a revolving publication fund established by the Pan American Sulphur Company and other friends of Latin America in Texas. Publication of this book was also assisted by a grant from the Rockefeller Foundation through the Latin American translation program of the Association of American University Presses.

Standard Book Number 292–78384–1
Library of Congress Catalog Card No. 68–59338
Copyright © 1968 by Agustín Yáñez
Printed by the University of Texas Printing Division, Austin
Bound by Universal Bookbindery, Inc., San Antonio

TRANSLATOR'S NOTE

The Lean Lands by Agustín Yáñez was first published in Spanish, under the title *Las tierras flacas*, by Editorial Joaquín Mortiz in Mexico City in October, 1962.

The action of the novel takes place in the early 1920's in the barren hill region of Jalisco, beyond the small town of Yahualica, the "pueblo" of *The Edge of the Storm* and the Clamores of this novel. Whereas *The Edge of the Storm* describes life in this small town during the eighteen months that preceded the Revolution of 1910, *The Lean Lands* deals with the struggles of the farmers living on the small isolated farms, so remote as to be beyond the reach even of doctors and priests, where the people rely almost wholly on superstition and their belief in magic.

The author, Agustín Yáñez, is one of the most important writers in Mexico today. Born in Guadalajara, Jalisco, in 1904, he published *Baralipton*, his first successful work, in 1930. Since then he has written about many aspects of Mexican living and thinking; he has deliberately set out to give a complete picture of "la realidad mexicana," the title of a series of lectures given at the Colegio Nacional in 1953. He has written about childhood in *Flor de juegos antiguos*, adolescence in *Archipiélago de mujeres*, the life of the city in *Ojerosa y pintada*, the life of a small provincial town in *Al filo del agua*, and the life of the countryside in *Las tierras flacas* and *La tierra pródiga*.

In the sense that he finds his inspiration in the familiar scenes, sights, and sounds of his province, even in that section of it he has made peculiarly his own, Yahualica and the surrounding countryside, Yáñez is a regional writer; but his concern with people as human beings, and his ability to make them live fully in the moment and milieu he describes, makes his work of special interest to the foreigner. By a curious paradox, his characters are both deeply Mexican and at the same time universal.

But Agustín Yáñez is not only a creative writer of great ability. His introductions to many of the books in the collection Escritores Mexicanos, published by the National University, as well as his analyses of his own creative processes in his lectures at the National University and the Colegio Nacional, reveal him as a penetrating and stimulating literary critic.

As Governor of Jalisco (1953–1959), one of the largest and most important states in Mexico, he proved that an intellectual could also be a man of action and the record of his administration, the number of schools built, and the miles of roads providing necessary links for the development of the country, is impressive. Now, as Minister of Education, he has set in motion a widespread reform of the nation's whole educational system.

The very qualities which make his work such a faithful record of the reality he is expressing—his exact and detailed descriptions of the countryside, his careful reproduction of the regional idiom with all its wealth of imagery, and, in this book particularly, the use of country sayings and regional proverbs—make it difficult to translate. But, since there is so much that can be conveyed, it was felt worthwhile to make the attempt.

Mexico City   ETHEL BRINTON

CONTENTS

Part One — BETANIA:
THE LAND OR THE MACHINE

Good morning and God bless you

"Hail, Mary. Good morning and God bless you. How are you this morning?"

The sun's rays were just touching the peak of La Tapona; soon the red disk would be appearing over the Sierra de Cardos. The valley reflected the rosy radiance of the sky as the last banks of mist rolled away, merging imperceptibly with the smoke rising from the houses. The bellowing of the cattle, echoing loud and long, could be heard above the crowing of the cocks and the barking of the dogs.

There was no reply, so the man dismounted, tied his horse to the wooden gate in the stone wall, and greeted the dogs by name. "Nero, Herod, Caiaphas, don't you know me?" He shouted again, louder, in the direction of the house. "Rómulo, my friend! Doña Merced! How are you this morning?"

A woman appeared, wiping her hands and forearms on her apron. "Hail, Mary most pure."

"Conceived without sin. What are you doing out so early compadre? Be quiet, you fiends!"

"I've been shouting."

"I didn't hear you, I was making tortillas. I came out when I heard the barking. What a row these dratted dogs are making!"

"And Rómolo?"

"He went around to see Epifanio, who's still set on having either the machine or the land, the stubborn old pig! But come in, neighbor, and have breakfast. Rómulo won't be long—he went before it was light this morning."

"Has he done the milking already?"

"What do you think we're milking? The last two cows had to go"—the harsh tone held a note of suffering—"and the yoke of oxen will have to go, too, and the hens, and the dogs, who knows, perhaps even the house." Overcome by a wave of bitterness, the woman added: "But he doesn't want that without the land. The worst of it is, this idea of taking the machine is only a whim, that's all. I've told Rómulo so. They can take me first. But come in, neighbor, do. What's the use of complaining about what God has ordered? I'll warm up a few tortillas for you. Thank God we still have those, and beans, and atole,* and peppers."

"You go ahead into the kitchen, comadre. I'll wait here in the yard for Rómulo. Get in before my tongue lets fly and the string of oaths that's sticking in my throat comes pouring out. I can hardly believe that even that barefaced crook would go so far. I'll wait here. Keep on with your work."

Doña Merced lifted the latch of the gate in the stone wall, saying as she did so: "What good does it do the poor to get angry? They just hit us harder. 'Tread harder on the downtrodden—that's the law of Caiaphas.'"

The sun had risen over the Sierra de Cardos and its light filled the plain. The woman continued, bitterly: "There's nothing left except to bear it. All we can do is hang on to what we love best and let them kill us before we give it up. And then what? Everything will still be the same."

* A thick beverage made with ground corn.

same neighbor, Palemón, was here, when the machine first arrived. They brought it in through this very gate in the wall. They unloaded it here in the patio, Rómulo and Palemón between them and a boy who came with the mule. Teófila squealed when she realized it had come and heard the shout, "Look what we've brought you!" and saw the box on the black mule. Her eyes were wide open and so was her mouth as she watched them lower the contraption gently and carefully to the ground, then lift it up and place it in the room with the brick floor. Teófila showed them where to put it. How she skipped about when the unpacking began, when the machine was uncovered, when the string was taken off the pedals and they moved! It was really hard to believe, enough to make you weep for joy, to see it here all of a sudden among all the old junk, like a miraculous apparition, such an unexpected article, such a costly article, so undreamt of that we felt the same respect and devotion, and even awe, that we'd feel if one of those priceless treasures you find in churches, which some people aren't allowed to look at and only the bishop's allowed to touch, were right there in front of us in this junk-filled house. I doubt if Teófila was ever as happy in her life, either before or after, as she was that day. And giving her that pleasure makes up for so many sorrows. It gives us courage now that we're in danger. When the machine was unpacked and all the cords were untied, Teófila couldn't take her eyes off it. She was eager and impatient, but when she reached out her trembling hand she just stroked the cover very gently, as if it were a newborn baby she was afraid of hurting. "Not the tiniest scratch," she said, turning to Palemón, her smiling eyes and mouth showing her gratitude and paying him for his care on the way. "It's almost a miracle—on these roads for so many days, and here to the end of the earth, as they say." She touched the drawers with the tips of her fingers. Then she amazed us. She lifted the lid, raised the machine and set it in place, fitted the leather belt over the wheels, threaded the needle, moved the pedal, set the machine going, brought it to life. She seemed like a different person. Her movements were deft and sure like those of a priest at the altar. Palemón compared them to those of a doctor while he's operating. We hardly recognized her. For the first time she seemed to be a stranger, very different from the girl we'd watched grow up from babyhood, very different from her father and mother —and all this was a mystery to us, something belonging to another world and hard to understand. But the girl wasn't afraid or nervous, she just brought some scraps of cotton, without saying a word, and drew up a chair, and then started sewing them together with a steady hand. We couldn't have been more surprised if she'd suddenly been changed into a queen with a golden crown. We could only stare at her. She'd stop the machine, then set it going again, slowly or at full speed, keeping the fingers of her left hand on the seam and carefully moving the top wheel with her right hand as her feet worked the pedal. Then she brought us out of our daze by saying, "There, I really did know, didn't I? Now I'll be able to help you, father, by making things for other people, but the first thing I'm going to make is a dress for you, mother." She made us cry, in front of Palemón. "Watch, now, I'm going to oil it." She looked in the drawers, unwrapped some little packages of brand-new tools, went through them, unscrewed something that looked like a lamp, took the stopper out of a bottle, poured out something like oil, screwed the lamp together again, and began squeezing some drops of the liquid into the little holes in the machine. All this took up the whole morning. Out in the kitchen that day the beans got burned and so did the corn. That just made us laugh. The house could have burned down and it would have been worth it. It was the happiest moment Teófila ever had in her life. Imagine seeing her changed into a queen and behaving like a queen, so different from the child we'd known. When I say to myself that the house could have burned down, I'm not including the machine—the machine they want to take away from us now. If they did that, it would be like Teófila dying again and being carried out to her grave.

It was Doña Merced who first went back to the subject, picking up the threads of the conversation where they had left off.

"And I don't want those creatures to say I'm just a cross old woman, that old age and poverty have made me cranky. If you can't make some kind of a bargain, I will, especially since it's only a whim, and the worst of it is, it's not even the old man's, bad as he is, but that ungrateful worthless girl's, even though it was here she learned how to sew, and for nothing, too, seeing her skinflint of a father would never buy her a machine because it was too expensive, he said, and a hard job to bring it here. Now they're trying to get hold of it, saying, 'No man knows who'll reap the reward of his labor. Take that poor fool Rómulo and his old woman, who went to all the trouble of bringing the machine here, and it's the most expensive model, too: they'll have to give it to us to pay off their debts. So then it'll be ours, and as good as new, being so well taken care of. No man knows who'll reap the reward of his labor.' And poor Rómulo and his old woman . . ."

"We may be poor, but we have our self-respect. I pay my debts and up to now no one's been able to throw it in my face that I've ever kept anything belonging to anyone else."

"You certainly don't owe Epifanio anything, and you've put up with his insolence besides, the dirty crook."

"A bargain's a bargain, even when you're so poor you have to agree to a bad one. It doesn't matter how unfair the interest is, I agreed to it and I have to pay it, even if it comes to ten times more than the loan. I can't be the one to break our custom of standing by a bargain, it's something that's handed down from father to son, and it lets all of us here in this region live in peace, trusting each other and helping each other, just like the members of a family, without needing any government or policemen or courts. We're so far away from anywhere, what would happen to us if we broke this custom that's been handed down to us, that all of us were born and brought up in?"

"Yes, but who's broken it," Palemón asked, "except the money-lenders?"

"Ever since I was little," Doña Merced remarked, "I've heard the priests say it's just as big a sin to agree to usury as it is to practice it."

up on horseback. The very day I was born our finest mare gave
birth to a colt, and my grandfather kept it for me. He gave it the
same care he gave me, as if we were twins, or even closer, a single
being. When the time came, my grandfather himself broke him
in. He had a small saddle made, a special one, for his grandson. He
lifted me up on what he called my "namesake," took the reins, and
led me about, first around the yard, then along the roads of the
plain. Finally, on my tenth birthday, he said, "Take the reins.
You're big enough to ride by yourself now." He gave me a riding
whip, a lasso, and spurs, all of them specially made for me. Soon
he didn't have to lift me up. I'd take the horse over to the stone
doorstep and jump on his back. I'd also saddle and unsaddle my
"namesake." And "Namesake" became his name. A fine chestnut,
a handsome horse, and we understood each other as though we
were actually a single being, alike in our thoughts and feelings.
So then I didn't have to ride over the land while perched on the
horse's rump behind my grandfather. When he went to saddle his
horse, his grandson had his saddled already. This pleased my grandfather very much and he never got tired of boasting about it everywhere. We'd ride all morning, and sometimes all day long, taking
food with us, eating anywhere, or sometimes we'd just do without
until we got home, hungry enough to enjoy our evening meal.
That's how I learned the highways and byways, the names, leg-
ends, and superstitions of the land before I reached the age of
reason, as they call it. I feel, and am, just as much a part of it as
any tree or rock. They can pull me up by the roots, and the day's
coming when I'll be uprooted like a dead tree or a rock in the path,
but this'll just be to place me further inside it, deeper down in its
shelter. The only thing that worries me is this idea of the resurrection of the dead and of having to go to the Valley of Jehoshaphat.
That's why I suggested that very name for the cemetery at Cuilán—
it's in a valley. I hope the trick'll work. My grandfather and Namesake, between them, taught me to understand the language of the
earth, its whims and fancies—for it has these, too. The horse would
prick up its ears as though saying, "Listen," and I'd stop and listen,
straining my ears to hear. At first I couldn't hear anything except

the wind in the trees, or birds singing, the sounds of the farm, the farm animals, the running streams, the rain, the thunder. I noticed that Namesake pricked up his ears before I heard the sounds and also when we passed through places where someone had died. Later I began to hear the blades of grass growing, the corn in the cornfields, and the movements of ants, worms, microbes, and pests—under the earth or in the buds, in the leaves of corn, and the beanpods, the peapods, or in the folds of a sprouting shoot. And I'd ask my grandfather about everything. "What does the air say when there's no wind, and the flies and butterflies when they stay perfectly still, and the dogs when they howl in a different way from their usual barking? And why does Namesake prick up his ears when there's nothing strange in front of him?" My grandfather would explain everything to me: the power of the land, the souls whose bodies are buried in it, the spirits dwelling in all the elements of nature—plants and trees, springs, streams, rivers, and marshes, fire, each of the winds, plains hemmed in by mountains, rocks and stones according to their shapes and colors, the earth according to its fertility. What I enjoyed most, and I never got tired of asking him to tell me more about it, was his idea of the marriage between heaven and earth and their constant interaction to shape the future, from the character of people at birth to the scars of the years in their faces and the harvests to be reaped. But while filling me with a love of the land he also taught me to master it. He taught me to know its harshness and its reverses so that I'd know how to reap its rewards. He trained my eyes to see things at a great distance; he made me put my ear to the ground until I could hear the steps of men or animals hours away and know whether they were friends or enemies, whether they were bringing good or bad news, whether they were cattle thieves or coyotes, lost cattle or strangers. There was no one like my grandfather for reading the heavens and smelling the air to learn if we'd have plenty of rain or a drought, and for knowing when the early drought would come, the rise and fall of the temperature, the coming of hurricanes, eclipses, hail, and snowstorms. People from far away came to consult him and had faith in him. My favorite pastime was to stand beside him for hours and hours watching the night sky, listening to him tell the names of the stars, the meaning of each one, its position at such and such a time, its effect upon the earth. One of his last prophecies was the coming of the comet that would bring about the Revolution. He died shortly afterwards and didn't see it. They also say he told about the great earthquake that destroyed cities on the other side of the ocean at the very moment it was happening. The only thing he never liked to talk about was hidden treasure, and he never answered any questions they asked him on this subject. "The only treasure hidden in the earth," he told me, "is the fertility of the earth itself, and the only way man can obtain it is by plowing it with oxen and watering it with the sweat of his brow—by hard, back-breaking toil." Hidden treasures, money won by gambling, debts—he hated all of them. He'd say to his children, and to me and his other grandchildren, and to his daughters-in-law and other relatives, over and over again, "Working with debt hanging over your head is like trying to carry water in a basket." Once—I can't remember the reason for the journey—we went to the other side of the Sierra de Cardos. I must have been about six or seven years old, and it was my first visit outside our part of the county. We had blankets and bags with us, because we were going to spend several nights away from home. My father, my uncles, and some friends were with my grandfather, and on the way they mentioned the names of villages I'd never heard of before. At the top of the mountain we stopped for a siesta. I don't remember who began to point out the villages, praising the comforts and advantages they enjoyed and comparing them with the neglected state of our farms and the poorness of the land we lived on. My grandfather got angry at this, as he did when they asked him to look for buried treasure. "Those are the thoughts of ungrateful sons and of cowards, leaving their own mothers and wives to look for a new mother and go running after other people's wives. Each man has only one mother and one lawful wife. Just as we're bound to them, we're bound to the land. In fact, we're the land itself, and our feelings toward it are of our own making, since they come from our not knowing how to treat it, or from not being able to treat it the way we'd like to and the way it deserves. We'll never find what we're looking for in distant places, and the very thought of abandoning the land is wrong unless it's to bring back to the land what it needs. I know these villages. I tell you from my own experience that they haven't got anything for us to envy, unless it's the dangerous temptation to try new inventions, but in the end they're disappointing because you get tired of them, and they also bring slavery. Those men and villages are enslaved to each other. They can't live by themselves, and they don't have the freedom we have. When they don't have charcoal, or gasoline, or electricity, they're frantic. If the stores run out of matches they don't have flint and tinder to start a fire, and besides, they don't know how. The women can't go out into the street without shoes and shawls. The men have to wear dark trousers. They can't live without stores, and police to keep an eye on people—an endless chain of slavery. Our land is poor, we often don't get enough rain, but this very insecurity and poverty teaches us to be self-sufficient, to make do with what we have, with what we can get from the land. We help each other, sharing what we have, but they're not like us. On the contrary, they destroy each other, and it's everyone for himself." That was the way my grandfather's sermon went, that day on the mountain. I used to help him with all the chores—with the milking, plowing, sowing, weeding, harvesting, threshing. I'd help him tie up the stubble, put the fodder in the barns, clean out the stalls for the cattle and the horses, feed the animals, shoe them, and shear the sheep. I'd even volunteer for jobs I couldn't yet manage. When I was quite small I learned to lasso, to make figures with a rope on foot and on horseback. And I learned to be a good rider, to race my horse against others on the plains. My greatest dream was to break wild horses, but my grandfather wouldn't let me while he was alive. He owned a good deal of land and some farms on the other side of La Tapona. That's why we were constantly going back and forth. 'When the master attends him the horse grows sleek' was one of his favorite sayings, and there were others constantly on his lips: 'The early bird catches the worm' and 'The sleeping fish is swept downstream.' I've often seen him get down from his horse

because these men have a lot of requests from all the farms around here.' I saw I'd have to hurry, and remembering the saying that you have to seize opportunity by the hair, I got up my courage and grabbed it by the only hair it had. That is, I promised to pay them four days hire and for their work. What with being waked up and being anxious to find you as early as possible I didn't get any more sleep the whole blessed night."

Despite the look of irritation on Rómulo's face, his neighbor added, "I didn't tell you I've arranged for them to come to my place today so I can bring them from there and we can talk at the Crossroads by La Providencia. It's up to you. I tell you again, I've got just the answer to your problems right here."

Rómulo scratched his head again, more testily, spat out of the corner of his mouth, and spoke grudgingly, making an obvious effort. "What treasure? I ask you again. And even if there was?"

"How stubborn you are, compadre! How can people be wrong for so many years? All the people around here have claimed—and proved over and over again—that your grandfather and your uncles buried treasure, at least your uncle Don Salvador, who never gave away so much as a drop of water even to save his soul—and he didn't have any children or heirs! What did he do with all he had? Anyhow, you've got nothing to lose by trying, if you'll just give us some idea of where it might be. You can't leave me stuck here like a bride at the altar, all ready for the wedding. And don't forget the expenses. Just think, at least two hundred silver pesos, and my pocket's no better lined than yours."

"I'd be glad to go along with your scheme, even though I don't believe in buried treasure and my grandfather warned against all that kind of thing. I've gone against his advice too often and it always turned out badly. But now that I'm up to my neck in trouble, I'd be only too glad to—yes, in spite of everything I'd be glad to— if only I had the least idea where to look. I'm telling you the truth. I don't have the least idea and I can't remember hearing anything that would give the slightest clue."

"Look, let's put our cards on the table and think this out. First, your grandfather's dislike of talking about the matter was to throw

us off the scent. You've talked to me so often about this that I'm sure
of it. He died with the coming Revolution in mind, and the French
invasion when he was a boy made him think that the mob would
come and carry everything off. In a case like that, you know, people
usually hide their possessions—money and jewels are buried and
young girls are sent away or covered up with rags. You also know
that the cash your grandfather left was nowhere near all he had.
He died suddenly, without time to reveal his secrets. Secondly, try
with all your might and main—remember how a woman struggles
to give birth—try to cast your mind back over the places where
your grandfather and your uncle Salvador, at least, preferred to
be, the places they visited most and returned to most often. That's
where the key lies. Thirdly, there's no witchcraft in it, if that's
what you're thinking, or anything against the laws of our Holy
Mother Church. This is something invented by learned men—a
kind of clock, like those instruments I've seen, though I can't remember right now what they're called, that point to the north. They
say sailors use them to get their bearings when they cross the sea.
Yes, it's an invention of learned men, based on magnets—you know
about those, I think you even have one, except that these magnets
are very powerful, according to what they've told me. On that score
you can have an easy conscience. The most important thing is for
you to search your memory and say anything that comes into your
head, no matter how unimportant it seems. Just remember what
women do, or those who are helping them, when they find it hard
to give birth and suffer for hours and even days."

Poor Merced, to go no further, when Teófila was born. We'd
been married for ten years or more. All her efforts were useless:
medicines, prayers, relics, processions, promises to the Eye of Divine Providence and to all the saints known and venerated around
here. She was so set on having a child that she did everything the
old wives from the neighboring farms told her. Drinking the sap
of different trees, gathered on nights when there was a new moon.
Using rare herbs brought from far away. Bathing in water poured
over her from gourds in a cemetery at midnight. Rubbing herself

with lard mixed with the hair and bones of who knows what venomous animals. Plasters made from animal fat and the yolks of turkey eggs of such and such a color, or the dung of a newborn calf or a bull in heat. Even spells or invocations to the spirits and to the devil himself, God forgive us! No use. We'd almost become resigned to the will of Divine Providence when His Eye, which is venerated in the Shrine at the Crossroads, performed the miracle. How delighted my grandfather would have been to know I'd given him a grandchild! Merced's time came. And the joy was driven out by more trouble, worse still. It began on her way back from the well with a jar on her shoulder and another in her hand. It was midmorning. All that afternoon and throughout the night her pains got worse and worse. One after another, women began arriving to help her. They decided to burn pepper so the smoke would make her cough and start it. They shrouded her in the bitter smoke. She nearly choked to death. We found her gasping for breath like someone with whooping cough or like a child who has cried too long. They let her rest for a while. All the women on the farm were there and others had come from neighboring farms out of curiosity or pity. Matiana, disrespectfully called Madre Matiana, was in charge. Poor Merced's body, and the room, too, were covered with medals, figures, scapularies, ribbons, little bags with relics of the saints in them, the bones and hair of wild animals, or magic herbs that they gave her to smell from time to time. She had the ribbon of San Blas around her neck and the measuring rod of Santo Domingo de Silos placed over her womb. Every now and then Matiana would touch her lips with the picture of San Ramón Nonato that they always bring on these occasions, even when it looks like an easy birth. My sister-in-law, Cenobia, brought from home the little copy of the Hand of Providence, made of coral-tree wood. It's all in one piece, a beautiful piece of wood, and it opens to form the Five Fingers. Some people even say it's miraculous. Cenobia would put it in her hand and make her hold on to it when the pain was at its worst. The kind people had brought along all the holy or miraculous things they had in their houses, because on these farms they all stand by each other like this when someone's in trouble. We even forget our own needs to go and help our neighbors. Many blessed candles, all that there were on the farm, were lit in the room. By the light of them the women looked like a circle of witches. They were walking to and fro, standing still, pitying the sufferer, most of them merely curious onlookers getting in the way. They let her rest for a while after burning the pepper in the room. Everyone's eyes were watering. After a while, seeing that nothing was happening, Matiana got up on the wooden bed, telling them to hold the supports firm. She bent over poor Merced and began to knead her womb as though she were grinding corn dough on a slippery metate. "You're going to kill her, don't be so cruel!" I shouted at her. She shot a murderous glance at me. "Stop meddling and get out of here," she muttered without stopping her kneading. "You're in the way and it's because you're here she can't get on with it. As if it wasn't your pleasure Merced is paying for, you meddling fool! Just like a man! When the consequences happen they can only wring their hands and roll their eyes. They ought to suffer like women. Get out! Do you hear me?" I obeyed. It still grieves me to think I was probably just waiting for an excuse to leave and not have to go on watching Merced suffer. There are times when a man is such a coward! There were many friends in the patio. Don Epifanio was first and foremost with offers of help. He made me take a good nip of brandy, and tried to comfort me with stories of worse cases. Kind soul! There was a new moon that lit up the patio and the troubled faces of Don Epifanio and other friends. A scream of agony from Merced cut short our conversation and we held our breath. We'd have liked to stop up our ears. I could see the wish in the eyes of the men beside me and I was tempted myself, but we bore it like men. Don Epifanio's bottle was soon empty and another was brought out. We all kept on taking sips. We finished my gourd of tobacco and my leaves of corn. Don Epifanio sent to his house for more. We kept on drinking and passing the bottle around every so often. The screams continued. A woman came out and walked through the kitchen, saying on her way, "They're going to hang her up. There's no other way." I started to go back to the room, but Don

My grandfather was called Teódulo, which means, so I've heard, "slave of God" or something of the kind, although he would immediately reply that he was no one's slave, not even the slave of Divine Providence, for the simple reason that God doesn't have or need any slaves, only devoted children who are his creatures. The fact is that it's the custom to give the eldest sons their fathers' names. Therefore I wasn't called after my grandfather, to his great annoyance. But my father was the second son, and the eldest had already inherited the name Teódulo. He certainly scolded that uncle of mine once, in my presence, because he'd gone without permission to the fair in one of the villages you can see from the top of the hill. The words remained fixed in my memory, although at that time I could not understand them. "Out of sheer stupidity you just bring back diseases that cause children to be born blind, without lips or arms, even with huge heads like Pánfilo's son. If you don't get syphilis, you bring back leprosy or tuberculosis. When did you ever know such diseases around here in the old days? Not even smallpox, which has left pockmarks now on half the people here. In this part of the country people used to die of apoplexy, colic, bladder trouble, old age—and the women died in childbirth or as a result of it. Natural deaths, because you have to die of something. But there were lots of adventurers over there, bringing in these contagious diseases, infesting the farms that would always be healthy, because of the good climate, if it weren't for these scourges of God. Because they're a punishment for the sins people commit there. That's all they go there for—out of stupidity, curiosity, and evil desires. That's the attraction those villages have for them and that's what they bring back. And for good measure they're done out of their money. It's a wise saying, 'Stay at home and you won't come to harm.' The idle go wandering off with the excuse that they're looking for business or entertainment, as though there wasn't enough to do here and nowhere to enjoy yourself harmlessly without running into danger. The innocent women are the first victims, then the children! It's a wicked shame! One day Divine Providence will get tired and rain down fire on those cursed villages." My grandfather trusted nobody. When he left the house he'd lock the door of the room where he kept his saddles, spurs, and machetes. He also had two guns there that he hardly ever used, but his papers and other keepsakes he always kept locked up in a small chest beside the bed where he slept. It was a heavy little chest. Yes, he did like to spend time in what was called the saddle room. He had a bench in it and some tools. He used to spend his spare time doing a little carpentry, chiefly in the dry season when there was less work outside in the fields. He was always of the opinion that the men and women of his family or in his service and any acquaintances who would listen to him should acquire a skill apart from work on the land, because, as he used to say, "Idleness is the mother of all the vices." And he would add: "First and foremost it breeds poverty if life on the farms, once the harvest is over, consists merely in lying in the sun on your back, waiting for the rainy season, when there are so many productive things to be done. We don't need to bring leather-workers from the towns, or blacksmiths, carpenters, solderers, masons, weavers, or women to spin, sew, and embroider." He assigned a trade to each one of his children and grandchildren. I was still a boy when I began carpentry at his side, even though I also liked leatherwork because it's so necessary on a farm. If he had anything to hide, apart from what he kept under lock and key, he'd hide it in the barn, in the hay. I've often watched him doing this, but I don't think the things were of any great importance because he never minded my seeing him, either because he trusted me or because he thought I was just a child. He always kept his money, I remember, in the small chest beside his bed. His gold, when he had it, he always carried in a belt, the kind they call snakeskin, and I remember his locking this away, too, in the chest, and putting his gun or guns and cartridges on it. My uncle, Don Salvador, on the other hand, never took me into his confidence. My grandfather would often walk along by the stream. He'd walk up and down the whole length of it because he had hopes of making a reservoir with the help of the neighbors who'd benefit from it. Yes, I've watched him touch the rocks in the riverbed and calculate their resistance many times. Once he took me to some big caves in the foothills of La Tapona. I never went

other hand, to go back to the house was to start the argument about the machine or the land all over again.

But Doña Merced was not in sight when they got there. Palemón jumped into the saddle and rode off with a mechanical, "We'll meet there, then, God willing," echoed by an absent-minded, "God go with you." It was uttered automatically, from force of habit, while Rómulo's real thought, hidden under vague reluctance, was the wish that his neighbor would not come back to involve him deeper in this mess, as if there were not enough to worry him already.

It was the dead season of the year, especially trying at the beginning, the season that stretches from harvest to seed time in the lean lands, which are wholly dependent on the rainy season. Empty days. As if the noise of a rushing torrent, or a strong wind, constantly beating upon the ears, had come to a sudden stop. As if the sea, roaring in the eardrums, finally burst them, leaving you deaf. Emptiness in the pit of your stomach. Giddiness. Dizziness. Dejection of idle hours, when there is nothing that must be done. Idleness stretching endlessly ahead. Nothing to do but obey the dictates of your own whims. Lie on your back in the sun all morning and all afternoon. Walk for the sake of walking, to kill time. Idle conversation. Playing cards. Drinking and drinking. Weeks, months of boredom. Neighbors leaving the region, the farms abandoned. The desolation of the land. The tragic splendor of the sun on the eroded fields. The shadows of the rare passers-by moving along like souls in torment. The desolation of huisaches and nopal cactus.

And it is worse still in a bad year, when the harvest is scanty or, like this year, lost. The feeling of emptiness is aggravated by disappointment in these first days of inactivity. It is some time before people become resigned and hope springs up again. "More was lost at the time of the Flood." "God willing, we'll make it up in the coming year." The men seem unable to get started on jobs that would bring in some money during this time of enforced rest from their agricultural labors. They are loath to begin getting ready for the next season or to start making repairs on the farms. They keep putting it off from one day to another, even when it is a case of necessity or duty. "Next Monday." "After the twelfth of December." "After Christmas or New Year." They try to make the need for rest an excuse for their idleness. "God's law itself tells us to rest one day in seven, and God Himself rested after He created the world, though it wasn't much work for Him, because He was God. So it's a lot more necessary for human beings who have toiled from sunrise to sundown for months and months." It is Nature's resistance to a change of work. They turn from the chancy work of the fields to idleness. Sitting or standing instead of walking, their souls filled with the disillusionment that comes from having labored in vain.

Aggravated by his private worries—(trouble and poverty have been dogging my footsteps for a long time)—Rómulo's feeling of despair—(I feel as if I'm in the middle of a thick white cotton cloud, I can't get my feet on the ground, it's as though I'd been drugged, and I'm talking to myself)—was increased by the coming of the dead season when inevitably he would have to face his problems without the opportunity all the work of the plowing season gave him of keeping them at bay, turning his back on them, fleeing from them.

"Some powerful men have arrived, with money and good backing . . ."

The further away Palemón got, the more irritated Rómulo became, and by the time his friend was out of sight he was definitely angry. Slipping away so that his wife would not see him, Rómulo walked around without heeding where he was going, a prey to the violence of his emotions. He began to consider how and why he had got so worked up, because usually he was so calm—his blood was made of milk and water, Doña Merced used to say. He racked his brain but could not discover the reason.

It had started when Palemón, after beating around the bush, finally brought up the business of the divining rods. Or, thinking it over carefully, it might have been before that, when his friend sided with Doña Merced over the machine. But Rómulo had certainly felt his irritation rising as soon as the temptation presented itself of finding the treasure so easily with instruments guaranteed to find it, and his irritation had increased when Palemón insisted, forcing him, like a woman in labor, to try to remember, and suggesting things that had not entered his head but that he suddenly realized were true. Yes, that was the chief trouble—he saw things so clearly now, things he had never thought of. He felt like a man rudely awakened by a dazzling lamp thrust before his eyes. He realized he had been so much more stupid than he thought, letting his tongue run away with him, letting himself be persuaded and dragged along against his will by Palemón's effrontery. He knew he had been cowardly and, even worse, stupid to allow himself to be trapped by his neighbor's eloquence. He had also been a coward in another way, for although this idea of getting money easily to pay his debts had appealed to him, he could not bring himself to admit it and had been afraid of the risks involved, alleging untruthfully that the rods were bewitched and forbidden by the Holy Mother Church. Yes, the fear of getting mixed up not only with Palemón but with strangers, too, and who knows what kind of people they are, where they come from or what they want—this may have been the reason for his anger against a man who had tried to compromise him and even get money out of him, although they had not mentioned Rómulo's contributing even a centavo to the project, whether because the conversation about the machine had revealed that he did not have a penny to bless himself with, or because his obligation to contribute was taken for granted just because he listened to the scheme. In law, the accessory before the fact shares the guilt with the criminal.

Or this might have been just the straw that broke the camel's back, everything coming together. Last year's bad harvest. His debts, mounting year by year like spray from a fountain. His being forced to give up the animals that were left. The demand that he hand over the machine or have another bite taken out of the land. Teófila's death, and the insufferable way Doña Merced had behaved ever since. The bull that caught rabies and fell over the cliff before the rainy season. The way Don Epifanio treated him about the corn, making him sell in August before it could be harvested. The ingratitude of other neighbors who refused to help him. All this.

Even the memory of old wrongs he had not thought of since he was a boy. 'Old age and poverty make us more sensitive, and even the air and the daylight hurt us.' His lack of sympathy with his father and their strained relations after his grandfather died. His mother's harshness, the slights of his uncles, the dividing up and progressive eating away of his inheritance. Relatives moving away from the land. The trouble he had had to arrange his marriage to Merced. The desertion of his brothers-in-law, who refused to stay on the farm. The laughter of his friends when a horse threw him, and when he had to give up the first bit of land. His father's rude jeers when he tricked him out of Namesake, the chestnut horse that his grandfather had given him and that he had thought of as almost a part of himself.

All of it. The illness of Merced and Teófila, the deaths of people he knew, the dangers that beset him daily. The despair of many of his neighbors, the wickedness of others, the abuse of trust. The thought of the day when the machine would be taken away. 'A man has few friends when he has nothing to give.' And finally, bad luck. The impulse driving him toward the divining rods. The misfortune of not being trusted by anyone and of not trusting anyone either. Forebodings that are like the invisible shadow of the powers that draw near and hurt and kill in the dogdays.

Rómulo felt weary and quickened his pace, his usual way of fighting off sleepiness, spurring on his horse when riding, and goading on his oxen when plowing. He fought all his battles fairly, on whatever front they presented themselves, and his anger lessened as his weariness increased. Why should he resent his friend's good intentions? Yes, there was no denying it, Palemón's good intentions were evident in his offering him first use of these divining rods that he had been trying so hard to get hold of and that would rescue them from poverty. Rómulo might not agree with him, though in the bottom of his heart he felt tempted and hopeful, but what he could not fail to recognize was the proof of friendship Palemón was giving him. He might perhaps make use of it if outsiders were not in the business. They were sure to be sharpers, coming from cities or large towns to take advantage of the ignorant farmers, thinking them little better than animals who suspected no evil and could easily be stripped of everything, even their lives. 'The farmer who deals with outsiders gets the worst of the bargain,' my grandfather used to say. They come to make fun of us, touching us with the toe of their boots and robbing us into the bargain. 'The burro was not born surly, experience made him so.'

His neighbor was not to blame. He was willing to risk falling victim to their tricks himself in order to help a friend in need. His persistent questions had stemmed from his keen anxiety to help Rómulo out of his difficulties, by getting back property for him that was legally his because it had belonged to his grandfather; and in order to do this it was necessary to have some clues as to where it was. No, it was not the questions and the interference in his affairs that had roused Rómulo's wrath. On the contrary, he was grateful for his friend's recognition of his right to inherit the late Teódulo's property.

Still less could the reason for his sudden flare of anger have its roots in the scars of past injuries. Time and the resignation of the farmer had healed these. There was not even any reason to remember them. None at all.

"I'm the one who's responsible for this. I have to face my anger and get over it, recognizing that I'm stupid, useless, that everything I touch falls apart. I'm always unlucky, and it's not so much luck as my own fault. Everything I do, I do badly, everything I touch falls apart."

He sat down out of sheer exhaustion on the side of the hill, and from there he could see the whole panorama of Betania* stretched out below him.

Houses sprinkled sparsely over the chalky landscape, different yet alike, nearly all of them sheltered by a guardian tree—these, with the others growing at intervals near the bed of the stream, temper the harshness of the scene, the unbroken monotony of drab tones, mud-colored, dirty white, pale ocher, with lines of walls running in profusion over the barren expanse. Mud-colored houses of

*Bethany.

adobe. One, here and there, whitewashed, gleaming in the sunlight. The hamlet nestling in the hollow made by the stream that divides it in two, four houses on one side and five on the other, in the middle of the vast plain stretching away to the smoke-blue mountains surrounding it, the Cardos range and the hill of La Tapona dominating. No roads are visible, but their existence can be guessed at from the long lines of parallel walls, set close together.

When it is fine one can make out in the distance settlements of scattered houses, recognizable by the dark dots to which distance reduces the tutelary foliage in the far-stretching perspective of uncultivated land, since there is no other point of reference big enough, no domes, towers, silos, or thick clumps of trees. The houses of the region, which are flat roofed, have at most a second story with a balcony.

Belén,* the nearest farm, is a league away from Betania. It takes a full hour to get there. The land, which looks flat, is stony; the extensive layers of hard, chalky clay on the surface are slippery or scarred with furrows; there are sandy stretches and areas covered with fine dust. All of which makes it difficult to travel over in dry weather and terribly hard going in the rainy season. When the stream rises it cuts off communication between the two parts of Betania, and sometimes it is a full day before the water goes down.

The system of ownership and the dividing up of the land with boundaries marked by stone walls is the reason for the lack of roads in many parts of the plain, and is the most frequent cause of quarreling between the owners and those who cross over the pasture lands, open the gates, jump over the stone walls, or go through the five-barred gates to get from one place to another. It is the custom here, arising out of necessity, accepted as an obligation, religiously carried out on the whole, to shut gates behind one. Traveling on horseback is more difficult on account of the detours one has to make. The footpaths and bridle paths are hard to detect except in the few cases of established right of way. It requires a special skill to make one's way over the plain through so many obstacles; only the local inhabitants manage it, since they know the topography like squir-

*Bethlehem.

because it reminded him of Palestine, even the people were like the people there, and he decided to stay here till he died. What no one has ever been able to find out is where they buried him. Each farm claims this honor and there's even quarreling over it, but this is dying down now as time goes on and people forget. I try my best to fight off the evil thought that none of this is true, since I can't understand why not even the name of this famous individual is known and why they can't even agree about what he was. At the risk of offending the majority of my neighbors and suffering from the violence of a mob out to defend its prejudices—all the worse when these are so silly they haven't got a leg to stand on—I'm one of the few who believe it was the missionaries who named the region the Tierra Santa many years ago, but I don't shout my opinion from the housetop. My grandfather himself remembered seeing a huge cross, painted green, called the Mission Cross, on the top of Getsemaní. The fact is that this land of ours has been known as the Tierra Santa for a very long time and to decide who did or who didn't give it the name is unimportant. My grandfather was one of those most active in defense of the new names of the farms against those determined to go on using the original ones. Grand fights he had, just like those in the olden days when the Christians fought to regain possession of the Holy Sepulcher, which they had lost, according to the stories my daughter Teófila used to tell us. My grandfather used to say, "Since I can't go to Confession or even hear Mass very often, because there's no church here and it takes six hours to get to the town and another six to get back, the least I can do for our Holy Religion is to defend its Blessed Names." And he used to treat as heretics those who persisted in using the original names. The matter caused a lot of quarreling among the people. Thank God it didn't last long because the religious group prevailed. Besides, the Holy Names are nicer and their very strangeness gives them an ecclesiastical, aristocratic sound. The only name that didn't stick was Jerusalén, although my family and I keep on calling it by this name and not Torres de San Miguel, a name due to the pride of the owners, whose name was

Torres.* But they were punished for their sin. Apparently it was the biggest farm on the plain years ago, that's why the Blessed Name of Jerusalén was chosen for it. The Torres in their vainglory rejected this. Providence punished them: they lost everything, the lands were absolutely covered with saltpeter, and today the only thing left standing is an uninhabited house, the rest is a heap of ruins, but they continue to call it Torres de San Miguel (not my family and I, to repeat), although not even in its good days, much less now, was there ever any tower there. They say that other farms in the region also disappeared: El Hebrón, Canán, Ascalón, and others. It's believed they were destroyed because of their irreverence. The people called them El Lebrón, La Canana, El Escalón.† We have plenty of irreverent people here, for our sins, but they're in the minority, thank God. After all, in spite of having such a job to make ends meet, to be born and live and die in this Tierra Santa is a Divine Favor, as my daughter Teófila used to say. Where else could we put up so with the lot we have to bear without rebelling? I've always believed this, both before and after my daughter said it, and I still believe it, although I've realized it better since Teófila read to us from her books about the real Holy Land, and mentioned the same places as those here where we are put to endure joys and sorrows. Teófila had a very nice voice, especially when she read aloud to us.

The sun was still high when Rómulo reached the Shrine at the Crossroads. He was early, and as he waited for Palemón he determined to have nothing to do with the business of the divining rods, although from time to time he was tempted to try to put an end to his poverty, though not to get rich. Inside the tiny Shrine at the Crossroads the sun shone on the Great Eye of Providence in its sky-blue triangle with the gilt border.

* A surname, but also a word meaning "towers."
† The Coward, The Cartridge Belt, The Step.

Keep calm, don't be impatient

"Keep calm, don't be impatient, don't get restive." The booming voice of Don Epifanio. Fright, panic-stricken flight of boys, women, and the simple-minded. The new petitioners do not know what to do. The old hands, pretending not to hear him, keep quiet, not uttering a word, when he shouts and waves his hands threateningly. 'A barking dog never bites.' Also: 'A violent storm is soon over.' Debtors and henchmen know this. When he is really in a bad mood, he neither shouts nor waves his arms. Tongue-tied, spluttering with rage, he sits in his chair like an idiot or a paralytic. Once he used to tear his hair and rush around in circles as though imprisoned in a cage.

Now he can hardly walk, he is so fat. He does not even want to, even though he was such a man for riding, one who all his life used to ride day and night as though stuck to the saddle, who loved to be active, to ride over his land every day in wet weather and dry, with no regard for Sundays or Church holidays.

There he is, stuck in his leather chair all morning and afternoon, grunting like those pigs that are stuffed with so much barley they can hardly move. His daily exercise is limited to walking with difficulty from the room where he sleeps to the kitchen and from there to the terrace in the patio. It is on the terrace that he spends the greater part of his time. It is there he receives visitors, attends to his correspondence, gives orders and reprimands, has drinks and snacks brought to him, takes his afternoon siesta, conducts his affairs with his habitual precision. He has become more exacting. He shouts and waves his hands more. Nothing escapes him, no one can fool him. He knows how many animals there are or should be in each grazing ground; how many sacks of corn, beans, chick-peas, bran there are in the barns and where they are; how many bundles of straw are left; how much firewood, pitch pine, and kerosene; when loans are due and when interest should be paid. He needs no paper to remember his accounts to the centavo, the names and faces of his creditors, likewise the ages, names, and faces of those both big and small who live in the neighborhood, even some distance away, and the countless heads of cattle, bulls, cows, oxen, heifers, calves, horses, mares, colts and fillies, jackasses and jenny asses, mules male and female, pigs with their litters, rams and sheep, cocks, hens, chickens, turkeys, farm laborers, sharecroppers, and tenant farmers—he remembers the lot, with the characteristic features and distinguishing points of each one. "God," say the neighbors, "has given him a good memory"—the implacable memory of Don Epifanio Trujillo of the Tierra Santa. He knows, too, the names of the dogs in the district, and people say in fun, and he is flattered, that he even knows the names of all the swallows that come to the plain, the doves, larks, thrushes, hummingbirds, and other wild birds; likewise the names of the butterflies, wasps, bees, flies, mosquitoes, fireflies, glowworms, dragonflies, crickets, crows, vultures, mice, rats, frogs, toads, lizards, fleas, ants, scorpions, centipedes, spiders, earthworms, caterpillars, gnats, harvest mites, and other plagues, one by one.

Though he spends the day on the terrace, the time he most enjoys is that spent in the kitchen, where he has two breakfasts, dinner, and supper. He has his "elevenses" and his five o'clock chocolate, in addition to the snacks he calls pick-me-ups that are brought to him on the terrace. He eats and drinks without restraint, and is a byword in the district. He gets furious when one of his relatives tries to curb his gluttony, saying it will do him harm. "What! Do you pay my bills? Do you want me to die of hunger? What I eat and drink is my own! No one lends me anything, no one gives me anything on credit or out of charity!" He is utterly beside himself, bursting with rage, his face swelling, his eyes flashing fire and seeming about to pop out of his head, his hands and body trembling.

Four proper meals and countless pick-me-ups. Chocolate, milk, crackers, tamales, a taco with salt, when he gets up. Then breakfast: meat with a peppery sauce, eggs, fried beans with pork sausages, plenty of tortillas. Between one and two o'clock, dinner: boiled meat and vegetables, an entrée, meat, beans, plates piled high, and plenty of tortillas. About eight o'clock in the evening, supper: chocolate made with milk, milk, meat, beans, more tortillas, and, frequently, chicken, stew, barbecued kid, pigs' feet. He can manage without some of the snacks during the day, but not without his elevenses: tequila or pulque if there is any; tacos filled with pork sausages when there is no pork crackling, barbecued meat, tripe, and black pudding. Nor will he miss his first breakfast: chocolate made with water and with an egg beaten up in it, a glass of milk, and bread, if there is any, or crackers. He likes to plan a variety of dishes so that he can enjoy a change every day. The only thing he is not mean about is getting snacks and having guests in to share his meals. Not a week passes in which he does not sacrifice, in addition to the ox necessary for the maintenance of the household, a pig, a ram, several hens, just for his pleasure. Without a thought he will open his purse to have brought from the hills a deer, hares, quail, which he himself used to provide with his gun or his sling. He is one of the few farmers who can send to the town every week for supplies to stock his larder with all he needs, bread especially, and he never misses.

Two or even three ordinary people can fit comfortably in one of his leather armchairs, whereas he has trouble squeezing himself in.

He always breathes heavily even when he is not exerting himself.

Needless to say, this is worse when he gets up, walks, shouts, roars with laughter, coughs, or eats. He snores like a rusty saw and has fits of choking when he is unable to breathe: his face turns blue and the veins in his neck swell. His stoutness and his struggling for breath exhaust him to such a point that his head falls forward and he finds it hard to raise it or move it from side to side. His double chin pulls his mouth down, so that it is permanently lopsided, and he is unable to stop drooling. This impairs the clarity of his speech, which is dominated by violent, inarticulate explosions, frightening those who are unaccustomed to them.

'The lion is not as bad as he is painted,' say his debtors and his dependents. His habit of shouting, waving his hands, and flying into rages conceals the gay humor, the fondness for jests and repartee, that Don Epifanio retains from his days as a muleteer. 'The fat man's humor,' they often say. Popular sayings, which he uses maliciously, are never off his lips.

His joking communicativeness disappears when he is really angry and when there is a new moon, for this affects him as it does women, something no one can explain. His nerves are on edge, he will not leave his room or see anyone except those who bring him his food, and he will not say a single word to them. The most extraordinary part of it is that during those days he will have nothing but tripe and cornmeal gruel, and brews made of orange blossoms and mint. However, he does have breakfast and supper, chocolate made with water but without beaten eggs. It is not quite clear why he tries so desperately to conceal what happens to him when there is a new moon, but apparently he becomes giddy and suffers from headaches, colic, and vomiting. Some say they are just nervous attacks, that is all. To question him about this is to provoke a dreadful outburst. If anyone dares to ask him about it, he threatens to hit him and never speak to him again or let anyone mention him, as though he would blot him completely out of his mind. Not even his family is allowed to ask him about it, or even mention it, and anyhow they would not dare to. It is just whispered from ear to ear: retaliation for injuries, hidden under laughter and furtive grins. The worst of it is that when he is affected by the new moon, he has no consideration for anyone, still less for those who are in his debt or ask a favor. He is brutal, and would be capable of killing anyone on sight.

Although he has a large family, he has never married. 'Only a fool will take a chance in the marriage lottery.' From his youth he has flitted like a honeybee from one woman to another, his conquests scattered along his muleteer's route and afterwards over the farms when he decided to settle down on the plain, sank his claws into the earth, and began to make money. Scores of women. Anyone else, not blessed with his memory, would have lost count in nearly half a century of philandering.

The patriarch's catholicity of taste in women may be seen in the appearance of the children scattered over the farms on the plain. They are white, honey-colored, brown, and black; with big eyes and small eyes, almond-shaped and slanting, pale blue, yellow, brown, black as sloes; with hair as blond as the tiny hairs on an ear of corn, or as red as the head of a match, or chestnut, or dark, and straight, curly, or silky; some are tall, others stocky, some good-looking, others ugly, some graceful, others ungainly; carefree and worriers, Indians and Creoles. Nevertheless, they all take after their father in some way, although it is difficult to pinpoint the resemblance in many cases.

Whether the ties were for a few days or for years, in all of them Don Epifanio stuck to what, with no trace of sarcasm, he called indifferently his "code," his "principles," his "rule of life." He took no woman by force. Yielding to persuasion, self-interest, or affection, women went with him willingly and he never took them without intending to keep his promises. He never liked casual affairs or professional harlots.

Since he never made any secret of his affairs, and since there was no one he need hide from because his procedure seemed to him perfectly natural, he succeeded in getting each of the women respected by the community as though she were his legitimate wife. He installed them in houses of their own and on different farms, far apart. He provided them with enough to live on at a higher standard of living than they had been used to, but not in idleness. He made them do their own housework, and set them to study the catechism or studied it with them. If they did not know how to sew, they had to learn. He treated them according to a fixed plan; he looked after them when they were ill, especially in childbirth, and punished them when they did wrong with a severity appropriate in his opinion to the fault.

Since he felt that he was invested with undisputed authority in matters concerning his family, he used his discretion in dismissing a woman after paying her an indemnification based on the number of years she had been with him and the quality of her services, unless the misdeed was grave or had made him furious. In this case he just sent her away summarily in the clothes she stood in. Local gossip holds him guilty of the disappearance and death of many of his women, but this seems unlikely. The power of the polygamist, which inspired fear throughout the countryside, and the resources at his disposal were circumstances that did not make for marital infidelity—which, according to the moral code of Trujillo, and this he openly proclaimed, is the only justification for the application of the death penalty to women, just as for men it is cattle stealing. In fact, not even the cruelest stories told about Don Epifanio include anything of this kind.

When he wanted another new woman and was about to start relations with her, he would inform the others and stop visiting them, at least during the actual honeymoon, or possibly for good. He also refrained from visiting the others and consecrated the months before the birth of his children to the mother-to-be. If his favorites objected to this he gave them a sum of money and sent them away. On the other hand, many women whom he had stopped visiting because of subsequent unions continued to live at his expense in their houses without interference, as long as they behaved like "decent widows"—Trujillo's own phrase. This supplanting of the old mistress by the new brought him into conflict with women who, out of self-respect or ambition, cupidity, lack of understanding, or a desire to make trouble, rebelled against the master's wishes. The speed, the drastic harshness against which there was no appeal, the bribes or threats, the active measures taken, ended these situations without adverse consequences and created precedents.

Don Epifanio's honeymoons lasted until he tired of them. No discussions or arguments were necessary to bring this about, and sometimes the woman had no idea what caused it. A word that displeased him, a look, a gesture, delay in serving dinner, its not being tasty enough, any trifle was enough to break the spell that bound the master. He always swore to himself that there was nothing capricious about it, no fickleness once his desire was satisfied, but rather, causes beyond his control, flaws discovered in his partner. This was when the polygamist would return, if the offense did not deserve absolute repudiation, to his other "pastures and drinking troughs," that is, his other women.

The surprising thing about the system is the skill with which Trujillo handled the social position of his children in spite of so many conflicting interests, influences, and tendencies, bringing them up as brothers and sisters in accordance with a patriarchal plan.

Before entering into relations with a woman—and he never did this without laying down terms—he would reserve for himself, expressly, unlimited *patria potestas* over the children. He kept an eye on them, one might say, even from before birth, just as he did on his cattle. He would calculate the day and hour when they were conceived, connecting this with the influence of the moon; he would watch over the behavior of the pregnant woman and be on the alert against any contingencies; he would not let her worry and he gave in to her whims; he petted her and forgave her faults and failings.

He was always present at the birth of his children and insisted on every precaution being taken: no lack of sheets and clean cotton, plenty of boiled water with ash leaves in it, a douche and cotton wool, bottles of alcohol and disinfectant, kerosene in the oil burners. He himself would boil the scissors and hold them over the flame before cutting the umbilical cord. He would take the child and examine it with minute care, touching the pubic region, looking at the eyes, opening the lips, rubbing the gums and palate; he would feel the bones, the crown of the head; notice the shape of the head, the consistency and strength of the spinal column; examine the thighs, the elbows, the knees, the muscles, the groin, the soles of the feet; and then store up these data in his memory.

For years he had been collecting names, and after much cogitation he would share these out among the newborn babies, provisionally, until it was time to have them baptized, which might be any time from three to ten years later. Some of his latest offspring are still waiting for this sacrament.

He would watch over mother and child during the nursing period. He noted carefully the progressive manifestations of instincts and temperaments, the baby's way of sucking, crying, smiling, and taking notice; observed how the infants stood the teething period, the summer heat, the cold; observed their precocity or tardiness in crawling, standing, walking, running, talking, beginning to think. He graded them according to almost the same procedures as he used for the offspring of his favorite animals.

Here, too, malevolent tongues have accused him of causing the deaths of children he abandoned when he discovered them to be defective. Even in the case of useless animals he was never guilty of this except on rare occasions; he preferred to send them away and let them die.

For some time, depending on the doubts he entertained if something was not to his satisfaction, the children remained in the position of godchildren. That is to say, he did not have them baptized as his children nor give them his name, but contented himself with being their godfather, presenting them as children of an unknown father, reserving the right to recognize them later if new facts, deductions, or circumstances caused him to modify the opinion already formed. This was the reason for the delay in baptizing them and giving them definite names, depending on whether they lived up to the prophetic design given by Don Epifanio to the names he had chosen from the *Lives of the Saints.*

The unilateral exercise of *patria potestas* implied the mothers' complete renunciation of their children. The father assumed the right to take them away at any time, even at birth or during the nursing period. Opposition, which in any case did not stop him from acting in accordance with his decision, frequently constituted the reason for repudiation, just as the commonest reason for taking children away from their mothers was the latter's dislike of putting their children with the children of the master's other wives. But this was a vital part of his plan to found a great family, one made indestructible through the unity of its members—a complicated undertaking, not so much because of their different origins as because of the contrasting destinies the father envisaged for his children in the whole pattern, taking into account each one's different attitudes and inclinations. For this reason it was essential to bring them together, let them get to know each other, accustom them to understand, help, and love each other, preferably willingly, or, if this proved impossible, unwillingly, no matter whether in the end they were to be brothers, sons of the same father, or only godchildren. It was no less necessary to take them away from the mothers who endangered or did not enforce the development of the dispositions that Don Epifanio thought he saw or wanted to see in them, in accordance with the role he had marked out for them in his plan.

In a region decimated by infant mortality no house escapes, still less the offspring of so many irregular unions. But he who should have been the last to complain and to break with tradition was the first to set a bad example, as he always was in everything, going to lengths no one else would or could go by denying and insulting Providence.

It was not remorse. It was not terror in the face of the mystery. It was not the fury of a bull when the branding iron sears its flesh, or of an animal smarting under punishment. It was the rage of a man whose hope is destroyed, the fury of a man accustomed to do as he damned well pleases, suddenly finding himself face to face with the inevitable, refusing to accept it, yet overwhelmed by it. The life of a child is such a small thing, yet so great that it embraces the future with its castles in the air.

None of the big scandals, none of the stones thrown in such numbers every hour, ever made such an impact on the people's minds as his behavior on the death of the children he had had with differ-

oxen who come in of their own accord, or like hens sleeping on a perch, when you throw down corn they come down, or like the poor deer who comes down to the water by day. If you don't follow your leader willingly, you'll be dragged along against your will. Then you'll come to ask for chips when you want to gamble. But remember, I dance to the music piped to me, and I have a long memory. I'm not like the women. If you want trouble you'll get it; keep calm and we'll be all right. In short, I like my accounts clear and my chocolate thick. Let's proceed with the cards face up on the table. Let me come around in my own time, just deal the cards slowly and don't be like the mouse that belled the cat and was afraid of the noise, or like those who play dead and then are afraid of the coffin, or like the person who vomits and covers up his vomit so as not to smell it. What do burned men die from? Simply from the heat, like you, you bunch of talkers. What fault is it of mine if the biggest cock is the one that crows the loudest? You throw it in my face that I have so many women, but you're all licking your lips and some of you are biting them till they bleed. It's like they say in church, "Let him who is without sin cast the first stone." The difference is that I do what I do openly, without hypocrisy or fear of anyone because I'm not one of those who stir up the water and muddy it without drinking. My motto is, 'Don't touch the water if you're not going to drink it,' and there's another saying, 'If you're not going to drink the water don't put it on to boil,' since I know from experience that a kettle that boils for a long time either boils over or boils dry. I boil only what I need, since I pay for it, not like you, you want to get it free, by stealth. You make a big commotion as if this wasn't called the Tierra Santa and as if you'd forgotten that Noah and his sons, patriarchs and prophets, had even more women and no one said a word to them, not even those who kiss the Bible, where those chosen by all these holy men are written down, they say. One thing is sure, you can't win the game unless you follow suit with a queen, and queens are my lucky cards. Besides, any furrow is a good place to sow seed. Why poach on the preserves of others? Leave that to the poachers. If you don't like a saddle, throw it away and ride bareback, and if you've got any hens, tie them up because the cock is on the loose. And why don't I get married? What's not written down in the civil register and the customs house is clear profit. I don't want to be one of those donkeys that won't bray because they're afraid of the harness, or one of those who are so stupid that they get on the donkey to go and look for it. I'd rather have people say, "He kicked over the traces" than "He kicked the bucket." The contented ox licks even the yoke; yokes are only for oxen. I prefer the saying, 'If one door is shut in your face, there are a hundred left.' One swallow doesn't make a summer and one angel doesn't make a Heaven; one leap is not a race and it takes many streams to make a river. If one is not to your liking, goodnight and goodbye, well, "Here, take this, it's all you'll get, just give me the boys according to the bargain." Tell me who wouldn't have more than one mount so as to change horses? On the other hand, why buy a blanket if it's going to get holes in it? Grasp opportunity when it offers, what's sauce for the goose is sauce for the gander. I may be shameless, as they call me, but I keep my word and don't pretend to be a saint. Not that there aren't some who have made a sieve of their blankets, familiar with everything outside their homes but rarely with what's inside them. They drive away their legitimate wives and children and pretend not to see them. They throw the stone and put their hands behind their backs, or they're like Pilate, they wash their hands up to the elbows. They pretend to be deaf like the old priest when he was reminded in the confessional of his faults. You also criticize me for taking so long to bring my children to be baptized, which means making them my heirs. I only ask how many years a friar spends in his novitiate. It's not a case of pass me another piece of bread. I'm going to confer my name on them, share out my possessions, my bits of land and the few *centavos* I've managed to scrape together by the sweat of my brow, as the commandment says, or as we say here, by working my fingers to the bone every day from sunrise to sunset, often going without sleep. So consider my point of view—you can see there's sense in it. Now let's look at the business of the children who died, which makes you so angry, just because I told them to accuse God of injustice and of not knowing what

Epifanio, it is also known as the House of the Trujillos. Some call it the House with the Terrace.

This is where the master would bring his favorite mistress, which in itself gave her special prestige, but brought greater obligation with it. Naturally she had to take complete charge of the Trujillos born of other mothers. This was why the house was nicknamed Bastard Barn, Limbo of the Lost, Home for Waifs and Strays. The inmates were called bastards, half-breeds, savages, brutes, cowards, bandits, animals, devils, scum, good-for-nothings; this last was the most common, along with bastards, outcasts and foundlings.

Here, together with his children, Don Epifanio gathered his best stud horses, pedigreed cattle, weapons, riding gear, farm machinery, furniture, china, and favorite possessions. The leather armchairs at Belén were made to order, out of suede and calf leather. In Belén he has a proper brass bed, with a quilt on it, one of the few beds in the plain. The parlor in the Big House is full of images and photographs, the most striking being those of dead people, especially old men and young children, mostly the latter. The mere mention of the macabre gallery of the Trujillos is enough to frighten children and those who are timid. There is no more effective threat on the plain than "I'm going to shut you in with Don Epifanio's dead people," although those who can boast of having entered the room are very few in number. The room is kept locked and only opened to receive guests of honor on high feast days, when the bells ring out (although there are no bells for miles around.)

Delays and excuses are Trujillo's answer to those who praise Belén as the perfect place to build at least a chapel to serve the neighboring farms, and then ask him to give land and head the contributions of workmen, materials, and money. The flattering remarks that, apart from its geographical situation in the center of the Tierra Santa, Belén has become the capital of the plain on account of its wealth and the activities carried on there, thanks to Don Epifanio, go in one ear and out the other. They point out in vain that the church or chapel would bring in the people from the farms; that nobody would question the exclusive right of the landlord to set up stalls, as there are none at all in the district, or to collect a fee from those who brought their wares, instead of traveling six or more hours to take the money for their provisions to the town and the same time getting back every week; that the money would stay here and also the profits made in other business—in animals, seeds, loans, exchanges, differences in weights and measures; in short, that he who does the sharing out gets the lion's share. He replies, "I'll think about it. Perhaps next year when there's a good harvest. Just let me get in the clear again, as soon as I'm paid what people owe me." This is what he usually answers. But they say he has actually said openly, "When horses talk and pigs fly," with such additions as, "You can pray in the meanest shack—and better still under the clear blue sky, with nothing to disturb your prayers. All the more so because we're too far away and too poor for the priests to come all this way. We'll have to keep going to fetch them when we need them. As the saying goes, 'From priests and the sun, the farther the better.'" Such remarks, when he lets his tongue run away with him, confirm his reputation as an unbeliever.

Naturally there are times when he is dazzled by such possibilities as collecting ground rent, just for the pleasure of being like the governor and making people pay willy-nilly.

The idea that gives him most pleasure is the possibility of inventing some miracle, the appearance of some image that will make Belén the honeycomb where bees as well as flies will gather, long lines of people, like ants, covering the walls of the chapel with holy pictures, the chapel blackened by the smoke of many candles, suffocating with the scent of many flowers, shining with lamps and silver ex-votos, and with its poor boxes full to bursting. He is not quite sure if it was his own idea or if somebody whispered it in his ear. Many people on the plain have tried this, imitating places on the other side of the mountain, but the attempts have been so clumsy that after the novelty wore off they became the laughingstock of the countryside, even though the people did not want the Tierra Santa to be left behind in the question of miracles and miraculous appearances.

"The time is ripe," thought Trujillo, "provided the hook is well baited—or, say, provided the sugar is well stirred."

Just thoughts flashing through his mind. He is not in the mood for new escapades. Tired, and having enough money, he is content to imagine the fun he would get out of imposing a string of taxes, and to calculate his profits. That is the least important part, since he has no need to get involved in squabbles, entanglements, or extra work in order to make more money. With or without the chapel, the poor come anyhow to pay their taxes, "weeping and groaning" as it says in the prayer. The business of the miracle would involve the risk of verification and difficulties with the parish priest and his curates, if it should cause enough stir to bring them to pay a visit, a thing they rarely do, and then it's a hasty one to give confession or the viaticum to a dying man. However closely they tread on his tail, Don Epifanio manages to avoid them and refuses to see them when they come to Belén. It would be fun to play a trick on them: knowing the character of the villagers, calculating their reactions, preparing the miracle carefully, getting credulity to nibble at the hook, and stirring up their regional pride. The opposition of the priests would arouse their anger and harden their determination to defend the special favor granted to the poor people exiled on this plain of tears, so Godforsaken, as the inhabitants often complain, that one day God must surely remember them and reveal His manifest mercy clearly for all to see.

Vain temptations! He might have done it in other days, for the consolation of the unhappy and to his own advantage, but now the ruler of the plain was only engaged in accumulating lands, cattle, women, and children, squandering his energies.

Leaning back in his leather armchair on the terrace of the Big House, contemplating the unending barrenness and unchanging features of the surrounding countryside, Epifanio Trujillo shuffled the past with the present; he laughed to himself at the thoughts that passed through his mind, the escapades he recalled. He remembered proudly his deeds of prowess; he remembered the opportunities he let slip by, unable to grasp them; he was irritated by the inertia into which he had fallen. He struggled for a moment against the pleasures of his present vegetating existence, with no desire to move around as he used to when he flitted like a hummingbird from flower to flower.

Eva
Sara
Rebeca
Rachel
Abigail
Ana
Amanda

Teófila! She was the one who should have been mistress of Belén. My mouth still waters when I think of her. You can tell a canary a long way off. Still waters run deep. What a pretty trout to find in such a dirty little pond. She was born good, you wouldn't even have to teach her. That's the truth of it! She was the only one who ever made me weaken and even consider marriage. Through her I became convinced that wedding veils and shrouds are made in Heaven. You don't get a girl like her born every day. I saw her come into the world. I stuck around during the long hours that preceded her difficult birth, for she was no wild rabbit or ordinary filly. How many times I took her up in my arms when she was very tiny, afraid she'd melt like a lump of sugar. I watched her crawl, heard her first cries, guessed her first words, better than those of the daughters I loved best. She was always charming and gay, from a tiny little girl. She'd come to me, stay with me, stick closer to me than to her own father. I used to say to Rómulo and Merced, "What a good thing you haven't asked me to be godfather, as that would make it more difficult for me to marry her, as I intend to when she's old enough. She's set apart and promised to me, mind." They didn't think it was at all funny; they'd purse their lips and refuse to smile at the joke. Then she got measles, afterwards smallpox, so badly that Merced consoled herself with the thought that it was better for God to take her than some man who would ruin her. I rushed off to Cuilán to fetch the druggist, who soon found the remedy and cured the disease, thank God. She had a few marks on her face, but they suited her. She grew tall like a shapely tree. She matured early like the quick-ripening corn in a well-tended cornfield and soon became a woman. She began to be shy with me. One day she asked me point-blank, "Why do they say you're worse than a hawk or a coyote, that there's no hen safe from you?" How innocent she was! About this time they let her go and stay with some relatives in Clamores for a while, or maybe Rómulo wanted her away to hide her from the many wolves beginning to crowd around, since love and money can't be hid. It wasn't till Merced was at death's door that Teófila came back. I still catch my breath as I see her again in my mind's eye, and find it hard to breathe. Then I really began to suffer. Fires not quite burnt out are easily fanned to flame. It was scarcely credible. She was now a young lady, careful in her speech, proper in her behavior, but still natural. The nice thing about it was that with all her education, she didn't think herself too fine to milk cows, carry water, sweep out barnyards, get up early and take her full share of the farm chores, mixing as before with dull farmers, coming down to their level with ease and patience and great sympathy for the ignorant, all with a cheerful smile always on her face, to the amazement of everybody. She talked of starting a school for the children in Betania, and began teaching the grown-ups to read and write. She never stopped. There had never been proper schools or teachers on the plain. From time to time the people in several settlements would get together and get some young girl of Spanish parentage who knew how to read to keep the young boys busy, paying her with corn, beans, hens, eggs, when and as they could. Children from the farms farthest away came to Betania in the mornings, from Monday to Friday. Teófila dedicated her afternoons to the older people. Then the people took to gathering together, especially on Sundays, so that Rómulo's daughter might read to them *The Christian Year* and other interesting books she'd brought from the town. She did so willingly, on condition that they'd learn the catechism and afterwards say the Rosary and the Holy, Holy, Holy. I was one of those who'd never miss while the earth turned on its axis, and I'd even learn the catechism again and get down on my knees and pray, providing I could listen to her voice leading the prayers, it was such a pleasure to hear her. The grass is always greener on the other side of the fence. But her most surprising and striking gift was her skill at dressmaking and embroidery, that was something out of this world, at that she was in a class by herself or, as they say, she rolled up her sleeves and set to work and you had to take off your hat to her. Rómulo told me he wanted to buy her a sewing machine with pedals, a new one, the best he could get. I encouraged him, opened my purse and let him have the money he needed. Love is shown by actions rather than by kisses and hugs. I would have given it to her and nearly said so, but bit back the words just in time for fear of arousing their suspicions, lest they should guess at the thoughts whirling around in my head, keeping me awake at night, and put a malicious construction on them. Fears run in one's veins like blood. It's a vicious circle, with no beginning or end to it. I didn't want them to say, "He's setting a sprat to catch a mackerel," or to discover the way my mind was working. I finally managed to make them believe that a contented cat isn't looking for mice and they needn't be afraid of the mouse falling into a nest of vipers. I swallowed my anxiety, kept quiet, and determined to bide God's good time. The blessed machine arrived. I was one of the first to be dazzled at the sight of a new Teófila when she set the machine working. I couldn't take my eyes off her: they followed her movements from side to side, unable to keep still. They were drawn from the contemplation of the sure swift movements of those rounded hands to the rhythmical swing of legs and thighs working the pedal, only to move back up the body to the head, seeking those fascinating eyes of Teófila, whose face wore a smile like that of an angel in a painting. With her head up, shoulders straight, and completely at ease, she looked very much a woman. I remembered the saying, 'Now the rustic violin is played by a master hand,' and the other, 'A bad musician finds even his fingernails in the way,' and 'Look for a jack and turn up an ace.' We had never seen this kind of foot-machine before, anywhere in the district. It was made of wood that gleamed like a looking glass, with lots of drawers and all the metal parts working smoothly, with hardly any noise. And there was Teófila handling it as though she'd been doing this all her life, as though she'd invented it. The most interesting thing was to watch her embroider, moving the cloth with the design on it, held between odd-looking hoops, from one side to the other, swiftly, without a pause, without letting the needle move off the guide-line. In less time than it takes to tell it she'd cover the section fastened in the hoop with flowers, leaves, stars, and other marvels. I wanted to kneel down and kiss those skillfull hands. Saint's hands, they seemed to me. With all due respect to the dead girl, I'd never felt this kind of an itch for any other daughter of Eve, pardon the expression. Now that I've known a really good girl, I soon get tired of the run-of-the-mill variety. I bided my time: a good pair of legs always carries the day. I didn't want the dove to get frightened and fly away, be carried away before my good intentions could take shape. I didn't want them left to pave the way to hell, as they used to say, unless it's the hell of despair, because of the morsels that slip through your fingers and remain stuck in the memory, night and day for ever and ever.

Out of kindness, and helpfulness, Teófila invited girls from the neighboring farms to come and learn to sew and embroider. Not one of my daughters, not even one of those who, just because they live at Belén, are known to be my favorites, was invited. I wasn't offended. On the contrary, I was delighted. I said, "Ah, I'll be damned if it isn't coming along nicely. The girl knows what I'm after and is off like a hare, though she won't let on. 'Give the fillies their head, they'll soon come back to the path.' 'The dove doesn't flutter where the hawk flies.' " There were other signs: she was too serious, too stiff, and she overdid her prudishness in conversation when I was there. She'd suddenly grow confused when our glances met or when I shook hands with her, and when, as a joke, I'd come straight out with a flattering remark or a compliment, like the day I said to her, "We have no eyes to see all the beauty God puts before us," and, on another occasion, "There are times when a stick of pitch pine will start a conflagration." She never questioned me again or even touched on anything concerning my life or my adventures, though obviously she was both longing to do so and re-

fraining from it. I may be a fool but I know women and the devil
has learned more from experience than by just being the devil. She
neither rejected nor accepted my attentions, but she blushed and
I think even trembled when I made my meaning clearer. "With
you, a field is a farm and plain water is wine. Let the man in love
not lose hope." I expected to be put in my place—she was good at
that—or at least to have my remarks ignored. She pretended not
to know what I was talking about. So my feelings weren't hurt because she didn't invite my daughters. I boldly took my daughter
Plácida to her. "Look, Teófila," I said, "I want you to teach this
girl to handle the machine as only you can, but I particularly want
her to learn the catechism thoroughly and to read *The Christian
Year*. I'll come back from time to time to see how she's getting on.
Tell her what to do and don't be afraid to pull her braids and box
her ears, as if she were your daughter. She needs it. As for payment, that'll be all right, your father can deduct from what he
owes me whatever you decide on. You can name your own price,
without even asking me." I didn't give her or her parents time to
reply. With this parting shot I hastily took my leave. Whether it
was because she enjoyed it, or because she felt obliged to learn, or
because she courageously set to work to make the best of it, the
fact is that Plácida made amazing progress and in the twinkling of
an eye learned to cut out, sew, and embroider. What she couldn't
or wouldn't do was read *The Christian Year* or get the catechism
into her head. With the excuse of taking Plácida over or fetching
her, there was hardly a day I didn't go to Betania. Teófila was ab-
sorbing more and more of my attention. Each day I discovered
new qualities she had. I remember one morning she came out all
dressed up with boots on, the high-heeled kind, laced well above
the ankle. Somehow or other I caught a glimpse of her calf as she
moved. She was wearing ribbed cotton stockings and the rounded
shape above the boot made such an impression on me that I felt as
though I'd been struck by a bolt of lightning. I was dumbfounded
and couldn't utter a word. My frequent visits troubled Rómulo and
Merced, they'd receive me with wooden faces and speak very curtly,

as though saying, "Take what you like from the fields, but you'll get nothing from our orchard." Teófila, on the other hand, behaved very properly, was cordial and began to act quite naturally with me again, but she always had Plácida with her and gave me no chance to speak openly. She always kept her place and managed to maintain a distance between us, which was not physical but a question of respect she imposed upon me by I don't know what art. I alternated between despair and hope, like a ball bouncing up and down. For the first time in my life I began to think of my age. It was true, I was thirty years older than she was, but was there anyone to get ahead of me? I felt full of life, strong, active, capable of giving the boys a run for their money, one by one or all together. It's true that the heart never grows old: it's the skin that wrinkles, and I had no wrinkles or gray hairs. With my black moustache, red face, bright eyes, firm hands, and strong legs, I was a stout oak, not to say a bull. So as my doubts increased I felt defenseless before Teófila. I was hypnotized the way coyotes sometimes are by the hens looking at them. Then I discovered that Felipe and Jesusito, my two eldest sons, were after Teófila. Suddenly I was furious. "If they cross my path," I said, talking to myself, "they'll get what they're looking for." The badly brought up boy will find someone to correct him wherever he goes. As your children get bigger, the more trouble they are. 'Some think they're well away and then find they're at the end of the line.' 'A few clouts in a house make for good order.' Jesusito was the same age as Teófila. Felipe was five years older. Even the saying 'Like seeks like' made me furious. This was enough to put a damper on my plans but not to make me give up the idea. I was determined to fight them for the girl and win her if I could.

"Dawn"
"Milkfoam"
"Honey"
"Morning Star"
"Cinnamon"

"Bridal Wreath"

The cows were coming back to the barns, crossing the small square in front of the verandah of the Big House. The deep voice of Plácida was urging them on. Plácida had made herself mistress of the Big House.

Trujillo confirmed this, treating her as his favorite daughter. He himself, grumbling and waving his hands like a spoiled child, accepted her tyranny provided that she did not try to curb his gluttony. Bossy, bad-tempered, apt to fly off the handle at any moment, unable to brook any opposition: this is what Plácida has inherited from her father to start with. She builds up and tears down. There is nothing placid about her: she is as inflammable as tinder or cotton.

Her brother, the dreaded Felipe, trembles before her. Her brother, Don Jesusito, the smooth one, drips honey in the presence of the woman whom, under his breath, he calls the Whirlwind, the Bitch, the Sergeant Major, the Boss.

Plácida also leads the rest of her relatives and connections by the nose, starting with Amanda, Don Epifanio's surviving mistress, whom he keeps at Belén—"because of her age and long service."

A mere shadow of her former self, Amanda looks like a frightened rabbit; she spends most of her time hiding away in corners where no one can see her; when she does appear she scurries by furtively, taking no part in what is going on around her. This woman, who used to be so pretty, so careful of her appearance, so sure of herself, so wise and patient, tireless in working around the house and waiting on her master, Don Epifanio, always ready to make a fuss over him, patiently putting up with his temper and moods until she managed to make him feel better, to restore his good humor, to get him to laugh and forget his troubles and stay in the house without a thought for his other mistresses; this woman now has no place of her own, is reduced to obeying, in silence, Plácida's commands.

To those who remember her particular liking for order and cleanliness, her present neglect of herself is pitiful. She was never a woman of many words; she spoke with her eyes and face and natural gestures. Now she is dumb and her eyes are expressionless; her face, arms, and limbs seem to be made of wood, with rusty hinges. She has been gradually going to pieces, like a bit of pottery becoming more and more unserviceable.

Amanda was fifteen years old when she first came to live with Don Epifanio. The master set her up in a house outside the Tierra Santa, on the Barranca Honda farm. Her eight sons were born there, three of them died there, and she remained buried there for thirteen years, which must have been the happiest years of her life.

Her lord and master had brought her to Belén with every mark of respect and placed her in charge of the great nursery of Trujillo bastards, her capacity for this post having been more than sufficiently demonstrated by her exceptional treatment of the sons of other women when her own had been taken away: she had been an excellent mother to them. None of his other wives had fallen in with Don Epifanio's plans in this matter as well as Amanda. Whether the children were hers or belonged to other women, Amanda treated them all alike: they were given the same food, and ate together; they were equally clean; she washed, mended, and ironed for all of them; she meted out rewards and punishments impartially; she made them feel members of the same family; she managed to banish even incipient quarrels and uncouth behavior. All this work never kept her from being always ready for the master, who never announced his comings nor had any set day or time to arrive. In a moment a meal was ready, served on dishes gleaming with cleanliness on a freshly ironed tablecloth in a house so spotlessly clean and silent that there seemed to be no children in it when there were actually twelve living there. If the master wanted to rest, the bed was always made up with spotless sheets and a water jar and glass within reach and a hand basin, jug, and soap ready for use. Amanda took even greater care to have a change of clothing always ready, and Don Epifanio preferred this to those in his other houses, even Belén. But what made him enjoy the Barranca Honda most was the children, well brought up, respectful, behaving like brothers and sisters, fond of their mother, silently cheerful in their father's presence, obedient. "These are virtues," Don Epifanio would shout, "better than those of Don Porfirio Díaz." And he would remain longer at the Barranca than at Belén or any of his other haunts.

Amanda's eldest was Don Jesusito, the last of the children to be taken out of her hands by their sire. She never saw him again or had any news of him or ventured to ask where he was until she was taken off to the Big House, where she found him, now the second son of the dynasty, complementing with his contribution the tasks assigned to the eldest, Don Felipe, who had been sent to the Barranca to take the place left by Jesusito and had spent two years there in Amanda's care.

In the patriarchal plan, the role of strong man was reserved for Felipe. "He would maintain," as Don Epifanio used to say, "the respect due to the name." Under this term he included all the interests of the Trujillos, lands, people, cattle, credit, countless ambitions of all kinds. Jesusito's job, on the other hand, was to gain his ends by hiding the iron hand under the velvet glove; he was the cat to Felipe's tiger. Don Epifanio decreed their titles: *Don* Felipe, *Don* Jesusito. The people were not slow to add to these. The first they nicknamed the Squeezer or, more commonly, the Bully. The second was called the Fixer, the Sneak, the Snake in the Grass, or Cat's Claws. And both of them were called all the names mentioned before: outcasts, vagabonds, bastards, idiots, brutes, foundlings.

Amanda found that Don Jesusito had become a stranger. Not only did he show no signs of being pleased to see her again, but actually seemed to resent her presence, although he concealed this and pretended it was not so. He took to calling her Doña Amandita, in honeyed tones so ambiguous that it was hard to say whether they expressed affectionate fondness or derisive scorn. What he was looking for was a way of not recognizing her openly as his mother without arousing criticism. He made clear from the beginning the distance that was to separate them from now on, and succeeded in doing this without words or gestures by means of a calculated coldness, all the harder to bear for being hidden under a mask of politeness.

It was not that Don Jesusito denied or was ashamed of Amanda.

On the contrary, he felt a satisfaction in knowing his mother when so many of his numerous half brothers did not know who had brought them into the world. He had excellent memories of Amanda, of her beauty and virtues, many of which he thought he had inherited; he looked back longingly to the joys of his childhood, spent in the cleanness and peace of the Barranca; he still missed the delicate care and tact with which he had been reared, delicacy and tact which he thought he also had; he would frequently turn over and over on his tongue, silently, the words "mama, mamá, mamacita, madre" as though they were delicious fruit, out of his reach, or lost treasures.

But during the years out of his mother's care he had acquired an outward layer of dissimulation and soft-spokenness. It was a deep layer, soft in appearance. "He looks as though butter wouldn't melt in his mouth, yet he's capable of tearing the place down." That is the way his father describes him, and, pleased with the success of his plans for Jesusito, he adds, "Better guile than force," expressing a deep-rooted conviction of his that it is superior to the role of brute force assigned to Felipe.

A shrewd talker, both in what he says and in the use he makes of his rather high voice, Jesusito speaks calmly, lowering his voice, half shy, half respectful, until it requires an effort to catch and follow his words. It is still harder when he becomes animated and speaks rapidly. He pours out a string of words, giving no time for interruptions, especially when he is determined to persuade, ensnare, or distract attention from the axe he wants to grind. He loves to beat about the bush and go around in circles, appealing to one's weak side, with special pleading invented to serve his own ends and lull the unwary. When he speaks he is all smiles, he wiggles about and blinks in wide-eyed innocence. He uses his hands, rubbing them together, and looks around ingenuously. They say he acquired these gestures when Don Epifanio, having decided upon his role, sent him to Clamores, where he spent two years under the care of the parish priest, in whose house he lived and whose orchard he looked after.

Don Jesusito is second to none at entering into the roles he is to play. No one can match him at showing sympathy, raising hopes and kindling desires, or at appeasing the discontented. He seems to identify himself with the joys and sorrows of others. Even knowing his trickiness and falseness, even fully aware that he means the opposite of what he says and promises, the villagers are dazzled, dumbfounded, dazed by the tongue of young Trujillo. He gives no breathing space, no time to answer, to think; he rushes off at a gallop, sweeping them along; he cuts short their observations and arguments, makes them laugh, leads them away from the matter they came about, leads them away from the point, makes them say "yes" when they meant to say "no." And they go away happy, saying what a fine person Don Jesusito is, how wise and persuasive, how different from his tiger of a brother, Don Felipe, who pays no attention to arguments and cannot keep a civil tongue in his head. Led astray by the eloquence and gentle manners of Jesusito—"my word, such a nice fellow"—and cornered and trapped more by the fascinating eyes of the cat than by its claws, they go away convinced that black is white. When they think it over and come back to discuss the matter again, it is too late: Don Jesusito has got his way and crushed them. They've given him their word, signed on the dotted line, sold out to him, they have no further rights, however much they complain, beating their heads on the ground, confessing they have been fools, realizing now, to their sorrow, that they have fallen into the jaws of the crocodile, though they should have known better. 'The quick-witted live off fools, but the latter work hard for what they get.' It has happened even to Felipe, even to Plácida. 'The bitch is fierce, she bites even members of her own family.' Only his father has escaped. 'The time has not yet come to beard the lion in his den or for the ducks to fire the guns.'

Not even her son's disdainful treatment of her, the worst cut of all, provoked a cry of complaint, or even the flicker of an eyelid, from Amanda. She redoubled her efforts to serve the ungrateful young man without his knowledge. What hurt her was not seeing herself humiliated—she was hardened to this, and scarcely noticed it—but discovering that treachery was habitual with Jesusito, finding him so different from the way she had brought him up; and it hurt her more than anything to see him making use of his training in kindness and good manners, which she had given him, as a cloak for his treacherous actions.

For the first time, quite subconsciously, Amanda set herself against the will of her master Epifanio, who had changed the natural goodness of the boy, had taken him away from her for this purpose, to turn him into a wicked man, a hypocrite, making use of the very qualities that his mother had encouraged and that were now only skin deep, making it easier for him to achieve his evil ends, like nets to snare innocent animals.

Another change was in store for her. It soon came, shortly after the move to Belén, for no reason. The master broke off all relations with Amanda. Then he sent her to sleep in an out-of-the-way room. He made her wear the old clothes she had brought from the Barranca. Her silence, her way of looking at him, her diligence in anticipating his slightest whim, which, up to that time, had always been able to pacify him in his rages, ceased to have any effect. Her self-confidence began to falter.

The worst was still to come. It came. There was no reason for this either. The master started acting as though he could not stand the sight of his former mistress. This behavior was followed by furious tantrums. To come upon her or see her in the distance drove him crazy. No, it was not the effect of the new moon. A curious disease. Nor was it the dogdays: there was still some time to go before St. Bartholomew's day. It was an unknown malady. At the sight of Amanda he was like a mad dog at the sight of water. When she went away he was better. She began to look like a hunted animal, took to hiding away in corners where she could not be seen, stopped even keeping herself clean.

As unexpectedly as he gave way to his outbursts of rage, one day the master sent for Amanda. They were reunited. From that time his attacks of fury at the sight of her alternated with imperious summonses to his side. These reconciliations were violent and led nowhere; the master would veer from a fit of weeping to a storm of shouts, threats, cursing, and blasphemy; from vile, stupid, fruitless actions to repentance and good resolutions. In his hands the woman was no longer a woman but a wornout rag; her eyes were faded and her nerves frayed; all the strings that had vibrated so tunefully before were now broken.

One of these frenzied reunions ended with her being sent away to the Barranca. Nothing could have pleased the poor creature more. But before a month was out he went to fetch her himself and brought her back to the Big House. Amanda did not utter a word; she made no complaint, showed no signs of any emotion whatsoever. Plácida was driving the cows home, as she did every evening, shouting at them in her deep voice, and hid her anger from the returning pair. Now, as he sat on the verandah, the harsh voice of his daughter, amplified by the echoes of the farm at this time, assailed the old man's ears:

"That machine of Teófila's."

"Teófila."

"Fila."

"La la"

"Aaaa"

If there are saints in Heaven, Teófila is one of them, no doubt of it. And I was the one, with my goings on, that caused her death. There's no doubt about that in my mind either. Not that I killed her. That would be presuming too far. God took her, but it was my fault. 'We lose soonest the things we love best.' Because of my monkey tricks. I remember it as clearly as when the bolt of lightning struck close beside me, killing my mare, Golondrina. How true it is that all good things disappear or die. That was two days before the darling took to her bed, never to get up again. I kept on all the more persistently with my refrain. 'Grab the mare now she's within reach, or she'll get away from you.' That day I managed to speak to her more directly, without Rómulo or Merced being there. 'When there's trouble ahead, and with women, it's best to come straight to the point.' The girl looked at me pityingly for some time, then finally she spoke. "Suppose God were to take me in return for getting you out of the mire." She spoke with the voice and face of a saint, the kind they call martyrs. I, in my madness, still laughing, returned to the attack. I started to say, "Believe very little of what you see and nothing of what you hear," but she'd run off, calling out to her mother that I was there. God immediately took her at her word. To tell the truth I didn't fully grasp her intention until it was too late. Not until after she died, and time went by. Never did I cover the distance between Belén and Betania in such a short time as when I learned that Teófila had brain fever. I tore along like a soul borne off by the devil.

Every day I went back and forth, taking all that was necessary from Belén. I showered money on all the local healers. I even sent to fetch the doctor from Clamores, and agreed to pay whatever he asked, although he always refused to cross over the mountain and come to this barren region. I left no stone unturned. My sins weighed more in God's sight, and He took her. I don't even want to think of it. Not even if lightning had struck me, not even if La Tapona had fallen on top of me, could the shock be compared with this, the end of the world for me, especially since I knew it was my fault. Teófila's words, two days before she got sick, were graven on my heart. And I couldn't tell anybody what had happened, although I wanted to tell the parish priest from Clamores who'd brought the viaticum and extreme unction. But he always hated the sight of me, and that day, in addition, I was furious for so many reasons that I was beside myself and shouted aloud at God and nobody could stop me. Later I learned that my despair had given rise to a lot of ugly gossip.

I was the one who insisted on her being buried as an angel. They were amazed that the suggestion should have come from me, as I'd always ridiculed the custom. "Teófila was not only an angel, she was a real saint," I told them. They replied that she was nearly twenty years old and would have to go to purgatory. It would be flying in the face of Providence, because God was the one to judge, and it was not right, it looked like mockery. Everyone would be scandalized. Some would laugh, others would have a lot to say about it, and who knows what else. I'd ordered the necessary things to be prepared. Rómulo decided against it, earnestly begging me not to persist, out of respect for the dead girl. I was so close to marrying, after all that dallying, and so sure it was the only way as far as the young girl was concerned, that at this time I got rid of various mistresses, pensioning them all off. Even Amanda was sent back to the Barranca, in spite of the virtues I know she has. It cost me a lot to make that decision. 'When you are used to the best you despise the second rate.' When Teófila died even the sun changed color, and the air had a different smell. I was filled with great listlessness, a listlessness that I still haven't got over, it gets worse and worse every day. And I'm getting so fat, eating and drinking like a pig; that was my only consolation, sitting like a stone, idly watching the hours go by. 'He who has drunk from a china cup won't go back to his earthenware mug.' I wasn't interested in my horses, in riding, in my mistresses. I ended up not going out at all. And now I couldn't, even if I wanted to. If I brought Amanda back to Belén, it was out of pity, she's a helpless wreck. Teófila herself would have approved of this act of charity toward a person who has nowhere in the world to go and can't look after herself, worn out as she is, not to mention her virtues and my sense of responsibility in fulfilling my obligations. This one can't be given money and sent away, because she'd die, like an old bitch, paralyzed. Besides, she's the mother of Don Jesusito and we have to have a mistress at Belén to stop people's tongues wagging. With Plácida there, even though she's mistress in name only, as is the case, there'd be no danger of her wanting or being able to be more than that, so we'll get out of the mire in this respect, as Teófila promised. And high time, it'll be said, but it's never too late to mend. I'd be willing now to build a chapel out of my own pocket, without anyone's help, if it were for St. Teófila, and if they'd allow her to be placed on the altar. But I can't tell anyone anything of what Teófila means to me, for, as the saying goes, 'What is for yourself is for nobody else.' Even this business of the machine. I have to make use of Plácida to conceal my own interest. Now I can understand the stories they tell of battles fought to get possession of relics. The saint's machine. It'll work miracles in Belén. That's it. They'll come from far away to touch it. And there won't be any trickery like the made-up tales and apparitions that occurred to me. It's the machine, the real machine of the saint. It will be as though she herself were to come down from Heaven and dwell in Belén. I even offered to wipe out all Rómulo's debts and start again with a clean slate on condition that he'd bring me the machine willingly.

"Bully."
"Sneak."
"Whirlwind."
"Outcasts."
"Idiots."
"Foundlings."

Don Epifanio found work for all his presumptive sons alike, without fear or favor, and had them trained in a skill even when they might still be considered small and were still far from being given a final position in their father's plans. As they grew bigger he would assign to each one a particular task until the time came to make them independent—that is, if they had proved themselves worthy of this. Then he would place them on different farms and give them a bit of land, some agricultural implements, a house, a horse, and weapons. The most important thing was to hand over to them, with some degree of solemnity, the right to his name.

To obtain this, they had, first of all, to pass the examination in "brotherliness and mutual helpfulness," as the patriarch described the test. A test continuing over many years, and consisting of minutely elaborated schemes and tenacious and implacable observation on the part of Don Epifanio, who was influenced by scores of circumstances and indirect, remote factors: it might be the opinions of insignificant neighbors, the shoeing of farm animals owned jointly by several brothers, the condition of the stone walls and five-barred gates dividing the bit of land owned by one member of the family from another. An invariable practice of the "system" was to set several brothers at the same task together and make them joint owners of lands. 'Wolves of the same pack hunt together.'

Those who did not come through this test with flying colors were disowned by their father, even if he had taken them to be baptized and given them their formal name. They had to leave the Tierra Santa or remain as sharecroppers or laborers, or were left to fend for themselves if not actually surrounded by hostility.

With his girl children, the proceeding was very similar, except that they remained longer under the supervision of the mother, their own or a foster mother.

The matrimonial alliances of his descendants were decided by examining each case individually. There were Trujillos, men and women, who were allowed to marry only as ordained by God and the government, while others, particularly women, were condemned to perpetual celibacy with no hope of release. Some of the sons were tacitly authorized to follow their father's example of polygamy.

Exercising his inalienable paternal authority, the head of the clan reserved for himself the right to unmarry and remarry his children—which he did repeatedly—by means of summary decrees, against which there was no appeal, concerning the mistaken selection and choice of sons- and daughters-in-law.

To refuse to accept the decisions of the head of the family in these matters of vital importance to the clan was to condemn oneself to expulsion, hostility, and persecution. The disobedient could not remain in the Tierra Santa, even as servants.

The principles on which Don Epifanio bases his judgments in these cases are no different from those learned from his experience as a muleteer and cattle breeder. They are contained in an endless stream of proverbs.

'Choose a cock, horse, and woman of good stock.'

'A horse should fill your legs, a cock your hands, and a woman your arms.'

'Food and a woman should appeal to the eye.'

'With a bull experienced in the ring, be very careful how you spring.'

'A woman, whether good or bad, needs a halter rather than a spur.'

'A blanket and a woman must be soft.'

'The woman who anticipates your slightest wish will rule you with a rod of iron.'

'The man with powerful protectors need not fear the malice of lesser men.'

'Have nothing to do with a balky mare or an arguing woman.'

'To your perch, hawk, and to your cabbage patch, rabbit.'

'Put a bit in the mouth of a mare and a bridle rein on a mule.'

'Better a donkey than a jackass or a balky horse.'

'Your daughter's son is your grandson, but who knows who your son's son is?'

'A stallion that doesn't neigh . . .'

A tale now almost forgotten even by the few who knew it is the story of Miguel Arcángel. Don Epifanio would have liked to forget it, too, as his rancor against his ungrateful son abated, but he is not a man to lose a scent and he has followed with increasing uneasiness that of his perverse son.

Miguel Arcángel—this was the official name he had him baptized by, and he was one of the few sons he had taken to be confirmed during the Bishop's visits to Clamores—was one of the first to receive Epifanio's surname, at a banquet in El Cabezón, as the master continued to call Damasco, either out of heresy or just to be different. Miguel Arcángel—the first of the names on the list Don Epifanio had started collecting before he had any children, even claiming that when he was a child this name was revealed to him in dreams, a name associated in the polygamist's mind with pictures of heavenly wars, the invincible lieutenant, the scales of justice, the flaming sword, vanquished monsters, eyes and arms like a bolt of lightning, shining raiment, certain victory—Miguel Arcángel was the patriarch's first great hope and a stimulus for developing his plan for his progeny.

Don Epifanio could see himself in the boy. He had had him with Sara. 'Choose a tall thin woman and a chestnut mare.' He met her on his travels as a muleteer. She was from a farm on the other side of Clamores, and used to help her mother sell food to the travelers. Their name was Gallo. When he took Sara, he gave her a house in Cuilán beyond the Sierra de Cardos. There the boy was born. Sara Gallo wanted to call him Jacob in memory of her father and because she had heard that the name meant "the strong one." The meaning did not displease Trujillo. "We'll see when the time comes whether he deserves it." He was wondering whether he would earn the name Miguel—not plain Miguel, that would be ordinary, but with the shining addition to Arcángel. Almost from the time he was born he began to show signs of being a prodigy. Or even before, if Sara's dreams and stories are to be believed. He would kick in her womb and she would hear mysterious voices; she could feel him galloping inside her, and strong hands seemed to clutch and tear at her; in her dreams she would constantly see the same little boy, tall, swarthy, wiry, who would sometimes overthrow a bull by the horns, sometimes run, swift as lightning, sometimes cut down whole forests in the twinkling of an eye.

Epifanio gave up muleteering. Sara was taken up to the Tierra Santa and installed near Torres de San Miguel. There the boy grew up. He amazed everyone by his incredible quickness, he was daring, strong, talkative, swift-moving, nothing was difficult for him, and at the same time he was upright, obliging, kind-hearted, and good at making friends.

It was in the early days of the "system" and Trujillo was more tactful in taking him away from Sara than he would be later, in other cases. His pretext was that he was going to take him to the city to school. Sara was transferred to Belén, where she remained until the break between Don Epifanio and Miguel Arcángel.

The patriarch saw that his son was endowed with both strength and cunning combined: brute force and guile, later to be divided between two people, Felipe and Jesús. He had no doubt of it— Miguel Arcángel was made to succeed him as head of the family.

So blindly did he desire this that he overlooked Miguel Arcángel's disdainful, superior attitude toward his brothers, a fault he would never again pardon. What he refused to tolerate was his insubordination when, all on his own, without a word to anyone, he decided to get married. In vain did he warn him time and time again, repeating the old saying, 'Do what I tell you or you'll regret it.' He took away the house and lands of El Cabezón that he had assigned to him and placed Felipe there.

Miguel Arcángel was not the kind of person to fight back, as Don Epifanio expected. He did not even say goodbye. Taking his mother with him, he calmly went off, leaving a message, "The world is wide, and I'm leaving even your name behind. I'll get myself another."

Epifanio would have liked to blot him out of his mind. Especially because of the insult to the sacred name, flashing like a comet across the August sky.

Don Epifanio feels that he is now drawing nearer and nearer, whether he comes as a coyote or an owl. He knows, and thinks he is the only one who knows, that since his flight he has been known as Jacob Gallo; that he has become rich, has a large family, and wants to get land in the Tierra Santa.

At the same time there is manifest restiveness in the clan, with Felipe, Jesús, and Plácida at the bottom of it. Like a gathering storm. Comings and goings. Pregnant silences. Shifty looks. Words on the tip of the tongue, checked before they are uttered. Secrets. Nervous gestures.

The old man senses the uncertainty, the restlessness, the unformulated ambitions of his heirs. Out of tune, weary, the strong voice tries to articulate words:

"Keep calm, my children, don't be impatient. Don't get restive, I know you as well as mules I've just unsaddled. Staying awake won't make the morning come any sooner."

Forward in the name of the cross

"Forward in the name of the cross. Let the dead bury their dead."
That is Matiana's customary greeting when someone comes to fetch
her.

"Please, Madre, come quickly, I hope we can get there in time.
The devil himself flew overhead."

"What Christian soul was his victim?"

"There may be many. The devil flew overhead and at once an
epidemic of diarrhea broke out. My grandmother's the worst, I left
her writhing in pain, she's at death's door. I saw him flying, too, and
the noise was deafening, I thought my ears would burst. Hurry up.
Just throw your rebozo over your head and let's go. I'll tell you more
on the way."

"And what about medicines? I'm not coming just to twiddle my
thumbs. Like a bilious attack, you say?"

The woman was lifting down from a hanging bamboo rack several bottles and jars and stowing them away in a canvas bag as she
spoke.

"The fright has given everyone diarrhea and colic. You should have seen the dreadful thing. We thought the end of the world had come. The only good thing about it was it didn't last long. A little longer and it would have been all up with us. Come on, Madre, don't be such a slowpoke."

"I've got everything now. Go on. So, what happened? I can't make any sense of your story except that there's an epidemic of diarrhea and the devil appeared."

"That's right. Isn't that enough? The devil himself, flying. We all saw him and heard the terrible noise."

The man helped Matiana to mount the burro, which was already saddled. They set off, the man behind, driving the animal before him with a stick.

"As if it were coming down over the house onto our heads. It moved along, throwing off sparks and smoke, with eyes glowing like coals. If you'd seen how dreadful it was, such huge wings! There's still a bitter taste in my mouth. By some miracle I and a few others haven't got diarrhea yet. Everyone came out to watch, young and old. And it just passed overhead, it was there for only a few seconds but it seemed like ages. People running around, weeping, praying, white-lipped, deathly pale. There wasn't even time to get the holy water and blessed candles some keep in their houses for an emergency. They went to fetch them because we thought it would turn around and come back again. Old Nestor tried to cut through it, making crosses in the air with his knife, like he does with the dust storms in the rainy season. No good. It just gave a small wiggle and went on like a buzzard, only it was the size of the Big House at Belén. They say that you yourself often see him but it can't be in the dreadful form in which he appeared to us in La Tarabilla."*

"You're one yourself. You must have caught diarrhea of the mouth. I can't get a word in to ask what really happened."

"The devil himself, I'm telling you. Our friend Tobías killed a pig and invited some of the neighbors. The farm is small—you know

---

* The Chatterbox.

it—and the houses aren't far from each other. There we were, celebrating the pig-killing, when suddenly we began to hear a buzzing from the direction where the sun sets, and soon a black dot appeared in the sky and got bigger and bigger, and the sound got louder, too. It wasn't a bird or a meteorite, it was headed straight for the farm. It looked just like a gigantic bird, judging by the size of the wings when we saw it close to. Eyes shone on all sides of it. "The Devil! The Evil One!" We began to cry out and run, and there was nowhere to hide. I realized, in the middle of the scramble, that if I went into the house I'd be crushed to death. A terrifying bird. I heard that he used to take the form of a beast of prey but at night and not visible to everybody, just as spirits aren't seen by everyone present, only by those they appear to. Tell me, in what shape does the devil appear to you?"

"And the pig wasn't diseased?"

"You're not listening to me! You're like that doubting Thomas of a Melesio. I was asking you in what shape the devil and the spirits appear to you. What do they look like?"

"In so many shapes that I don't even bother about them any more. Nearly always when someone is going to die or is in danger."

"So your prophesying skill comes from him?"

"Nonsense, I'm his worst enemy. Our Lord permits me to recognize the Evil One in whatever form he disguises himself, and gives me the power to detect his evil schemes in order to frustrate them. It's incredible, the number of cunning schemes he invents."

It's impossible to tell of all the things I've seen and experienced during the course of my eighty-odd years. As the saying goes, 'The devil knows more because he's old than because he's the devil.' When Teófila died, for instance, I was going out to warm up a poultice, when who did I see in the yard but Don Pifas in the shape of the devil, covered with soot, with a tail and horns, grinning with delight. I took to my heels, forgetting poultices and everything else, and ran back into the room, beginning right away the "Go forth, Christian soul" and the other prayers I usually say for the dying. I barely got there in time. I'd left the girl fairly calm and I found her writhing about as though trying to keep from being dragged away. I went in, made the sign of the cross, gritted my teeth, burned some sweet-scented marigolds cut in August before St. Bartholomew's day, walked around the room sprinkling all the corners with palm branches blessed and dipped in holy water, praying aloud all the time. When I drew near the dying girl she'd stopped twisting and turning. Her face was tranquil, smiling, and she drew her last breath like that. She died peacefully, a happy expression on her face. Then the trouble began with Doña Merced and Don Pifas: the one fidgeting around like a lost soul, begging for death and crying out that it was for *her* sins alone that God had sent them such a punishment; the other, possessed by the devil, insisting on burying the dead girl according to his fancy, declaring she was a saint—he was a nice one to talk!—prowling back and forth like a mad dog, waving his hands, raving against God. He nearly killed me, tried to grab me by the scruff of the neck, lost control of himself and actually kicked me. He was frantic, and it served him right.

The farmer continued:
"I'd begun to doubt if he really existed, at least to doubt if he could actually be seen except in our imaginations, conjured up through fright. That happened to me once when they filled my head with the idea that the devil himself was after me. I could see vague shapes and hear steps in the road or behind the stone walls, and I could see shadows prowling around the farm at night. The worst of it was the way my animals behaved. The old gray horse would prick up his ears and I couldn't make him budge though I nearly killed him. The cocks and hens would cluck, ruffling all their feathers, and the oxen bellowed as though stung by gadflies. Worst of all, the barking of the dogs was just like when they know there's a mad dog around, exactly the same. In the mornings there was no sign of coyotes, bobcats, snakes, boars, cacomistles, or other animals that do damage for all our sprinkling sand and setting traps, and nothing happened to the suckling pigs and hens we left out on purpose. The kind of cries I thought I heard didn't sound like any familiar animal, and the odor I smelled was more like pitch and brimstone. I got

more and more frightened. The truth is that my conscience wasn't easy, I'd been behaving like Judas and the last thing I'd done was to seduce a young girl on the Trancas farm with false promises . . ."

Matiana's head and body swayed gently to and fro, keeping time with the monotonous gait of the burro. She bore no resemblance to the famous old woman whose reputation extended to the boundaries of the plain and even beyond. Her head fell forward on her weary neck, nodding rhythmically. As in a trance, her eyes were fixed wearily on the narrow space around her; barren ground, showers of pebbles, the ups and downs in the path, small creatures scuttling out of the way, anthills, processions of tiny ants—these things passed endlessly before her eyes, but, lost in thought, she did not seem to see them. Normally cheerful, lively as a squirrel, quick and authoritative in her remarks, sharp-tongued and sarcastic, outspoken, the sybil of the plain was now absorbed in her own thoughts, hearing nothing, saying nothing. And these silences are ominous, inspiring dread and terror.

But the man, undisturbed, continued his tale, unaware that the old woman was not listening to him.

"One night I said, 'To hell with it!' I took my courage in my hands, and a gun. In front of the farmhouse two big embers were shining and on the other side a huge shadow moved about in threatening fury. I took aim and fired. Are you listening, Doña? Don't laugh . . ."

Matiana's smooth face, smooth as a stone in the river where the women wash, an unwrinkled face worn smooth by years of weeping, worn thin by long days of sun and wind. Matiana is always ready to set out and go—be it near or far—to the bedside where calamity has struck—in rain or thunder—with no thought of reward, unconcerned about leaving her house empty. Her eyes, something like an eagle's, something like an owl's, are set deep in their sockets and not all can face their keen gleam. Tears have hollowed two channels running down her gaunt face. No one has ever seen her weep but her countenance has been carved out by centuries of weeping. Her face is sunburned and clean, and bears marks like those left on the washing stones in the river, the result of daily scrubbing with soap and lye for years and years. Matiana's door is open day and night—to those seeking advice and consolation, healing, spells to ward off evil, communion with the unseen. Her hands, strong and bony, carry their burdens from this world to the next and back again, a terrible privilege, consuming yet sustaining the energy of the mediator. Birdlike in appearance, yet with the strength of a mesquite. From time immemorial Matiana has always been Matiana. Grandfathers and greatgrandfathers say she has not changed from when they knew her as children. "She will bury our great-great-great-grandchildren," they say, "and still be as tough as a branch of quince." With her hard fingertips she feels the hidden movement of the spirits which harm or help the living. Nobody on the plain and in the region around it knows, as she does, the good and harmful properties of the three kingdoms of nature—nor how to use them or counteract them. Gossip has it that Matiana goes down into hell by night and when she seems lost in thought.

What greater hell than the thoughts of men's minds! If the just man sins seven times a day, I've never in my life met seven just men, seeing that all the fairly good commit their twelve sins a day, for instance, and that's nearly always because they haven't got strength for more, except in thought. My eyes grow weary and they smart, driven unwillingly to examine, search, and scrutinize the inner workings of men's minds. Don Pifas' insistence on getting possession of the machine is sheer vengeance, wicked vengeance. He believes, though he doesn't say so, that it's affection, even devotion. Others think it's just ordinary avarice. The two-faced creature has managed to persuade himself, without getting up courage to put it in words, that it's remorse, because according to him God couldn't find any other way to get Teófila out of his clutches, and she offered her life in return for the conversion of the old billy goat. So the girl owes him her enjoyment of Heaven. In fact, it's not remorse, it's sheer presumption! And he's puffed up with the idea that he's changed his way of living because of Teófila's miracle! You can't see into his heart. In his younger days it was a stable with devils in the stalls, and now it's a sink of iniquity overflowing with wickedness. That's what made him give up his running around. Unbridled drinking, the fattening of his heart, bladder trouble, bad blood, ingrained evil made worse by so many evil deeds. For instance, this latest determination to get hold of the machine, out of wicked vengeance for old and recent injuries: the fight Rómulo and his brothers put up for what was theirs at the time of Teódulo's sudden death, a useless struggle in any case, since Pifanio snatched it all away from them by crooked means. Then Merced, feeling sorry for Sara Gallo, kept her in her house for a few days when she fled from Belén, until her son Miguel came for her. Later there was his fancy to have Teófila and in this he came up against a stone wall, which he never forgave or forgot. His hatred was increased when he sensed Merced's intentions. She was made desperate by the constant fear that one day the old goat was bound to dishonor them by seducing the girl, and kept invoking the Eye and the Hand of Divine Providence, begging them, day and night, not to forget to strike down the evil man with a bolt of lightning or send him by some means or other to the next world. She made vows to all the saints she knew, and combining faith with work, she kept praying to God while she took her own measures too. She kept following Epifanio around, trying to take his measurements when he wasn't looking with a ribbon which she would at once hang on the miraculous statue of San Benito de Palermo, venerated in the Chapel at Cuilán, always ready to grant his worshippers the favor of removing from their paths, in no more than fifteen days, the neighbor whose measurements they brought him. The man would inevitably die, however strong and healthy he might be. Reliable little Black Saint! Merced had prepared the wax and the offering for the task, but the main thing was lacking: she couldn't get a chance to measure the man she hated, and there wasn't anyone to help her, since she didn't want to tell anyone about her scheme. It was at this stage that Teófila's illness occurred, followed by her death. This drove Merced mad, for she believed that God was taking away from her what she loved most dearly as a punishment because she'd schemed for the death of the dirty old he-goat. This, in his opinion, was the worst thing anyone could wish him, worse than if someone had actually tried to kill him. He had a vague suspicion of Merced's intentions and something she let out in her despair gave him the final clue. No one told *me*, but I gradually put two and two together—the ribbon, the black wax, Merced's cries beside the body of her daughter—"This is what I get for wishing harm to others"—and more than anything else, this cursed power and my habit of seeing into the minds of others. The old moneylender is fully aware that while Merced won't part with Teófila's machine for all the wealth in the world, Rómulo, given the choice between the machine and the land, won't hesitate to keep the latter. This is the worst of it, that Rómulo and Merced, fighting like cat and dog, should be at odds with each other when they've been so united. It's easy to speed up the pace of Justice and cut the thread on which the life of the scoundrel hangs. But no, a different fate is in store for him, a worse punishment: his own children will cut this thread. We have to wait. I can scent their approach in the air. I can see them coming, Miguel Arcángel, Felipe, Jeusito, Plácida, followed by the countless swarm of bastards. Not one is missing. What worse hell could there be!

"My fears soon vanished. The cat turned out to be a neighbor's and the ox had Trujillo's brand on it. Blessed discovery! So I doubted the devil's existence until yesterday, when I saw him plainly with no room for doubt, and I wasn't the only one! You'll soon see the evidence of so many sick people. Are you asleep, Madre? Can you hear me?"

"Have you heard of a man called Jacob Gallo?"

"Sakes alive! What have you been dreaming about, Madre?" Her companion scratched the back of his head as a sign he was thinking. "I think I have, a somebody-or-other Gallo, looking so very much like a Trujillo that I wouldn't trust him an inch. He passed along by La Tarabilla, coming this way toward Betania, a little while ago. To be on the safe side, I kept my mouth tight shut, didn't say a word."

"How did you manage that, a blabbermouth like you? And that Gallo, what did he ask?"

"Now, Madre, let me think. Well, now, I believe he asked about the price of land and how we got our seeds for sowing."

"Did he ask about the Trujillos?"

"Something. Something. I don't remember. Yes, if there was any quarreling among them, between Don Felipe and Don Jesusito, between the children and their father. To tell the truth, I don't remember very well."

Justice is Matiana's province. She metes it out in favor of the weak. She never has to be asked. When complaints are brought to her she makes no answer, not a muscle of her face moves. At most she asks a brief question, without emotion. If the injustice is the result of wickedness, a flash of lightning may be seen in her enigmatic eyes. She neither promises nor threatens. She withdraws into herself, concentrating with all her mental powers. She examines the cases in the light of her conscience, weighing the evidence. Without bias, calmly, dispassionately. She judges each case on its own merits, by itself. It may be months or years before sentence is pronounced; it may another equal number of months or years before it is carried out. The "Judge" must have her doubts resolved. She waits patiently for the enlightenment that makes the case transparently clear with no mixture of personal emotion. At other times judgment is passed and the sentence carried out with lightning speed.

Her sentences need no rod or whip. Her frequent minister is Death. Or paralysis. Paralysis or death of men, animals; land, seeds, tools made useless. Before the sentences are carried out, nobody knows, nobody can find out, the stage of the trial nor the time before the judgment. Still less if the request is made by one of the defendants.

"Doña, why are you sometimes so quiet? You're like the muledriver who answered the question after three days on the road."

"He must have taken three days to find the answer."

"What they asked him was, what was the name of the solitaire thrush."

"It could just as well have been what the mule he was riding was called. I'm not talking about names, and things. People, too, and even feelings are stored in the memory, not for one or even three days, but for months, for years, or for always."

"Madre, your words are shrouded in smoke. No one can understand you. Or, as we say, they tell us neither one thing nor the other."

"Smoke, dripping water, and a prattling spouse drive a man out of the house."

They were now coming down the side of La Tarabilla. They could already see the cluster of houses in the background, scattered in among the orchards. Up above was the Tierra Santa with its bare earth.

"And you haven't said a word in answer to my question about the devil, Madre!"

"You haven't answered my question about the pig."

"I told you that you'd said something like Melesio, who came back from the North believing in nothing. The very thought of it makes me mad, and I think it's a sin to repeat it."

"Then shut your mouth."

"How do you manage, Madre, not to be curious?"

"By guessing what I want to know."

"Guess what the doubting Thomas said."

"I'm not interested in knowing that."

"He said an outrageous thing."

People were coming up the hill to meet them.

"She died, after all."

"Her time had come."

"Rosenda's newborn child, too. Her milk must have been turned by the fright she got from the devil."

"Can you hear me, Madre?"

"The oldest woman and the new offshoot together!"

"The Day of Judgment!"

"Bless the whole ravine, say a prayer to stop the devil from coming back. Stand on the brow of the hill or in the middle of the river, wherever you think it'll be most effective. A prayer like the one you said blessing the whole plain from the top of La Tapona at the time of the Spanish influenza or Carranza disease, and which proved a blessed relief."

Having no priests, no doctors, no judges, no police, what would the plain and the harsh country around it do without Matiana, the miracle-worker? Her service is manifold: she has the gifts of a prophetess and exorcist, defender, chastiser, healer, adviser, comforter, and midwife, and can perform the burial rites. In public and private disasters, in this land of huisache and cactus.

Illiterate. Yet she can read and has taught others to read the outward appearance of people, things, and agreements; to make mental notes and calculations. She inspires admiration for the speed and accuracy with which she performs arithmetical operations and calculations to determine the seasons and feast days.

She is the people's calendar, in a land where few houses have printed calendars, so that it is difficult to keep count of the days, to know what day it is and when it is a day to be kept or remembered. Most of the farmers are used to not knowing this; in the isolation in which they live their routine lives it does not matter to them, except when it is something very special. They can barely count the days of the week in order to know when it is Sunday, and that is only in order to perform certain domestic tasks, since few are able to undertake the long journey into the town to Mass and market. They have neither the time nor the money. The calendar they are interested in is of another kind: the phases of the moon, the position of the stars, the coming of the cabañuelas,* the near approach of the rainy season or its delay, the dogdays and the drought, the renewal or ending of the rains; the effect of these signs in the heavens on the birth of livestock, the preparation of the land, getting the tools ready

---

* The days of January, thought to predict the predominant weather for each month of the year. Between January 1 and 12, January 1 represents January, January 2 represents February, et cetera. Between January 13 and 24, the months are counted backward, with January 13 representing December, et cetera. Between January 25 and 30, each day represents two months, counting forward. On January 31, each hour represents a month, first counting forward, then backward.

neighing, braying, barking, the birdsongs, the high-pitched voices of the farmers, all continue as before. This returning cycle brings back the dead to our minds, and we see them in their accustomed places, doing their accustomed tasks as we saw them before, especially in September when the fields begin to turn yellow and are filled with marigolds and sunflowers, the days grow shorter and sounds are heard more clearly, and the Day of the Dead draws near. Just like the year when we escaped the turmoil of the Revolution but fell victims to the Carranzazo, which is what the people here called the epidemic better known as Spanish influenza, which created havoc among us. That was when I climbed La Tapona with the weight of the holocaust on my shoulders, amid the terror of all, and the weeping of widows and orphans, bearing the invocations of the living and the dead, and I spoke to God and placed our great distress before Him and told Him that we were well punished and asked Him to turn aside His anger from us and tie up the devil again. I drove out the evil spirits, put a spell on the land and the winds that brought the germs and the waters that kept them alive and propagated them. I kept my arms uplifted as long as I could with the burden of petitions and suffering, while from all the farms and all the houses where anyone was left alive, smoke arose from blessed palms, crosses and wreaths of marigolds, clothes and infected straw mats. The cry from the plain was heard, the wind changed, the evil spirits returned to hell. How time passes and nothing changes in the life of the countryside, with its annual cycle of seed-time and harvest, endlessly repeated and accepted, year after year, day after day; lands, people, defenseless cattle, all at the mercy of and helpless before the mystery of disease, seasonal ills, usury, all kinds of injustice, all kinds of evil, water shortage, pollution, recurring infectious diseases and epidemics, sometimes worse than others, depending also on the months. The dogdays are the worst and there are years when the mortality is heavy, especially infant mortality, since there aren't enough hands to look after them all or, on the other hand, to drive away Satan and the other evil spirits who are constantly prowling around the plain, getting stronger and stronger all the time, seeking to destroy souls. Amen. They say that I'm a witch and there have always been some who have tried to destroy my influence, to stir up the innocent farmers against me, to strike at me, many deadly blows, from which, thank God, I've managed to escape, miraculously, because I have the people on my side, and they're the first to protect me and give, I won't say their eyes, but their lives and more. I've never been afraid of anybody, not even of the devil. I'm weary of walking alone, with only my thoughts for company, along roads and footpaths, at all hours of the day and night; weary of being present at deathbeds and watching by the dead; weary of standing firm against the most arrogant. After all, it is they who are afraid of me, they don't dare to face me but try to find someone to act for them. They throw the stone and put their hands behind their backs, although they're well aware I can see in the dark and find out secrets. They also know that sooner or later they'll need me. I don't know what they mean by "witch." I don't know if I am one according to their ideas. What I do know is that I have no pact with the devil, because it's not from below but from above that the sudden vision comes, vision that enables me to help my neighbor, who pays me what he can when he can. I make no charge, and ask for nothing. I myself am poor, I live on my herbs, my fruit trees, and what people feel like giving me. I live on little and never refuse to help anyone, cost what it may. The troubles of others distress me, I forget my own. I accept neither credit for my successes nor blame for my failures. No one need ask my help. What I cannot forgive is injustice. The punishments based on my judgments come from above, which means they are just and even I can't stop them, though I've often wanted to. "Vengeance of the witch," say the sufferers. Our Lord knows that this is not true. The people know it, too. Our Lord and the people protect me from the assaults of the Evil One and the schemes of the wicked.

"Yes, you ought to know, so you can offer up your best prayers, the one most fitting for the occasion, from the most suitable spot. I have to tell you what that heretic Melesio said, roaring with laughter, standing there with his arms folded, bold as brass, as he watched the devil go by with that horrible noise, making fun of our terror, laughing at my grandmother kneeling out in the open countryside, her arms stretched out in the form of a cross, beating her breast, scared to death, beside herself with fear. All of us kneeling down, following her example, beating our breasts in repentance, terrified at the sight of the devil, yes, the devil himself, passing over our heads, above our houses, and changing his course as though he saw us, hovering like an eagle or a hawk, ready to pounce. The heretic began to move away and if it hadn't been for the gun he was carrying and his coolheadedness, which held us back, we'd have hurled ourselves on him and lynched him, because he kept saying, the heretic, that we were all a bunch of ignorant fools. There was no reason to be frightened, he added, since what was flying above was not the devil but one of those things called airplanes that he'd seen in the North and that he knew had come to Mexico."

"Ear-what?"

"Airplanes, I think he said, and then to call us all fools into the bargain, the unbeliever!"

"Don't forget that when Melesio said the Revolution hadn't reached this side of Cardos, it wasn't because I prophesied it wouldn't, but what would it find here? Roads? Not even those. No good horses, no food, no enemies, not even flies. That didn't make me angry, remember? He might have been right or my opinion might have been based on the same reasoning as his. Who knows?"

They reached the afflicted farm. When she had attended to the sick, Matiana busied herself praying for the dead child, dressed her as an angel, and complied with the general wish that she utter an incantation standing in the middle of the river, turning her head and hands, first to one side of the ravine and then to the other. Her duties done, she set off on her return journey as the light was beginning to fade. She walked in silence beside her companion. She did not speak until they reached the top of the pass.

"Didn't I tell you? The pork was bad."

"I wouldn't have believed you could have gone over to the side of the unbelievers," her companion muttered in a tone of mingled sorrow and anger.

They walked on in silence. Night had fallen over the plain. Shortly before reaching the old woman's house in Betania, they concluded their conversation.

"Whether it was Satan himself or an airplane, it's all the same, the latter's merely the former in another shape. Or worse, the devil entered into men, making them fly through the air."

"Nothing of the sort. Don't let's beat about the bush. It was the devil, alive, wagging his tail and puffing out smoke. Don't be so disbelieving, Doña. It doesn't suit you, you less than anyone. Without you, we'd have no one to ward off the calamities that fall upon us every day without our knowing even which direction the blow comes from, and then what would we do, especially the poor, without even the comfort of someone to turn to?"

Part Two — JERUSALÉN:
THE RETURN OF MIGUEL ARCÁNGEL

Struggling along

"Struggling along. It's the same old story, from the moment we're born till we breathe our last. We can't get away from it, no one can change our lot. While every year the land gets stonier and harder, and it's no good letting it lie fallow for a season or two or even longer. And the sky as well, less rainfall every year, more uneven and more deceptive. Frosts more frequent and droughts earlier, longer and more destructive all the time. The ponds dry up earlier each year and there's not a trickle of water in the stream. The wells get lower earlier. It's harder to get a tree to take root. The women have to go farther and farther to get water and have to go down to the ravine to wash. It takes them all day to go and come."

The Great Eye of Providence, in its blue triangle with gilt borders, was listening. Like a huge Ear painted at the bottom of the wall it listened to the talk of the men.

"God tightens His hold on us but He doesn't strangle us, my grandfather used to say."

"Those with this world's goods grow harder and harder, and are never tired of trying to get more at the expense of the poor, grinding them down without mercy, leaving them like dishes at an inn, scraped clean, face downwards. Now we're really out of the frying pan into the fire. Farming tools sky high, corn sold before it's cut, with the buyer driving a harder bargain, the renting of land or oxen harder, not to mention the conditions the tenant farmers have to put up with."

"God is present where all else is lacking, and speaks for the man who is silent, and He may delay but He doesn't forget: these were little sermons of my grandfather's."

"No matter how hard we struggle, in every way, we can't even manage to make the necessary repairs, to scrape together enough to eat. I cover my hungry yawn with the sign of the cross. No matter how hard we work we can't get enough to keep us alive."

"But we haven't come to join in your complaining, my friends, and it wouldn't serve any purpose. So . . ."

"I was coming to that, to cut Rómulo off and stop his complaint that he's struggled so hard all his life for nothing. I say, it's our own fault we make fools of ourselves—some out of laziness, running around in circles, pretending to work, and others out of habit, since no one can stop them doing what they've seen others doing all their lives. They don't realize that things change, which means you have to look for other ways of killing fleas, as they say. 'A willing heart goes all the way.' We struggle along, groping blindly, trying to see what will work, although we know well enough, for example, that sowing seed in pure clay is like trying to catch up with the sun to give him a letter, and worse than plowing a lake. As the saying goes, 'It's worse than sowing seed in the river: you won't even get the seed back.'"

"Listen, friend, I'm beginning to think you enjoy being like the people on the plain. The afternoon's almost gone in idle talk. Remember, I'm not from the plain. I like to go straight to the point and, if necessary, take the bull by the horns."

"Isn't that what we're doing? Aren't we seizing the opportunity to continue the struggle to satisfy our needs by safe, guaranteed means, like the magnetic rods?"

ing with her, as they say, like a ball in their paws, even though
Teófila was quite capable of keeping her dignity and making people
treat her with respect. But with those Trujillos you never know what
to look for. They're there, watching, even when they don't interfere,
and they trade for what they don't buy. God forgive me. There are
times when I'd rather have her dead than think of her—Hail Mary
most pure—connected with those creatures. It's one thing for me to
dislike getting mixed up in squabbles and to be cautious, not speaking ill of anyone, but it's another thing entirely not to see their
faults. I'm under an obligation to them—for all their 'It depends,'
they've done me favors—but that doesn't mean I have no reasons
for distrusting them. I have lots of them, and they go back a long
while. The way they seized the property belonging to my father and
my uncles, to go no further. I'm willing to grant that my father and
my uncles were mainly to blame—my father especially, God forgive him—because they were wastrels and squanderers. But it's true,
too, that Pifanio behaved very badly. He coveted their property and
took advantage of their necessity, if he didn't actually steal it outright. When my grandfather died, squabbling broke out between
the brothers. I think it would have been the same even if my grandfather had had time to put his affairs in order and divide the inheritance between them. They were hard to handle, envious, un-
brotherly. They weren't at all like their father, who had been so
reliable, so open, such a gentleman in all his doings, in his relation-
ships with others, in his conversation, whether he was speaking
seriously or joking. My father never liked the favoritism my grandfather showed toward me. When my grandfather died I felt like an
orphan even though my father took me to live with him and my
stepmother. So I saw for myself how soon the estate that my grandfather built up by hard work and patience fell to pieces. I remember how I suffered as each bit of land was sold. It was like having
pieces of my flesh torn away. I couldn't forget the old man's pride
as he showed me the boundaries of our land, telling me how he'd
acquired it all, bit by bit. What hurt most, and still hurts, even after
all this time, was the loss of my chestnut horse, Namesake, and my
grandfather's house at Belén, which I refused to enter again for a

long time. It hurts so much, I'm determined not to think of it. 'Things that humiliate should be forgotten and never mentioned.' But it's Merced I've got to think of now. She must be worried, not knowing where I am. Palemón arrived at just the right time so I could put off telling Merced about Don Pifas' generous offer. I can imagine the fuss she'll kick up when she learns of it and sees in my face that I mean to accept it. There's no way of getting into her head the great difference in value. I couldn't believe my ears, but these crazy fads and fancies seem to sweep over Epifanio from time to time—the way he offered, this very morning, when I went to see him early, to wipe out all my debts and start with a clean slate in return for the machine, while he considered the only bit of land I have left a trifle, not even enough to pay the interest, so it would be only postponing the agony of handing over the house, too, and eventually the machine, at whatever price he likes to fix. I don't know why women can't use their heads to think things out properly. I realize how sad and how hard it is to part with the thing, but keeping it won't bring Teófila back to life again. Strange women from the farms all around will sew on it. It won't bring in the money she was giving me. What a good daughter she was! How pleased she looked when she gave me her earnings! "You see, father, I wasn't just dreaming when we bought the machine. We'll soon have it paid for, and what I earn then will be our own." Then she'd let her imagination run on, building castles in the air. God's will be done! No, I don't say Merced is wrong, but she ought to understand that in time of war there's no quarter given and it's no use crying when you're drowning. Let me think how I can persuade her. Meanwhile, what can I do about these people? I've already said no, definitely no! But they're pigheaded. The worst thing is my growing suspicion of their leader, for his likeness to the Trujillos. It looks very fishy to me, their not charging anything for the hire of the divining rods on condition that we go with them and hold them, too. I'm going to get up the courage to ask him what his game is, who he is and who sent him . . . In the end I didn't have to; he beat me to it, telling me what he was after, showing me what side he was on.

Pifanio had sent him to sow his wild oats after he came back from the parish priest's. What everyone expected happened. Miguel Arcángel ran away with Florentina Sánchez. But he treated her with respect. He was an honorable boy. Since Pifanio refused to consent to the marriage under any circumstances, simply out of sheer capriciousness (there was nothing against the girl—on the contrary), the young man took her into the town and they were married. He came back again to fetch Sara, his mother, who had sought refuge with Merced, in my house in Betania, when she fled from Pifanio and the house at Belén. Then they disappeared. No further definite news was ever heard of them. There were tales and rumors, all contradictory. All this happened when the revolt was at its height, and although it missed the plain, we were cut off for weeks and months. Gradually we began to forget the affair. From time to time, isolated scraps of news reached us. Since many turned out to be lies, we ended up by not believing any of them. As when people die, after the first despair you stop talking about them, even though you don't mean to. You get used to living without them, as though they'd never lived. Gradually their habits, their voices, their faces, even their names are forgotten, until they turn to dust and are wiped from the memory. 'Out of sight, out of mind.' Haven't I just made up my mind to forget Teófila, my only daughter? Yes, to part with her machine, which is the same thing. One fine day the past rises up in the memory, things past appear vividly again, like the full lips of Florentina Sánchez, her turned-up nose, small, curious, like a mischievous, affectionate child. I shook hands with her only once. She had soft hands, both firm and smooth. She had a cute nose. A pretty woman! I'd like to ask after her and hear what happened to Sara Gallo—tall and slim, as Epifanio used to call her. These girls of the Tierra Santa that I knew as a boy! How many of them have died, gone away, or grown old! A farmer's life doesn't give him much time to notice how time flies. Then, one day, talking about ages or reckoning up years, noticing wrinkles or thinking in what a short time the youngsters have grown up into men and women, we're amazed for a little while. 'White hair may fool you, teeth may lie, but wrinkles tell the truth.' I remember Florentina as a girl just reaching womanhood. Above her lips and at the beginning of her jaws you could see the same down as on peaches. We're also aware of the passing of time when some wanderer returns home after many years, ragged and down at heel, like the prodigal son. We feel that time has slipped through our fingers like water. We begin to get ready to die when God wills. The houses don't usually have mirrors in them. Some men, very few, carry small ones in their pockets, round ones. Some women use them, too, chiefly girls, but they keep them safely hidden as though ashamed of being known to have them. I don't know where Merced keeps Teófila's mirror hidden. It was big and square, and could be hung up or stood on the floor. I sometimes looked at myself in it before Teófila's death and she used to laugh at me, affectionately, and she herself would sometimes put it in front of me, saying, "Look, what a handsome young man you are, father." I let my daughter treat me affectionately, like a child, God keep her in His holy kingdom. She was more like a town-bred young lady, perhaps even city-bred. "A pity," they used to say. And now, reappearing, young again (I only shook hands with her once), in this man who has many of her features, although he is also the living image of Miguel Arcángel—at least I think he is. The truth is, I hardly remember what he was like, whereas I can see Florentina in my mind's eye exactly as she was. Always as if she had just washed, fresh as a daisy, always looking as if her hair had just been combed and braided. And what braids she had! How she used to twist them in circles around her head, her own idea, no one had taught her, she wasn't imitating anyone. The only thing I remember about him is the few moments at dusk when he came dashing to Betania to fetch Sara, his mother. What Sara told us about the hell she had suffered at Belén! How different when my grandfather was the master there! Although I didn't say anything (I make it a practice not to say anything when something happens until I see clearly the danger approaching, threatening, pursuing me, even if the blow is the one I can least endure or put up with, the worst evil that can befall me), the tales Sara told us were the cause of the anger in my breast, and I'm quite sure, although she didn't say so, of my wife's anger when Pifanio jokingly made up to Teófila under

my very nose, hiding his intentions by pretending to think of her as
still a babe in arms that he'd carried about and considered as his own
child. We couldn't get rid of him. He'd come on one pretext or another, looking innocent, pretending sincere affection for us. There
wasn't a day when he wasn't there. I on my side, and Merced on
hers, tried to avoid him, and Teófila, certainly, on hers, but it was no
use. Teófila hadn't even been born at the time of Sara's visit. The
outrageous behavior of that Pifanio brought it all back to our minds
with a shock. During the days when she took refuge with us, it didn't
even occur to me that the shameless creature might take it out on us.
Sara couldn't speak of anything but the hell Belén was. I can't remember if I associated Florentina with these things at the time,
delighted that she'd escaped the danger of falling into a similar
frying-pan, or pitying her because, after all, she'd fallen into the
hands of the same pack. The man who assigned the Holy Names to
the farms, whoever he was, would have been amazed to think that
Belén, in the course of time, would be considered a hell on earth—
far removed from all the associations called up by the very name:
angels, shepherds, hermits around the Holy Child. I think, or rather
I'm sure, that if my grandfather had lived a few years longer, Pifanio wouldn't have risen so high in the world or committed the
folly of having so many women, producing a string of children so
tossed about from one to the other that they didn't know for sure
who their own mother was. And of course I wouldn't have been in
such straits with the machine, forced to hand it over. And to him.
To anyone else wouldn't have been so bad, but to the one who made
us suffer so much over Teófila. And to have to give it to him. 'I can't
shut the gate, the whole wall's fallen down.' To hide the rage seething inside me because I can't get my affairs in order, because I'm
helpless against old Pifas, I keep telling Merced about the favors we
owe to the Big House. For some time I've been reading in Merced's
eyes, although she won't say it in so many words, that she thinks
I'm a coward. Ah! Now the men with the rods are going, with Trujillo Gallo at their head, giving me no time to refuse to accept the
bargain Palemón made in my name. No, it was I who didn't get up
the courage to turn it down. Now it's too late. Florentina Sánchez'

son has disappeared into the darkness. Only the hoofbeats of the horses on the hard barren clay can be heard dying away in the distance. Why blame Palemón for getting me into this without my consent? I told them definitely no. Ah, Florentina Sánchez!

Because the night was clear and the road familiar, Rómulo sped rapidly along his homeward path. A winter sky, sparkling clear. In the bright starlight he threaded his way cautiously across the bed of the stream, over the slippery stones so easily dislodged.

In few of the scattered farmhouses was there a light showing or any sign that the fire still burned. Except Matiana's, of course. It must be late.

Rómulo hurried home, braced for his wife's outburst. He certainly deserved it. The dogs barked their greetings. There was a faint light coming from the kitchen. Cautiously, the man opened the wooden gate in the stone wall, crossed the yard, and faced his wife. There was no outburst, but a mysterious expression of joy on her face. She merely smiled and asked him, "Did you see the devil? Did Miguel find you?" She added, as if talking to herself, "Miguel Arcángel!"

Rómulo was taken aback, bereft of speech. Merced appeared to be absorbed in her own thoughts. It seemed ages before she spoke again, still talking to herself.

"Teófila's miracle! What else can it be? A real miracle! When I least expected it. I'm sure of it, the passing of the devil is part of the bargain. Between God and Teófila. I didn't see or hear it. I must have been in here making tortillas. Those who didn't see him claim that they heard him, or smelled the pestilence at least, from different parts of the plain, and they say people are dying in various places as well as in the ravine. May God find us ready!"

Her husband was amost paralyzed with amazement. He opened his mouth and ventured to ask, "Was Matiana here?"

"No, Miguel Arcángel."

"The young one?"

"No, the older one, who says his name is Jacob now. I don't like this changing his Christian name. His surname, yes. I didn't recognize him. But the things he told me and showed me left no room for doubt, and I began to believe him. He was the first to bring the story of the devil. Where did you see him?"

"Arcángel?"

"No, the devil."

"I didn't."

Doña Merced roused herself, fastened her bright eyes on Rómulo. "What? You didn't see him?"

"Or perhaps I didn't notice him . . . you know, he takes so many shapes! Maybe I did come across him . . ."

"You're still a . . . Christian soul. In the sky, flying round, puffing out smoke—they say that's the way they saw him, flying over the plain, sowing pestilence."

"And what about Matiana?"

"If what they say is true, she went down to the ravine to bless it and look after the dead and injured. People were coming to and fro with the news all afternoon." At last anger appeared on Doña Merced's face. "Where on earth have you been all day?"

"And what's Teófila got to do with this?"

Merced's face grew gentle; a kindly smile appeared.

"It's her miracle. Nothing can persuade me it isn't. The miracle of Miguel Arcángel, I mean. He himself must have told you—we don't have to worry, or hand over the machine. He'll arrange everything with Epifanio and you're not to bother about the land. He'll rent it or buy it from you without quibbling about the price and give you a well into the bargain. Very determined, he is, with lots of money, apparently, from what he says."

Doña Merced let her tongue run on, reliving the unexpected visit, omitting no details: the affectionate friendliness with which he had treated her, behaving from the beginning like one of the family; his knowledge of the situation; his sorrow at Teófila's death; his knowledge of how the dead girl had been dressed; the news he brought of Sara, of Florentina, and of their children; his tall black horse, his gleaming spurs and shoes—yes, he was wearing shoes and not huaraches—his spurs shone like stars and jingled like bells; the bit, and the bosses on his saddle, those of a prince. He was in his prime, strong, with hands and arms of steel, slender legs, head set firmly on his shoulders, and very sensible in all he said. He was wearing a good suede jacket and a hat edged with braid. He was clean-shaven. His saddle had bosses of gold and silver shining like flames from a spirit lamp against a blue background. His spurs, bit, stirrups, and the silver plates on his riding harness were all from Amozoc. Yes, he wore pants, not the white breeches they wear around here; a jacket, not just a shirt; a hat with braid on it, not just straw. Very friendly, he was, very kind, remembering that we took Sara in like one of our own. He asked about things now forgotten, wanted to see our daughter's machine, opening his eyes wide in wonder and saying that the wood is called birdseye, a very fine wood, something I never knew or had forgotten . . .

His yawns, together with a sinking feeling in his stomach, reminded Rómulo that he hadn't had a bite to eat since morning. He did not want to interrupt his wife's soliloquy. Unobtrusively, he got some tortillas and placed them on the embers in the hearth. Unobtrusively, he began to eat them.

Mechanically, without pausing in her tale, Merced put the jar of beans and atole on to warm. "He's made up his mind to settle here." She brought a dish and a jar. "He had a pistol with a pearl handle and an embroidered holster, and his cartridge belt was full, and a machete and a gun hung from his saddle." She brought over the dish of green peppers. "He had two big men on fine horses with him." She served the beans and atole. "He's proudly ready to challenge anyone to drive him out of the land where he was born." She put more tortillas on to warm. "He's determined not to put up with any interference." She lit a stick of pitch pine to give some light in the kitchen. "And I tell you again what he said many times, that he wouldn't argue over the price you ask for the land, either to rent or to sell it . . ."

"Sell the land?"

"Would you rather have it taken from you? Isn't it better, as the saying goes, to 'take a step back to make a better leap'? In any case, the question of renting or selling is apart from his promise that they won't take away my daughter's machine from us, not for anything in the world."

"No one lends without interest."

"There are times, Rómulo, when I pity you. I don't think you really are ignorant—you just pretend to be. Suppose it isn't true, what he said about the debt he owes us for taking in Sara when she escaped from Belén, do you want more interest than to crush that monster who cut him off out of sheer bad temper?"

"Merced!"

"Rómulo!"

"In any case I don't see what miracle you're talking about or what it's got to do with Teófila."

"You still think it's a little thing? They're certainly right when they say there's none so blind as he who doesn't want to see. When we're being helplessly swept downstream and a man suddenly appears on the bank, a man we didn't even remember, and he not only stretches out a hand to us but stops the current that was carrying us off . . ."

"And to be under an obligation? And such a big one?"

"Look, it's no use talking like that. You make my blood boil!"

"My one desire is to live in peace. I'll put up with anything rather than start a quarrel."

"That's just what we've done, and nice fools we look because of your stupidity."

"Disputes between neighbors living on adjoining farms are the worst of all. Isolated as they are, they're dependent on each other's help. It's like quarrels in a family. God preserve us from that."

"Leave God out of it."

"We have to defend the Tierra Santa from quarrels like those in other parts where families destroy each other, and old scores are passed down from father to son, to grandchildren, to cousins and nephews, until the last branches of the families disappear. Where our only safeguard is the trust we've built up in each other, let's not destroy it . . ."

"Trust that will snatch away your only daughter if you don't look out!"

"Why are you so stubborn?"

"And why are you so eager to give in? What a good thing this man has arrived, this man appearing like St. Michael to fight the dragon!"

"I can't see what the devil all this has to do with Teófila and what you mean by a miracle arranged between her and God. I don't understand this story about the devil flying overhead and people saw him. How? Where?"

"In the sky. A clear sign that the Trujillos' hour has come and the devil will carry them off."

"Flying overhead? The devil? Where did you hear that he flies overhead? He crawls along like a snake, or at best he runs here and there like a mad dog."

"There you've got a clear sign that it's a miracle, for God to allow him to fly over the plain to tell us of great and wonderful things, as the Magnificat says. Who else but Teófila could get God to do this? She lived and died here, and suffered the horror of the shameless old goat and is looking down from Heaven now at what's going on here, the corruption spreading from Belén, the swarm of bastards, and from up there she can hear Plácida's voice, her devilish voice, and see her long nails reaching out for the sacred machine. Who else in heaven can know this corner of the world and succeed in bringing God's Justice here? You can't deny it: she persuaded God to let the devil fly over the plain as a sign that the Trujillo's hour has come."

"What do we gain if the Trujillos go and the Gallos come? It's the same story all over again. As my grandfather used to say, 'Better the evil one knows.' How many of these changes for the worse have we known in the Tierra Santa! There are things that can't be helped— they are as they are and no one can stop them or right them."

Rómulo realized that his voice sounded hollow, as if he were talking into a jar or standing under a vault. Without body. This happens to him when he lets himself get carried away by his thoughts. He never knows if he actually utters the words or merely thinks them, if he is talking to himself like a madman or just sighing, faced with the inevitable.

The stick of pitch pine crackled, almost burned out. Merced was in another world, with her own thoughts.

Listening to the same old story all one's life—there's no escape till we die. All we can do is fold our arms, waiting patiently for God's will to be done. At least that's this one's attitude. A good person, but good for nothing. He won't even try the impossible, and things very rarely are that. Otherwise, how is it that in the same wretched land there are those who have all they want and those who haven't even a rag to fall dead in? Some act and others just stand by, the smart ones and the lazy ones. Not that Rómulo's lazy. It's just that he's like those donkeys that draw the water up out of the well, that can only keep going around and around, or like the water-carrier's donkey, weighed down with water and dying of thirst, or like the charcoal-burner's donkey, more work, less food. He spends his life sighing for the days of his grandfather. This has been bad for him. The slightest setback always makes him think it's no use going on. He isn't like those who stand up to bad luck, who are willing to take risks and accept the consequences. That's what I didn't like about him from the start, to think that he'd never abduct me, not that I wanted him to, it wouldn't be right, but this showed me how weak he was and still is, incapable, needless to say, of dragging me off by the hair of my head, or even of raising his voice to me. I used to wink at him, lie in wait for him, slip off to the spring alone, or bathe alone in the stream, pretending I didn't see him following me, to see what he'd do. It wasn't only that he didn't reveal his presence or spy on me from a hiding place, he'd even take fright and run away, as he did whenever we were likely to meet. When he couldn't escape, words would fail him, his color would come and go, he didn't know what to do with his hands or his hat. He never got up the courage to speak to me, yet there wasn't a day that he didn't come to Betulia, where my family lived, to catch a glimpse of me in the distance. 'He who is content with looking doesn't even think of trying to win.' Don Teódulo, his grandfather, was the one who came to arrange everything, asking for my hand, marrying us. "That one couldn't get the ox out of the ditch," my uncle Agapito used to say. Between the engagement and the wedding I gave him a hard time of it. I got my brothers to pick quarrels with him, I got my father to postpone the wedding, I sent a lot of messages to say no after all. To see if I could make him shake off his lethargy. I spread the rumor that I'd rather marry a man from the other side of the hill. At the party at Getsemaní I snubbed him many times and even played a trick on him with some young men from Cuilán. His grandfather took part in the game, which made me even angrier. But we were meant to marry and we got married. Pity us poor farm women, we never really know why things happen, we only see them coming, like storms; they come and we have to accept them the way we accept the coming of the dogdays—we accept our lot and scarcely realize the passing days and months, the rainy seasons and the dry seasons, the winds and clouds, the movement of the stars in the heavens. We're not surprised any longer when there's a flood, hailstorm, or drought, when year after year more earth is washed away, leaving the plain more barren, less able to bring forth seed, or when people and animals die and no one knows why. Why did Teófila catch meningitis? Why did she die of it? She was strong, so sound and healthy, so clean, so methodical. And her marriage? Although I don't think that the usual fate of women on a farm would have been hers, because she was very different, superior to the others, she could read and count, could read the thoughts of others in their faces, and besides, she had other qualities, not because she was my daughter. She wasn't like either her father or her mother in this, thank God. But there are times when I prefer what happened, when I think she might have got married and had a bad time of it. Getting married to one of those around here would have been bad enough, but to someone from outside who would carry her off where we wouldn't be able to look after her, worse. Marriage is nothing but suffering for women, from the beginning. What pleasure is there in it? Children, perhaps, but long after they're born. But that's something different from marriage, which boils down to battling with a man, putting up with him, giving in to him. At least I don't know of any woman on the farms around here, among those I know and have talked to about these things, who's discovered the key to the mystery or found the pleasure we expected to find underneath so much secrecy, although we didn't know exactly what it might be. Nothing but suffering. Until the day and hour that's bound to come. I can't even bear to remember the day Teófila was born! I don't know which is worse, to suffer but still hope to find some joy that was hidden before, or to become resigned, submitting mechanically, just like doing any other task, no matter how painful or boring— like grinding corn on the metate, chopping wood, getting water from the well, carrying the water, going to the river to wash, carrying the basket full of clothes. A woman's work is never done. Dry season or rainy season, she never can rest. Even when the harvest's in and the men spend their days lying on their backs, they still eat. One child is scarcely born before another comes. After the pain of childbirth, there's the constant sorrow of losing your children. As the years go by and they take us more for granted, the men are more demanding and more inconsiderate. They don't know how to give us pleasure, they can only wear us out with their demands. There are times when without realizing it women begin to feel like widows, bored and lonely on the farm, and many are without even the advantage of having the freedom to rule the house, neglected and shackled to a drunken, gambling, woman-chasing husband or an even worse one. I'm like some of the old village women or young girls I talk about this to, I think there must be some pleasure in marriage some- where in the world. What happens here is that the men don't know how to treat women, don't try to give them pleasure. They're con- tent to satisfy their own needs like animals, and don't care what the woman feels or doesn't feel. They'd rather see us suffer than enjoy ourselves. We're only saucepans or metates to serve them. Like slaves. Before, we didn't rebel. We would if we weren't accustomed to endure, like animals who can't even kick. If one rebels she doesn't dare to break away, out of fear that she'll miss what she thinks is hidden behind the mystery in the temptation of marriage. Sara, Sara Gallo, the only one of the women in Epifanio's herd that

I've spoken to, never stopped telling of atrocities, and if she found
any pleasure at all, she didn't mention it—Miguel Arcángel's
mother.

Their increasing yawns brought Rómulo and Merced to the reali-
zation of the prolonged silence that had fallen between them.

"Tomorrow's another day. It's time we went to bed." Blowing on
the embers of the fire, the woman lit a stick of pitch pine.

"I told you this morning we were out of kerosene."

"I forgot."

"Just as you forget everything, even that you have a wife. You're
like the man in the story who was happy 'With a bit of meat and the
heel of a loaf.' "

There was a cold breeze when they went out into the patio toward the room where they slept, the room where they kept the
sewing machine. The barking of the dogs, which were stationed at
regular intervals, reached them from all sides. Herod, Caiaphas,
Nero, rousing themselves, made sure that everyone was in. Rómulo
stopped in the doorway, contemplating the stars. From inside the
room, as she lit the candle, Doña Merced called out: "And how did
you get on with that wicked old man at Belén? What did he say?"

"That he'll give me a few days' grace."

Afraid that, in answer to more questions, he might blurt out the
money-lender's offer to consider the debt settled in return for the
machine, Rómulo began to whistle nervously. Doña Merced remained silent. Some time passed. Rómulo shut the door and said as
he was coming into the room, "This new moon will be the Christmas
one."

He got into bed and put out the light. Half asleep, Doña Merced
murmured, "Shepherds and a hermit, and the devil. I can see them
all in my mind's eye."

A long silence. Outside, the barking of the dogs went on and on,
endlessly.

"Ah, you, always thinking you're fooling me, making me out
more of a fool than I am . . ."

Take your music somewhere else

"Take your music somewhere else," Epifanio Trujillo had told those who came to see him about making arrangements for the Christmas pastorals, usually held each year at Belén, the various groups in the district competing. No, this year, at any rate, he wanted no mummery in his house.

At first it was thought that the refusal was the effect of the moon on the testy old man. Hopes sank all through November as the phases of the moon came around and no one could make the master of the Big House change his mind. The news of his decision spread through the farms and stirred up bad feeling, especially because people were already upset by the contradictory reports of the devil flying over the Tierra Santa and the deaths occurring in those places where the Evil One had been seen. The producer of the Christmas pastoral organized by the people of Betulia went around making speeches.

"Not that we need his dirty old courtyard or the supper he gives the shepherds who go to Belén. We've got more than enough places to hold the competition. That's the advantage of our Tierra Santa: not a soul to bother us, not a dog to bark at us, we live as we please, far from each other, our houses independent, each on its own bit of land, since there aren't any haciendas on the plain where just one person rules and is master of the wills of others. Here, apart from those indebted to them and those who fear their loud voices, we can do very well without the Trujillos. The plain is big enough for us to breathe freely without them. What's infuriating is that a custom that goes back further than anyone remembers, and that serves to bring together all the farm people, must be broken because of the whim of a madman. It even provides an opportunity for buying and selling, the only one except during the May festival at Getsemaní. No, it isn't right to break the tradition handed down by our fore-fathers and entrusted to our keeping. Less than ever, now, when we need to make our peace with God, who's let Satan loose on us—yes, it's as true as I'm standing here. And whose fault is it? Just look around you and you'll find the answer. Which one of us openly keeps several wives, none of them legal? Who fathers bastards all over the place, dropping them like dung, braggarts with no respect for anyone or anything? Who takes advantage of those in need, charging exorbitant rates of interest for money to buy seeds, to hire yokes of oxen? Who seizes other people's goods on the slightest pre-text? You know what's happening over Teófila's machine. He wants to take it away from her parents! I won't keep you any longer. Who knows what other troubles lie in store for us, announced by the appearance of the Evil One flying about the sky? Who knows? Not even Madre Matiana."

His listeners were roused by these arguments: their faces reflected the expression of the leader and their heads nodded as his had done when he was speaking.

Plácida, Don Felipe, and Don Jesusito intervened eagerly—eager to crush their father—in favor of having the competition held at Belén. Making themselves the mouthpieces of the growing dis-content, they paid no attention to the furious command to be silent, not to interfere in what was none of their business. More eagerly still, they joined forces, raised their voices in sudden rebellion, demanding to be heard, throwing in their father's face the endless succession of unreasoning demands they had put up with all through their lives as puppet children.

Don Jesusito's tongue was the most cutting, though he pretended to give conciliating advice.

"Yes, father, it was all very well for you to treat us like hypocrites who were doing your bidding with an eye on your property. You had every right to do so. I'm not objecting to that. You're master in your own house, master of your cattle, your wives, your children, and you always have been. Nobody disputes that. But we'll have the pastorals here because we want them here. That's the way you've taught us to act when we get an idea in our heads—it has to be carried out even if the sky falls. You've brought us up as your children and we have to be true to your training. Now that you've got so fat, you don't always say the right thing and there are times when you act like a silly child. After the many good examples we've had throughout our lives, we're not going to spoil it all now at the eleventh hour by going against the respect for religion that you taught us, helping you destroy the little religion that remains in this place. The mummery of the shepherds and hermits with the instructive quarrel of the angels and demons in the presence of Temptation—the one you like to tease, making her forget her part, remember? And they say there's a new group coming from the other side of the mountain with a Temptation who looks like the late Teófila, but prettier. Come on!"

Ignoring the interruptions, grunts, and gestures of Epifanio, Jesusito continued. "Don't you think the mummers should come, now more than ever, since the stories have got around that the devil is loose, flying over the plain? So that people can see how St. Michael struggles with him and overthrows him! I ask you for the sake of Doña Amandita, in memory of the blessed Teófila, or because anyhow the feast must be celebrated, simply because it must, if there aren't any other reasons."

Don Felipe and Plácida were more outspoken, more brutal.

"We've come to the end of our patience with your ruling that this

me—I see things when I'm awake or just getting off to sleep. Hallucination or dream, it left its impression upon me. I was as stunned as if I'd fallen off a colt that wasn't broken yet, not even remembering my usual sayings, which I need in order to feel alive the way you need air to breathe. I was wide awake now, remembering only what I'd just seen and kept on seeing in front of my eyes, though not so clearly. No—things past and present came crowding into my mind, forming a confused conglomeration with fears and desires for the future, making my head whirl, taking away not only all desire for sleep but even the wish to eat. My whole life was there, I couldn't say now if everything was going around and around, or if it was the presence of the portraits of the dead, stiffly there in their places all around me, not moving, lit up by the candles, that beat upon my brain. Some had hanging jaws and sunken eyes, like my first wife, Doña Eva, who bled to death from a miscarriage. I've got an enlarged photograph of her next to the painting of San Jerónimo with his skull and the trumpet for the last Judgment. Others had their mouths and eyes open. Some were even swollen, because it isn't easy to get the photographer from the village in a hurry and sometimes he doesn't even want to come because it's so far and the road is so hard, although he knows I'll pay him whatever he asks, even more, so as to have even this remembrance of those I'll never see again. This is one of my pleasures, and many people criticize me for it, the way they criticize everything I do. It's chiefly in the rainy season, when the rivers and streams are high and the roads full of mudholes, that the photographer takes a long time to come, and he sometimes arrives when the bodies are disfigured and decomposing and I have to take a strong stand against those who try to make me hurry up with the burial. This was one of the things that annoyed me most when Teófila died, that nothing on earth would induce Merced to have a photograph taken and the photographer I sent for at my own expense made the trip in vain because there he was with the others, just there, doing nothing. That night, although the photographs were in their places, bright as day with all the lights there in front of my eyes, my glance wandered over them without seeing them. The world of hallucination hid them from my sight. I was paralyzed, like those who have a stroke, and can't move even their tongues, but the stream of thoughts and figures kept passing in front of my eyes, as when you have a fever and your temperature is rising or you can't get to sleep, troubled by some worrying thought, of which there are plenty in this life. St. Michael, machete and all, and Temptation, dressed like a singer at the fair, and the ring of devils, shepherds, and shepherdesses, and Madre Matiana, and even the blessed Teófila, they were all driven back, thrust to one side, by the horde of other images that came crowding into my mind. Among them I kept seeing all the opportunities I'd missed, beginning with the young girls, this one, that one, the other, this one here, that one there, why should I remember their names now, what they looked like, all the details that made them so attractive? The girls, lands, animals, business deals, schemes, and profits that slipped through my fingers, even the desertion of Miguel Arcángel and Teófila's machine, all my schemes that didn't come off, the attempts that ended in failure. "No, by Heaven!" I said to myself. "The business of the machine isn't settled yet and nothing on earth can get it away from me or make me give it up. 'When I look at my crates I remember my hens.' " Matiana came back into the dance. I realized that whenever I've dreamed about her—and it's always something bad, I hate her so much—some misfortune has followed. The bad spell passed, but I was filled with presentiments that drove the past out of my mind. This business of the machine, it'll go badly, and this one or that one'll try to get out of paying what they owe me, and the business of Miguel Arcángel, and my determination to have the machine, that's going to cost me dear, and the way Matiana looked at me, and the expression in the eyes of my children. . . It was all gone in a moment, but I had a feeling that Felipe and Jesusito had slipped noiselessly into the room and were standing behind me with clubs in their hands. I pretended not to notice anything in order to see what they were up to. Chiefly because I didn't want to show surprise, still less fear, I controlled my impulse to turn around, and listened to the noise they made trying to hold their breath. Then I heard Teófila singing in the courtyard where the Christmas mummers were, it was her very voice and the same song I often heard her sing when that music teacher was going around to the farms on the plain, gathering people together and getting them to sing, very nice it was, like after a fall, when you're bruised and aching in every limb, and you suddenly remember something good that you've seen or experienced, something that cheers you up, helps you bear the pain, the shame, your anger at falling, so to hear Teófila singing the way she did before was to have someone to keep me company when I knew the boys were creeping up behind me, watching for me to fall asleep. As the candles in front of the dead burned low they guttered out. To light them when it gets dark, or before it's light in the morning, is our way of celebrating the Day of the Dead—and to pray. I don't. I don't know how and I don't want to, but in nearly all of the houses they do. The very poor have tallow candles stuck on the floor, the rest have paraffin or wax ones. There's no grave-yard near the farms of the plain, they're all far away on the other side of the hill. We don't visit them and we don't want to. Why should we? There's only bones there that don't see or hear or feel anything. After the funerals nobody goes back, and there aren't any flowers on the graves as in other places—that's the way we are, and in this I've got the same opinion as the others. When the candles sputtered I jumped up and half turned around, with clenched fists, sure I'd see them there, ready to beat them back. There was nobody there. The surprise of finding myself alone in the empty room, the sputtering of the candles as they burned out, the lights themselves just like when a dead body's there, the flickering that made the faces of the dead seem to move, as though they were trying to break the glass in their frames, to come down off the wall and seize hold of me—I don't think I could even cry out, I was so panic-stricken. If I called out, no one in the house heard me, no one came to my help. I stumbled out of the room, my legs like lead, making a useless attempt to run, hampered by my terror and my size. Outside I saw the new moon. "Now it's got me again!" I cried, and shouted out to the women, "Amanda! Plácida! Sara Gallo!"

"Look, children, don't try to deceive me, because I'll just wait until you stop talking nonsense. I know the real reason you're digging your heels in, kicking over the traces, lashing out; you're trying to wear me down so I'll divide your inheritance among you in my lifetime and make over what I've entrusted to you. The fish isn't swallowing that hook, not even nibbling at the bait. Speak out clearly. Don't come to me with this business of the Christmas plays, which you care about less than I do. You've always made fun of this mummery. It's even less use making fools of yourselves over this nonsense about the devil flying around. That's all very well for the peasants who come down the hill beating their drums, but not for you, you know the world and you've seen these flying machines that run on petroleum. Why are you so religious all of a sudden? Ridiculous! 'When the saint slips. . .' It was a wise man who said, 'Never fatten a small pig, he'll just get bigger,' and the one who said, 'If you raise crows, they'll peck your eyes out.' I'm to burst like a toad from anger, eh? That's what you want, so you'll be left with everything, with a free hand to cut the cards and deal them the way you want. 'As you do unto your parents, so will your children do unto you.' I'd like to oblige you, and die without dividing my inheritance among you. Do you hear me? Leaving you alone to bite each other, to destroy each other in your squabbles, you three and my hundred other bastards together with Miguel Arcángel, who will certainly join in the fight if he hasn't already joined up with you to overthrow me. And then we'll see. Don't forget, 'What you sow, you reap,' and for my part, 'I'll die in harness even though I die before my time.' So don't come any nearer. There's fire, you may get burned. You know the old song, 'They may take my life, but who knows when they'll get my property?' "

Jesusito infused more honey into his smile, looked at his father in wide-eyed innocence, lowered his voice, which was honeyed, too, and, gesturing gently to Felipe and Plácida to keep quiet, played the bull, giving him his way, seeking an opportunity to stick in the banderillas:

"My dear father, why are you so determined to see trouble everywhere and visions in broad daylight? If you've given us more than we need, and atole with laughter is better than chocolate with tears, well, who makes you rich? He who supplies your food. Get these stormclouds out of your head, it isn't the rainy season now. You don't need to beat around the bush when you're such a big tree, and what a big tree trunk you are, father..."

By using a string of sayings, he was confusing the old grumbler, cornering him, getting him where he wanted him. 'God preserve our honeycombs from those who don't eat honey.' He came back to the business of the Christmas play, tackling it from another angle: "They'll go to another farm. Belén won't be the center of attraction any longer. It'll lose control over the people..."

"What you want is to make a fool of me. If I've said no and then I say yes, they'll say, 'What an old faker he is, he hasn't got any say now in his own house.'"

"There's something else you haven't thought of, father. Why do we need to quarrel or offend our neighbors, who are used to having the rigmarole here? You know better than anyone that you can't interfere with women or the festivals of the people. They rebel. Don't forget that there isn't much to entertain people around here. Music? No. Bars, pool rooms, public houses? Still less. No serenades, no dances, no gatherings, with the exception of an occasional bull-tossing competition, a few horse races—and for years we haven't even had those. We've got only two festivals—the competitions between the groups of mummers here on Christmas Eve, and the dances at Getsemaní on May 3rd. It's not only fair, it's necessary for our peace to keep up these entertainments for the country people. You have to have some pleasure when there's so much sadness." The gruff old man showed signs of giving in. Then he started off again, entering into an interminable duel of old sayings with his sons.

"Don't chop so much wood for me, I no longer have a hearth. Don't talk to me about bitter things that set my teeth on edge..."

"Time is a good counselor and will reveal the truth..."

"Since the atole's mine, I'll stir it with my own stick..."

"Some hens do a lot of cackling and never lay an egg..."

"The man who's really a man doesn't look for a boost..."

"Don't let yourself get hurt and make matters worse..."

Don Jesusito tried an appeal to his avarice. "Father, some time

began going around the farms the people were suspicious of him, they talked about him, thought the worst, muttered that he was a Protestant, or Spiritist, or Socialist, who knows what else, though no one around here knew the meaning of the words. They refused to give him anything to eat, shut the door in his face. Teófila was one of the first to be on his side, to help him break down their resistance, to second his efforts, singing herself and getting groups of people on the farms to sing, a thing they've always done by themselves, for pleasure, with no one to teach them—but they'd get shy when asked to sing. Gabriel and Teófila did everything they could to get them over this. Naturally, at the beginning I wasn't at all pleased at this friendship between the girl and the musician, I fought it in every way I could think of, trying to drive him away, declaring that yes, he was certainly a Protestant at least, and adding that no one was to speak to him or pay any attention to him, since I'd learned of the harm he'd do because they'd told me so in the town. But he came to see me, talked to me, got around me, convinced me of his good intentions, and without his mentioning it I realized that Teófila wasn't his type. He'd traveled a lot, even to the real Tierra Santa, and knew those things they call theaters inside out. He didn't put on any airs, but you could see he was somebody. The upshot was, I went over to his side myself. He had me looking for musical instruments, and I had a hard job scraping a few together, most of them stored away and needing to be fixed. He got me to buy a gross of mouth organs in Clamores. Following his instructions, Rómulo made reed flutes, two violins, and even a double bass, and collected iron rods, bottles, tin cans, sticks, for making noise. On every farm he'd gather groups of singers, calling them choral societies, one day in one place, another in another. Every afternoon and evening he'd make them sing. For the first and only time the plain was alive with music. The farms were full of sound at night, fields and orchards were filled with songs, the sower and the plowman sang, the women sang in the kitchens, and when they took their lunch to the sowers in the field, and when they went for water or washed in the stream. The boys sang as they ran and threw stones at the birds. The milkmaid and the gleaner sang, the

and her enthusiasm in helping the musician. At heart I was still rather jealous, comparing myself, so self-willed and domineering, with the gay, lively foreigner who did everything so well and was so charming. We were full of curiosity to know and hear what he was going to do with the heap of old, useless instruments from all over the place. First of all he mended them. How surprised I was to hear him playing on the broken mandolin without keys or strings that I'd taken him, finding it one day on the farm of a friend, crushed under a pile of old saddles, yokes, plow handles, and other stuff. I'd never heard such music in my life, apart from Teófila's voice, of course. I was dumbfounded, carried up to heaven, and I wanted it to go on and on. A few days later I heard him tuning the guitar, the violins, the clarinet, and an accordion. When he'd fixed all the instruments he could get hold of, he put to work all the young men with some talent that he'd got his eye on. All through the length and breadth of the plain music groups sprang up, there wasn't a cluster of farmhouses where more or less tuneful music couldn't be heard. At the beginning it was sheer confusion. The ever-lasting faultfinders kept saying that there was no head or tail to it and never would be. The teacher gathered them together in groups: string instruments, wind, and what he called percussion—those were the last. They beat sticks, tin cans, bottles, pieces of tin. The disbelievers showed signs of bowing before the evidence when, one Sunday in Betania, the group of boys with mouth organs played, and the teacher accompanying them on the accordion. What a master Gabriel was, he could bring anything to life, and in what a way! The next week it was the strings—the violins, the guitar and mandolin, followed by the bass fiddle. Everything was going better and better, to everybody's delight including the former faultfinders, though they still couldn't see how Gabriel would fit in the people with the sticks and bottles and so forth. "Don't worry, my friends," I'd say to them. "How can you have the roof before you have the foundations and the walls?" Another Sunday in Betania the reed flutes made their first appearance, first alone, then accompanied by the mouth organs. Something to make your mouth water, it turned out, some first-rate little pieces. I begged Gabriel, and he agreed—

to have the full rehearsal in Belén, though he'd thought of having it at Betania—to keep in with Teófila, of course. So he did, one Sunday afternoon. More people came than to the pastorals we've been talking about. They came from the other side of the mountain, from Cuilán, like flies in search of honey, even from Clamores and other distant towns. Of course, there were people selling things, lots of them. The clapping was louder than at a bull-tossing competition, and all the people were shouting and yelling. The strange thing about it, though, was that in spite of such a huge crowd, it was so quiet while the music was playing that you could hear a pin drop, except for a few babies in arms. Maestro Gabriel and his pupils were a great success. When they finished, every farmer, even the most stupid, wanted to play something, or at least to whistle. I felt tempted to shout at them, "Don't whistle it, it's meant to be sung. It isn't only muledrivers that whistle." I was too happy to spoil anyone's pleasure. The only fly in the ointment was to see the expression on Teófila's face, her eyes sparkling as she turned them toward the music master. "Water finds its own level," I thought. Then I took comfort from the saying, 'The animal sets the pace when the road runs uphill; but when the ground is level, the master has his will.' And it wasn't at all to my liking that the first public performance was in Betania. I didn't say anything so as not to go against the current, since one of the advantages of being old is to have the patience to wait till the swallows fly away. I invited Maestro Gabriel and his musicians to a party in the Big House. I killed a calf and four pigs—tasty, they were. It was very gay. Teófila was there, of course. The truth is, there never was such peace on the plain, so much harmony among the farmers, all united in the enjoyment of what they sang, played, or listened to, trying to get music out of the very stones, fascinated by the novelties Gabriel thought up every day, and by his charm. Even though Teófila realized the distance separating her from this globe-trotting charmer, and how impossible it was that he'd be seriously attracted to her, I'm sure she was madly in love with him. I felt sorry for her.

The suspicion was correct: Miguel Arcángel or Jacob Gallo had been talking to his half brothers, chiefly Don Jesusito and Don Felipe, indisputable leaders of the Trujillo bastards.

Jacob both dared and flattered them as he described his plans for the future and the resources at his disposal: first, his three grownup sons, three sons like colts eager to be let loose, ready for anything. They came to work, not fight. They would like to share with their kinsmen the results of the improvements that, with new systems, they would make in the land. If this was unwelcome, let them say so now, clearly, and then keep to themselves. He would not put up with any double-dealing—as he said this, Jacob Gallo fixed his eyes firmly on Jesusito. If they discovered any trickery, the Gallos would not respect any ties of family relationship. It would be to no one's advantage—least of all the Trujillos', who were certainly living in a glass house—to start trouble. He came to tell them this, to persuade them not to start a fight. The Trujillos would be likely to lose, tied together as they were, yet not united. In any case, what did they stand to gain by opposing the Gallos? What did they hope to get, since their situation was growing worse and worse with the capricious temperament of their father? What definite rights did they have? They were nowhere, cast out into the street, with no security at all. It would be better for them to work in harmony or with mutual respect.

The question of the Gallos' settling on the plain did not come up. They were already settled there. The only thing Jacob wanted to be sure of, so as to know where he stood, was whether the Trujillos wanted noise or silence; alliance, war, or a respectful distance between them.

If they decided to become allies, the Trujillos would have these advantages: Jacob's help in settling the matter of their heritage and in modernizing their methods of agriculture; access to new techniques and products, among which Jacob mentioned reforestation, soil conservation, introduction of new crops, perforation of wells, construction of dams, opening up of roads, agriculture in place of cattle-raising, a variety of money crops, use of fertilizers, improved seeds and machinery; industrialization, exploitation of the forests in the Cardos mountains, investigation of the mining possibilities in the region; political power and influence; money and financial credit.

Seeing a mocking smile of disbelief on Don Jesusito's face, while Don Felipe drew his brows together as though saying, "Try those lies on some other fool," Jacob raised his voice:

"How easy it is to see that you're still living in the good old days when dogs were tied up with strings of sausages, and that you haven't seen anything of the world! Will you bet me your uncertain heritance that within a year I'll accomplish almost everything I said? But it has to be an official bet, signed in the presence of a notary, in which I undertake to do this, that, and the other, and you renounce your inheritance in my favor."

Don Felipe and Don Jesusito bit their lips, stroked their moustaches, shifted about uncomfortably. Don Jesusito tried to make a joke of it, to go off at a tangent, to flatter his half brother.

Cornered by Jacob, they agreed—the Sneak being the spokesman—that the idea of joining forces appealed to them. They just needed to consult some of the other brothers in order to draw up a formal agreement.

"And the bet?"

"Do you imagine we doubt your word? Not a chance!"

"Don't try any slippery tricks or it'll be the worse for you."

Don Jesusito slipped away immediately to rouse his half brothers to make common front against the interfering bastard. He found the ground cut from under his feet. Jacob had stolen a march on him. Even those on the fringe of the Trujillo clan and the people on the different farms were dazzled by the reappearance of Miguel Arcángel. Don Jesusito and Don Felipe were furious with themselves. How could they have fallen asleep and let the coyote catch them unaware when they least expected him? To have to admit that they were the last to learn of his arrival! They wondered if Don Epifanio was just pretending not to know of it. Why? They finally agreed that they would pretend to do what Gallo wanted, without committing themselves, thus giving themselves time to see how things would go and how far Jacob would turn out to be merely an empty threat, full of idle talk.

Gallo asked them to show their good faith by persuading Don Epifanio to change his mind and allow the pastoral competition to be held at Belén, or by deciding to have it there even in spite of the opposition of the master. This, according to Jacob, was a necessary step toward later obtaining his signature to the documents giving them their inheritance during his lifetime, to everyone's satisfaction.

"Of course the competition will be held," Don Jesusito said. "How can we let him get away with such a senseless bit of willfulness?"

"If we let him have his way this time, we might as well give up," Don Felipe said.

They went off to see about this, and started to argue with their father. In the end the old man, in order not to give in, would not say yes but did not say no either, a sign that he would let his sons go ahead.

"But before you go, there's just one thing I want, since you're such good sons! I want the sewing machine that belonged to Teófila brought here. You'd forgotten all about it, I suppose, you bastards! I need it for Plácida, who wants it here. It'll please her, and we need it in the house. Why should the women have to sew and mend by hand when there's this machine that's not even being used where it is, and with all Rómulo owes me. But he doesn't want to hand it over, in spite of the fine terms I'm offering him in return for it. Merced's the one who's making most objections. I've held off from taking my usual measures, I'd rather try to persuade them to bring me the machine themselves. But day after day goes by and there's no move. I'm beginning to believe they take me for a fool and think I won't make any move out of respect for the dead girl! And here's Plácida, keeping on about the machine, dinning into my ears every day how much she needs it. Give me the machine, for Heaven's sake, the woman's worn me out. It's time to take the matter seriously now. They've had more than enough time. I want you, Jesusito, with your smooth manner, to get them to bring me the machine, you'll find a way—and if you can't, I'll leave the matter in Felipe's hands. I don't want to do it myself. So now you know. Let's see how you get on."

"It's not for nothing that they call this one the Sneak and me the

Bully. So you can count on us to do the job." This in the harsh tones of Don Felipe.

When, a few days later, there were plenty of people to bring Don Epifanio the stale news that Miguel Arcángel, his rebel son, was trying to settle down on the plain, he nearly choked with laughter when he heard that the Gallos had bought, cash down, and talked about cultivating, the stony, salty lands of Torres de San Miguel, boasting that they would restore them to their ancient grandeur, under the name of Jerusalén. His roar of laughter nearly choked him. When he got his breath back, he spat out:

"My curse has followed him and driven him mad, the ungrateful clod, as a warning to bad sons. Ah, what supporters my master has, and more are coming to join him . . ."

Like a file of ants, the people

Like a file of ants, the people wound their way to the house of Madre Matiana, and the chorus, echoing from lip to lip, sounded beyond the plain, on the other side of the mountain.

"Did you see it?"

"A bat the size of a house?"

"Sowing death in its wake?"

"Still flying around in circles?"

Few got up the courage to ask, "How is it they're saying that you're one of those who don't believe?"

The house on the river bank was seething with the curious. Those whose questions had been asked and answered remained to hear the questions of the newcomers, who kept coming, and the replies they received, or to ask for more news.

Frank with some, mysterious with most, Matiana, instead of appeasing the curiosity and easing the general anxiety, added fuel to it. Those who heard the true story of her journey to La Tarabilla refused to believe it, because it defrauded them of their hope of learning that the region had become the scene of extraordinary happenings, the like of which had never been seen before. They were sure the prophetess was concealing the truth, especially when they compared other enigmatic answers she had given at the time.

"It's not only now, the Evil One's always at large, and it's strange you haven't come across him, as you say . . ."

"It's when he enters into human beings we should fear him, not when he's flying around . . ."

"If you haven't seen him, it's easy enough to imagine him like a bat and you don't need to know if I saw him or not . . ."

"I see him coming by ways that make it easy for him to travel through the air or over the land. He's always here, not merely flying, but talking, whispering day and night in the ears of each one of us, tempting . . ."

"If you search your memory and examine it carefully, you'll know what truth there is in all this, and what the coming of the Evil One means . . ."

"The coming of Antichrist and the end of the world, beyond any doubt. Perhaps we'll see it, there's lots of signs that it's near. Then even the blind will see what was seen in La Tarabilla, and the deaf will hear what was heard there, and the paralyzed will run the way those in the ravine ran away in their fear . . ."

Consumed by curiosity, or because they had nothing better to do—the event was an excuse for prolonging the idleness that follows the harvest—many could not resist the temptation to go to the ravine to learn more about where and how the Evil One had passed by. They came back from La Tarabilla puzzled, troubled by the alternate version that Melesio, the unbelieving northerner, had sown—*not* the devil, but an airplane—while most of the people shrieked, "Yes, the devil himself, in the shape of a huge bat, with glowing coals for eyes and a tail that made a buzzing sound."

From the villages on the other side of the mountain came the rumor that there *had* been an airplane, the first to fly over this out-of-the-way region. This version, too, was likely to give rise to endless tales for the imagination to feed on. Nevertheless, the story of the devil was more in keeping with the superstitious character of the region, and this was the one that predominated, imposed by the stubborn will of the majority.

Go away, good souls. You'd be better off finding something to do, not just standing idle in the dry season. Find some occupation to bring you in something. We'd be better off and less dependent on Providence to get us out of our troubles or satisfy every stray itch of our blood. You come wailing to me when you get discouraged, as if miracles grow on bushes whenever you clasp your hands and purse your lips. You want to get out of me the secrets only God knows, because the just judgments of God are His alone, and because without His permission not a leaf stirs on a tree, still less a dry leaf like me. You come running to me for help when everything else fails—and it's anything from finding a lost needle or cow to bringing the dead back to life and foretelling the future. I'm not my own agent, and God doesn't always act through me, or give an answer every day to all the prayers I offer on your behalf. Study your catechism, I tell you. We don't understand it, you reply. Learn it by heart, and in times of trouble your need will help you understand it and apply it. In that way you'll be able to read the future yourselves, as I often do, without bothering God, simply by practicing looking carefully at faces and actions. The proverb says it clearly: 'God helps those who help themselves.' There's another saying, too; '*Ask and ye shall* . . .' Don't come to me the way Felipe and Jesusito did once, each one separately, wanting a charm to make the musician who had Teófila under his spell either die or go away, leaving them a free field. "It'll have to remove Epifanio, your father, too, because he's also after the girl." I told them. They bit their lips and insisted I should make a wax effigy of the musician and stick thorns in it. "And what about you? Haven't you got hands to do it yourself?" I asked each one. "Good pistols are what I've got," Felipe replied. "Then what are you waiting for?" I asked him. "Ah, yes, Señor Gabriel has friends in high places so it's risky to do away with him like any poor peasant." They thundered out threats. "I don't care how you do it," the Bully told me, with a threatening gesture, "but you'd better get this so-and-so out of our way at once—you can

manage it any way you like—if you don't want something to happen to you. A stumble, a fall, and nobody the wiser. There's lots of
cases, you know, of people being found dead one fine day and no
one's ever discovered who killed them." I raised my hands and my
voice and said, "When have you ever heard that Matiana is afraid
of the devil or of scorpions, much less of you, you're not even fit to
be a doorkeeper in hell, or even a scorpion, a centipede is the highest
you'll get to be." He turned purple with rage but he didn't hit me,
just raised his clenched fists, spat out a stream of yellow bile, and
muttered through his teeth, "You've been warned." Then he turned
on his heels, jingled his spurs, and struck the handle of his riding
whip against his leather chaps. I wasn't worried, I sent him off with
a flea in his ear, sure that only what God wills comes to pass, no
matter how hard men struggle to have it otherwise. A few days
later the musician went away of his own free will. The Trujillos
spread the tale that my spells drove him away. Teófila believed this,
though she didn't say so to my face. The first chance I got, I had a
word with her. "Listen, girl, how have you managed to get this idea
in your head? It was perfectly natural. A man who's traveled
around the world and studied in the city where the Pope lives, as
I've heard, and used to a very different kind of life, with lots of excitement and gaiety, like the actors in those places they call theaters,
which I don't know anything about—I think that's the kind of person Señor Gabriel is, and I've thought so ever since I first saw and
heard him. A man like that couldn't stay buried in a place like this
for any length of time. I don't know how you ever dreamed he
would. Water seeks its own level. It's keeping him here, without
all the things he's used to, that you'd need witchcraft for, not for
sending him away." She didn't reply, but I've got reason to believe
that Teófila kept her illusions about him to her last breath, and
suffered, even though she never spoke of him. He wasn't the kind of
man you meet every day. His place wasn't to be taken by any of the
Trujillos. Teófila filled it with her death. Go and look for something
to do, good people. There are things I can't tell you, and others I
can't understand myself, although they trouble me. I tremble when
I feel God wants to make use of me, and the pains I suffer when

Some say that merely seeing Matiana's house in the distance, or passing along beside it, fills them with an awe that is mingled with a sensation of foreboding or fear. As you enter the walled patio, a feeling of reverence seeps in through your pores, imposing silence. This may be due to the reputation of the inhabitant rather than to the house itself. There is an eerie atmosphere, an eerie smell, an eerie stillness. An expectation that some extraordinary phenomenon will suddenly appear. Apprehension, at least uneasiness. At first the smell seems to be due to age, then gradually you become aware of dampness, mustiness, staleness, a smell of things kept for a long time in boxes of fragrant wood among herbs no less fragant for being dried. And there are other smells, unknown or vaguely familiar. Copal, burned wax, resins, lotions made from flowers, and what they call perfumes; herbs, flowers, wood, medicinal oils and fats; cooking oil and oil for lamps; the fat of squirrels, porcupines, peccaries, coyotes, leopards, of a thousand fabulous creatures; grease made from the fat of hens, wild ducks, swallows, parrots, owls, hawks, buzzards, sparrowhawks. The mysterious vast realm of salves and ointments—some fragrant, others foul-smelling—and of powders, with a long string of magic names: Balm of Fierabante, of Judea, of María, of Guayacán, of Aloes, of Musk, of Tears of Incense and Myrrh, of Virgin Almonds; Balm of Gilead; Ointment of Pity, Oil of Angels; Unction of Archangels, Thrones, and Dominions; Holy Unction of the Seraphim; Balm of the Cherubim; Milk of the Lady; Pilgrim's Liniment; Gold Water. And potions to prevent fear, anger, overexcitement, the breaking of limbs; poultice of calves' cauls, Plaster of the Prophet; powders bringing good luck, aphrodisiac powders; powders to bring a Blessed Death, made from the ashes of palms, cotton, rags, and other consecrated things; powders made with bones of the unburied dead for All Souls' Day; powders made from the bones, fur, feathers, hoofs, and nails of birds and beasts of prey for the Day of Judgment.

They say that many, bending down to go under the low door, have fainted on reaching the main room. The room of Mysteries. Few are privileged to enter; fewer still are those who dare; and still smaller is the number of those who can give a reasonable account—no description is exact—of what they have seen. To enter is to become dazed, lost in a thick cloud shot through with rays of light. Rarefied air. Sublimation of a confusing blend of fragrances. Sacred. Funereal. Floral. Pungent. Pleasant. Enervating. Rancid. Nauseating. Eternal twilight, accentuated by the unearthly flickering of an oil lamp, red, deep, oxblood, almost black, whose flame rises perpetually toward a shadowy image or an indistinguishable host of images. There is one man who says he has seen a live heart beating inside a glass. There is another who talks about creatures the size of mice with children's heads and animal bodies, or vice versa, in cages. Another has seen a coffin covered with a pig's skin, its bristles as big as thorns. They say there is a mound of skulls and animal bones all heaped together, and a chair like a throne, made of coiled snakes. No, a small rug made of snakes, laid on the floor where Madre Matiana sits and walks up and down. They say that Matiana is told what to say by two owl-like fiery eyes, and takes her questions to them. That the coffin is covered with a kind of pennant or flag, with a red devil painted on it. Others say no, the flag is red and what is painted on it is a black monkey. Others say no, the cover is purple and there is a white cross on top. Perhaps this is because of the saying, 'Behind the cross, the devil.' No, what I saw was a devil. No, a cross, but not a white one; dark green. Something white, but not a cross, a complete skeleton, from the skull and ribs to the bones of the feet. The Lone Soul surrounded by real flames and you can hear its chains clanking. No, not the Lone Soul, the whole of Purgatory, I saw it. Matiana uses spirit flames to give light and heat and to cast her spells. Everything there moves, comes alive. In the darkness Matiana's eyes shine and flash fire. Cat's eyes, owl's eyes, or tiger's eyes. With so many Saints there, the walls look like the Courts of Heaven. No, not a single saint, only figures of Temptation, of animals, or strings of teeth, horns, heads, paws, tails. I swear that at least, at the very least, the Prince of the Heavenly Host is there; San Martín with his poor man; San Jorge with his dragon, protector against the stings of poisonous insects; Señor Santo Santiago with his devil underfoot; all these saints on horseback; and San Nicolás with his tub and two headless children in it; Santa Barbara, protec-

tor against lightning and flying sparks; even Santa Rita, advocate
of lost causes, and, although I cannot remember seeing him, San
Ramón Nonato must be there. You must have them all in your
house. I did not see them. What I saw were ancient idols. With
devil's faces. Idols of stone and clay. Which talked. A mass of
contradictions.

The main room is always shut. Locked. A big heavy key, that
Matiana keeps well hidden. She opens it only when she is going to
bed; in the daytime, only to consult the oracles or to cast spells, or
when she has to get something. If she opens it for any reason, she at
once locks the door behind her, so that no one can get in till she
comes out. At night, or when she is consulting the oracle or casting
spells, she bars the door with a crossbar as well, and pulls the mesquite latch, like a miser guarding and counting his gold.

Matiana spends most of her day in the kitchen, the patio, the
shed, and the orchard. In the shed she keeps the things she uses
everyday, her ordinary drugs, and discarded rubbish piled up in
orderly fashion.

The orchard behind the house slopes down to the river, in terraces
reinforced with stone. Guava trees, pear trees, lemon trees, pomegranate trees, sweet and bitter oranges, orange-limes, citrons. On the
top terrace, on the same level as the house, beehives; on the bottom one, near the river, a vegetable patch. This is enough for Matiana, who lives chiefly on fruit, honey, vegetables, peppers. Although
they are not strictly necessary, she never lacks other foods: corn,
beans, brown sugar, salt, cheese, lard, given to her by her neighbors
in return for her services, or as a sign of affection, or from a desire
to propitiate her. She frequently has milk, meat, bread, crackers,
chocolate, and various tasty morsels, which she shares with those
who come to see her—"so as not to get into bad habits," she says.

The other things connected with her profession—spices, alcohol,
pitch, turpentine, petroleum, tallow, grease, candles, wine, olive
oil, flour, vinegar, incense and copal, camphor, gum arabic, alkali,
creolin, glue, yeast, chlorate, sulphur—she gets from those who request her services and from close friends, but makes her requests
only when they ask her what she needs.

Although she cannot read, printed papers fascinate Matiana, especially those with pictures. She covers her door and windows with them, and also with sheets printed for religious festivals and programs for bullfights in the small towns nearby; reproductions of saints, heroes, and public figures; advertisements, newspaper photographs, a few lottery tickets. On the walls, a profusion of postcards, illustrations of religious and profane allegories, landscapes, alternating with bunches of paper flowers, fans, and garlands, which Matiana also likes.

She lives alone, without even a watchdog. At one time she had a lot of animals—a cow and calf, a donkey, pigs fattening, a henhouse full of hens, cage birds, rabbits, watchdogs. "I was strong then and could look after my plants and animals. Now I've only got my bees, to supply wax for the Feast of Corpus Christi and the honey I eat in my old age. What do I want with dogs? If God won't look after me, it's useless for others to try." When her two last watchdogs were found one morning with their throats mysteriously cut, such fearful calamities followed that the watchful care taken of Matiana and all her belongings by the Eye of Providence became an article of faith. After that dread vengeance fell on innocent and guilty alike, no one—not even the Trujillos in their worst fits of rage over some injury they attributed to the witch—has unsheathed his claws against her; no one goes near her house at night except those in urgent need of her services. Travelers avoid going by it, especially late at night, when, above and around the dwelling, lights can be seen and moving shapes, and the noise of weapons is heard and voices calling out, "Who goes there?" Sometimes the house seems to be on fire, with flames issuing through the cracks and lighting up the whole.

"Doña Matiana, Señora Matianita." Someone was calling, knocking at the small door.

"Forward in the name of the cross. Who's calling me in such a strange fashion?"

"Someone who hopes."

"Hope often ends in despair."

"Someone you're expecting."

"I'm not expecting anyone or anything."

"Yes, you are. Come close so I can speak to you through the crack."

"You're Miguel Arcángel, or Jacob Gallo."

"Jacob Gallo, himself. You're right."

"Why come so late at night?"

"It's better this way. You know why."

"You sound like Jesús, disguising your voice."

"You're insulting me, Doña Matiana."

"You're not Jesús, I know, but your voice sounds like his. I've been told that already, and there's nothing strange about it, you're the same blood, after all, and you can't deny it."

"Someone else is denying it. That's why I've come. But you know about it anyhow because you can read it in his behavior, and this isn't the time or place to go into it with you calmly, and it isn't what brings me here. I've come to greet you and tell you we're here, myself and my sons, to serve you, and we ask you to bless us and put the unseen powers on our side, to help us and not turn a deaf ear to us when you're interceding for justice, which is what we're seeking as much as you are. Just put your hand out through the door and I'll be back to see you in the daylight and we'll have time to talk."

"If you're going to give me something, tell me first what it is and why."

"First of all, I want to touch you so you'll give me strength and luck."

"You're making fun of a shriveled-up old woman."

"Listen to me. It's also so you can feel my intentions in my pulse and judge them."

"Why should I judge you?"

"Why not just because I want you to and ask you to?"

Crossbar and wooden latch creaked and the shutter in the door opened. In the darkness the man touched the firm bony hand.

"In addition, a small present, to be used for me."

The hand was swiftly withdrawn. There was a metallic sound.

"So you were lying from the beginning. I asked you."

"What do you mean lying? I was answering you and you interrupted."

"I don't take money, much less what I heard fall. What are you trying to pay for in advance? Some things can't be sold."

The shutter was closed, bolts and crossbar replaced. Jacob raised his voice in order to be heard: "You'll hurt my feelings if you don't accept this little offering, not to spend on yourself, just to distribute for me and to pray for me."

Silence.

"Don't be offended. Don't answer if you'd rather not, Señora Matiana. God knows my good intentions. I'll leave my offering on the stone outside the door. It's not mine any more. You'll know what to do with it. I'm not asking you, and I won't ask you, for anything else except what I said: your blessing in the struggle for justice and progress in the land where I was born. We're at your service when you want anything done, if you need us, at any time."

Jacob spoke loudly and slowly, standing close to the crack so as to be heard.

"Listen," the woman said finally, without opening the door again, "instead of giving me something, since I haven't done anything to be rewarded for, and you're surely not imagining you can make me obey you, there's one thing you can do: go and find out about an act of injustice your father wants to add to his list, concerning the sewing machine belonging to a daughter of Rómulo and Merced. Go and find out about that."

"I know about it, and I can promise you they won't take the machine away from Doña Merced. I'll answer for that. And listen, don't hurt my feelings by refusing to accept this offering. I'll leave it there."

"And then they'll say I stole it. Take it away. Later, if you want to, you can bring me some handfuls of corn."

"At least take care of this. I've given it to you."

"If you're stubborn, just imagine how stubborn I can be at my age."

"Well, it can stay here and I hope someone who needs it will find it."

them in his heart, though he was always attentive and very courteous to them, even teasing them in the friendly way that was natural to him. They enjoyed seeing him, listening to him, guessing what he'd be like to live with, comparing his ways to the ordinary ways of the farmers. This was what the latter couldn't forgive. They were jealous of him, and afraid. Of course, he won over most of them, fascinating them, entertaining them with music. Jacob Gallo, resurrected, brought all this back to my mind. With all their differences, I suspect they were alike in this. I know what he was really after—to get in touch through me with the invisible powers, because he has faith in me. I understood him. If I pretended I didn't, it was in order not to make it too easy, and because he doesn't know me and I don't know him, though I've got a pretty good idea what he's like. I know why he's been sent from above, which even he himself doesn't know since he's only the instrument, as we all are in this vale of tears, the instrument of the Hand and Powerful Eye. And since he doesn't know the Plans that bring him here, he doesn't want to confide in me and I don't want him to think, "This grasping old woman stretched out her hand as soon as she heard the clink of the gold." Not that he'll say so, but just in case. I'm not used to having money. Everyone knows that. And I don't need it. Still less, gold. What use is it around here? It's only the people who want to save it that have any. Who else? The fuss there'd be if a poor inhabitant of the plain should try to buy his tools with a gold coin. He'd always be suspected of stealing it. Doors'd be shut in his face here, just like in the towns. As the saying goes, 'Poor man yesterday, rich man today—how did the money come his way?' Suddenly I decided to pick up the coins and take them over to Merced, late as it was, so she could keep the machine. Or at least keep them for Jacob when he came back. I wouldn't look at them or count them, just pick them up before anyone came and took them. No matter how safe people's property may be around the plain, what lies on the ground is a temptation here as everywhere else . . . No, let them lie there. If he hasn't taken them. I'd like to be sure. If someone finds them and picks them up, then they're his. God will have helped him. The money's still there. How much is it? It may be thousands, for all I care. The devil's not going to prevail. Get thee behind me, Satan. Tell your story to the Trujillos, and tell them, too, that Miguel Arcángel is risen from the dead, that he was here, that he left this here and will soon come to bring back to our minds the story of the Trujillos—the never-ending story. I don't even want to remember it. Maybe Jacob Gallo will finish it, who knows, I think he will, or Miguel Arcángel, risen from the dead, who resembles Señor Gabriel. I hope he won't stray from the right path or be corrupted, and his coming be in vain.

Early in the morning, an upstanding young man appeared, followed by three companions, all on horseback, with a laden mule. The young man said he was sent by his father, Jacob Gallo, and, at a sign from him, the mule was unloaded and four bags taken off. The young man said two were corn and two beans, a gift from his father.

Matiana answered, "Yes, I'll accept those, tell him, and look, boy . . . what's your name?"

"Miguel, Miguel Gallo, at your service, legitimate son, the eldest, of . . ."

"Look, Miguel, just around the corner, by the small door that opens on the path, you'll find something to be taken back to your father. Go and get it."

The young man went and came back with a package.

"Here it is. I was only told to bring you these things. You can settle the other matter with my father when he comes. We Gallos don't talk much but we're very stubborn. We'll see you later, Madre Matiana."

"Pig-headed fools!"

The package lay on the ground, and it was impossible to get the young man to pick it up or to persuade him and his companions to stay and have something to eat.

"When my father rides this way, you can give it to him. Excuse us, we're in a hurry. Some other day, with pleasure. With your permission . . ."

"So young, and already so stubborn, so hard-headed . . ."

There was nothing she could do but pick up the package and put it away without opening it. The door of the main room creaked and Matiana entered her kingdom.

Infusion of frankincense gum for pains in the side, and white tragacanth for pneumonia, with oil of turpentine liniment, turpentine plasters, and decoction of pitch pine. To ward off the evil eye, buds from the mesquite tree and the red flower that is actually called the evil eye flower. For puerperal fever, and there is so much of it around here, frequent douches with water in which ash-leaves have been boiled, as much as the patient can stand, till she almost bursts; and water to drink in which the same leaves have been steeped. For sunstroke the same thing, with poultices of ash. They are remedies found in nature. Only those found in nature. Corn silk, plantain, pearl barley, melon seeds, sweet-scented marigolds, sage, hibiscus, bearberries, in drinking water and in poultices, for bladder trouble. For ulcers, gum from the sheath of the acacia flower, which may also be used for rubbing one's gums. Perfume, too, is obtained from this same acacia flower. The fat and tongues of swallows for mutes and stutterers. Wine kept in gourds, and cordials of red wine of Sanlúcar, for asthma. Ointment of San Rafael with the oil and scales of fishes for the blind. Damiana and rue for wind and parosela for the stomach, together with horehound and sagebrush, mint and mouse-ear. Just a few, only those found in nature. Orange blossom for sadness, pomegranate and bitter orange peel for biliousness, foxglove flowers for the heart. For fever, borage and enemas. Fox-liver extract for weakness. Great mullein, ribwort, and alcohol on sugar for a cough. For rheumatism, the roots of the sweet-scented marigold, crushed in alcohol and left for a month, and the stings of ants, bees, and wasps. Also good for colds. Just a few remedies, only those found in nature.

Part Three — BELÉN:
VIOLENCE UNLEASHED

There were shepherds in Belén

There were shepherds in Belén and the moon was full. The plain had some beautiful nights.

"A pity, considering what happened."

Other years it has rained so hard that the competition had to be held on the covered terrace at one end of the Big House, which made it very crowded.

"The Big House everyone hates."

This year, not a single cloud in the sky on any night, on any of the four nights, December 25 and 28, January 1 and 6, when the performances were given.

"They nearly didn't have a single performance because of the outrage that took us all by surprise."

In other years the rains have come early and put a damper on the entertainment and spoiled it.

"That bare-faced outrage put a damper on the devotion."

This year there was not even any need for artificial light.

"The old skinflint saved even on that, but it didn't stop him from doing what he did in such a wicked way."

The patio, gleaming in the bright moonlight, really looked like the night of the Blessed Birth, with the angels, surrounded by light, telling the shepherds the good tidings, and with the star shining.

"It's hard to believe they could choose that particular night to fall on the poor when they were least expecting it."

The night was still, the sky clear.

"Guilty consciences."

Although, as is natural in December, there was a clear sky with a full moon, it was cold enough.

"Not as cold as the Trujillos' inhuman behavior."

In the silvery moonlight, the devils—some small, most of them huge—with their red masks, their black cloaks sprinkled with glittering spangles like sparks from a brazier, and their horns, looked more like devils than in other years, more like shades emerging from the cave of night into the lighted patio. The beards of the hermits shone very white. Temptation, enveloped in crimson veils blowing in the wind, moved here and there like burning tow.

When it became known that there would be pastorals after all, the commotion started again. The murmur ran through the plain.

"They got their own way, the crows. Don Felipe, Don Jesusito, Plácida, they won out over the old man by showing their claws. What creatures!"

"The Trujillo team. One's as bad as the other."

Soon the rumor took on a bitter tone.

"Yes, and at what a price the old miser gave in."

"We might have known. They might have told us before."

"Outrageous, unbearable."

"It's outrageous, a really outrageous crime they committed, and as usual, against poor people with no means of defense."

A general uproar was about to start. No one could understand it.

When did anyone in the Tierra Santa hear of anyone trying to collect money from people taking part in a competition, making them pay for what they get from their own work?"

"They say it's a contribution."

"Nonsense! That doesn't even happen in the town, where I never go because it's all fines and fees for this and that, even for breathing."

"They say the Trujillos even wanted to charge an entrance fee, the good-for-nothing scoundrels."

"We should have made them swallow their entrance fee, hammered it down their throats, but everybody gives in, bows down before them, the way they did on this occasion."

"In no time they'll be wanting to levy a fine, like in the town, because you wear white cotton trousers and huaraches. That's just what happened to me a short time ago. I went in one Sunday and they put me in jail for being indecent, they said, in my white cotton trousers. There was a bit of paper at the entrance to town that said they're forbidden, as though anyone knew what's on those papers. So I paid a fine of two pesos to get out, away from all the drunks, and I didn't buy my provisions. I tell you I didn't even get to Mass, I was shut up there till there was nothing to do but give them two pesos, they let me out without paying the other one they'd asked for. When did anyone hear of a thing like that, and just for walking around in white trousers and a sash like we always do. Soon they'll be making us wear suede pants with silver buttons. Just to get money!"

"And they've got a thing there they call law. But here?"

"The law here is what those cursed Trujillos damn well please!"

"In the town, the man who doesn't wear shoes has to pay a fine. When a man can't wait, and finds a corner to do what he has to, he's taken off to jail and pays a double fine. And the man who lets his animals stop in the square or the street spends double time in jail and pays a fine, too, and it's a miracle if they don't take his animals away from him. And so on. If you even just stop for a moment and look around you, it's 'Take him to jail!' If anyone just looks like a bumpkin from the country, with no one in the town to speak up for him, that's enough."

"That's all we needed in the Tierra Santa, where luckily there aren't policemen or anyone else to stop us living the way we want to.

We may be poor, but each man can do what he damn well pleases."

"Above all, not having to pay for what we have or do."

"They want to get even more out of us, as if we didn't have enough to put up with already."

"They think they own even the air and the sun and the stars. Didn't they want to make us pay for the moonlight?"

"Charging for room. When did anyone ever hear the like of that in the whole Tierra Santa?"

It was such a complete surprise, and done in such a wicked way.

Just as in other years, those selling food and other things had been arriving before the actors and setting out their wares: guitar-carrying vendors of printed ballads, prayers, and birthday songs; people with herbs for sale, knicknack peddlers, barbers, dentists, dicethrowers; people selling lottery tickets, fortune tellers, tinkers, knife grinders, tinsmiths—a whole noisy throng of vendors and artisans, whom people came to seek out just as much as they did to watch the pastorals.

That first day—Saturday, December 25th, to be more precise—more people were there than in other years. By the middle of the afternoon, Belén looked like an anthill. The people were agog with curiosity, for different reasons; because of the danger that even at the last minute Don Epifanio might suspend the festivities; because it was Christmas and the next day was a Sunday; because there was such a bright moon, which meant they could go home late with their families, walking back over the roads of the plain as though it were daylight;because they wanted to see for themselves if, as people said, the pastoral from Damasco, the famous one, that was being performed that night and had won without a break for the last four years, would hold its own and not to be ousted, not lose to the new group formed in the mountains and constantly on the tongues of those who swore they had seen the dress rehearsal. There had been betting on the farms for days, as though the competitions were horse races. There was something strange afoot. How, for instance, could the betting have reached two to one in favor of the unknown pastoral when the one from Damasco was so famous and popular, and when it was known that in order to make sure of winning they had rehearsed morning, afternoon, and evening for weeks, had completely renovated their costumes, had added to their choruses, and had prepared a number of secret surprises, like miracles, to astound those present? There were rumors of mutual spying, for neither side wanted to lose ground and both wanted to seize the lead. Nevertheless, no one could give a clear account of where the mountain pastoral came from, or who made up the troupe, or how or when they held their dress rehearsal.

The chain of surmises, favorites, gossip grew. Back again with renewed force, rising noisily, dominating the crest of the shouting, came the topic of the flying devil, more exciting after all, than the other tales. What better occasion to examine it and verify it in the various accounts brought in by the other congregations. Except for those of the ravine, the people from other farms who claimed to have seen the apparition contradicted each other, and were vague when they tried to give details about the circumstances: it was midday, no, midnight, it was like a dragonfly, no, a worm with wings, it was coming this way, no, it was flying toward the mountain. There were an unexpected number of people doubtful and reticent, even openly disbelieving, concerning what only days before had been an article of faith. Now it turned out that many were familiar with flying machines but without knowing exactly when or where, without daring to maintain that that was what the monster must have been.

More and more people kept arriving, more traveling vendors. In such a lively throng, sales were going well, with tales, rumors, prophecies, betting, meetings of neighbors who had not seen each other since before the seed-time. Peddlers and artisans did not have enough to sell. A dense circle of men, women, and children were listening, fascinated, to the couple selling ballads; it was the greatest attraction. They were singing of the terrifying appearance of the devil, Satan, in the guise of a flying monster, causing death wherever he passed above the farms of the Tierra Santa. The listeners crowded around, asking if the paper had illustrations on it showing how it all happened; the peddlers, a man and a woman, replied that they just had the ballad in their heads, for they had heard it from the poet who made it up and had added some new details, and that

"And their singing—it's as if we were back in the days of Maestro Gabriel, as if he himself were their leader."

> How wide the plain! It seems this lap
> Of our journey is ended, without mishap,
> Without mishap.

Hermits and devils pushed back the curious, frightening the little boys who wanted to touch the brand-new costumes.

At this moment, while they were hurrying up with the preparations so that everything might be ready and the performance begin, and while they were once again listening to the peddlers crying their wares and games—while the people were absorbed in all this, *Bang!* Out came the collector demanding payment. The couple selling ballads were repeating the verses about the moneylender:

> And with repentance sincere
> Let the moneylender prepare
> His conscience now to square.

> Let him who has swindled his neighbor
> Restore his ill-gotten gain
> For money will not avail him
> If obtained by another's pain.
> To warn us of coming Judgment
> The devil flew over the plain.

Thinking that someone was trying to play a trick on them, the man went on singing and strumming his guitar. The rude insistence and coarse language that followed made him think that Trujillo, the moneylender, believing the verses referred to him, was ordering them to shut up.

"What! Haven't you got ears, you jackass? Can't you hear me telling you it's fifty centavos? Cough 'em up! Don't stand there looking stupid, you idiot!"

As though big black spiders and scorpions had suddenly emerged from every direction, swirls of people could be seen crowding together, jostling each other; shouts were heard. What it was all about no one really knew. They became confused and started to run away.

"By what right?" the man selling ballads asked.

The answer he got was a violent one. A hand seized his guitar and broke it over his head before a voice roared insolently, "The right of my strong right arm. I can do what I damn well please, you son of a bitch."

It was Don Felipe Trujillo, in a rage, with his hand on his pistol.

"If you don't like it, clear out, go back to wherever you came from, you dirty bastards."

The hanger-on who was collecting the money started to kick at the wares on the ground; he danced on the printed papers. The man's wife turned from tears to inarticulate yells of rage, then to bellowed insults and foul language.

Taken by surprise at the sight of arms, the crowd instinctively drew back, abandoning the victims of the attack. They overturned a box of wares which the peddler, on all fours, tried to gather together again, cursing as he did so. A man selling ends of cloth and bandannas lay face down with his arms outstretched, struggling to keep his stock from being trampled or stolen. The poorest were the worst off, the old men and women selling seeds and toasted peanuts arranged in little heaps; their wares were pitilessly stamped on by the agents of the Big House. Those with pastry and sweets for sale ran from side to side, skillfully lifting up their trays to save them from harm. One woman selling tacos and enchiladas waved her tongs with a glowing piece of charcoal in them, in a fierce gesture. Pleas, insults, threats.

Recovering from the untimely incident, the crowd began to surge back, muttering threats, the anger of some at odds with the timidity or indecision of others. Indignation increased, gained ground, overcame mere passive curiosity. The idea spread, the cry, muffled or outspoken: "By what right?"

Like a red-hot iron, branding it on their minds, came the unbearable announcement: "Contribution!"

"And the worst of it is, when your neighbor starts to give way you think the battle's lost."

"No. By what right?"

Indignation mounted, sparks were flying. At any moment battle would be joined.

Those in charge of the pastorals had gathered together, trying to calm people down, to restrain the aggressors. Don Jesusito Trujillo, joining them, talked and talked, changing his expression and his tone as the situation required, ceaselessly rubbing his hands together, blinking in wide-eyed innocence, shaking his head as though he would not hurt a fly.

At first he had stood up resolutely to the peddlers, without Don Felipe's insolence, but with equal stubbornness. When the cry "By what right?" became general he maintained that it was by right of ownership. "This is a private house, not a public square. How can you expect to take all the profit without contributing to the cost? It isn't fair." The words *justice, right, equity, respect for the property of others* were constantly on his lips.

When the directors of the pastorals intervened and the first moment of surprise was over, Don Jesusito, seeing that the people were gaining, turned from demanding immediate compliance to persuasive pleading, trying to sound out the feelings of the people, to divide them, to gain time, to see if it were possible to get money out of the peddlers, whom he began to blame for the trouble. The Trujillos were merely acting in the public interest, threatened by those who were exploiting the public by selling at high prices, taking advantage of the need and ignorance of the people, deceiving them with damaged goods and food gone bad, unfit to eat, even poisonous, and also deceiving them with various tricks when they measured or weighed, when they played cards or roulette, as it was easy to prove. By every means in his power Don Jesusito tried to persuade the spectators to hurl themselves on the profiteers, poisoners, tricksters, or at least not to make common cause with them. The peddlers alone were guilty of the disorders because they were out for themselves and would not respect other people's property. They had begun the quarrel, they themselves had destroyed their wares in order to start the fire going and get the others worked up. It was not right that because of a few greedy, ravenous, unprincipled swindlers the people should have to go without their festivities. It was not right to play their game, to defend them. On the contrary: Down with those who charge high prices, enemies of the public health!

"Come here, smell this chicken, this sausage! They're bad. Pity the people who've eaten these filthy things! They must be writhing in pain. And look at this bottle of so-called fruit drink: it's colored with aniline dye, which you know is harmful. And look, bugs! It must be water from a dirty puddle. What crooks! And even so, you don't want my brother Felipe to punish them."

Don Jesusito directed this battery of words toward the belligerent and those who were undecided. He cut short the denials and explanations with which the accused tried to defend themselves, not giving them time to catch their breath with his stream of words, emphasized by soothing gestures.

Someone rushed to break the bottle, to throw the fried food on the ground, while their owners yelled, helplessly:

"Lies! It isn't dyed and there aren't bugs in it . . ."

"Fresh chicken, just boiled . . ."

"Clean water allowed to settle . . ."

"I raised them myself. I killed them this morning."

"It's pure hibiscus with white sugar in it."

"You all saw the bugs!"

"Liars!"

"You can still smell the rancid lard."

"Filthy Trujillos!"

"Bastards!"

"Children of the devil!"

Don Felipe took out his pistol.

"Brother, calm down until they're convinced we're doing this for their good and justice is on our side."

The directors of the pastorals insisted that they should suspend the fee-collecting and particularly that they should put a stop to the vandalism.

"It wasn't us—it's the anger of the people against those who are selling poisoned food . . ."

"Against those who steal part of every yard of muslin and percale they measure..."

"Against the dishonest gamblers..."

"What we want is to give guarantees to those who come to Belén..."

The people were divided in favor of and against the peddlers, but most of them were content to watch and listen passively.

"Well, let them pay this time and we'll see about the other days."

The directors of the pastoral would not agree. They kept on arguing.

After a lot of discussion, Don Jesusito proposed: "At least let them admit that we're right to charge them and let them guarantee to sell good things cheaply, to abide by the law and not sell food that's gone bad or things of no use."

The directors deliberated; they decided that things should go on as they had done every year.

"Then let them get out of the patio, carry on their trading outside of our boundaries."

"And who knows," asked the leader from Betulia, "where your boundaries are?"

There were smiles all around, either open or concealed.

Don Felipe started to attack the questioner. Don Jesusito held him back.

"Did I say something I shouldn't? Was I impolite? According to you, everything is yours. Just tell us where. That's all I want to know, in order to avoid further trouble."

The enquiry proved useless. Most of the peddlers had gone and the rest were clearing their things away.

The pastoral was hurriedly begun. A string of firecrackers drowned the arguments. A shower of lights filled the sky with colors. The angel choir appeared, headed by Lucifer, all dressed in dazzling white: "Brave Archangels, created in my wisdom, the time has come. Shall we not, my valiant ones, fight zealously and hurl from this sky him who calls himself the Almighty?" And Sin replied: "Lucifer, mighty Angel, Thou art the king we would have and we will destroy God."

Lightning, thunder, fighting, and the voice of the Archangel, Michael: "Silence, hapless coward..."

But it was not the same. There was a bitter taste in every mouth. The performance had lost its savor. Many had gone with the peddlers. Those who remained were bewildered; their tongues and throats were dry; they were not paying attention; they moved from one side to the other, restlessly, a prey to helpless rage, to forebodings of more injustice to come, realizing their moral cowardice in not rising up in defense of those attacked.

Some—among them Rómulo—were unable to bear their thoughts and left in the course of the performance, in which they had lost all interest.

Filled with shame, with a sense of defeat, muttering to himself, Rómulo made his way toward Betania in the moonlight.

Pack of cowards! Why not face the truth? That's what we are. And we deserve all we got and more. That's the honest truth. What I'll have to listen to from Merced when I tell her! She'll give me the rough side of her tongue, as they say, and I'll never hear the end of it. There's no dignity left in the Tierra Santa. Even hope is lost, and we've lost all sense of shame. What is left now? The only fate left us is to be branded tomorrow like oxen. Who ever saw anything like it? If my grandfather came back from the dead he'd die again at once, of anger, and even more, of grief. Never in his life would he have agreed to it. First of all, he would have made them pay damages. No, in the Tierra Santa there's never been another like the late Teódulo Garabito, loving protector of those in need and declared enemy of the oppressor. He never hesitated to call a thief a thief, and couldn't be held back from running to lift his hand in favor of those who suffered injustice or wretchedness. In his time there wasn't any envy in the whole region. Teófila used to say that envy is begrudging other people their good fortune. On the contrary, everyone was glad when someone did well. This is still the general rule, just as we're sad when our neighbors have misfortunes, and help each other in time of need. If I don't have such and such a thing, I don't worry, since so and so will lend it to me, gladly. Envy began when Pifanio started to thrive, to be harsh toward others, refusing to lend remedies for the sick—the enema apparatus, laxatives, medicinal herbs. The bad example spread. We began to hear of neighbors who refused a handful of sugar and salt, a jar of oil, a stick of pitch pine, which no one up to that time had refused to lend from one house to another as though we were all one family, especially in the matter of medicines, which people offer at once without waiting to be asked. Then some people didn't bring back what they borrowed or didn't return favors, and this caused a cooling in friendships. We began to distrust each other. People began to lose confidence in the words of others. Thank God not all of us, there's still a lot of us who live as our forefathers taught us, but if we keep on like this, it's goodbye to the peace and harmony here. What's just happened is a blow to the unity among the farms. I was reminded of what Teófila used to read to us, how King Nero burned Rome and blamed the Christians, just as Jesusito's doing now. According to him, we should all destroy the peddlers. That's what they call "sowing discord." My grandfather used to say, 'Sow the storm and reap the whirlwind,' and also, 'With what measure ye mete, it shall be measured to you again.' I'm not saying they'll come to harm. I'll leave that to God's justice on those who oppress the poor. Someone has to look after them and stand up for them. Because we, their neighbors, are a pack of cowards, of good-for-nothings, as Merced says. Oh, and in my anger I forgot the warning Don Jesusito gave me before the set-to with the people selling their wares. As soon as he saw me he beckoned me over and I went. He put on a flattering expression and clapped me on the back, saying, "Ah, Rómulo, how goes it? Listen, I've got some business of my father's to discuss with you, and for goodness sake don't make it worse than it is already. He says you're making a fool of him. You know what he's like when he gets an idea into his head. He wanted my brother Felipe to handle the matter, but I offered to settle it in the proper way. Felipe's rough-handed, you know, and sometimes he goes too far. I said, 'We must treat Rómulo as a friend.' Let's try and have a word

nally he outdistanced them. Or he escaped from them by taking a short cut, engrossed in his unexpressed irritation, his self-communings, under the beautiful moon.

"What do you think of the incident?" (There's no dignity left. He would die again from sheer grief to see this.)

"And you, such a supporter of the Big House." (He hasn't come back to life.)

"I won't go back for anything in the world." (There was no envying, no grudging the good fortune of others. Teófila.)

"If Teófila were alive it wouldn't have happened." (King Nero.)

"Not even the comfort of Matiana is left." (Merced, the rough edge of her tongue.)

They walked in groups. The children asleep in their elders' arms. There was weeping. Barking of dogs on all sides. Christmas Eve moon. And dogs barking, near and far.

"Don Rómulo, why are you on foot when you're such a horseman?" (When I had money . . . it can't be helped now . . .)

"And Doña Merced? Didn't she come?" (There's no way out.)

A short distance away from Belén, a woman started shouting through her tears: "Bastards! Everything I had! Bastards! Better to have killed me! My pottery! Bastards! My dishes! Bastards!" (A pack of cowards!)

Rómulo hurried along as though pursued by wasps that were stinging his ears, eyes, lips, and hands.

"We might have known." (For getting mixed up in it, Merced will say.)

"We lived such a peaceful life." (Settle the matter with the boys.)

"Each one at peace with his neighbor." (It's no longer anything to do with me.)

"In perfect agreement." (I've got no say in the matter now, Pifanio will say.)

"Stretching out a helping hand, each one concerned for his neighbor, like one family." (My father's given me a message for you, he said.)

In other years, by moonlight or in the darkness, people had sung on their way back from Belén, repeating the songs of the pastorals—

When, oh when, will come the time
When Lucifer, Prince of Darkness,
Will again be called Star of the Morning?
Oh when?—

and telling about the doings of the devils and the shepherds, refer-
ring to the amusing tricks of Bartolo, the lazy shepherd, the temptations of Temptation, the fight between Bato and Gila. This year
only curses could be heard.

"Curses on the Big House." (What an outrage!)

"Curses on the Trujillos." (One as bad as the other.)

"Curses on Belén!" (Cave of monsters.)

"Curses on the Tierra Santa!" (No one to turn to.)

"Curses upon curses." (Abomination after abomination.)

What pity they aroused—what feelings of remorse, those ill-fated
peddlers who walked along in the moonlight, bowed down with despair and carrying what remained of their merchandise on their
backs. (When the time came we all bent before the storm, we all
gave way, withdrew and left them in the lurch. We didn't have the
courage to stand by them and prevent the outrage.) A peddler with
ribbons, thread, and so forth was running along in panic with his
empty box when he stopped, turned around, shouted like a madman,
muttered to himself, cursed. The man selling baked goods had only
saved his oil burner, which he was carrying high above his head,
moaning. Some, unable to walk any further, were resting by the
side of the road, utterly beaten, sobbing, with their heads in their
hands, while others stared at the moon, dumb and motionless, as
though turned to stone, and the moon shone down on faces with
wide-open eyes and countenances indelibly stamped with despair.

"By what right?"

In the moonlight the impenetrable whiteness of the barren clay
was cruel. (Not as cruel as the Trujillos.) And the dark masses of
the acacia trees were threatening.

("By the right of my strong right arm, you son of a bitch.")

The dogs were barking on all sides. (By the right of ownership,
good people.) It *would* be on this night of December 25, the day on

which Our Lord was born. (Worse than if it had been on a Good Friday.) Not even a cloud in the sky to soften the harsh light of the moon. (No one to turn to.) Curses, barking, weeping, sobbing, wailing, footsteps in the night on the roads leading from Belén. The cold was growing more intense.

"Yes, a real chill. I don't know when I'll get there." ("That's what you get for being mixed up in it," Merced will say.)

"Is there any truth, Don Rómulo, in the rumor that they're trying to take your daughter's machine away from you?"

"It's not my business any more, it's Miguel Arcángel's."

"The Captain of the Heavenly Host preserve us!" (Florentina Sánchez, what a fine girl! They'll soon ruin her!)

"My old woman still has a dress Teófila made for her with her blessed hands." ("Father, we'll soon pay for the machine, and then it will all be profit, to help you with.")

"They'll have to do it over my dead body." (Yes, I've got a chill.)

"And there we were, all asking questions, dying with curiosity to know what was foretold by the devil flying in the shape of a dragonfly with eyes like glowing coals. Now we know, now we're undeceived." (I'll have to stay in bed.)

"How right they are when they say that troubles never come singly." (These pains will be the death of me.)

"Take the machine away from you—we might as well say, 'the relic'. The day they did that there would be a revolution on the plain, there certainly would be! (Don Felipe says now, and don't make it any worse, for Heaven's sake.')

"We wouldn't leave one stone of the Big House on another, and the same with all their other miserable houses!" (Pack of cowards!)

"How different it was in the days of my grandfather! Belén was everybody's home, and everybody would come there, everybody loved and respected him as a father and benefactor of the poor."

"So he was, I remember."

"That's what I hear, everywhere."

As they got further away from Belén, a growing rumor, barely audible, rising above the murmuring, prevailing over complaints and curses, gaining in clarity, made itself heard:

"The Gallos are coming, they've already arrived at their old land . . ."

And, growing louder:

"Gallos against Trujillos! That will be worth seeing . . ."

Hope dawning:

"They'll put the upstarts in their places!" (Merced thinks so.)

"God grant your prayers . . ." (Merced swears it.)

"A man called Jacob, a powerful man . . ." (He carried off Florentina.)

"Miguel Arcángel . . ." (Ah, Florentina Sánchez, with the big black eyes.)

Consolation of those in trouble:

"They'll put them in their place."

No more cowardice:

"Let them fight with them and not the defenseless poor."

Trembling all over, shaken by shivering, Rómulo could just make out the outline of Betania in the moonlight, could distinguish the familiar sound of the barking which greeted him. (She'll give me the rough side of her tongue, and there'll be no stopping her.) Following that scene of wicked injustice, the dear familiar smells unloosed the fount of tears. Blaming himself for his cowardice, like a child reaching home after some act of naughtiness or experience of danger, Rómulo burst out crying as though his heart would break. With a lump in his throat and shaken by sobs, he reached the stream which since his childhood he had been able to run lightly across at any hour of the day or night, at any time of the year. (Whose fault was it that I was there to see such wickedness?) He tried to recognize the shape standing on the stones on the other bank. Impetuously, he jumped from a slippery stone, lost his balance, and fell. He heard a familiar voice speak his name.

"Rómulo."

The shape moved towards him, looking like one of those blackbirds that hop across the stony river bed. Agile and black, like a blackbird, accustomed to leaping over the stones in the stream. Bony hands (Death is close behind me) and skillful.

"You're all worked up, my friend."

Recognizing her, he was reassured, but he wept louder, like a child running to its mother's lap after some naughtiness or escape from danger.

"Matiana, why did I have to go?"

With the woman's help he rose and crossed over the stony bed.

"I haven't got a bone unbroken after that fall and I'm shivering all over."

"And after what you witnessed without lifting a finger to defend them."

"Yes, that's true."

"The wicked creatures! But weeping won't do any good. Come and let me give you some medicine. Forward in the name of the cross, neighbor."

He limped after her.

"Too bad it happened, and with such a moon."

"It wasn't long before they came with the first call for help. They told me that some people were killed in the shooting and a lot more wounded or beaten up. I put my rebozo over my head, picked up the bag with the things for accident victims in it, and hurried as fast as my years would let me. The news I heard on the way kept getting worse and worse. That the bastards had ganged together and were molesting the shepherdesses. That the Gallos had arrived and were having their first encounter with the Trujillos, shooting in the middle of the crowd. That the people were so furious they set fire to the Big House and tried to drag out Epifanio, Felipe, Jesús, and other bastards at the end of a rope. The people came running like terrified animals. Near Belén I began to meet peddlers, running away, struggling under the weight of their merchandise. I got more and more details. I didn't want to see the faces of the wicked creatures. There wasn't any need. I stayed there for a while to see if my services would be needed, if there'd be any more news of the commotion. The little quassia I had with me was all used up in a moment. No way of getting enough, so many needed it—like you, now. I treated several people who'd been knocked around in the brawl. I used arnica. There weren't many of them. One woman, older than I am, who'd hurt herself trying to run. A man whose shoulder was out of joint from the mauling by Felipe and his men. Some with sprains and more with bruises from being trampled on. I still can't understand why on earth, with all of you there, no one stopped the fight."

"It happened so suddenly, and was done so brutally . . ."

They went straight to the kitchen. The moisture on the water jars gleamed in the moonlight. Rómulo drank three, four mugs of water, and was still thirsty.

"You were frightened and angry, weren't you? I came back slowly, helping a woman selling tortillas with her load. She had a baby at her breast and another three children. What a wicked thing! I'm going to give you some orange water with quassia and valerian in it. When you get home, let Merced give you some purging pills, take them with really hot atole tomorrow. Be very careful when you pass them. Wash them well and give them back to me. I'm certainly going to need them. It wouldn't be a bad idea, when the sun comes out, to stand on an anthill until the ants bite you, to ward off the shivers. You have to be well for Twelfth Night."

Rómulo asked why.

"To go back to Belén."

"I'll never go back. I don't think they'll have anything after what happened."

"Yes, there'll be the performance of the new pastoral. You've got to go. Take this blanket and go home. Not another word."

She went back to the path with him.

"Don't try to learn anything more. Cover yourself up well on account of the cold. It's dangerous to try and see into the future. The just judgment of God. It was a good thing I stayed on the bank of the stream for a while, enjoying the moon. Tomorrow, as soon as I can, I'll drop by your house. Cover yourself up well. Forward in the name of the cross. What a lovely moon!"

Moonlight and dogs everywhere in the Tierra Santa. Madre Matiana remained near the stone wall, recalling the past and looking into the future.

The sleeping earth. It makes you sad. The way death steals slowly over the body, numbing it inch by inch. Like the sleeping boldness of those who used to enjoy the reputation of being firebrands. It makes you sad to recall other days and other faces and make comparisons. It's the fault of the moon. It stirs up memories and drives away sleep. The moon brings back swarms of memories, reviving joys and sorrows. What mad ideas it has! Since it doesn't grow old, it brings to life even things you're not sure ever happened, things that may have been only wishful thinking. For example, I rarely think of the time when I was a girl. I sometimes feel it's impossible I ever was a girl. And this moon has been bringing me visions all night long of those years and the happy days when I didn't know anything about dead men or illnesses or cures, struggles, envy, threats, disasters, or fears, nor anything about the other world, or the assaults of the devil—I doubt if I even knew of his existence. The plain hasn't changed, except perhaps it was greener in those days, less barren in the rainy season, the rainfall has always been scanty and irregular, with droughts, as always, though I think there were more trees, and people had more energy, there was more business, more enjoyment, more choice. Or it may have been because I was a lively girl. Sometimes my spirit overflowed with happiness, and sometimes I felt sad for no reason, but it didn't hurt, I liked it. People would smile at my strength of will, but kept scolding me for my uneven temperament. I remember they'd say "You're very capricious" from time to time. It stuck in my mind, and just for fun I'd pretend to be capricious all the time and without any reason. I never went outside the plain, I've always lived inside its boundaries. Not even when the French came. I was still a child. They said I was born the year the Americans stole a great deal of land from us, but I could see that the pasture lands were still there and the mountains hadn't changed their positions. How could it be possible to steal them, to carry them off? How could anyone steal me? The French carry me off? That's what my family was afraid of. I heard them say the French troops stole horses and saddles and imposed forced loans, but why should the French want me? Why? I began to catch my family's fear. By then I knew what it was to get excited, to suffer because I wanted something, some fancy material, or long earrings like the older girls. But what I remember best is the fuss I kicked up to take part in the pastorals. What a job I had! My family didn't want me to go. I managed to get permission by being stubborn. We were living at that time on a farm called La Canana which was abandoned later, and every year they used to have famous pastorals. First they let me sing with the chorus. My voice amazed everyone with its true and penetrating notes, surpassing all the others. Even my family were surprised and finally agreed to let me be a shepherdess. Soon, that very year, the girl taking the part of Gila became ill and I took her place. I can still remember how thrilled I was to hear Bato singing to me. "Know, Gila, that I adore you, more than my bull, more than the lamb I eat, you are my life, my treasure. More than your ducks and your hens—more than your doves and swallows." I answered, "More than the flowers growing in the meadow—more than the nightingale you love so much—more than your cows and your calves." It was thrilling. And next year they made me Temptation. My family didn't want that either. They objected. I was stubborn and wouldn't give in. I liked it and did it very well. "Come forward, fascinating Temptation," said Lucifer in a deep voice, "and silently enter this fertile and treacherous land, my daughter." I would come forward, singing in a treble voice, "Like you, breathing only vengeance; like you, without faith, without hope; like you, fallen, I weave my fascinating charm about men's hearts, and they will forfeit God and Paradise." Why on earth am I remembering all this at my age! Oh, how I loved to watch the admiration on the faces of those present as they listened to me and followed my movements and my affectations! And the eyes of the men, young and old, fastened on me, following me about, glowing like live coals, never leaving me, like gadflies, like these creatures that fly about at night that we call fireflies, how thrilling it was, although being so young, I didn't realize just what those hungry eyes meant and wanted, the mysterious attraction of those who devoured me with their eyes, filling me with a happiness I couldn't explain. My family used to scold me. I could hear them say, "It looks as if she's a slut, as if it's in her blood. God save us! And God save you from going around with your defenses down, it'll lead you straight to perdition, that's the truth. Take care not to slip, child." They talked angrily of so many lost women. How could they get lost, men or women, here on the farm where the distances between one house and another are so short and the paths so well known? What did they mean by "lost"? I felt as though I'd been born dancing and had been dancing all my life. Even on the first day the curiosity with which people looked at me didn't bother me. I didn't mind going out, beginning to sing, walking from side to side. It was as if I'd been doing it all my life. I didn't find it difficult to change my expression, sometimes being happy, sometimes sad, sometimes mischievous, sometimes innocent and frightened. It was just as easy to move from singing to speaking, as if I'd been born to it. I was surprised myself at the natural way I could change from being Gila, an ordinary shepherdess, to being and feeling like the daughter of the devil, twisting like a snake, putting on a flattering, hypocritical expression, speaking in a voice like an angel's to offer the apple to Eve and make her swallow a bite and give Adam a bite while the people fidgeted in their seats and the men's eyes gleamed brighter and their bodies seemed to break out in a sweat, their throats dry, their hands and jaws clenched. Adam and Eve ran to hide. Lucifer chuckled, facing the Archangel. "Tell God to make universes and men like these, Michael." So one year, just as naturally as I'd been Temptation, I took the part of Eve, hypocritical and provocative. Another year I was given the part of the Virgin Mary. Yes, it surprised me most of all to discover the ease with which I jumped from one role into another, completely possessed by each one. Or rather, I didn't jump into them, I wore them, like different dresses that I'd put on, changing them so rapidly that it was hard to believe I was the same person. The fact is, I felt I was the Virgin myself, and didn't have to make any effort to appear full of grace, purity, humility, since the appropriate virtues, gestures, tones of voice seemed to spring from the depths of my being. The same thing happened when I was Gila, or Temptation. No one taught me the twistings and gestures that occurred to me, they welled up as if from deep springs, flowed through my nerves and veins, inspiring my movements. As the Virgin, I was ready to sacrifice my life to save the Christ Child in my arms. As Lucifer I was dominated by a hatred of St. Michael, even of God, and my voice shook with real fury. But the audience, especially the men, liked best to see me as Temptation. They said they'd never seen anything like it. The same words my family had used ran from house to house, whispered or spoken by gossiping tongues. Some repeated them shamefacedly, others pityingly, and there were many who gaily, insultingly, mockingly repeated, "Tart, bad woman, whore, slut." I didn't know the meaning of the words, although I had an idea from the way they were spoken, and I was dying with curiosity to find out, trying to get at the meaning without the courage to ask, and I wanted to know why, as they spoke them, people seemed to be talking of something bad and at the same time pleasurable, enjoyable. I was reminded of the saying, 'Forbidden fruits are sweetest.' There were so many forbidden things all around me! The secret desires I'd aroused both pleased and embarrassed me, the former more than the latter, to tell the truth. I was flattered to discover that their eyes declared and repeated the opinions hidden underneath their words. One thing I was sure of, that whatever it was, I was the cause of these thoughts, sufferings, desires, reflected in their eyes, their open mouths, the constant agitation of their lips, hands, and bodies, in their dry mouths and panting breasts. I can't deny that I liked to feel I was the cause of those expressions and fidgetings. God forgive me. The words they used kept whirring around in my head like mosquitoes, biting and stinging. Or rather, like moths, stubbornly flying around and around a flame, whether they get burned or not. That's how I started to be a prophetess, reading people's intentions in their faces, guessing the meaning of their words. Soon they began to say, "She's a witch," and call me Madre Matiana. What stupid fools to say this, when they were the ones whose manner gave away the past that shamed them and the future that set them on fire. What fools! All I did was get used to reading their faces, their words, their silences. What fools! Getting back to the French again, the fear that they'd carry me off started a new fuss, like the one about the pastorals, or trying to find out the meaning of the shameful words. I never got tired of asking who they were and when they'd finally come. "You crazy girl. Don't be so curious. You're too inquisitive." I'd join in the conversation of the older people. "You're poking your nose into something that doesn't concern you." I wanted to know why the French carried off farm girls. I got no answer to that except furious glances. Then I began to picture it all, with confused images of war and violence. I discovered impatience and learned the meaning of it. I tasted it, setting it beside the sense of triumph in the struggle—the taste of salt and pepper. "You're so restless and impatient, you want to go too fast," my family would say, "as though the peppers burned your tongue." "Or, I've got fire in my blood," I thought. Eventually, after so many false alarms, it was known for a fact that the French had occupied the square at Clamores and would come to the plain. My family hurried me away with some other girls to hide us on a farm lost in the windings of the ravine. This experience brought me all kinds of unknown pleasures and fears in the company of the other fugitives, who were just as fanciful as I was and most of them older. Oh, what endless conversations took place on that flight, how it stirred our imaginations and our emotions! Since there were no signs of the French, how eager we were to be betrayed! How bored with being shut in! We wondered what they would be like—white or black, with blue eyes or dark, bearded or clean-shaven, polite or bad-mannered. It's strange how things turn out. There, with those girls, all from respectable families, I came to learn the meaning of the words that had bothered me so much! Eventually it was learned that the invaders had reached Cuilán, had come to the Sierra de Cardos, and were advancing toward the plain. My family rushed on with my wedding. Just think! I was barely fifteen years old or thereabouts.

No one could understand it. In spite of so much shouting and bad feeling and squabbling, so much coming and going and bad temper and gossip, they still went on with the pastorals at the Big House in Belén. Even when there seemed little likelihood of many people coming—which is exactly what happened on the evening of the twenty-eighth, Holy Innocents' Day, and on the first day of the year. Only the farm servants were there, and only because they had to come. The shepherds of Betulia and El Tabor worked hard at their performances. For what reason? For what purpose? So that the audience would yawn and fall asleep? Their persistence seemed inexplicable.

But underground rumors were rife. Mute, suppressed expectation could be divined on farm after farm, on face after face, and in the dazed eyes of the ignorant.

As though there were a conspiracy afoot, the roads started to fill early on the Feast of Epiphany. Even peddlers appeared with their wares. It is true there were not many women, and that was unusual, although at first nobody seemed to notice even that, nor the serious faces and sparing conversation of those who came, looking as if they were afraid of an ambush or were anxiously waiting for something to happen.

Neither on Holy Innocents' Day nor on New Year's Day did Don Felipe or Don Jesusito appear in public. "Their behavior wasn't anything to laugh about." Don Epifanio did not put in an appearance either, although he watched the Temptations from behind a small shutter in the parlor. "They weren't worth it, though." Disjointed words and phrases, indicating their state of mind, fell from people's lips as they walked along the road, lost in thought.

"You can hear the river . . ."

"Authority! My foot!"

"There's something in it."

"Whatever it is, if he's in it, it's bad!"

"Where are they from, anyhow? Who are they?"

"The same sort."

"Will there be any shooting?"

"Fighting."

"It'll be his birthday present."

"I've come alone, on account of the uncertainty."

"Skirmishing with guns and machetes."

"I didn't want to bring my wife either."

"Cut them to ribbons."

"Out of curiosity."

"We'll see."

"What we get."

Some, as though learning to read from their first book, joined words together:

"There are lots of fools . . . talking of great and wonderful things . . . what's going to happen? . . . there's a lot of mystery . . . you can feel the same terror you feel when a bad storm comes on with its gusts of wind, flashes of lightning, and thunder . . . Saints preserve us! . . . and the earth gets dark . . . Blessed Saint Barbara! . . . and there are flashes of lightning that leave you blinded, waiting for the thunder . . . the pastoral isn't important . . . sheer camouflage . . . so is all this, to rouse our curiosity . . . and it may turn out to be nothing at all, that's often the case when there's so much fuss . . . when the skies seem ready to fall on us and it all comes to nothing, all hot air . . . too bad my old woman was frightened for nothing . . . she wouldn't come for anything on earth and the children stayed with her, crying . . . as though they'd never see us again . . . but there are some who say it's true . . . we won't have to wait long to see him get the present they're bringing him for his saint's day . . . it may be more hot air . . . or the same . . . there are officials here again . . . we'll have the good old days back . . . Good God, we're getting along well enough without all this claptrap about the law . . . almost forgotten . . . only used to meddle in other people's affairs and stir up trouble . . . panting to do or not do something . . . I'm sorry I didn't pay any attention to them for fear of quarreling with Utimio . . . who sneered at me, saying I was probably afraid to go, probably one of those who'd given in . . . no, of course I wasn't . . . I'm not afraid of anybody, and I'm going if it's with a lump in my throat . . . I won't give in.

Incendiary remarks were dropped among the disjointed words:

"The situation's going to be interesting."

"They'll act out the story of Cain and Abel, where father Adam is the one who kills his son."

"Every little chapel has its fiesta."

"Today's the day of Epifanio's and his children are giving him his birthday present."

"And the story of the disobedient son who claims his share of his inheritance."

"We've seen churches fall. How much easier to overthrow this hut!"

"Don't fail to go and see the destruction of Belén by Lucifer."

"It's the story of Christ's robe . . . how they cast lots for it."

"Brother against brother, fighting for possessions."

"Sons against fathers . . . or the end of the world."

"Look. Here's his present!"

Remarks adding fuel to the fire, stirring up curiosity.

Belén was filling up. The expressions on the faces of the crowd were full of suspicion, and an uncanny silence reigned throughout the multitude. There were many unfamiliar faces. Jerky efforts at conversation, forced, strained laughter, ill-disguised attempts to overcome the tension, soon died away. An uneasy silence prevailed, as in a crowded church before the liturgy begins, a silence broken by coughing and nervous throat-clearing. The moon was late rising. It would be later still. The mystery pastoral was late, too. "Where can they be from, anyhow? Who are they?"

A few torches were lit . . . the miserliness of Epifanio. The accusing voices continued:

"Injuries must be avenged."

"When the dog is dead there's no more rabies."

"Acts of injustice, like the machine that belonged to Teófila, who died."

"Profaning Christmas evening."

"His gift. Today's the saint's day of the Epifanios."

"Ready. Keep your eyes peeled."

"Let him have his gift!"—and obscene gestures followed the words.

Hopes were fulfilled from the very beginning when wind instruments properly played by a proper band were heard in the distance. The memory of this kind of music was dim in most people's minds.

They approached, playing a military march that raised people's spirits. There appeared a mass of lights such as had never been seen before, inspiring fear as well as curiosity, since it looked like a heavenly phenomenon. A large troop of well-shod horses was heard. Wonder almost bordered on panic when a troop of shining white shapes was seen. They were angels, dressed in silver robes that shone in the beams of the amazing round lights they carried, high in their right hands, in a triumphant gesture; they rode on white horses, so well matched that it seemed impossible to tell them apart, and their trappings and harnesses were dazzling. What was incredibly marvelous was to see the angels moving their huge wings in front to cover their faces and then back until they folded together, and upwards and downwards in time to the music; and to discover that they were of real feathers, very white. Behind the heavenly company walked the shepherds and shepherdesses, escorted by the musicians in double file. The hermit brought up the rear of the procession, riding on a donkey that he spurred on by shouting and digging his heels in his flanks. As though hypnotized by the angels, the audience paid little attention to the colorful pomp of the shepherds or to the fact that the devils were not present in the procession.

Amazement grew as the pastoral entered the patio of the Big House. The lights were all extinguished at the same moment, the wings stayed uplifted, and the angels jumped to the ground all together, as though flying, without touching the stirrups. They took the horses by the silver reins and formed two lines facing outwards; and moving in circles in time to the rhythm they sang:

> Come, shepherds, come,
> To Bethlehem let us go
> To see in this child
> The glory of Eden.

The performance was so rapid and carried out so precisely, with no sign of hesitation or the sound of a command, that the surprise was expressed in unaccustomed applause which kindled people's spirits.

With airy lightness the angels jumped on their horses again, the puzzling hand-lamps were suddenly lit once more, wings moved, and, straightway the dialogue began: "How long shall we suffer this horrible bondage? This abominable treatment meted out to us each moment?"

At these rebellious words the angels formed two columns and hastened to join battle, for the first time, on horseback. St. Michael's voice rose:

> Get ye back, ye traitors,
> Here ye meet might.

The bands drew apart, golden swords gleamed, and the tremendous battle was joined. The rhythmical skill of the movements and the complete mastery over their horses filled all present with admiration. (No one was aware of the exact moment in which Don Epifanio came out onto the verandah, nor of the presence of Don Felipe and Don Jesusito.) Face to face, St. Michael and Lucifer maneuvered their horses, made them dance, brought them to a sudden halt, and raised their swords; and a fearful clap of thunder shook the earth, and a huge ball of fire burst, sending out great tongues of flame, with thick clouds of smoke in their wake. The spectators, terrified, ran for shelter; loud voices told them to be calm; without a pause the show went on. Falling into the midst of the flames and smoke, instantly transformed, the devils, dressed in red and black, were writhing about, with bats' wings, heads crowned with horns, with no lanterns in their hands, tails between their legs, long tails that lashed from side to side in desperation.

Out of the middle of the fallen angels rose Temptation. At the sight of her, illuminated in the crisscross rays of red light from the devils, there was a general exclamation. With flowing hair and sinuous movements, and clad in soft folds of silk, red, coppery, or purple as the lights changed, and with appealing eyes, a tempting mouth, and soft attractive hands, she held her head up proudly, with an expression at the same time imperious and smiling:

> My presence circulates
> A poison that penetrates
> Sweetly into the soul.

The voice was warm, disturbing. The woman turned and twisted about like a snake, like a circus contortionist. Another new experience was to watch her trailing along the ground after Adam and Eve, to watch how she coiled herself around the Tree of Paradise, how gracefully she cut the forbidden fruit and held it out to the rash wife while the music imitated an infernal laugh, accompanied by the shrieking of the devils and evil-smelling gases. The unaccustomed effects kept the audience in suspense, carrying them from surprise to surprise.

The round disk of the moon appeared on the horizon, ingeniously used as a background for the figure of the Eternal Father who, from the top of a wall, cried out:

> Adam, Adam,
> Why have you hidden yourself from me?
> Why have you fled from my presence?

The couple was cowering behind a large flowerpot. The man answered:

> Why, because I am naked
> And so is the woman.

The scenes followed upon one another rapidly. The speeches were brief, the endless traditional monologues being suppressed. Action dominated, emphasized by unexpected effects of light, sound, thunder, smell. Everything was planned and carried out with precision in order to create illusion and keep the spectators spellbound. A world both real and magic. Something never seen or heard before. A string of miracles. Fantasies taking shape before their eyes. Entranced, the people forgot the omens announcing revenge.

But conveniently distributed throughout the crowd, the mysterious accomplices and trouble-makers who had been working, for weeks past, in the service of a hidden power now started a rumor.

"This demonstration of efficiency and great resources isn't just for its own sake—it's only the beginning . . ."

"Oh, look! . . ."

After the expulsion from Paradise came the unexpected episode of Cain and Abel, never included in the pastorals. Adam appeared. The accomplices got the audience to ask why.

> The disobedient son
> Wanted to take your inheritance.
> Bang him right on the head.

When the murder had been committed, the angels came out with their lamps; they wrapped Abel's body in a shroud and carried it off. St. Michael the Archangel announced:

> Did you see that? This cannot be.
> The just man, sacrificed, will return,
> As you shall see.

Insinuating voices: "The cock* can't crow any clearer—and you know which Gallo."

But no sooner had the funeral procession of the angels disappeared than the chorus of joyous shepherds entered from the opposite side.

> Bird that sings in the forest,
> Greeting the dawn with such glorious sound,
> If you meet the Good Shepherd, bid him
> Chain up the enemy and keep him bound,
>   Keep him bound.
>
> The devil with his loud shouting
> Makes the earth quake in dread
> Because he knows the King is born
> Who will trample on his head,
>   Trample on his head.

Strange, primitive instruments of great sweetness accompanied

---

* In Spanish, "gallo."

the singing. Finally, the costumes of the shepherds and shepherdesses were seen in all their splendor; until then they had been over-
shadowed by the dazzling presence of the angels.

Fine, shiny material in bright colors, harmoniously combined:
grass green, flesh-color, fuschia, coral, pink, sky blue, yellow, tur-
quoise, purple, separate and mixed, combined in skirts and tunics,
stockings and trousers, cloaks and hats, huaraches and shepherd's
crooks, girdles, ribbons, borders, flounces, trimmings, appliqués, in
joyous, frenetic extravagance.

"Ah!" A new exclamation of amazement. "These are real shepherds, not false or imitation ones."

"Yes, they are—a real demonstration—but what's the reason for
it? What's the purpose of it?"

"We'll soon find out, the best is yet to come."

"What?"

"I don't know. Who knows?"

"His present."

The contrasting idylls of Gila and Bato, Flora and Bras, were
charmingly acted; also the intrigues of Temptation among the shepherds and her assaults on the hermit; the cheekiness of the devils;
the laziness of Bartolo, jarred out of him—as the nerves of all those
present were jarred—by a loud triumphant chord of music, accompanied by the lighting of a huge star and the appearance of an
angel in a blaze of light, floating in the air, diving down resolutely
in a dizzy diagonal line. A cry of anguish burst from the throats of
all there, sure that he would be dashed against the earth; this was
followed by a sigh of relief. Safe and sound, slowing down in his
flight, spreading out his wings, the luminous figure set foot on the
ground and joined the other angels carrying their round lamps. The
chorus surrounded the shepherds, singing in clear voices:

> Glory, glory, glory unto God
> And throughout the plain be peace.
>
> Come, Shepherds, let us raise
> This our fervent hymn of praise.
> With glory and splendor the fields are ablaze.

The shepherds and shepherdesses joined in the chorus; the fleeing devils howled.

Through thick strings of Bengal lights the Manger could be seen.

> A branch grew from out a tree
> And on that branch appeared a flower
> And from that flower was born this day
> The Divine Redeemer, who will set us free.

Kneeling shepherds and angels sang:

> Hail, Beautiful Child, Hail, Light of Heaven,
> Comforter of Man, Glory of the Father.

When all thought the performance was over, a procession bearing colored torches entered the patio with a noise of firecrackers; groups of men advanced in mottled tunics and turbans, carrying bundles on their backs; behind, escorted by warriors with lances and shields, came the Three Wise Kings, richly appareled, on magnificent horses. The Red King rode on a sorrel horse; the Black King, on a dark chestnut-colored horse; and the Yellow King, on a prancing black charger. They dismounted in the patio and walked with imposing bearing, jingling their spurs, toward the Manger, and bowed before it; the air was filled with incense; the chorus sang:

> The Three Wise Kings from the East have come
> To render homage to the Almighty One.

Dozens of spiral rockets of all colors rose up and burst in the sky; this artifice was unknown in the district. The wealth of lights made the night like day and dimmed the brightness of the moon.

"If my anger the other day didn't do me any harm, all this excitement will be the end of me ..."

"Wait, the best is still to come—the present." The Kings rose. The music continued. The Kings moved towards the verandah of the Big House. The Manger was hidden. The Red King turned toward the audience and gestured for silence so that he might be heard. The music and the noise of firecrackers stopped. The Red King spoke in a loud voice:

"Today, since it is the day of the Wise Men and the saint's day of our host, we have come together to enjoy ourselves peacefully, since it so happens that the Three Kings who are now here are natives of this land and we would like to see it emerge from its poverty. We are not come to compete with pastoral groups who have been at this for many years, or who are, you might say, 'veterans.' We have come to demonstrate what can be done with good intentions and hard work. There is nothing miraculous about what you have seen. The lights the boys have in their hands are flashlights with electric batteries, which anyone can get for a few cents; the big globes and the star in the Manger are kerosene lamps; the angel came down by means of a pulley with a double rope; the 'bomb' was made of inflammable gases, which are harmless if used with care, and it served to form a smoke screen, to give the devils time to take off their angels' costumes; and so on—a matter of organization and knowing how to do things well and quickly. There was no magic about getting the Manger ready and putting up the poles for the angel's descent without anyone realizing it. There are other inventions that some of you know about already and that all can know about if they take the trouble. As a pledge of these things, the Kings are going to distribute their gifts: corn, beans, salt, sugar, cotton, and other things; but it must be done in an orderly way and without any confusion; we have brought enough for everyone. I will begin, as is fitting, by giving his present to the master of the Big House, since today is his saint's day."

He made a gesture of command. One of his followers came forward, his back bent under a heavy load. The King deftly slipped off his cloak, tunic, and crown, revealing a brand new charro costume with silver buttons. He strode resolutely toward Don Epifanio's chair. The King—who would have believed that he had been wearing a mask—raised his hands to his face and the old man turned into a young one.

"Felipe! Jesusito!" called Don Epifanio, panicking at the approach of this hateful guest, but neither Don Felipe nor Don Jesusito were anywhere in sight; no one knew the moment when they had faded away. The one who was there, half hostile, half curious, was Plácida.

A man can have no worse enemy

A man can have no worse enemy than a member of his own family
set against him. The disturbance on the plain assumed proportions
greater than those of the usual incidents that feed the insatiable
curiosity of the villagers, who are always ready to welcome any novelty because these are rare in their humdrum lives. This time it was
not like those heavy but passing storms that disappear when the
sun comes out, leaving the sky clear and serene. It was rather like
a stroke that leaves the face twisted, or a severe beating that causes
permanent scars, because the events were not of the sort to be forgotten as soon as they are over, their echoes fading in the memory
with the passing of time. Battle had been joined, not only between
members of the same family—Adam, Cain, and Abel—but also
between different ways of viewing the future of the land—St. Michael versus Lucifer—and a power, forgotten, feared, and desired,
had been re-established: civil and military authority. "Yes, that's
what we . . . let's see how it works out."

Although the Feast of the Epiphany had left so many lasting impressions, the most amazing was the knowledge that Jacob Gallo came with the double office of commissary and captain of the militia; the company of soldiers with spears and shields turned out to be police equipped with rifles.

Then began the fitting together of pieces to reconstruct the story of the son who had been disowned and cursed. Like a file of ants, people brought forward their tales, even those who had never heard the story. The effort to remember—in which the whole region joined—took on the aspect of a difficult birth. Everyone from Don Epifanio, the repentant father, to the adolescent girls and boys, had his head full of visions or dreams or questions. Hopes and fears were centered on the Red King.

Those who voiced the opinion that 'A man can have no worse enemy than a member of his own family set against him,' that 'The bulls of Tecuán will only be overcome by horses of the same region,' were opposed by those who remembered the sayings 'Like father, like son,' and 'Six of one, half a dozen of the other,' and 'Wolves from the same litter.'

Fear of the restoration of authority—there had not been any since the Revolution began—produced reactions unfavorable to the intruder and favorable to the Big House at Belén, and found excuses for the excesses of the Trujillos. But opinion was divided, and the group influenced by the gifts, promises, and warnings that Jacob and his gang lavishly scattered around were in the majority.

Don Felipe and Don Jesusito made themselves scarce in the days that followed the sixth of January. Don Epifanio, needless to say, shut himself in, without even stirring from his bedroom.

"What a fine present they gave him on his saint's day!"

"It's a miracle he didn't have a fit!"

"They say what annoyed him most was being caught unaware in public for the first time. He'd always been so alert to everything that was going on. He was caught napping. And in spite of the fact he was expecting it. For some time he'd sensed the footsteps of the coyote drawing nearer. He'd even seen his footprints. The antennas that made him a legend failed him for the first time."

"That was the fault of his wicked sons, Felipe and Jesusito. They'd thrown sand in his eyes, his ears, his nostrils, so that he wouldn't see or hear or get wind of what was coming. They're in it, right up to the neck."

"Just drooling to get their inheritance."

"They'll get their come-uppance."

"Whom the gods would destroy they first make blind."

"A man has no worse enemy ..."

"What a present! They might as well have hanged him at once!"

The echoes joined again to trace the history of the noble Red King.

"When his father disinherited him, Miguel Arcángel went off to the States."

"He wasn't disinherited because of his disobedience. Don Pifas, the dirty old man, had his eye on Florentina. For his favorite son to get ahead of him was something he couldn't forgive ..."

"Who knows if it was then or later. The fact is, he did live in the North and that was where he learned all those tricks he's flashing in front of our eyes."

"He came back with a nice lot of money and bought lands on the other side of the hill, and ended up making a fortune in business ..."

"No, he found buried treasure."

"No he didn't. He came back in the thick of the Revolution and climbed to the top just like that!"

"He became the right-hand man of a famous general ..."

"And he still has powerful friends in the Federation."

"That's the reason he's come here with so much power."

"The devil looks after his own."

"He's sworn to get revenge on all his family ..."

"And to strip them of all they have ..."

"And take over the whole plain ..."

"He swore when he changed his name that he'd come back, that they'd see ..."

"Ah, Jacob Gallo!"

" 'A man has no worse enemy ...' "

" '. . . a member of his own family . . .' "

Firmly ensconced behind the thick walls of his bedroom, Epifanio Trujillo was also racking his brains, chewing on memories and superstitions, bellowing like a wounded bull.

'Once a thief, always a thief.' I knew it before he was born, but I simply fooled myself, let myself dream. 'The cow gives birth to a bull, not an ox.' And I wanted him to be a bull, I looked after him like one of my stud bulls, though all the signs warned me I should make him into a plow-ox. 'I bought a pig in a poke.' When I wanted to change him, it was too late to act on the saying that 'When the horse is groomed, saddle him or keep him in the shade.' He turned against me. It was my own fault. The best horse needs a spur, but at the right time, and 'A horse that won't carry a saddle shouldn't get any oats.' He was a rebel even in the womb, he'd kick and kick—and his mother was so happy, no pains of any kind, no nausea, no headaches, no fancies, no vomiting, and her legs and face didn't swell. On the other hand, I had an awful time of it while she was carrying the child. I had plenty of headaches and dizzy spells, I felt lazy, my bones ached, and I kept stuffing myself more than ever. But I didn't understand, I wouldn't pay attention to those warnings of fate, or to the dreams that God or the devil sent me—a dog chewing at my guts, a bull trying to gore me, a chestnut horse trampling me underfoot, a bolt of lightning striking the house, a house collapsing. And the bad things that happened to me that year—long droughts, cattle dying, harvests ruined, one of my wives running away, the only time that happened, I don't even want to remember her. That year a colt threw me, a thing that never happened before or since, and my stallion died, the only one I had then. How excited I was about the son that Sara was going to bring into the world after the dogdays! "If it's a boy," I thought to myself, "he'll fulfill the dream I've had ever since I was little, and I'll call him plain Miguel, and if it's an easy birth besides, I'll add the name Arcángel." I wasn't expecting it would be, though. From what Sara said about the way he kicked in the womb, and the way his strong little hands clawed at her, I was sure he'd come feet first, the wrong way around, and then we'd have a lot of trouble to get him out. How surprised I was when he shot out like a bullet! His mother didn't even bleed very much and had hardly any pain. On the other hand, I had bad cramps in my belly, I don't know why, and I'd scarcely had anything to eat all day. "Nerves," said Matiana, who was on friendly terms with me at that time. So it was a boy, and a very fine one. I was crazy with joy—and blind, too, I know now. So blind and so crazy that I didn't put two and two together—my dreams, so different from Sara's, and then the voices she heard, and the bad things that kept happening to me. I didn't even pay any attention to the traits and skills he showed signs of almost from the day he was born. So crazy about him that I didn't notice how he was showing his claws, how he was fulfilling Sara's dreams—a youngster who could run like lightning, who would seize the young bulls by the horns and almost knock them over, who chopped wood as though it was straw. 'The old hawk doesn't screech, he just folds his wings.' There's nothing I can do about it now and it's no use crying over spilt milk. It would have been so easy to give him a little something in his milk and increase the number of little angels with a San Miguelito Arcángel, beautifully dressed up, no expenses spared. Or later, even, with all the risks he ran. If Matiana could read my thoughts now, she'd laugh at me in her solemn way and say, 'Meditations for after death,' or 'Locking the barn after the horse is stolen.' I'm like San Roque's dog, howling and howling, with the ear of corn in his mouth. 'If you're born a fool, you stay a fool.' No use thinking what I should have done or not done. The thing is to do what I'm going to do, and undo what I'm going to undo, now, right away. You don't grow old without learning something. That's what hurts me most. Another cock will crow. To make matters worse, I'm perfectly certain that all those devilish children of mine have been working together for some time, and they're not even clever enough to fool the old man, coming to me with their soft talk, first Felipe and Jesús, they're a punishment for my sins, and then that hypocrite of a Plácida, who won't give back this damned machine. What did the dirty bastard say? "I'll smooth it over, and that way I'll make friends out of those who worship Santa

if there's anything I can do for you, and to spend a little while talking to you, which is our custom around here . . ."

"I haven't got any time to lose and there's nothing I want at the moment."

"It's obvious that you hold the winning cards, King of Diamonds, and you're forgetting unfulfilled promises."

"Say it in plain words and don't try to be funny."

"You sounded us out about the competition . . ."

"No, I wasn't sounding you out. You gave your word that it wouldn't be stopped, as a pledge that you wanted peace with me, and I'm at your service."

"If I remember correctly, we agreed that you'd arrange the division of the inheritance."

"I offered to help you, not to handle the matter myself. You know perfectly well that it's nothing to do with me."

"You didn't even mention the matter to him . . ."

"It wasn't the right time, and you people—the ones concerned—weren't there."

"You didn't even tell us about your plans."

"There was no reason why I should."

"You're talking to me in a very unfriendly tone . . ."

"The tone of a busy person who likes to go straight to the point and call a spade a spade."

"It wasn't like this the other time . . ."

"The other time and every time. It's up to you to reply to my proposals. I'm not going to beg anyone. That's not the way I do things."

"You think yourself so safe because of the handfuls of corn and lengths of cotton you distributed."

"Look, Jesús, it's no use playing games, so don't beat around the bush or try to butter me up. It's even less use to try and scare me. I'm not any greenhorn. Tell me clearly and plainly what you want, what they've sent you to me for."

"You didn't tell us about having a post of authority either . . ."

"Just as you didn't tell me about charging for the right to sell things. That was the last straw for the people."

"Let me speak. You're interrupting me."

"You talk too much. It's a bad habit. And I know why they've sent you. You've come to find out exactly where you stand. And so that you won't get yourself tangled up, thinking you're going to get me tangled up like a skein of wool the cat's been at, I'll tell you again, in a few words, my proposals—not bargains, as you call them. I don't want to pick a fight, but I'm not afraid of one. And I'm certainly not trying to bother Don Epifanio or get revenge."

"And yet you're just about killing him, and he's your father, too."

"I have enough means to save the plain from want. What happened on January 6th demonstrated that."

"And win the people over to you . . ."

"I'm ready to share the benefits. That's all."

"If I remember correctly, you spoke of an alliance with us."

"With you and with anyone else who wants it in good faith. But don't make me say 'Once bitten, twice shy.' "

"That's changed."

"No—unless by alliance you thought I meant complicity. Tell Don Epifanio to come, and Felipe, and the others, and we'll immediately draw up agreements for wells, reforestation, machinery . . ."

"I thought that by arranging for the competition we sealed the bargain—I mean the bargain to work together."

"Of course, on my side. But to work together to get things done. But your people, and you especially, haven't played fair. Why do you want proofs? I don't like wasting time. Come on, I'm going to show you what's been done in just two months, so you can get an idea of the bargain we can seal."

"So what? Tell me, what do you intend to do with this post of authority and your armed peons?

"Establish order and justice. Security. For this once, I'll overlook your lack of respect and bad manners in calling the police peons. Don't forget that things have definitely changed. Oh yes, there's something you can do for me: tell Don Epifanio not to keep on with that business of the machine and not to collect money from people on the pretext that they didn't tell him what was going to happen. If you don't give him my message, I have ways of getting it to him, you know."

"Remember that he's *your* father, too."

"But *I* didn't disown *him*. You know very well that my name is Jacob Gallo. Even if it weren't, as an official I also don't recognize relatives. Not even my own children. So now you know just where you stand."

'God is man's only friend, and his only kinsman a peso.' 'You have to learn how to lose before you can gamble.' 'In conversation, like friends; in business deals, like enemies.' 'Pepper or a needle, it's all the same; they're both sharp, and the one who's pricked says Ouch!' 'Carry it carefully, devout young men, that figure of Christ is worm-eaten.' 'Don't think I'm so old, I'm just badly preserved.' 'Out of sight, out of mind, and when you're dead you're buried.' 'An evil thing never dies, and if it dies it's not missed.' 'Bad news has wings, good news can barely walk.' 'Courage, let the sun rise so we can see what kind of a day it is.'

What was thought impossible by the throng of advisers, the reconstruction of Jerusalén, was finished with the greatest dispatch. The main house was repaired; a building for the town council and a block of twenty dwellings for laborers were constructed; vast areas were terraced with heaps of black earth brought from Cardos by strings of mules; the different levels of the series of huge terraces were protected from erosion by walls of stone and mortar; two lofty silos, shaped like towers, were rising at great speed. "Now there *will* be a reason for saying 'Torres de San Miguel' when they mention the farm." Stockyards, stables, pigstyes. Two spacious barns, already filled with fodder and modern farming equipment.

The greatest miracle was to have found water. "Don't they say the magic needles are no good?" Although the greatest miracle for everybody was to see how they built an iron tower that Jacob calls a windmill. He says the fans will turn in the wind and bring up water, and it will be cheaper than when he can pump it up by electricity.

Electricity! The word is exciting. Jacob also says he will bring it before the rainy season, and there will be light bulbs and a corn mill and a kind of entertainment that he calls cinema and who knows what else.

Those who saw his pastoral, and especially those who missed it but heard the exaggerated praise on all lips, began to believe blindly all the announcements the King of Diamonds made.

Don Jesusito bent over backwards to express his amazement and admiration: his stepbrother was nothing less than a Wise King himself. "You really are. The hell with anyone who doubts it."

Inside, hate was gnawing at his entrails—"Damn the woman who brought him into the world, the dirty bastard." Jacob laughed. "I can read your thoughts. But I'm also keeping my word. I'm ready to sign a contract to build reservoirs, an electric plant, and retaining walls, and to give you guarantees, this last without a contract, merely because it's my duty as an official." And Jesusito was think-ing, "The son of a bitch can't even take a joke. Let's see whose arm is longest. And aloud, in hearty tones, "Thanks, brother, thanks a million. Of course! How kind you are, King of Diamonds!"

Blinded by rage, deafened by the noise of masons, blacksmiths, carpenters, stone-cutters, Don Jesusito Trujillo beat a hurried re-treat, bewildered by the mocking laughter of the renegade, and swearing revenge.

'If you're made of straw keep away from the fire.' 'Don't make a monkey of yourself just to please others.' 'Once bitten, twice shy.' 'The cock is not to blame, but the one who tied him up.' 'The horse that can't stand being kicked will never make a good stud.' 'It's the frog most trampled on that makes the most noise.' 'No use locking the barn door after the horse is stolen.' 'I'll get there in my own time, only don't push me.' 'You can tell the lead ox in the first trial.' 'Let's see if pruning the tree will help it or kill it.'

"A fine mess you've made of it, look at you, you sons of bitches!

What the devil do you come to me for? Are you out of your minds? What in hell's name do you want? Get out of here, get out of my sight, you Judases, you devils, you double-crossers! Go back to that dirty bastard and lick his feet. Don't forget, 'The dog that keeps on licking, ends by drawing blood,' you traitors, you yellow-bellies, you ass-kissers! Just look at what's happened to you. 'Starting off like a horse and stopping like a burro.' 'Look for the grain of the wood and the weak side of a fool.' How easy it was to find yours! Sold out! What did you tell yourselves? When the tree falls we'll chop it up for firewood, we'll butcher that fat old pig, we'll squash him like a toad. And you're not even men at all! You want someone else to pull your chestnuts out of the fire, you cowards, you rotten fairies! All cut from the same cloth. Didn't you hear me? Get out, you sons of bitches . . ."

"Keep quiet, Felipe, he's our father, after all, and up to a point he's got reason to think . . ." (Now we're really getting it—'Pecked at by the cock and trounced by the turkey!')

"Shut your mouth, you hypocrite, you're the last one to talk. I know you're here because that bastard really put you in your place."

"Get it all off your chest, father, and you, Felipe, control yourself."

"You stinking hypocrite! Did you come here like the centurion to make sure I'm dead? You, Felipe, say something. I'd rather hear you lying to me than listen to this crooked son of a bitch."

"There's no way out except to fight him . . ."

"That's what you should have done from the start . . ."

"He pulled the wool over our eyes . . ."

"With the inheritance!"

"No, by promising to send weapons."

"You boneheads!"

"Look here, you've had a fine time insulting us. I've had enough of it."

"Felipe, calm down. Look how he's treated me, and I'm putting up with it . . ." (Until my patience runs out, and there's a limit to it.)

"Let's get down to brass tacks. We've got to stop this bastard in his tracks because he's trying to take over, and what we need is a firm hand on the reins, a leader to give the commands even though he leads us over a cliff. And what can *we* do? What right do we have? What are we owners of? We'd just be called meddlers. What papers can *we* ram down his throat?"

"How well you know your lesson, boys! That bastard sends you here well-prepared. Of course. And what else? When are you going to kick me out of my house? Will you let me keep what I'm wearing? Go on talking, boy!"

"Oh, do what you like. I'm going away, a long way away. And you'll see what'll happen. Come on, you, or are you staying?"

"Listen to reason, father. If the fuse wasn't already lighted we wouldn't be talking to you like this. We've never mentioned the subject till today. Listen to us without yelling at us. That only makes it worse. Let Felipe finish and we'll respect your orders, on my word of honor."

"Whether you like it or not, your age and your health make you unfit to handle this situation even if you wanted to. You can't even move, and that guy's as full of tricks as a barrel of monkeys, as you saw on the feast of the Epiphany. 'No hawk is fat, no coyote pot-bellied.' "

"What a pair of no-goods! How long have your hands been so paralyzed that you can't act like men?"

"Señor, speaking frankly, from the time that we realized that in our position it was no use trying to fight that so-and-so. That's why we tried to come to some arrangement with him for the future, hoping to keep it from you so you wouldn't be hurt. What more could we have done? What definite decision could we come to? Even after his bursting into this house, we tried to convince him of how wrong he'd been, tried to get him to beg your pardon and offer to go away. That cruel son of yours won't listen to reason, and he hasn't got any feelings. The other day he even told me he won't recognize his own children if they cross his path. What can you hope from such a heartless person? The only thing to be done here, as

Felipe says, is to confront him with a single power, legally accredited."

"I've given you this power long ago."

"Without putting it in writing?"

"Ah, how you children keep pestering me—and you look like grownups!"

"You see, even you don't treat us as grownups."

"It's useless, Jesús. I'm getting out of here. You can both look after your own skins. I'm going to look after mine."

"Felipe, don't play-act."

"Father, it's clear you don't know him. Nothing will make him come back."

"And what about you? Are you going away, too, leaving your helpless father all alone?"

"No, I'm not going, but it's maddening to stay and let him have it all his own way while we stand with our arms folded. The Trujillos!"

"Well, give me your advice."

"There's no use. You've got it into your head that we're just play-acting. Felipe and I weren't made for the roles of the Wise Kings in a play. We have our dignity. I've done my duty in telling you the situation is worse than you think."

"Make Felipe come back."

"You know what he's like. You can read him better than your favorite horse. Felipe won't come back unless you treat him properly, and show that you appreciate him. Neither of us wants to be the master here. That's your place. But you've got to realize that you'll have to hand over the reins to someone capable of standing up to that son of yours and beating him. If neither of us deserves your trust, appoint any other of the young men who are your sons."

"We were getting along so well . . ."

"That's what I say, but there was bound to be a fly in the ointment."

"Bring Felipe to me. We'll settle the matter peacefully. There's just one thing I ask you, son. Take that machine to that dirty clown and ram it down his throat. Teach him he can't interfere in my affairs. I have my whims, too, and one of them is to get hold of that useless bit of junk of Rómulo's, even though they give me its weight in gold for it, do you understand? Or if you'd rather, take the machine to Rómulo and bring me the one that belonged to the dead girl."

"All right, father. I will, if Plácida will let me take it. I think there'll be a fight with her, and that'll make matters worse."

"Even if you have to walk over Plácida's dead body, do what I tell you. Take that damned thing out of the house."

"All right, father."

When Jesusito had gone off, apparently resigned, the old man went back to his grumbling.

Cut from the same cloth. I'd been told how alike they were, especially in their voices and in certain gestures and movements, the kind that flatterers and swindlers use. That day, like today, how quickly I knew it was one or the other, or both together. That's why I was so furious with this one, sensing the presence of the worse one behind him, he was acting out his game for my benefit, just like the night he came to see me, speaking in Jesusito's voice, saying, "I've come to work in peace, forgetting the past, but I'm ready to defend myself, and I've got the authority of a commissary and I'm captain of the militia. I'm putting myself under the orders of my fellow countrymen, earnestly begging them not to make me use force. Help me to bring justice and peace to the plain and accept this gift as a token that I want to help some friends in a matter they want to settle with you." That's what he said, and who knows how much more, his words flowing on like a stream of water, without giving me time to answer. He bowed low, like Jesusito, and walked out. But he's a lot like Felipe, too. Now, all of a sudden, my plans are wrecked, my plans and attempts to found a respectable, united family that would make the name of Trujillo known and feared throughout the ages for a hundred leagues round. That's why I was so careful about crossing the breeds and why I was so strict with the women. A mare who's been badly mated is worthless, even as a gift.

In the case of this girl Florentina, it's true I did have an eye on her, but in the way you start to hope when you see the ears of corn first forming, and you know that it takes time before the kernels are tender and firm and you can eat them roasted with salt, or boiled, or in sweet tamales. 'Give the ears a chance to grow, but when they're ripe, don't wait.' The reason for my anger wasn't that the boy— he was my favorite son at the time—had got ahead of me with the girl. No, I was angry because he got out of the stable and kicked over the traces, but even more because of the pride and defiance with which he suddenly threw my name and surname in my face, along with everything I'd given him, obtained through many years of hard work, and all the hopes I'd placed in him. I overlooked his boyish escapades. I gave in to his whims. When I punished him for this business with Florentina by taking away his house and lands, it would have been a horse of another color if he'd come and humbled himself and begged my pardon, or even stood up to me and started to argue, but the rotten son of a bitch just went away and took his mother with him—and worst of all, he changed his name from Trujillo to Gallo, when I'd made the dirty bastard my legitimate son according to all the requirements of the law. 'As the dog returns to his vomit, so the fool returns to his folly.' 'When the cat's away the mice will play.' And now the double-crosser wants to blot out one name with the other, declaring war between Trujillos and Gallos. The evil there is in the human heart! But in my heart of hearts, I sympathize with his insolence, because it shows he's got good blood in him, my blood. Oh, even now, if he'd only make his peace with me, and admit his errors, and repent, I'd put all my property in his name, I'd raise him again to the place I planned for him long before he was born, long before I knew Sara, his mother. Felipe and the others would be under him, or he and I would send them the hell away from here, far away, because I'm fed to the teeth with their double-dealings, their treachery, the cowards! They can't stop the man who's trying to destroy them, so they think they'll escape by appeasing him. They're trying to push me into going along with them and to grab their heritage from me, throwing it in my face that I'm old and infirm and no good for anything.

Look at the two who want to put themselves at the head, to seize the reins. Reins! I'll force them down their throats, I'll whip them with them from head to foot, the no-good bastards. 'Take a man by his word and a bull by the horns.' 'They can't carry the candlesticks and they're trying to carry the cross.' 'Can the leopard change his spots?' 'When it's God's will for a man to die he's even worse off alive.' What can have happened to Sara, poor woman? 'A hurt should be forgotten and never mentioned.' And Florentina? 'What's not spent in tears is spent in sighs.' Such a promising little filly! My son did well to grab her and carry her off. Why should I want the temptation? Ah, I remember—in fact, from that day to this I haven't been able to get the Temptation in the last pastoral out of my mind. Florentina, perhaps, or one of her daughters? Florentina!

Curiosity and necessity brought a stream of people to the new Jerusalén. There was work there for anyone who wanted it, and of the kind they wanted. There was entertainment for those who had nothing to do. They could get the tools they needed. There was a constant stream of fresh gossip to feed the curiosity aroused by the King of Diamonds. (With so much to aggravate him, Don Jesusito Trujillo had the consolation of a kind of vengeance when he heard that the nickname he had invented to make fun of his hated enemy had been generally adopted, although the people repeated it without sarcasm, as a form of popular admiration.)

Those who had seen the mysterious pastoral—but even more those who heard tell of its marvels and were kicking themselves for not having seen it—were the ones who led the search for the mystery behind it all. It was as when a puppet show or circus performance is over and the curious try to find the source of the illusion and pursue the heroes, anxious to touch them, to re-capture the enchantment and prolong the emotions of the performance; or when, after a fireworks display, those who cannot resign themselves to the end of the magic all crowd around the charred remains of the fireworks castle, struggling to explain and reconstruct the magic of the lights that kept them open-mouthed with wonder. So, young and old went to Jerusalén, hoping to see the blazing descent of the angel and find the framework of similar miracles—stars and hand-lights, movements of real wings, instantaneous transformations of devils, the sinuous twistings of Temptation, fantasies of costumes and finery.

They found another miracle, the swift rebuilding of Jerusalén—a host of works and workers, constructions completed overnight, of greater moment than the sights of the pastoral at Belén. The news of these events spread rapidly and more and more people, from farther and farther away, gathered to behold them.

The King of Diamonds was not an easy person to see. This increased the eagerness to hear of his doings, and there were skilled lips that praised him to the skies.

Each visitor, even if he was obviously of little importance, received his quota of things to wonder at, according to his status.

"Oh, yes, he's a man in every sense of the word. The sun always shines on him, he makes a success of everything, he's good at everything, nothing frightens him. And what a leader! How generous, how kind to the poor and needy, how brave in attacking the wicked, how just to evil-doers. He's a lucky man, there's no doubt of it, but at the same time he has his head and his heart in the right place, and his feet firmly planted on the ground, with legs and arms of iron. What he decides to do, he does. He's the first to start work and the first to run a risk. He's an excellent shot, and sets an example for all of us when it comes to riding and taming horses, lassoing cattle, cutting the maguey, milking the cows, sowing seeds, pruning, building. He's tireless himself, and he tires out the most experienced hands. His shrewd remarks surprise everybody and make them laugh. He doesn't give you time to rest or shut your eyes, and won't pardon any delay or let anyone question his commands—but how well he pays those who are faithful to him, how he helps those who serve him, how he encourages those who are having a hard time! A man in every sense of the word!"

Those who were looking for stories got them at first hand.

"I've been with him almost since the time he was driven out by his father. I can tell you how he became rich and powerful by sticking at it and not letting anything stop him. He was lucky at everything: business, the land, industry, politics. He kept his eyes peeled and succeeded in turning all the ups and downs of the Revolution to his advantage, buying, selling, lending, bartering one thing for another, from arms and cartridges to foodstuffs and army vouchers. He didn't really take part in the Revolution, not with a gun in his hand, but he lived side by side with the principal leaders, and he's still a great pal of theirs, the ones that have become heads of everything now. He carried out dangerous missions for them in the worst part of the troubles. I don't know how he managed to keep in with both sides, with Villa's people and Carranza's. At that time he was doing business in Zacatecas and Aguascalientes, although he didn't neglect to take a look from time to time at some lands he had under cultivation in this area, on the other side of Clamores, because he'd always wanted a farm. When things began to quiet down a little, he bought some well-watered land cheap, in the basin of the Juchipila river near Jalpa, and some fruit orchards in Calvillo. With the unsettled state of the country, wonderful bargains could be picked up at that time for cash, and the master had his money in hard cash. Bargains? All the landlords wanted to do was sell their property for what they could get for it and clear out. It's true enough that money makes money!"

Some of the old people asked after Sara and Florentina.

"Ah, what a pair of women, real women, none better," said another of Jacob's oldest followers. "What stuff they're made of! It's a pleasure to talk about them, to remember how they helped the master from the moment they left the plain, when all they had was the clothes they stood in. Yes, they helped him in the struggle in thousands of ways, in Cuilán and Clamores first, then in all their wanderings, even in the land of the gringos. They sold food, did other people's washing and ironing, worked as sowers, harvesters, even as smugglers, they didn't care what they did, hard or easy, it was all the same to them: scrubbing floors or carrying heavy loads, working late, getting up early, or going without sleep for days and nights on end, working in hospitals and boarding houses, selling things on the streets or in the squares. Always cheerful, always making the best of it, and, above all, helping the master in his work, when he was working as a laborer here on the other side of the hill, and when he took it over himself. Doña Florentinita! What a head she had for figures and bargains! She always understood the most complicated sums as easily as she could add, subtract, and divide. She was the bookkeeper in the businesses in Zacatecas and Aguascalientes, with Doña Sarita as the storekeeper, and she was stricter and more suspicious than a customhouse official. Even now, when they can rest—and how well they deserve it!—they're as busy as bees. Who do you suppose thought up the miracles of the pastoral and did all the organizing? Doña Florentinita, of course, who else? She's still as fresh and lively as a girl. She doesn't even look old enough to be the mother of her sons, such good-looking young men."

The question of Jacob's political fortune aroused greater curiosity.

"He's very fond of keeping his own counsel, and since he's so full of life, so strong-minded, so industrious, so obliging, he wins the confidence even of people who are suspicious by nature, and makes firm friendships. Look at the way he made friends in Aguascalientes with General Obregón, the man who's now in Don Porfirio's seat." (Quite a few people on the plain were surprised to learn that Don Porfirio was no longer President; they heard this important bit of news for the first time.) "They're such great friends that not long ago the master visited him in the Palace in Mexico, and found him seated in the Golden Chair itself, and they chatted and even joked, God in Heaven! What won't he do with other, less important people? I think they wanted to make him Governor, but he doesn't need the money and he doesn't like that kind of nonsense. Being his friend and being able to go and see him any time he wants to is enough, and more useful to him."

These stories had a greater effect than the bomb that fell in the midst of St. Michael's struggle with Lucifer. There was no lack of doubters to ask why, if he really had such power, such wealth, Jacob Gallo would prefer to come back here and exile himself on the plain. His men had quick answers.

"The master has always wanted to live on the land. Business, his trips to the North, the industries he started, were ways of making money to invest in the countryside. This is where he can really breathe, this is where he feels at home. And he's always dreamed of coming back to the plain, he'd always grieved over the backwardness of this place, always spoken of setting up systems he learned in other lands and of bringing improvements. No, it really isn't revenge that drives him, or the desire for money. He has plenty of farms, in better regions. But who wouldn't enjoy being a prophet in his own country? That's what it is."

To the farmers whom he considered influential he gave an abundance of details; and as he showed them the way the work was being done in Jerusalén and Canán, they were more anxious to have similar advantages brought to them: wells, protection against erosion, soil improvement, fertilizers, pasture-grounds, good breeding animals, credit.

Jacob Gallo would appear unexpectedly. He would ask questions, give advice, make promises, give gifts, dazzle, ignore gossip. He personally gave out gifts to those who complained that they had not gone to Belén on January 6th. The favored persons received lamps of the kind carried by the angels and were able to move on their own shoulders the wings that had filled them with wonder. Jacob laughed heartily.

He refused only one thing—proposals to buy corn before it was ripe.

"No, I'll lend you seed corn and tools, and I'll help you to improve your crops, and it won't cost you a thing. Only the lazy ones will lose their seeds. But we have to do away with negative ways of doing things, like selling crops before they're ripe, and contracting foolish debts. Naturally, I'll lend to the man who can guarantee a yield because he'll work the way I tell him. And so you can understand better what I'm trying to do, this year I'll lend without interest. And in the years to come, at only 8%. What I want is to see you wake up."

The suspicious sowed seeds of doubt. From Belén to Jerusalén gossip spread back and forth: that Jacob was up to no good, that Don Epifanio threatened this and that, that Don Felipe, that Don Jesusito, that the sons of the King of Diamonds . . .

Formal complaints rained down upon Jacob as the man in authority: This man did this to me, that man took that away from me, such and such a man is bothering one of my daughters . . .

"Disturbances, problems, unrest. And we were living so peacefully!"

" 'A man has no worse enemy . . .' "

The storm winds had begun

The storm winds had begun, those that announce the coming of Lent. It was now the middle of February. The cabañuelas* had been promising. Nevertheless, not even the flies made their way to Belén. Sharecroppers, those selling their crops before harvesting it, those in search of oxen or farm implements, none of them had gone with their usual petitions. Nor had the artisans—not even Rómulo himself, always so punctual—kept the promises Don Epifanio demanded as extra interest for their loans. By this time, every year, Belén was full of masons, stonecutters, carpenters, leather workers, blacksmiths, tinsmiths, farmhands, all forced to give unpaid labor to repair houses, stables, farmyards, walls, equipment, tools, to brand cattle and to cart material, under penalty of not getting help for the next seed-time, or of being outlawed and handed over to the persecution of Don Felipe and the other bastards.

The only ones who came were those who spread poison, like mosquitoes spreading infection.

* See footnote on page 78.

"The King of Diamonds went straight ahead without paying attention to anyone. He said there wasn't enough water in the sea to put out the fire when he burned down the Big House and all the Trujillo farms. That was why he had support in high places. He'd put them all in chains, from Don Epifanio down to the least of their followers. He'd do this, that and the other, he didn't care anything for anyone, they could criticize all they liked, he was the cock of the walk and was still hoping to dance in what was left of the verandah in the patio where he'd been humiliated. All the Trujillos were cowards." They placed their stings and went off, leaving the sores to fester and swell.

Disaster on disaster struck the Big House. Through their own fault, their own fault, their own exceedingly great stupidity. As if the bad feelings they stirred up at Christmas with their use of force had not been enough, they added the squabble over the machine, outraging the feelings even of those least interested in the affair.

Who knows what scorpion stung Don Jesusito into deciding to obey his father, this time abandoning his usual hypocrisy and proceeding with greater brutality than if Don Felipe himself had taken things in hand.

With the devil's own fury he stomped into Plácida's room like a storm wind one morning and without explanation ordered the hefty men with him to pick up the machine.

The old battle-axe, the old dragon, as Don Jesusito used to call his sister, turned on them in a rage, with blows and curses that would shock the most hardened ears. She leaped forward, nails out. A swift blow, hard and unexpected, stopped her in her tracks, knocked her down, winded her. She quickly recovered, sprang up like a panther, seized the wooden bar used to fasten the door, and leaped on her brother. He, pistol in hand, ordered his men to tie her up as best they could. He stood there, furious, eyes blazing, brooking no delay or argument.

Four strong men fell upon the fury, disarmed her, and with great difficulty tied her up with a rope. Don Jesusito ordered them to gag her; they forced a bit of cloth into her mouth and tied up her jaws in a bandanna; they fastened the rope to a hook, so she could not move.

At this moment, Doña Amanda appeared, silent, wraithlike, her sunken eyes glistening in mute pleading.

"Get back inside, Doña Amandita, that's all you can do," the son advised his mother. "You keep your nose out of it. In time of war, there's no quarter for anyone." He himself pushed her back, warning her not to attempt to untie Plácida. He locked the door himself.

When the machine had been loaded onto a mule, Don Jesusito told two of the men to keep their eyes on it, with strict orders to let nobody near. Followed by another two men, he set out along the path to Betania.

With the stealth of burglars they circled Rómulo's house and entered the patio. They shot the dogs trying to defend it, silencing their barking with death, and then searched the kitchen and the farmyard. They found the rooms of the house locked. Don Jesusito ordered them to force the locks and, if necessary, to break down the door of the room where Teófila's machine was. They battered down the door, burst into the room, took out the machine Don Epifanio coveted, and unloaded the gift of the King of Diamonds. Just as they were placing the new burden on the mule's back, they heard the wild shrieks of Merced, who was just coming back from the well with one jar on her shoulder, another in her hand. She put them down on the ground and ran towards them in a frenzy, invoking all the saints in Heaven, cursing Jesusito and the bandits with him, threatening them with all the Powers of Heaven and Earth, begging them not to commit this crime, begging them to kill her first. She howled, she wept; she picked up a stone and hurled it at Trujillo, who took out his pistol to fend her off and raised it to shoot. Doña Merced tripped, fell, lay on the ground without moving, not attempting to get up, her cries stilled. Don Jesusito and his gang retreated as fast as they could.

They were crossing the stony bed of the stream when renewed curses rained down upon them. Matiana, inflexible, awe-inspiring, drawn up to her full height, was standing on some stones at the entrance to her house.

"I hope your damned feet kick from the gallows, you devils! This time you've gone too far, you filthy animals!"

Trujillo turned around, took aim at Matiana, and emptied his pistol at her. Matiana remained motionless, fearless, arms raised, threatening, challenging. Maddened, Trujillo reined in his horse and stuck in his spurs to go back. The horse reared, slipped on the stony ground, and fell, throwing the rider. The bastard's companions fled, leading the loaded mule by the bridle.

Whichever of the many stories that they circulated is the true one—that a shining light hid Matiana and Betania from Jesusito's sight; that the horse, getting to its feet with difficulty refused to go back; that the rider was deafened by voices and claps of thunder; that a powerful force set him on his horse and deposited him on the other bank—the fact is that Trujillo, shaken by the fall, gave up the idea of laying hands on Matiana and contented himself with shouting out: "Just wait, you old witch, you dirty old whore, you'll see me again soon and you'll get what's coming to you, you stinking old bitch."

The stream of abuse flowed on and on as he retreated. The insults alternated with those hurled at the cowards who had abandoned him at a critical moment. It was right there that the series of miraculous stories began, invented in self-justification by those who were with Don Jesusito. He had raised his whip to strike them, and another mystery is why he repented, beside himself as he was, so unlike himself, so completely lost to all reason.

That was not the end of the affair. When they were in sight of Belén and were least expecting it, they were stopped by a voice from behind a stone wall. The muzzles of guns appeared, and they were ordered to dismount and put their hands up. The threat was so sudden and unexpected that Don Jesusito and his followers obeyed like automatons, the men throwing down their weapons on the ground.

"You damned Judas! I know what made you start off doing your dirty work—but doing it like a fool, without rhyme or reason, like a mad dog that even bites those in his own house, not sparing even your skinny old mother. You tried to get ahead of me, didn't you? Getting in good with the old man so he'll make you boss and squeeze out the rest of us so you can put your foot on our necks, you sneaking son of a bitch . . ."

Fright soon gave way to anger, which was all the greater when Don Jesusito, who thought he had been held up by the armed troops of the Gallos, recognized his brother Felipe.

"So it's you, the Bully! What do you hear from Horns of Gold, your new master, whose boots you're licking?" Diverting attention as he talked, he made a dash to pick up the pistol he had thrown on the ground. In a flash, Don Felipe, heavier, quicker, pounced on his younger brother, knocked the weapon out of his hand with one blow, and then taunted him, twisting his arms behind him.

"See, you can't even get off to a good start, you coward. And in addition to being a coward, you're a traitor. Is this the way you're going to get ahead of me, you little rat?"

"Well, what do you want with me, then?"

"To hammer it into your skull that you can't get away with trying to put anything over on me, you double-crosser."

"All I'm doing is trying to give my father what he wants. And you, you act *so* brave but you're just out for yourself, and playing dirty . . ."

With a violent wrench that made his joints creak, Don Felipe forced from his captive a yell of pain; then he gave him such a push that he fell on the ground three yards away. Standing over him, pistol in hand, he added: "I'm going to give you one last chance. Come over where no one can hear us . . ."

The muzzles of the guns still pointed from behind the wall. Don Jesusito's men remained with their hands up. Standing motionless in the middle of the road, ears pricked up, was the mule with the machine on its back.

Those shots at such close range—it was unusual to hear shooting on the plain—had startled Betania. One by one the neighbors had gathered in a crowd at Matiana's house. But when she saw the aggressor withdraw, she had abandoned her hieratical attitude, come down off her pedestal, and shut herself up in the room of the Mysteries, deaf to the voices outside, to the anguished calls.

I never saw the French I heard so much about—in the end they didn't reach the plain. All I had was the excitement. Just as the

Revolutionaries, long afterwards, didn't even show their noses, in spite of the stories and rumors. Just as the shots of Jesús went wide of their mark. But my wedding was hurried on, not postponed, out of fear of the French, who abducted girls. My family had got the idea firmly fixed in their heads, and were set on it. I didn't even know what it was all about. "You're such a tomboy, so full of curiosity, so likely to get into trouble." They were more afraid of my character than they were of the French. They were afraid I had the makings of a whore. I remember my father coming up to me one day and yanking my rebozo over my face and shoving me into the house so I wouldn't see how the bull struggled to mate with the cow. This increased my curiosity and made me want to understand mysteries I hadn't even thought about before. I was full of hazy notions, and sometimes feverish ones, and I was restless all the time, like a spring where the water bubbles up—a high-spirited young girl who had started to get a bad reputation but was actually completely innocent, just impulsive, that's all. So it was fear that made them act so hastily, without telling me or giving me any say at all in the matter. They chose a mature man, and they often mentioned him as an old, intimate friend who lived some distance away, so that I got him mixed up with people who were already dead, people who were talked about as if they were still living but in far-off places. I met him on the day of the wedding, which they'd told me about a few days before in the same voice they'd use to say, "Get ready, tomorrow we're taking you to the dances at La Cruz, or to wash in the river." They only told me about it because they'd received the wedding presents, and they showed them to me. "All right," I said, without feeling either pleasure or displeasure, believing this was the natural way these things were done. For the first time I stopped imagining what it would be like, stopped making up stories of my own and getting all excited. It didn't keep me awake, either, the way other things often did even when they weren't any business of mine. One night they took me straight from the farm in the ravine, where they'd hidden me, to Getsemaní, where the wedding took place. That had been the difficulty, I learned afterwards, because my family and the gentleman were afraid to take me very far—and even more so to cross the hill to the parish church at Clamores, which was the proper place, because the French had been there and might come back any day. Finally the man arranged for the introduction to be made by proxy, which my father agreed to, and also for skipping the marriage banns. They got a priest to come to Getsemaní, the only place on the plain where there was a chapel. When the day came, we got up very early, in fact the business of saddling the burros began shortly after midnight. I can still hear them saying, "How nice, we're going to have moonlight all the way." And we did. One of those early morning moons, bright yellow, that dazzle your eyes when they're still unused to the light. I remember it very well. We had to reach Getsemaní before dawn. They talked about everything except the reason for the journey. They were so absorbed in their conversation that they didn't bother about me and let me remain silent. All the way. I was surprised I could get sleepy on a journey that was made to order for a girl who loved novelty and new experiences, and also surprised at myself for not joining in the conversation about attacks, ghosts, comets, and northern lights, and all the other stories and tales of miracles they passed the time with, trying to drive away their fear of the shadows and the big shapes that seemed to move or lie in wait. "This is the safest time to travel when the roads are dangerous and there's a revolt going on." I heard them say it several times. When I wasn't dozing I enjoyed the journey, watching the face of the moon, discovering strange shapes in shadows and reflections, combining them according to my fancy, feeling myself creator, mistress, and sovereign of a world that first became a complete circus with giants, dwarfs, acrobats, lions, monkeys, pyramids, giraffes, camels, elephants, bears, and other wild beasts —I'd never seen a circus but I imagined it from what I'd heard— and then changed into a fairy tale like those I'd also heard, with castles, monsters, and everything. Or it took on the shape of a large army with horses and huge machines, or became a town of the kind they call cities, with palaces and towers that I've never seen in my life. With these fancies of mine the journey seemed short. From time to time I listened to the conversation, chiefly when someone was pointing out directions by the outline of the hills or by the position of the moon and stars in the sky, naming roads and places, fixing the position of distant regions. The moon was still shining and there weren't any signs of dawn yet, but the barking of dogs and the movement of lights and people told us we'd arrived. We went straight to the chapel. I was full of curiosity to discover the face of the man among those strange faces. All I knew was that he was called Don Concepción. All the good qualities they'd talked about so much didn't help. No one thought of pointing him out to me, and I couldn't get up the courage to ask, until finally the priest came out and said, "The bridegroom here, and the bride here." I saw him out of the corner of my eye, but I quickly lowered my eyes and kept them fixed on the ground during all the talking and the Mass. I answered without raising them, saying what I was told to say and doing what I was told to do. I let them put a ring on my finger, opened my hands to take a handful of coins, took a few steps forward, knelt down. When it was over and we went out, it was lighter but I could see the moon disappearing. Don Concepción had vanished again. When he came back he was wearing leather leggings with spurs, had a riding whip in his hand, and wore a wide-brimmed hat trimmed with braid that came down to his ears and tied under the chin. There was a horse behind him, saddled and another with a pack saddle. I heard them say farewell. I felt persons helping me to mount, saying, "A real woman," seeing that I wasn't crying, that there wasn't even a pucker in my face. Don Concepción's voice: "I've got to get there quickly and it's a long way off." I was almost afraid. Was it fear? It wasn't pleasure. Ah! That Jesusito! I even feel sorry for him, the poor man! How's he going to get out of this mess? It's at least sixty years since that early morning. Someone's sure to say I was frightened to death today. What a bad shot the poor fellow is!

"I don't know a thing, I didn't hear a thing," Matiana answered when she was forced to open her door by the shouts of those begging her please to come out. Doña Merced was in a state of collapse as a result of the crime of the Trujillos, who had carried off the machine and even killed the dogs.

"Forward in the name of the cross. Stop bothering me. I've told you, I didn't hear anything and I don't know anything."

Nor, with the passing of time, could anyone move her from that. Not even when the attack was proved and the endless wonders surrounding the retreat of the assailant were known to be true. But Matiana's eyes gleamed with sinister sparks, cold as the gleam of an upraised dagger, inexorable, increasing the dread which the sacred impenetrability of the arbiter inspired.

"With her on hand, there wasn't any need for Miguel Arcángel and his soldiers."

"What will the King of Diamonds do?"

"Ah, Jacob Gallo, he's powerful!"

"Never leave us without your help, Madre Matiana. Protect us from our enemies forever and ever."

His intimate friends used to call him Chon or Choncho. I always called him Don Concepción. A serious, quiet man, he was very considerate and patient with me. I learned many things from him: how to wait and let things take their course—'If you won't live in the present, you don't deserve the future'—and how to overcome my fear of brute animals—'It's better to tame them than try to change them.' He taught me how to break up the heavy clouds in the sky, to avert plagues from the fields and cattle, to recite the Trisagion, the Litany of All Saints, the Magnificat, the Prayer of the Just Judge, and other prayers and invocations. He was a hard worker, very conscientious about keeping the bargains he made. There wasn't anything of a womanizer about him. He didn't like drinking or playing cards. He had a saying, 'Cards and tobacco, wine and women are the ruin of a man.' Or else, 'If you want to be a good horseman, eat little and drink less.' He was very careful in his spending, because, as he used to say, 'Where there's no fire, there's no smoke, and in the house where there's no fire, those who live there make their own fire, and where the fire has been, the ashes are warm.' Maybe his heart was telling him what would happen, because he'd repeat to me, 'It's harder to keep it than to get it.' He was a lovable person. I began to love him. I didn't have long to enjoy the pleasure of finding that hidden affection, which I tasted like honey or a lump of sugar, afraid it would be gone or that someone would see me with it and steal it away from me. And that's what happened. He was taken away from me, by the press-gang. I learned this a long time afterwards. All of a sudden he just disappeared, just didn't come back from a trip to Cañones to collect a few cents he was owed for some cattle. I didn't hear any news about him for months and months, only the rumors they tried to console me with. I was isolated on that ranch way up in the mountains and I lost hope. It was almost a year later that I learned the truth. They'd taken him off to fight, and in a skirmish between the guerrillas and the French he met his end. Then I remembered other sayings of his that were often on his lips: 'No man, however great, can escape his death, his fate; hence I fear not the thunderbolt but the appointed end of my days.' So much fear of the French on my account, and see who it was that finally met them! 'The man who is destined for the gallows will not be drowned.' 'To each man the evils that fall to his lot.' I wouldn't let them pity me or try to console me or help me with my burden. From the time he went I held the reins of the farm in my hands, and when I knew I was a widow I took an even firmer hold. They didn't think I could manage my share of the estate, and there were relatives who threatened they'd sue me for the inheritance. They thought it would be easy—a young girl widowed before reaching her seventeenth birthday. The suitors thought their job would be even easier, and there was a long line of them, with good or bad intentions. They pestered me for years and years, and still do, even in my old age, because, as they say 'Anyone who sees a horse without a saddle will try to saddle him,' thinking 'A man should persist even though he's turned down, for if he persists long enough, no one can resist him.' I held out against lots of no-goods who kept quoting sayings to me: 'Look after the stalk even if the corn is gone; better for men to eat it than the worms.' 'This grass is so dry it needs to be watered.' 'A pan that isn't stirred will burn!' Epifanio, to go no further, was one of the stubbornest. Even when he was still after Teófila, he suddenly said to me one day, "Ah, Matiana, how hard you are, and I haven't got any teeth left." "No, only their roots," I answered. Time covers up everything. There's no one now who remembers that Don Concepción ever existed. For longer and longer spells of time I forget it myself and fall into the confusion reigning in the plain over the mystery about whether I was ever married, if I'm a widow, or if keeping my virginity is the reason why I can master the invisible. But I know what they've all forgotten or never knew. That's the source of my strength, and also of the pain I suffer all alone. Silence increases my powers, it's necessary for controlling the spirits. In this way I've seen plotting defeated, storms broken up, enemies fallen into perpetual death like the leaves on the trees each year. Forward in the name of the cross, Christians. There is One above who metes out justice.

What Doña Merced was suffering from was shock, rage, and especially a feeling of helplessness for not having defended, for not having snatched away, the profaned relic. Of less importance, although it had left her face bathed in blood, was the blow that knocked her senseless when she fell. As she recovered, and there was someone to take care of her, her sufferings at the time of Teófila's death returned with renewed force, and when the sight of the machine loaded onto the mule came back to her mind, however hard she tried not to think of it, she again suffered the sharp pain she had felt when they had taken out the body to bury it.

"Better if that robber'd killed me and then killed me again." That was her only cry, repeated with a degree of obsession that was agony to those who heard her. Matiana arrived. Unafraid. Majestic.

"Why are you making such a fuss if you know they'll bring the machine back? Yes. They'll bring it back! It was necessary for this to happen so that God's just decrees could be carried out."

I had a plan. These Judases made it go wrong with their hasty actions. My prediction that they'd give trouble to their mothers came true even earlier than I expected. And it turns out they're even making trouble for their father. They're so anxious to get their inheritance, they're worse than dogs tearing each other to pieces over a scrap of rotten meat. How the boy Jesusito showed his teeth and claws—worse than the horns and hoofs of Felipito. I knew they had it in them, but I never thought that Felipe's savagery, still less that of Jesusito, would put me to shame and even make me repent of having bred such abnormal sons. More than anything I was furious on account of their stupidity. 'He who washes an ass's head, loseth both his soap and his labor.' It's driving us straight to destruction, in addition to giving an advantage to the other damn bastard my plan was aimed at. It was very simple: turn the people against him by letting it get around that he owes his evil arts to a bargain with the devil. He made the devil fly and then said it was a machine like the ones they'll soon have in the plain. His pride raised up towers like those of Babel, and along with the electricity they're talking about they'll be the ruin of our poor land. Haven't you heard about and even felt the electric shocks you get from little boxes of powder? Well, what will happen with bigger machines? Everything will be electrified, no one will be able to move without risking a death worse than being struck by lightning, the cattle will trample everything down, the seeds won't grow, the few trees in the region will die, the rains will stop, frightened away by these inventions, and for the same reason, children will be born crippled if they're born at all, and there won't be any cure for the sick, no absolution for the dying, no indulgences for the dead. It's a lie that he got his bags of gold in business when the Revolution was at its height. The Masons gave it to him to come and pervert us, to make us devil-worshippers. 'It's easy to tell a wolf in sheep's clothing.' It's a lie that they're natural things, those marvels he produced here at Belén and goes on producing in the name of Beelzebub to deceive the ignorant. He's trying to take away our faith and our acceptance of God's will. It's the Lucifer of the pastorals shouting out, "Who is there like me?" It's a lie that he's not trying to favor anyone, sheer trickery and promises, pacts with the devil at the bottom of them, sugaring the pill with miserable gifts of things we could make here, and better. 'Anything can be called a supper, even if it's only a taco.' Because I also had the idea of going around from farm to farm, promising to forgive and forget debts, to renew friendships so we could oppose and get rid of that damn intruder. We'd leave violence for the last resort, when we were strong again, counting on the people. One day they'd burn this, the next day, that, and they'd gradually bump off the police, a few at a time, until the rest took flight. Ah, if I were a young man! These were my specialties, and the reason I got control of the land in spite of all the cowards who tried to get in my way. How long did they last? They were caught in the trap, swept away by the wind, not a trace of them remained. My hand knocked them down like houses built of cards. Not any more. I counted on my older sons. I've thought about the others—there's so many of them!—and I can't find a single one who's fit to come into the business. They can't even stand up to their brothers. I realize it's my fault. What was I thinking about, bringing them up with such care? After what's happened, I'm tempted to forgive Miguel Arcángel, although he hasn't asked me to, and lean on him, and give him all I am and all I'm worth. Sometimes I can't see any other way out. I just get a glimpse of one, and I'm turning it over and over in my mind: Plácida, who's as mad as a whole pack of wolves thirsting for revenge. She's like a crazy person, she can't even bear to be alone, she tore out of the house and she's moving heaven and earth to get back at Jesusito. Her anger's my only hope, if I can convince her I had nothing to do with the business, I didn't hear her cries, that's why I didn't run to help her, and if I prove it by naming her my only heir. She's got the claws to stand up to her brothers, give them what they deserve, keep them in order, not even letting the intruder escape, that big bluffer trying to frighten us with streams of gold and electricity. Poor Epifanio Trujillo, you can't use your own hands, you're like a man dangling from the gallows, you'll have to give up all you've gained with such hard work! One by one all your dreams are being destroyed!

Lent went by in a dead calm, broken only by rumors. The deploying of armed forces in the neighborhood of what had been the main lairs of the Trujillos was the only novelty. The villagers who had withdrawn into their houses at the beginning, accentuating the emptiness of the plain in the dry season, began to come out, anxious for news, with the long faces of those who cautiously approach the scene of a disaster to contemplate the results, careful not to take personal risks.

Since the outrage nothing definite was known of Don Jesusito or of Don Felipe. Either they had gone back up to their hill farms or were shut in behind the stone walls of their respective fortresses of Damasco and Galilea. It was not only definitely known that Plácida, set free by Don Felipe, had fled from Belén showering curses even on her father, but that many people on different farms had seen her and more than a few had talked to her—or rather she had sought them out to empty into their ears the dreadful things that had happened to her, and to broadcast the announcement of her vengeance. "They can all go to the devil but I'm not going to let it stop there," she was reported as saying in her rage.

From mouth to mouth, all over the plain, ran the proverb, 'A house divided against itself cannot stand.' The farm people repeated these words with reverent awe, marveling at their discovery.

Murmuring started and began to spread among those who were in despair because of Jacob Gallo's leniency, his failure to punish the depredations of the Trujillos, especially the theft of the machine, and also because of the displeasure with which he received complaints against the Big House, the abruptness with which he cut short the stream of gossip they brought him.

People had expected to see resounding punishment: to see Jacob's armed men descend on Belén, rescue the machine, and rain down bombs like those of January 6, leaving no stone on another; and to see not only Jesusito but the whole gang of Trujillos led away in chains to have the ley fuga* applied to them, or at least to see them left to rot in prison.

When March came, things were still not very clear for those seeking credit or wanting seeds and tools, nor for the sharecroppers trying to get better terms from the Gallos than they had from the Trujillos, as they were led to believe they would. The only thing certain was the good wages paid in Torres de San Miguel to artisans

---

* "Escape law"—when a prisoner is killed by his captors and they excuse the murder by claiming he had tried to escape.

and laborers; also the digging of wells and the construction of channels with reinforced banks in certain places on the plain, for the benefit of a few friends of Jacob, Rómulo and Palemón among them.

News of proposals to capitulate to the Big House also spread, held in suspense only by the expectation provoked by the quarrel in the Trujillo family and the challenge thrown in Jacob's face. He was attacked in his double position as authority and friendly go-between in the matter of the machine, which was supposed to have been ended with the handing over to Don Epifanio of a brand-new one on Twelfth Night, in the presence of numerous witnesses.

Matiana came in for her share of criticism, too. How could she remain with her arms folded, deny the facts, and content herself by uttering mysterious sayings in which the veiled threats might be against the evil-doers or might not? What was stopping her from raining down fire and lightning on the houses and fields of the Trujillos? Why did she fail to take action in some mysterious way: a wrenched limb, a fall, a stroke, or something of the sort, not only for the one who had fired at her but for the whole cursed family, their cattle and flocks, even their dogs and cats, birds, lice, worms? What was the matter with her? What obligations kept her, not so much from punishing the crime that had been committed, but from fulfilling the warning mission God had entrusted to her for the teaching, well-being, and example of the defenseless Christian flock?

There were all kinds of rumors flying around: that Jacob denied the presence of the devil flying over the plain; that Jacob had been given money by the Masons to corrupt Christian customs and bring people to ruin; that Jacob had made a pact with Satan to use electricity and other diabolical instruments to place people, animals, and land in danger; that Jacob was a common swindler; that what he wanted was to seize the whole Tierra Santa; that the return of authority and men legally armed would end in unbearable tyranny; that he would end up by coming to an agreement with the Trujillos to ridicule religion and morals.

Palemón, who had been one of the first active agents in the subversive work in favor of Jacob, wondered and discussed with him whether the wave of objections, especially those springing from ignorance and long-standing superstitions, were spontaneous or the effect of discord treacherously sown by messengers in the service of the Big House?

Things were so unsettled that few villagers made the journey to town to visit the seven altars and take part in the Holy Week processions, which on other years emptied the farms.

As the rainy season drew near, hands trembled more, the knots in people's throats scarcely let the anguished question be heard, "What are we going to do?" Dry lips. Eyes big with fear. The only ones untroubled were the children and those in love. The children still ran about, got into mischief, played the games of the dry season: pitchpenny, hopscotch, marbles. Lovers watched out for each other, sought occasions to meet, to exchange words, to give each other a brief demonstration of their mutual affection. The same thing happened when the men were being forcibly recruited, or at the time of revolts or great trouble in the houses, on the farms. The same thing always happens.

Part Four — BABEL:
THE DAY OF JUDGMENT

They stood gazing

They stood gazing at the plain stretching out before them, at its driest now as Lent drew to a close. The transparency of the light and air magnified the far-off hills and brought them closer, giving a greater sharpness to distant details. The clumps of trees outlined on top of the hills and surrounding mountains were so clearly visible to the naked eye that one could count the trees and note their species, distinguish between branches and leaves, as if at this season of the year the eyes became telescopes or magnets, drawing to them all far-off objects so that every detail stood out sharply, even the branding marks on the cattle moving about like toys in the distant fields, the faces of passers-by, or the distinguishing features of houses scattered on the remote slopes. The eyes are like magnifying glasses focused on the fine etching of walls and furrows which, rising and falling in straight lines, divide the landscape into squares, looking as if they had been sketched by a childish hand. Behind them the drama lies hidden, the long story of ambition, strife, death, and transitory survival, blotted out by forgetfulness but once the cause of tribulation. Now, only the scars remain on the landscape, scars that no longer offend the eye but serve as a spur to new ambition, bringing about strife and changes in the lines of the walls and furrows where the victor replaces the old scars with new signs of his ephemeral mastery of the land.

For those exiled in this corner of the world, Lent is when one is aware of the colors with which the dryness covers fields and mountains, clothing them in glistening solemnity. According to the time of day and the weather, the great luminous veil softens or adds luster to the tints. In the morning the sun, shining obliquely at the beginning of spring, bathes in blood-red splendor the high rocky cliffs, the scars and clefts in the mountain chain, glowing like bits of glass or chunks of coral burning in the heart of a fire. To the east, the scattered clusters of houses gleam white. In the east, as the sun rises, the tones of copper, lead and tin which meet the eye are paler, while in the west, facing the sun, the colors deepen, taking on brighter tones as the light strikes them. In the dry air, where objects and distances offer no resistance, the light pierces through everything, stretching to the horizon, dilating the deep, glowing, Lenten colors of repentance as morning moves on toward midday. The implacable harshness of the reflected light increases and reveals the barrenness, the desolation of the land, its skin broken in every direction, dotted with patches of inflammation and gangrene, like a Nazarene fallen in the hills, his body bleeding from the blows he has received, brutally flogged by masses of huisaches cruelly invading the scene. The sun crosses its noonday meridian; the retina is assaulted by the glaring colors all along the length and breadth of the horizon, the evening crucible of molten metals where reds and purples, ochers and yellows, and the hues of sulphur and flint jostle each other in gathering clouds, increasing in volume as the end of the dry season approaches. Colors forged in the fire. A blood-red scab, tinged with gold, covers the plain. When the three hours' agony is over, the colors cease to struggle, become softer, play on the huisaches, the paths, and the stone walls, run up and down the hillsides, gently lick the wounds and scabs of the landscape, define perspectives, make outlines sharper. The blood-tinged ocher is softer. As the sun declines, it sheds the purple tones it had gradually acquired. Bronze and golden hues give place to scarlet, green, purple, and pure violet, in stark colors with reddish gleams. Reaching its vernal triumph, the conquering sun lengthens the days so that the colors may prolong their battle. The world is again divided: the lands to the west fall prey to the swift-approaching darkness; the east rises in defense of light. The sky reverses the pattern of the earth: in the west, dazzling beacons; dark shadows looming in the east. Violet is tinged with saffron and indigo. The great veil is purple again, corroded with rust and scabs, advancing from west to east, bringing mourning in its train.

There are some days—in March, in April—when there are no coppery tones, only a silvery light floating over the darkness below, struggling at the same time against the invading bronze of the west, blending it gradually with the silver without dimming the brightness, which is heightened at times and perceptibly linked with that of the day. It is the Holy Week new moon. The moon that guides the return of those who have gone to the distant services and processions in the far-away town. The first moon of spring, made from silver of the old stamp.

In this atmosphere the country people, moved by these Lenten color-effects, anticipate, grow impatient, commune with the land, feel the imminence of the rainy season, try to foretell the future, to find in the different paths of the sky, in the color of the sky, signs of how and when the rains will come, although they are still many long weeks away. Men and women spend the idle hours of the day devoutly scrutinizing the signs in the heavens.

The lofty clouds, compact, metallic, like women of great height, imposing, but sterile. The flight of the swallows who arrived or will arrive on the day of San José and hastily build their nests in the chinks in the houses. Swallows of good omen, fortelling the future! The day of San José! Green, yellow, and full of miracles! San José! Madonna lily in his hand, like his statue and image—only his statue! Oh, if the earth would only grow green again, if only lilies could grow on the plain! Let us see if this moon or the following ones have their halo or nimbus around them, a sign of rain, just as fleecy clouds are, and the larks when they build their nests on the ends of the branches farthest from the trunks of the trees. Or the sinister sign of the "anvil," the huge cloud given that name on account of its shape, or the sinister sight of the "palms," those large dark clouds high overhead, long fingers with pointed tips stretching out. Ah, the enigmas of the firmament, cause of anxieties and hopes!

Enigmas of the winds. The wind storms have stopped. Now the air stirs up eddies, in columns that look like towers on the march, or in spirals sometimes so violent that their approach inspires terror, like serpents seizing and destroying all they meet in irresistible fury. Panic as at the passing of drunken giants, contorted, blind, with implacable claws, walking at random, rearing up like dust devils. Twisting columns swirling across the landscape. Eddies, spirals of dust, straw, leaves, brambles, thorns, birds, lopped-off huisaches, sticks, tiles, pieces of roof. Riddles of the dry, burning, suffocating wind; or the refreshing breeze, harbinger of hidden moisture; or cold air, appearing like the ghost of months now buried.

Hopes and anxieties depending on the flight of birds and bees, on the paths of ants, on cocks that crow at different times, on the way the oxen open their nostrils to sniff the direction of the rain.

All eyes fixed on the signs in the heavens; familiar sayings on all lips: 'The farmer looks at the sky and the merchant at the ground.' 'He who laments at seedtime has forgotten the cabañuelas!' 'When you see spiders on the ground, look for clouds in the sky.' 'Mist on the hills, rainstorm coming; mist on the ground, a good summer.' 'The corn that doesn't sprout in May won't even serve as fodder for the horse.' 'You can't depend on the rainy season.' 'When the rainy season is good, even the herdsmen give birth.' 'Red sky at night, sailors delight; red sky in the morning, sailors take warning.' 'While there's life there's hope.' 'Interest runs on swift feet.' 'A busy ant does more than a sleeping ox.' 'The problem is not to begin the task but to bring it to a good conclusion.' 'Seeing is believing.'

The surprise, that year, as Lent drew to an end on the plain, was to see the tall structures—incredibly tall—that changed the familiar landscape. They had to be seen to be believed, and even then the people were amazed at the distant sight of a star in Torres de San Miguel, on top of a soaring steel contraption near the other two tall

them from any attack. In this they possessed a virtue the people of the Tierra Santa are losing, that of being jealous in looking after their women, since 'A woman and a guitar belong to the man who plays them.' It's a pity that the old customs are dying out, and that the Trujillos are the reason people have lost their respect for women, especially Don Epifanio with his shameless goings on. But this has made people think, and it's this more than anything else that's caused the anger everyone feels now in the whole of the Tierra Santa, not so much because of the theft of the machine, or because of Merced, or what happened to Plácida and Matiana. No, it's the killing of the innocent dogs that still makes us furious after all this time. But I can't pacify Merced. She's made up her mind that since Jacob didn't make mincemeat of the Trujillos it's up to me, since according to her I've suffered the greatest injuries. The more I think about it, the angrier the business makes me, but I still can't see what I can do—although I'm willing enough, because she's really right. I'm the one who's suffered most. But I've never been a quarrelsome man, still less so now that I'm old and getting more and more useless all the time. At first I had hopes that Jacob would take the punishment into his own hands. He's the man in authority, so it's his duty, and in fact the injury was directed mostly against him. We got the backwash. I was sure that as soon as he heard the news—and that was why I went to tell him right away—he would have come here in a rage. It was his chance to strengthen his position and not let anyone get around him and then laugh at him afterwards, which is just what happened. How surprised I was when I got there, to discover he knew more than I did and wasn't bothered at all! I wasn't the only one, there were lots of others around, Palemón among the most insistent, begging him to make an example of them, using his authority boldly from the start, so that from then on no one would be left in any doubt, or make fun of it or of him. He should make it quite clear that lawlessness in the Tierra Santa was over and done with. He just listened as if he was hearing it raining but wasn't getting wet, and just said everything would be settled at the right time, and better than we had any idea of. I was anxious to know how Merced was getting on, and seeing we weren't getting anywhere I went back to Betania, thinking he'd come with me to look into the matter, to make some inquiries, or at least to visit Merced and Matiana. I described to him, as best I could, the cruel way they'd killed the dogs and my desperation at seeing them lying there, the rage still in their eyes, which were still open, and in their bared teeth with their mouths covered with foam. It was no use. He didn't offer to come and he didn't come. I told Matiana about it. "Why do you want him to get mixed up in the quarrel?" she said. "Just letting them tear each other to pieces is sufficient." She may be right, although I don't know why I didn't say that that takes time and the important thing is to punish them right away. Merced wouldn't give me any peace in the house, insisting I should go over there, not so much to get back the wretched machine as to demand satisfaction. She kept it up so long that all I could do was grab my hat and go out, walking in no special direction. When I got to the bank of the stream I sat down to think. If nobody was giving out any information about the chief criminal, where should I start to look for him, without weapons or a horse? How could I go and beat up a helpless old man who for all anyone knows may not have had anything to do with his bastard's savage attack? What I did was go and look at my dogs and drive the buzzards away from them. I felt so sorry for them. The passers-by wept out of pity, but it roused their anger even more. They sympathized with me, and some of them even got angry enough to suggest we should join together and go and burn down the Big House. I hardly managed to get up the courage to say that Jacob had promised to see that justice was done. I think they were sorry for me because I couldn't make up my mind to take justice into my own hands. So I spent the rest of the day beside my dogs. Memories came back to me of each one: Nero, the oldest, with the loudest bark, the most faithful in spite of his name, and the boldest; Herod, the most cunning, who could smell things a long way off; Caiaphas, the most mischievous and active, the most excitable. Now I'm sorry I gave them those names. I did it to avenge myself for other bad moments that Epifanio had made me suffer, and they stuck to them, but it was out of affection, because I had no intention of offending anyone except the owner of the Big

House, and that only in secret. When night came I went back to the house. Merced was still sobbing loudly, surrounded by neighbors who'd left their household tasks to come and keep her company, or who'd come out of curiosity, eager to learn the details. As soon as the story was known, people started coming, even from distant farms. I had to keep telling the story all over again and answer more and more questions. The visitors, too, had lots of news: the fight between the two evil brothers, the wild rage of Plácida, the idiocy of the old stallion. And then, in a chorus of exasperation: "What are we waiting for? Why don't we put an end to these filthy brutes?" I pretended not to hear them and began my story all over again. I was walking along in the field, which was lying fallow this year, when I heard shots in this direction. I ran in a panic, feeling in my bones that something had happened in the house. On the way, I met Nicandro coming to look for me, and he blurted out, like a shot from a gun, "I think they've killed Doña Merced." I felt the earth going around and around, but in spite of that I ran faster. I got here and the first thing I saw was my innocent dogs lying in a pool of blood. The first people who arrived on the scene had taken Merced into the room. She was just coming around, after having her face sprinkled with alcohol. "Apparently it's only the blow and the fright," I heard them say. At that moment, like a stab in the back, I noticed that Teófila's machine wasn't there. I was beside myself and I shouted, "Yes, they carried it off, the crooks, and left the other new one there in the patio." I heard them repeat the story, and I understood. Merced began to yell, "The machine! The machine!" "I'm going to get it, right away," I told her. When I was sure Merced wasn't hurt, I went out to look at the other machine and the mangled bodies of my dogs. In my state of confusion I scarcely heard the words buzzing in my ears, they just brushed past me. "The shots were fired at Matiana—nothing happened to her—they went to get her some time ago—if she doesn't come it's because something's happened . . ." I stayed out in the patio, unable to make up my mind to go in and face Merced in this state, unable to resolve to cope with her heartrending cries, unable to find anything to do, hardly hearing what others were talking about and asking me, answering them with distracted remarks that made them think I'd lost my mind, and they said no wonder. It seemed high time for me to try to find Jacob, to ask him for help, the only solution that occurred to me, but I couldn't just go off like that without saying goodbye, leaving Merced in that state. Finally Matiana arived, followed by a throng of people. The people who'd been with me crowded around her, asking if it were true that they'd shot at her. More mysterious than ever, she went into the room, paying no attention to the curious, merely saying, "Forward in the name of the cross." I followed her. "Let's have a look at you, woman," she said, ignoring the talking as if it were prayers. She examined Merced, went over her from head to foot, placed her hand on her left calf a moment, said, "We don't die from this, woman." I ventured to say, "I'm going to let Jacob Gallo know." Neither Merced nor anyone else answered, so I hurried out, glancing at my poor dogs on the way. Nero had fallen in front, Caiaphas and Herod behind, one on top of the other. Innocent creatures! The horror of death and the violence of the struggle was reflected in their faces, in their eyes and their stiff paws. At least the criminals have got a new nickname as the result of their crime. They now call them "dog-killers," and people have remembered Matiana's dogs, which were found mysteriously slain some time ago, and the Trujillos are blamed for the deed. When I got back from Jerusalén, Merced was still shouting, "Better if the robber'd killed me and then killed me again." Matiana had gone. They told me she'd prophesied that the machine would be returned and said the evil deed was necessary in order that God's justice could be done. The bodies of the dogs were also gone from the patio. I asked what had been done with them. They'd been thrown into the arroyo down below. In this part of the country it's considered a lack of respect toward God to bury animals as if they were beings with a soul. I mastered my longing to break the custom. What nobody can take away from me is the pleasure of going to see them every day—in spite of the smell, which is worse and worse every time—and the consolation of being able to drive away the buzzards for a while, although it doesn't really do any good. Ideas that get into your head.

When she was barely able to undertake the journey, Merced went to Torres de San Miguel in search of Jacob. (What a person, not even a message or a greeting!) Sara's son received her with a great show of pleasure at seeing her recovered and well. (I simply can't understand this man, in his speech and manner he's so like the other crook, but he's so completely different from him.) Jacob met Doña Merced's resentment and complaints with persuasive words, and gestures:

"You're mistaken in thinking that I'm not and have not been very much concerned. More than you imagine. The fact is, I'm not going to take action before the time is ripe. Have you already forgotten what I said about letting things take their course?"

The woman held to her point, stubbornly:

"Then it'll be just the same with you, we'll just hope for things to get better by themselves, or get worse. I was hoping . . ."

"Remember that I was born and brought up in this region . . ."

"I know and I'm sorry . . ."

"Ah, Doña Merced, don't be angry! Why are you in a hurry to get the machine back if you don't use it?"

"Well, what a coward you turned out to be! Don't you realize that what makes it all the worse is to think that having got his hands on it at last, the dirty old man will keep fondling it as if it were . . .? How easy it is to see that you haven't let yourself be bothered and that you don't know what it is to have a daughter!"

"What's the good of re-opening the wound and driving yourself crazy thinking about punishment?"

"Once again, I've come to ask if you will see that justice is done. I know it's Rómulo's business, but the less said about that the better. If there aren't any men left here on the plain to take a strong line, we women will do it, and I will lead them in punishing cowards even though I fall in my tracks. This is no life!"

"Well done, Doña Merced. That's what I like to hear."

"We had such great hopes that you'd set things right."

"But you can't right the wrongs of years in a minute. Remember, 'With time and a trick or two.' "

"I'd like to see it, but there's no sign of it."

"You'll see it, Doña Merced, the way you can see these towers now. It really is Torres de San Miguel now, although you're so impatient."

"I've had enough of patience. I'm fed up with hearing that tune ever since I was born."

"Patience is the only virtue the farmer has left."

"Because he's a helpless fool."

"For whatever reason you like, but his strength and dignity lie in his patience."

"Don't make me laugh. You can tell you're rich! Dignity! With what's happening before our eyes? That was in the old days. Yes, there was dignity then. We didn't have much but at least we had that."

"Doña Merced, Doña Merced, 'The man who loses his temper is lost.' "

"But it's worse if he lets them walk all over him."

"It's one thing to let them walk all over you and another to fight a battle on ground that someone else chose."

"The battle is fought where you're attacked. Anyhow, you're the one who came here of your own free will and chose the ground. Lastly, I've been told that you don't like wasting your time talking, and I don't know why you're going on with this conversation. Just answer me one thing: What purpose was served by the gift of the machine you took to them? I say it just puts you in a worse light."

"Say what you please, Doña Merceditas. I'll just make this reply: I'm balancing my accounts. And I'll tell you more. Rómulo's account with the Big House is settled to the last centavo and I've got a formal receipt."

"Receipt? I don't understand. And still less this business of centavo for centavo. The machine, then . . ."

"Never mind getting yourself worked up trying to understand. You'll understand soon enough. Would you like to see what we've done on the farm?"

The woman remained motionless, unsatisfied, not daring to say any more, not fully understanding what she had heard, unable to make up her mind to go or to stay. Finally, as though waking up from a dream, she asked after Sara and Florentina. She wanted to see them, to greet them. She learned that Jacob had not wanted them to come before. They would soon be here and one of their first visits would be to Betania.

"We Gallos pride ourselves on our good memory."

"Then . . ."

"It's necessary to lead women."

"To behead men."

"Or to put the head in its proper place."

"The head and everything else." She raised her face, the tone of her voice became harsh again, and her eyes flashed, glinting with reproach. "Jacob, since neither you nor Rómulo nor anyone else can or will take pity on me, and since none of you have any guts, I'm going straight there myself to get back the machine as best I can. I don't care a bit if they stop me and if something happens to me or the machine, you and Rómulo will be responsible, chiefly you because you're the authority, they say, and a powerful person! I leave you with . . . with God, no, with your vanity, which won't even get an ox up out of the ravine."

As if a sudden supernatural force flowed into her nerves and muscles, the old woman set off with a rapid, vigorous step. There was no doubt she would do what she said. Jacob followed her, trying to restrain her, to make her listen to him, to make her see that her action would destroy plans about to be brought to fruition. Doña Merced walked on, impervious, unheeding, not looking back. Jacob tried to take her arm. The woman shook him off.

"The only thing you'll get out of this will be the destruction of the machine. I'm sure of it. Leave it to me. I'll get it for you."

The old woman, still furious, took a few more steps. Then she stopped short, and spoke as though to herself. "That's the only thing I'm afraid of. Not what may happen to me, but that something may have happened to the machine to stop all the trouble and it won't belong to anyone."

"The machine is safe and well looked after."

Doña Merced hesitated. Then she cried out, "You're trying to fool me like all the others you've promised so many things to."

say. Nobody doubts there are—or were—treasures hidden in the Tierra Santa. Trying to forestall the inquisitive and suspicious, Miguel Arcángel asserts and insists that there's no sure treasure below the earth but water, and above it only the sweat of human beings. We laughed, even though not openly, those of us who were sure he'd found buried treasure, and we've been told that when he pretends to be looking for springs he's looking for mines, which there also are in the Tierra Santa. We're sitting on gold and silver, you might say. What else could be the meaning of these colors that the plain has, especially at the end of the dry season? Burnt colors like those of mineral ores, like the colors found in places where there are mines, as I've often heard those who know these places say. This is something we've always believed, that there are mines here, undiscovered or completely forgotten. Now it may also be true what my grandfather used to say, 'If you want to lose money, start working a mine.' And how angry he'd get when someone would start a conversation about reporting these hidden treasures and suggest he should go into this kind of business. I was influenced by his attitude, although that doesn't mean I didn't toy with the idea that an unexpected discovery of this kind might get us out of our difficulties, if it was the will of Providence. In this case there wouldn't be any sense in opposing it or in thinking that something that came from above was evil. Even if the use of divining rods is wrong, this doesn't prevent me and a lot of others who've seen them in action from being amazed at their going straight to the place and wiggling like serpents sniffing out the scent. Yes, there's something in it. And if they're as good at finding mines as they are at discovering springs where you'd never think, Jacob will certainly get richer in less time than it takes a cock to crow. It's the custom here, as I learned from my grandfather, to look for water by wrapping some cotton around a branch, soaking it with brine, drying it in the sun, then putting it on a saucer, placing the saucer in a covered jar, and storing it in a hole. If the cotton is wet next day it's a sign that there's water there. The worst of it is that wherever we look, all through the Tierra Santa, the cotton rarely gets wet. I used to hear my grandfather tell how he was sometimes shown in a dream those places where he found water by digging a shallow hole, and some of these wells of my grandfather's are still in use. I'm tired of looking, it's many years now since I stopped trying to find water on the land belonging to me, that same land that's shrunk and shrunk, like a poor man's shirt, from constant washing and patching. Now there are only shreds left, pitiful shreds, blessed be God. I only laughed when Miguel Arcángel announced one day—to console us, of course, after Jesús raided us—that he was going to dig me a well in Betania. I didn't want to contradict him. It must have been Easter Week—to tell the truth we don't know the calendar here, if we don't ask Matiana the dates—when the men with the rods arrived and after a short time they said, "Here." The rods behaved like those cardboard snakes the peddlers bring around at Christmas time, that the children like so much. They all pointed, moving in the same direction. Miguel Arcángel's men began to dig, to the laughter and doubts of those who passed by, and after three days good water welled up, lots of it. I didn't know whether to attribute it to Teófila, because since she died—something I'd almost forgotten—I'd been asking her to perform the miracle of giving me water chiefly on account of my longing to have some real evidence the girl was enjoying heaven. And now, when I start wondering if such a long delay means she spent all this time in purgatory, I'm very troubled and I rack my brains trying to think why this could have been, because she was a model girl and I can't find any reason why she should pass through the flames of purgatory unless she'd begged to be allowed to suffer for the sins of others. On the other hand, Merced said she offered up her sufferings on that day when that brute was about to kill her, on behalf of the Blessed Souls in Purgatory, and only God knows if that helped Teófila. There's one thing Merced doesn't have any doubts about, and that is that we owe the water to a miracle of Teófila's. She goes around saying it everywhere.

The rainy season was upon them. Later than usual, because of the work undertaken in Betania and other farms at the Gallo's expense, but chiefly because the rains had caught them unprepared and empty-handed, not a few farmers decided to make formal agreements with the King of Diamonds. "Let's see how we get on." Others, the minority, had no help for it but to go and seek aid from the Trujillos.

They found Don Epifanio completely helpless. He had gone back to his childhood. He knew it. He began to realize it, but refused to accept the fact, when the sons he most relied on left him. He had had the sensation that first his arms had gone, then his legs, and last his head, so that he could no longer think and plan. He tried not to give in; on the contrary, he tried hard to think, to make his tongue work, repeating that without him those Judases would have neither feet nor head, that they would fall on their faces in whatever they undertook. The truth was that after a few days of not having Plácida, Felipe, or Jesús to count on, Don Epifanio did not dare to leave his room. There he ate and did what he had to do. Without Plácida's restraining influence he got fat again. 'What one eats and enjoys is all one really has.' He wouldn't let Doña Amandita stir from his side. 'He who suffers much is consoled with little.' He did not let the bottle of brandy out of his hand. "I'll make the most of the little time I have left in whatever way I can." He had bright ideas, got excited over a thousand arbitrary ways of putting things to rights, of punishing the rebels, of summoning them to him and settling matters with them. Then he realized he had no feet and hands to work, to command and enforce obedience as he had been obeyed before, in spite of everything, by Felipe, by Jesusito, by Plácida. He missed Plácida's harsh company, her tyranny. He had no one to trust, even to fulfill a simple command. He couldn't move. 'What will you whistle with, if you haven't got a whistle?' He took refuge in Amanda, in eating and drinking. It was going to his head. 'With love and wine you can drown all sorrows.' His states of excitement and grumbling grew less, he was calming down.

The ragtag and bobtail of the Trujillos, even the unacknowledged bastards, began to flock around the Big House, sniffing about like suspicious dogs, hopping around like crows. They put up with expressions of mock surprise. 'Like the blacksmith's dog who snores through the hammering and wakes up at a whisper.' They were meek, anxious to be of some help, to win favor with their father and master, sucking up to him, wearing themselves out trying to anticipate and carry out his whims. As they found no great resistance, they gradually took on various responsibilities: they bargained with the sharecroppers who came to render accounts, paid for corn in advance, sold seeds and fodder, hired out oxen and farm implements, extended credit terms, won over those who came to Belén, and even took measures in case the older Trujillos should show up.

It was definitely known that Don Felipe and Don Jesusito, at bay, threatened by each other and by the supporters of the King of Diamonds, had barricaded themselves, the first in his house at Damasco, the other at his birthplace on La Tapona, the other side of El Tabor. Once out of the clutches of the Bully, the Sneak ran off, determining to keep none of the promises extorted from him under duress and resolving to make himself strong enough not to be taken by surprise again. Teófila's machine was the only thing he left in Felipe's power on the morning of the assault.

On that day, after the violence with which Don Jesusito was humiliated, his soft-voiced approach triumphed again. When he listened to his brother saying to him, "I'm going to give you one last chance. Come over where the others can't hear us," and abruptly drew him to one side, the Sneak saw his opportunity. He felt he was being led onto his own ground. He let Felipe talk and talk until he was tired; he said nothing to contradict him, and even nodded to show his approval of the torrent of absurd suggestions he heard.

The Bully suggested that they should go together to the Big House and force Don Epifanio to give them their share of their heritage. Don Jesusito would know how to present the matter so that they would not make things worse and have to resort to harsh measures. Don Jesusito would refuse every suggestion of his father's to name him his representative, administrator of his property, executor, or anything of a kind to give him supremacy. Don Jesusito in fact was not to accept, or to renounce, any part of Belén that might fall to him, including, of course, the Big House. Don Jesusito would agree to strive to see that Plácida would inherit nothing and that the other Trujillos would get money but not land. Don Jesusito would retire to his farms of Galilea and La Tapona and never set foot in the center of the plain. Don Jesusito would promise to live in peace with his brother even though at a distance, and prove his good faith by giving him a safe conduct allowing him to travel in safety to Torres de San Miguel, which would cause much talk and serve as a turning point to determine whether Don Felipe would decide to unite with him to attack the Gallos in a war without quarter, a war of blood and fire. This last was the major obsession of the Bully: a surprise attack, ingeniously prepared so that no one would suspect who or how, and all would be amazed at the boldness and filled with respect. For instance, blow up the tower with that devilish machine they called the weathervane or one of the other towers the renegade had built in his pride. They might also set fire to the houses in the middle of the night, destroy the experimental plants and installations, or poison the water and the best animals, or steal money or valuable things, or fall unexpectedly on the police, lynch a few and give the others a good trouncing, to make them run off and appear ridiculous. This was the main thing, to make a laughing-stock of the King of Diamonds, his authority, and his supporters. Don Felipe let himself and his imagination run on imagining the commotion. It would not be the first time Jesusito had executed an affair of the kind brilliantly. He began to remember with pleasure attacks that had inspired respect for the Trujillos and of which no trace of blame could be fixed on anyone. "Yes, that's what I want, to have fear and disgust serve as a warning to that so and so of a brother of yours." Finally he proposed that they should think about abducting Florentina, the wife of their enemy, and if it seemed feasible, carry off the mother as well. "Now, that would be a good idea. They say that Florentina's still attractive, almost as attractive as when father wanted her for himself."

Don Jesusito paid out the string, gave him more rope, so that Don Felipe would go on talking.

Of course. It would not take him long to think of the best way to teach those in Torres de San Miguel a resounding lesson. But it would be better if they planned it together, as on so many other occasions, although the carrying out of it would be, of course, the responsibility of the Sneak. Running off with Florentina would be best, although not easy, and should be their principal aim. "I like it, I like your idea very much, it's what I suggested from the beginning. It's right down my alley and I'll show you with this that nothing has really changed between us. That would be the worst thing that could happen to us." The easiest thing, perhaps the best, because of the shock to the country people, would be to destroy the windmill and burn down the barns full of fodder, converting them to ashes. It would also be nice to steal their best weapons and saddles from them, more than their purses of gold. "Just imagine how people would look at us, riding on those saddles with silver bosses, with their automatic pistols with shell handles stuck in our belts in the holsters embroidered with their initials, and with their carbines and machine guns, even their uniforms with the solid silver buttons and braid." Of course. It would not take long to make preparations, just a few days to plan it properly, because Jacob is as clever as a fox and it is necessary to think of everything. Afraid? Not a bit! But it never does any harm to take precautions and make use of all one's advantages. Everything, everything will be all right. Agreed on everything.

"Come on, then, to Belén."

This was where Jesusito showed his greatest slyness.

"All right, let's go, and you'll be convinced it was all done at the old man's command. With me there he won't be able to deny it. Right there I'll renounce any advantage I may have in your favor." These were his words, but after they had gone a little way he began to hem and haw. Thinking it over calmly, maybe that day was not the right day, considering what had happened, to get anything out of him, either for good or bad, unless they killed him, and that would complicate things and make the situation worse. Just imagine the state Plácida must be in and her presence would make everything difficult. The foolishness of the shots fired at Matiana would have brought many people to the Big House, which would prevent a formal interview with the old man, one that might have positive results. He moved along tranquilly, giving Felipe plenty to think about.

"Look, take the machine. You can even tell him it was you who rescued it and take the credit for it and make sure of getting into his good books. I'll go to your house at Damasco here. I'll wait until you let me know how things are going, and as soon as you say the word I'll come running to join you."

"I can see you're up to your usual damned tricks. You're trying to put one over on me."

"Put one over on you? How, in what way, if I give you all the advantages and agree to everything you think of without arguing whether it's right or reasonable? I'm even giving you this damned piece of junk, this whim of my father's, that's given me so many headaches, beginning with the bad thoughts it put into your head against me, when what I did was to do what the old fool ordered me to do in your presence, against my will, against the reasons I had pointed out to him so often, as you know. Well, here it is, I leave you the reason for your false suspicions, so that you can be the one to give it to him, although it was another who pulled the world down on his head trying to get hold of it. What more do you want?

"Well, I want—I told you you were an awful fool to take away the new machine, which is worth money—I want you to go and get it and bring it to me at Damasco. But leave me your men and take two of mine with you, since the tighter you're tied the safer I'll be in case you try to play any tricks on me or make a fool of me, the way you often do. I'll instruct them to knock you out if you attempt any treachery."

Don Jesusito protested against this humiliating threat, but he agreed, rapidly working out a plan to trick the guards. He did this when they had scarcely reached the first house in Betania, where he persuaded them to wait for him, telling them it would be dangerous to arrive together now that the attacks on Matiana and Doña Merced would have aroused the neighborhood. By himself he could use his cunning better to get hold of the machine, and he would summon them to help him when the victims tried to fling themselves upon him. He peppered his rapid speech with guile and flattery. Without giving them time to think, he set off for Rómulo's, and then, hidden by the wall that goes as far as the Shrine of La Providencia, he started to run along a short cut and was lost to sight.

Afraid of what would happen to them at Don Felipe's hands, the men he had tricked decided to join the Gallos.

After his fruitless wait, Don Felipe preferred to spy out the land, to take soundings, to maneuver from his fortress at Damasco. His rage abated as he thought out schemes to get what he wanted out of the machine he had in his power. That whim of the lustful old man would cost him dearly. He would have to eat crow in order to get it back. Don Felipe would make him plead and despair before giving it to him, and then not until he named him as his only heir, with all due formality. And since he had been the one who set Plácida free and helped her recover from the attack, Don Felipe thought he could count on her to help him overthrow that crook Jesusito once and for all.

His first surprise was to find Jacob's reserve corps lying in wait for him, the more to be feared since they just remained on guard, that was all. At most, they searched and disarmed some passersby. The second surprise was not to receive any answer from Plácida, nor any sign of her exact dwelling place or of her intentions. On the other hand, he learnt that Jesusito was preparing to checkmate him. He tried to come to an understanding with Jacob, agreeing to accept any terms he wanted. He failed to get any definite answer or any hope of reaching an agreement. Even the requests that the soldiers be withdrawn or that they not molest his people were useless.

Successively the news reached Damasco of those who were hastening to sign a contract with the Gallos and those who tried to give themselves to the Trujillos. Soon Felipe learned of Don Epifano's prostration, the arrival of the string of minor Trujillos, and their taking possession of Belén, their daily encroachments. He could not contain his rage. Today, tomorrow, very early tomorrow, Felipe kept promising himself, he would descend on the Big House and get rid of that swarm. "I'm going to hang half a dozen at the least." He was held back by the suspicion that Jacob on the one hand and Jesusito on the other would get ahead of him, would hunt him down. A similar thing was happening to Jesusito.

The blow fell from the side where it was least expected. Plácida stole a march on them and took possession of the Big House. She brought to heel the lesser bastards, but she did not send them away; on the contrary, she conciliated them in order to count on them as allies and tools. It was said that she acted in agreement with and on the advice of the King of Diamonds.

Flocks of swallows winged their melodious flight through the sky in sweeping curves as the days grew longer. The long idleness of the dry season was passing. The people were shaking off their sloth. The men made haste to perform the tasks they had postponed: mending the roofs and gutters of the houses, mending walls and gates, fixing tools, roughening the stone surfaces of metates, mending leather articles, getting supplies of wood, preparing seeds and animals. Men, women, children, and animals looked more closely at the sky, at the horizon, into their own hearts, in search of omens. Formations of swallows flew to and fro in curves as long as rainbows. The frolics of the wind died down in the heat haze, which was tinted a hundred and one colors. Impulses to sing, to shout, to run.

> My wife and my horse
> Strayed off one day;
> My wife, God forgive her,
> My wife did this;
> My wife, the devil take her!
> It is my horse I miss!

The long idleness of the dry season was coming to an end. The cattle were getting restive. Ants hurried about their business. Clouds were massing in the sky.

The clouds, the deceitful clouds

The clouds, the deceitful clouds. They would appear, gather quickly, look like rain clouds. Then fly away and disappear.

The same old story.

Hope refusing to admit disappointment.

Stubborn faith.

Blind love for the lean lands, covered with huisache trees, nothing but caked clay.

Mouths, voices, hearts clinging firmly to the miraculous virtue of the Trinity.

With the Seraphim, Cherubim and Thrones: "Holy, Holy, Holy, Lord God of Hosts, Holy, Mighty, Immortal, Have pity on us."

The chorus, repeated from time immemorial: "We worship Thee, venerate and bless Thee together with the Three Angelic Hierarchies and the Three First Choirs: Loving Seraphim, Learned Cherubim, and Lofty Thrones . . ."

Together with the Dominions, Virtues and Powers.

With the Principalities, Archangels, and Angels.

"They are Three who bear witness in Heaven and these Three are One."

Soloist: "Sanctuary of the Lord Most High, where none may enter, where the curtain may not be drawn aside, all we Thy creatures must worship Thee from without, in deep sincerity . . ."

Chorus: "O Lord God, the Cherubim, Angels and Seraphim praise Thee in gentle strains, saying, 'Holy, Holy, Holy.' "

Antiphon: "Eternal, pure Divinity . . . The ages proclaim Thy pity and tenderness . . . Thou, upon iniquitous man . . . Our fathers have sung the story of Thy marvelous works in their hymns of praise . . . When Thy just vengeance . . . Thy Great Blessings . . . Who should burn in the Sacred Fire of the prophet Isaiah . . ."

Soloist: "Blessed art Thou, O Lord, in the firmament of Heaven."

Chorus: "And all the earth is full of Thy glory."

She's said these prayers since before we were married. On Sundays and the first day of each month, in honor of the Divine Providence. House, clothes, and food. And from the time the clouds begin to announce the beginning of the rains, she lights three candles and lets them burn out. And when the clouds appear above the hill. When there are dust devils and hail, she adds the Magnificat and the Litany of All Saints to the Holy, Holy, Holy. She has always longed to have an end of paschal candle, to keep for storms and a good death.

In time of storm: "My soul doth magnify the Lord and my spirit hath rejoiced in God . . . For He that is mighty . . . He hath shewed strength with His arm; He hath scattered the proud . . . He hath put down the mighty from their seat; and hath exalted the humble . . . He hath filled the hungry with good things; and the rich He hath sent empty away . . ."

Ah, how well Teófila knew all this. Better than Matiana. I don't know where the book of Lavalle where she read it is, where she learned the prayers for the dying and the litanies. I liked to listen to her, no matter how hard it hailed, or even though the sight of the dying was enough to break your heart. I feel as though I can hear her still.

"Go forth, Christian Soul, from this world, in the name of God, in the name of the Angels, of the Patriarchs and Prophets, today take your place in peace and your dwelling in Holy Zion . . ."

The solemn words of moments of anguish: "St. Michael, St. Gabriel, St. Rafael, All the Saints, Angels, and Archangels . . .

Chorus: "Pray for us."

"All the Holy Orders of Blessed Spirits . . . All the Holy Patriarchs and Prophets . . . The Holy Martyrs . . . The High priests and Confessors . . . All the Holy Doctors . . . The Priests and Levites, Monks and Hermits . . . All the Holy Virgins and Widows . . ."

Chorus: "Pray for us."

"From sudden and unforeseen death . . . From the assaults of the devil . . . From the spirit of fornication . . . From lightning and tempest . . . From everlasting death . . . In the Day of Judgment . . ."

Chorus: "Lord deliver us."

"Forgive us . . . Pardon us . . . Free our souls and those of our kindred and benefactors from everlasting damnation . . . Deign to give and preserve to our use the fruits of the earth . . . Grant eternal rest to those dying in Thy faith . . . Deign to hear us . . ."

Chorus: "Hear us, we beseech Thee."

My flesh creeps when I remember and hear again the chanting of the psalms that are sung in times of calamity, at death beds, at the rosaries where the relatives and friends of the dead person gather on the evenings after the funeral. These gatherings have their good side. That was how I met Merced. They'd taken me to her farm when my family went to pay a visit of condolence when an uncle of hers called Petronio died. There, that very night, listening to her pray without losing her self-control, and watching her afterwards coming and going among the people, I fell in love with her, and although she's always denied it, she took to me that same night in spite of my shyness. I wasn't used to paying visits. 'Love is like the measles, we all have to go through it.' My grandfather was very good about going to see the neighbors in their bereavements. He wasn't much of a man for prayer, but on these occasions he prayed sincerely, kneeling for the whole of the rosary, his arms outstretched in the litany. I still seem to hear his hoarse, deep voice making the responses: "Grant them, O Lord, eternal rest. Let Thy perpetual light shine upon them, and from Thine abode in Zion, defend them." When I recall those prayers, I feel so many who have died come alive again. Teófila knew them by heart. How clear her voice was when she said them, never making a mistake. It was she who would lead the prayers, wherever she was. Even Matiana gave her her place in this. What a pity my grandfather never knew her. He would have been crazy about his great-granddaughter. He was so quiet and reserved when it came to showing his affection, but so ready to enjoy lively conversation. Yes, a world of memories, faces, customs comes alive again each time I hear those prayers my grandfather heard as a boy, prayers that were handed down—as he used to say—from father to son, joining generations in the same feeling, by means of words, unchanged by time but filled with more and more tears, more and more hope. What a consolation to repeat them when we feel troubled or neglected and to know that when not even our dust remains, when we're completely forgotten, they'll go on being repeated, unchanged, the very same chants, whether it's a question of asking for rain or appeasing Heaven, putting enemies to flight or watching by the dying or praying for the dead and for the fulfillment of our needs.

The treacherous clouds would glide over the plain, settle on top of the hills, and go away. "Hear us, we beseech Thee." The Festival of the Holy Cross at Getsemaní came and went, with its set of dances. "Angels and Seraphim say, 'Holy, Holy, Holy.' " Many were expecting a surprise from the King of Diamonds like the one he had produced at Belén. It was said that he would put on a showy dance in order to impress people and that he would hand out gifts. The Festival of the Cross was disappointing; there were very few people. "Deign to give and preserve to our use the fruits of the earth." The barren clouds saw May out. Neither birds, nor cattle, nor ants gave any sign of awareness of approaching rain. Lips redoubled their prayers and the Eye of Providence in the Shrine at the Crossroads felt the increasing weight of candles and flowers. Eyes grew hollow in despairing contemplation of the sky, and fixed their gaze on the distant hills where the flashes of lightning appear, precursors and sure sign of rain.

The greater preoccupation relegated all other considerations (quarrels, stories, diversions) to a secondary place. What does the world matter if the year is lost? "Deliver us, O Lord." When the rainy season comes, there is no time for the idle to invent stories for their amusement.

Soil and sky unyielding. "Deign to hear us, hear us, we beseech Thee." The whole of life is centered around these months.

The land was prepared, the furrows broken by the plow, trampled by the yoked oxen. The seed was ready. The obstacles of usury and poverty had been overcome as always, year after year. Only the clemency of the sky was lacking. "Have mercy upon us." The miracle hoped for, year by year. "Hear us, O Christ. Listen to our prayer, O Christ." What is the use of doing one's duty to preserve one's self-respect if the land is destroyed for lack of rain?

Let Rómulo say he's fastened to the ground with thorns like a huisache and won't change it for anything. What do I care about that lie about hope never dying, that if this year's lost the next one may be good? Now that my machine's gone. It's nearly four months now. "Soon now, tomorrow, the next day." They all keep telling me the same thing. The worst of it is, they don't know where it is, whether Felipe has it or Jesús, or whether they've broken it in their quarreling. One thing is sure, it isn't in Belén. I went there. Nothing could stop me. Poor old Epifanio. I even felt sorry for him. Without my machine, what do I care about the land, the foolish hopes of all the years in these barren lands, getting more worthless and more barren all the time? Let it all be lost, let it all just blow away. Even Plácida took pity on me. Even Plácida offered to give it back to me. But when? Now I don't believe anything. I don't even hope any more. Yes, I do, I hope it will all be swept away. Barren lands, sterile lands, in the likeness and image of the sky, one matching the other. Sterile.

The late coming of the rains, the piling up of barren clouds that scurried rapidly away, were regarded as signs that it would be a bad year, with scanty and intermittent rain. This seemed to confirm the belief that electricity and the other products of witchcraft brought by the Gallos would be the ruin of the Tierra Santa. Jacob was indeed a Mason, a Protestant, an enemy of Christianity who should be driven out as soon as possible and his possessions burned, destroyed. Salt should be thrown on Jerusalén so that no one would ever try to build it up again. Therefore, the Trisagion, the Magnificat, the Litanies of All Saints, and the exorcisms and charms of Matiana were all useless. Nor would they be of any use until the Gallos were driven out and the memory of them utterly eradicated.

Jacob's supporters had their say, too, and they were just as vehement. Those who made such a fuss about the lateness of the rainy season were accused of being puppets in the pay of the Trujillos. It was nothing out of the ordinary, but perfectly natural and normal; some years it had not rained even in June and the harvest had been good. How strange that they should forget something so well known as the barrenness of these unproductive, dried-out lands and the irregular rainfall due to so many bald hills completely stripped of trees, and then try overnight to put the blame on the very man who proposed precisely to improve the soil and even the rainfall. So determined is he that there is his money poured out in all those projects, which were completed in the twinkling of an eye; there are the piles of money promised, as a help in many other works, to those he trusts, so that they will sow or will rent him lands that for a long time have not been cultivated because of their barrenness. A little reflection will show who threw the treacherous stones. It is absurd to let oneself be led astray by mere unfounded gossip. It is a matter of waiting patiently for a little while. Jacob swears the year will not be a bad one. If he says this, he knows what he is talking about; he is not one of those who leave things to chance, who set out, without counting the cost, to try their luck, to see what fate will bring them, as has always been the custom here and no one will change it. Nor is he incredulous as far as prayers are concerned; but he does not believe that prayers alone are sufficient, and he even says they are the pretext and refuge of the lazy, repeating the well-known saying that 'Faith alone is not sufficient, you must also have good works.' He gets reports from far away, from the capital and even from the United States, that forecast the weather; they are made by scientists; there is also an instrument with a strange name that foretells cold and heat, rain and dry weather; that is science too. The good thing about it is that what it says agrees with what Matiana announces. This year will not be a bad one. And no one has to go far to know this. When the clouds gather in May and no rain comes, that is a sign the rain will be evenly distributed. The bad sign is when the rains come early and stop just when the seed is sown, stop, and calm weather returns. That is something we know well. Finally, the best proof is that Jacob has large tracts of land prepared to sow. He would not take that risk if he were not sure.

The doubts of his opponents were muttered aloud. Prejudices sprang up. It seemed Satanic pride to try to change the heavens, and to receive reports from the gringos, that is, the Protestants, which foretell the future, and to have instruments to forecast the weather, that is, to improve on the plan of Divine Providence, defying God.

Jacob Gallo's challenge spread like wildfire: he asserted that it would rain without fail on the last day of May if not the day before. Matiana had never dared to tell God the day on which it must rain. His audacity was so incomprehensible, and left the country people so amazed, that it did not even give them time to think about bets; but it did give them a chance to joke and nurse heretical suspicions of the King of Diamonds.

Whatever they believed, the prayers of the Trisagion, the Magnificat, and the Litanies of All Saints increased on the farms. Jacob's supporters could say that with this they tried to sow confusion as to whether the fulfilling of the prophecy was the work of prayer or of the improvements brought to the plain by Progress. This word, used for the first time, was on all lips.

Doubts remained. Who could guess what each one thought? The good thing about it is that it rained on the day announced. 'That's that, so forget the rest.' And the people's respect and admiration for Jacob grew, whether they wanted it to or not.

The first signs that the prophecy of the King of Diamonds would be fulfilled appeared in the granaries: the moths in the corn changed into grubs; then signs of the bees and ants began, the latter hurrying to clear out great quantities of chaff, the former speedily returning to their hives. Then toads appeared in great abundance.

That day, May 31, the cocks crowed at nine o'clock at night. In a short while lightning flashes were seen, a long distance off, far behind the Sierra de Cardos. The cattle trembled and it was some time before their lowing stopped. The dogs barked with joy. Goats and rams huddled together, bodies touching. Jacob's ill-wishers lost hope.

Nevertheless, day dawned in a cloudless sky. The ill-wishers took hope again. Faint hopes. Destroyed on midday of the thirty first when huge fleecy clouds formed out by the ravine.

Epifanio Trujillo died at three o'clock.

At that very hour the first clap of thunder was heard. 'At the first clap of thunder that's heard in May, the hare leaps and the horses play.' Stentorian chorus of neighing. Long drawn-out mournful howls. The owls flew in the daylight. Loud braying of donkeys could be heard, the frenzied males audible above the rest. The flocks of swallows flew away as though driven from their nests. Fresh, damp winds arose, blowing things about. A black cloud advanced, growing thicker and thicker, driving before it the last breath of the dry season. What a smell, offensive, corrupt, fertile, vegetal, animal! Smell of earth, of air! At this hour, three o'clock in the afternoon, the cocks crowed. The stallions at Belén leaped over the fences.

Don Epifanio's death was swift, there was no time to fight against it.

It seemed that the clouds were waiting until the dead man rendered his account at the Judgment Seat before they burst.

What a terric storm! "My spirit is filled with joy." What thunder and lightning! "For He that is mighty hath magnified me." What light from the lightning flashes! "He hath put down the mighty from their seat." The earth was soon soaked through, drenched to the bones. "He hath filled the hungry with good things, and the rich He hath sent empty away." The old people could not remember when it had rained like this. "Holy, Holy, Holy, Lord God Almighty." What a wonderful storm to rejoice all hearts!

If God preserves us, tomorrow we'll go straight out and sow, God helping us.

There is no escape

'There is no escape from death and fate, either for the humble or for the great.' No one can make Doña Amandita stop repeating over and over again that saying. She was the only living soul who witnessed Don Epifanio's death.

Verónica, Salomé, Cleofas, Andrea, and other pious women who have come to help, ask her to keep quiet out of respect, because the body is still warm, the soul is rendering its account to its Creator. They gaze at the dead man and picture in their own minds what is taking place there above the bed, a few yards away: the Seat of Judgment with the Just Judge, the Guardian Angel on one side, the right, and on the left, Satan, accusing; the accused, prostrate, humbled, seeking celestial advocates to help him, to answer for him. From the face, the mouth, the open eyes—"No, they musn't be closed yet, he musn't be touched for a while!"—the women try to guess the pleas and the outcome of this awe-inspiring moment. Sighs, sobs held back. The bystanders repeat tales, reminiscences of the dead man. The women take Doña Amandita, with her compulsive refrain, out of the room. Plácida is there, standing impassive, brows drawn together, hands clenched. The storm beats against the room, the wind enters. The lowing of the oxen can be heard, the barking of the dogs, and above it all the bellowing of the stud bull. The muttered prayers increase in volume as more candles are lit.

"Yes, that's true. But I had my moral code, with its principles, according to which I thought I did right. I certainly never deceived any of them and I kept my promises to all of them. Besides, I kept to the saying, 'In the end it's up to them to say when.' I looked after them, was strict with them, and always remembered 'An open door makes a dog a glutton and a woman a whore.' I made them learn the catechism so they could teach it to their children. I forced them to understand that, 'A woman's modesty is shown by her dress.' I know that what I enjoyed most in life, what I enjoyed most in the world, was to watch them, wanting lots of them, the way you want flowers, one isn't enough because others have colors, charm, scents that the first one doesn't. And I couldn't see anything wrong in that, because to me they were all God's work, like birds, to be put together in the same cage, or flowers, to make pretty bouquets like I've seen on altars. To me they were the best of all created things, they were almost like angels or at least like a kind of bird of paradise, so pretty, so mysterious, that I never tired of watching them and seeking them. No, never, not even when they turned out to be ungrateful, or when I was too old. I continued to watch them, as the most precious gift God has given to men. I heard that it was a sin, yes, but my nature was never convinced, in my heart of hearts I could hear the command to go after them, tirelessly. How could I be deceived by a logic so constant, so in keeping with my strongest impulses? Besides, I could see this in animals, which are living creatures like us, after all, with the same instincts, obeying gladly, in the most natural possible way, without hypocrisy, the command of our Heavenly Father, "Grow and multiply," as I learned in the pastorals and in sermons. I multiplied, not shrinking from the burden of children and responsibilities. I spent my strength in this and kept nightly vigils. So, I did much of what I'm accused of, mixing blood of different races, removing influences, making selections. I proposed to form a powerful Big House that no one could destroy. I did everything I could. It wasn't my fault but my lack of skill and limited vision that caused my downfall. I didn't abandon any of my children, no matter how unworthy I considered them. I just didn't give them the place they didn't deserve or in which I learned they didn't fit, according to my scheme of things. God humbled my pride or the weakness of my judgment. But thinking over the matter carefully, I'm not sure it was my fault, because the boys are big now, they know what they're doing, I'm not the master of their wills or their actions, however much I'd like to be. That would be to blame God for the treacheries of Christians, as my fellow countrymen believe. And it's exactly because I didn't agree with blaming Him for our laziness, vices, and the rest that I got the reputation for being foul-mouthed and heretical, or was accused of vulgar sayings like 'Borrow not even from God and beg not even from the devil,' and 'What do I owe the sun for warming me?' and ' "It's something, at any rate," said the devil, and made off with a bishop,' and 'The priest is not going to blacken me, not even on Ash Wednesday,' and 'Even Bishops run to get a free gift,' 'What can St. Sebastian give when he hasn't even got any trousers?' But I repeated and acted on many others containing good teaching: 'Since there are many devils and little holy water, one has to carry more,' and 'The paschal candle is made up of many drops of wax,' and 'There is time enough for everything if one knows how to use it.' My intentions were good . . .

Verónica and the other women piously prolonged the silence, calculating the time required for the rendering of such a long account; but they were unable to check the impatient steps pacing to and fro, the questions, the signs of uncontrollable restlessness.

The rain started to pour down in torrents. Flashes of lightning lit up the room; the rays quivered over the bed of the dead man, manifesting the presence of the Divine Majesty. Nearby, in the courtyard, the old donkey, head of the herd, brayed stridently.

Plácida could contain herself no longer. With firm tread she strode out of the room, then marched back in, her mind made up.

There were many, many instances, as I've confessed, and apart from the attraction I felt toward the loveliest of God's creatures—an attraction I couldn't resist—I just couldn't let anyone get the better of me in using that power which, forgive the comparison, made me feel I'd been created in the likeness of God Himself, who created all things. That's exactly what I felt, the everlasting joy of being able to create and go on creating, with gusto, with unfailing appetite, because of the beauty of the creative act and of the creatures chosen to share the wonderful task of creation. That's the reason for my struggle against those who take it for granted that children must die, a struggle they criticize me so much for, calling me a heretic. Anyone who confers life must strive to keep it sound and healthy. There are my children to bear witness to this. I once heard them in church praising I don't know who because his offspring were as numerous as the branches on the vine, the stars of the sky, the sands of the sea, or something like that, and if I remember correctly, I think it was there I also heard them say that the saints of old, like St. Abraham, St. Jacob, St. David, St. Solomon, and many others, had lots of wives. So . . . But I won't mention these examples, although they serve to quiet my conscience, and have helped me draw up my "code," and have encouraged me not only to have as many children as the stars in the sky and grapes on the vine but countless cattle and houses, and lands and domains. This meant establishing my power, like the queen bees in the hives, the cocks in the barnyard, the stud bulls in the corrals. That's what I'm thinking of. It wasn't really so much that I wanted to, but in my struggle to dominate the land I had to give evidence of my power to them all. There were many instances that weren't far away like those of the Saints of old but right here, among respectable folk devoutly fulfilling all their religious duties, people you know well. I'm not talking about others who had no religion, like that General García who grabbed the Totache region here, out by Cañones. He was a terror for years, and didn't have a match for wickedness. There's no point in recalling his murders and thefts, his lust, his love of wild living, of spending his days and nights dancing and drinking. What a man! He made it a rule to celebrate every birthday by marrying some young girl, and that's saying nothing about his almost daily affairs with women. Since he had no respect for anything, everybody was terrified of him. He was getting on toward eighty and kept up the custom of having a new woman every year, followed by eight days of continuous feasting. He killed herds of animals, wine ran like water, and he brought musicians in from the surrounding villages and they played in turn without interruption and the dance went on and on but he never got tired. He had another custom: on this occasion every year he'd have all his daughters there, all dressed alike, and the year I went to the party there were thirty-seven of them. His goings-on began when he seized the hacienda of Liebres and its three owners and married them all at the same time. I still remember the horror the triple wedding caused, the scandal even reached this place, and what was most amazing was that the three were young ladies, very well known and brought up in the capital and in other countries. They say that he threatened to kill them unless he could have all three of them together as wives, and that he didn't let them even show their faces at the windows of the house. The fact is, they were never heard of again. Liebres was spreading like a grease spot, its boundary getting nearer the plain, there where the hills rise. I know it's no excuse but it helps to explain. That was when I began my struggle to rise in the world and the general's reputation was a measuring rod to measure the stature of the men who wanted to try their luck. I know I didn't have much religion either, but with my own "code" I never sank to the general's vices or abuses and cruelties, he delighted in doing evil, or to the hypocrisies of the respectable neighbors. The Sovereign Judge knows it. I did it to satisfy the needs of my nature and for the pleasure I got out of the most attractive part of creation. I felt something in me like a river welling up, I couldn't control it and I wanted to flood the world to fertilize it. An overwhelming desire to create, to grow and multiply, as well as to draw near the lovely things God put in the world and to enjoy them, believing it was for this purpose they were there, for me to look at and enjoy like the stars, the clouds, and the rainbow, the mountains with their colors and the variety of birds, flowers, trees, cattle, all in great numbers. I never broke or went back on

mind the saying, 'Some run after the hare, and others catch it without running.' I used to say, 'Don't dance unless you have music,' or else, 'If you want to be a woodcutter, first get yourself an axe.' But they'd say, 'Nothing ventured, nothing gained,' and thought I'd be stupid enough to fall into their trap. How were they going to catch me in their trap if they couldn't even get ahead of me in sayings! 'For one who runs there's another who flies.' 'For one who gets up early there's another who doesn't go to bed.' I can't deny that one of my principles was, 'When you're the anvil, bear; when you're the hammer, strike.' For a long time it was my bad luck to be the former, and when I got the chance to strike, I did so in self-defense, as a preventive measure . . . I'm accused of keeping other people's goods, of having driven a hard bargain with my neighbor. For instance, there were loud complaints because Don Teódulo Garabito's children, proud but not very capable, got mixed up in lawsuits after he died and engaged in unsuccessful schemes, in deals that fizzled out, until finally they lost everything and I was left with Belén and other lands of theirs. They were ruined by having so much pride. They were like old barrels that still have their hoops and their smell: you can sniff what used to be in them, but they're empty. Rómulo Garabito still claims sometimes that I tricked them out of their inheritance, although he himself admits I didn't hold a pistol to their ribs to force them to ask me for loans. What happened is that they wanted to appear what they weren't. They had to buy their cloth on credit even though it cost a fortune. They took as their motto, 'Get all you can while you can,' and they thought I would think, 'What's lent is spent,' even though they heard me say, 'When I stopped giving I began to get,' as well as, 'A fool and his money are soon parted.' With me it was a case of not looking for figs on thistles. Finally it turned out the way it always does: 'Do a hundred favors but fail to do one, and you will be treated as though you did none.' You're considered a thief, but 'Better to blush once than suffer a hundred times,' and 'Better to be seated badly than standing and at ease.' It's just ingratitude for services received, or the envy of those who are weak and can't bear to see the strong and enterprising win out. As it says in the proverb, 'Never a shepherd, always a sheep,' and 'If you've never worn huaraches the straps will make you bleed.' How I had to work to hold on to what I'd gained! 'Although the shirt is wide, the elbows still wear out.' And they're surprised I should try to have a watchdog like Felipe to look after my cattle. I wanted Miguel Arcángel for this, first. Doesn't every farmhouse have a dog to frighten off robbers as well as coyotes? Really, Satan, I'm amazed that with all your knowledge of everybody—look at all the things you accuse me of—you don't know a simple thing like that. Why doesn't my Saint Teófila come to bear witness in the affair of the machine, which they're also laying at my door . . . ?

The storm was growing worse, increasing in fury, drowning the monotonous funeral chant: "Pray for him Pray for him Pray for him . . ."

Doña Amandita came back into the room and her compulsive muttering of "There is no escape . . ." alternated with the "Pray for him" of the litany. Plácida kept walking to and fro, getting ready the clothes to dress the corpse in.

"Pray for him . . ."

My Guardian Angel will bear witness to the whole story, and chiefly to my intentions from the beginning. 'Money and love cannot be kept hidden.' 'Out of the heart the mouth speaketh.' As for wanting to keep the machine, I didn't want to torture Merced but to have a relic which nobody had a better right to than I did, if I'm right in believing—and the Supreme Judge will say if it is so—that Teófila offered her life to rescue me from my evil ways . . .

The noise of the storm drowned out the treble voice of Verónica: ". . . leaving us the signs of Thy Passion in the Sacred Sheet in which Thy Holy Body was wrapped . . ." She broke off to speak to Plácida when she approached to start placing Don Epifanio in his winding sheet:

"Wait until we finish the prayer, it's almost over."

The music of the storm accompanied the plaintive: "When Thou wast taken down from the Cross by Joseph . . ."

One of the younger bastards burst in, soaked to the skin, his face the picture of woe, and threw himself, spurs and all, upon the bed of the dead man.

The shrill voice of Verónica, after the brief interruption, continued: "Grant us, O Lord, O most merciful Lord, that by Thy Holy Death and Burial, the soul of Thy servant, Epifanio, may be taken to rest in the glory of Thy resurrection where Thou dost live and reign . . ."

The bastard rose and shouted: "How did this come about? What happened?"

"For ever and ever . . ."

"Amen," added the chorus.

"I left him healthy and well a moment ago!"

"There is no escape . . ." Doña Amandita muttered sadly to herself.

The thick hail drowned out the bastard's jeremiads.

I was a light-hearted man. I wasn't cruel. I'd make people do silly things to tease them, to try them out and see how much they'd take, how far they'd got and how far they'd go, but not to make them suffer just for the sake of seeing them suffer, and it was the same when I shouted and shook my fists. I liked to study people and things, to watch men's faces and behavior, to track down secrets hidden by smiles or blank faces, to note people's features, the motions of their bodies, the tones of their voices. The same with women. I wanted variety. No matter how good the dishes were, I wanted to try different ones every day, although I knew very well that 'Too much eating and too much drinking lead you straight to the graveyard.' But I remembered, 'The only things you're sure of enjoying in this life are what you've already eaten and drunk,' and the saying that goes, 'He whose belly is full cares little for the grumbling of his family.' I admit I'm a glutton, and that's all I have to say. I confess my sins and I repent. Just a minute, Beelzebub, don't get fidgety. The Angel can't say anyone was ever refused food in my house. Just the opposite. We'd always make anyone who came there stop and share whatever there was in the kitchen, especially those who were really destitute, in spite of my children complaining, when they grew up, about what they called waste, and sneering that the Big House was an inn where anyone could get free room and board. No, there wasn't any meanness in my house when it came to feeding the poor, still less the poor souls who arrived white-lipped and faint with hunger. This had always been a custom of mine even before I'd made my fortune, when I still didn't have a rag on my back. This isn't boasting, just the plain truth, to the best of my knowledge, and You, O Good Judge, will decide, since no one can deceive You. I say that if it hadn't been for me, in the worst years of the Revolution when everything was scarce and people didn't have enough to eat, a great many people would have died of hunger if I hadn't given them and their families enough to keep them alive. Well, of course, not exactly given, they wouldn't have wanted that, but their most urgent need was to keep alive and I helped them do this. Many of them never paid me a cent and if I demanded money or work from the others afterwards, that was only fair. I'd run the risk of not getting anything back, knowing that this was more than likely, out of Christian charity to those in need. But 'One must make the best of a bad bargain.' I don't see anything wrong with that. And at that same time when there was an epidemic of Spanish influenza and half the people on the farms were dying, who else bought and shared out medicines, alcohol, creoline, and other things that are said to be good for what they also called Carranza's disease? Who else put their efforts and money into getting these remedies? You, Lord, know that at least at that time I wasn't moved by self-interest, and I didn't make capital out of those favors . . .

"All of you go out while Verónica and I dress him!" ordered Plácida in a harsh tone. The storm was abating and the noises of the animals could be heard again: joyful neighing, barking, cackling. The lowing of the bulls, now with their cows, sounded calmer.

They say around here that I refused to build chapels. That's true —but why should I be the one to start? And what good would they be anyhow if we couldn't have a priest living here? It's difficult enough to get one to come, even when he's urgently needed. I say you can pray anywhere to You and the Saints, since we haven't got the things for a Mass or baptism and other ceremonies with a priest and all. People can lift up their eyes to the clear sky and pray, that's good enough and more direct. Perhaps I've been wrong to think and talk like this, but I assure you I didn't mean it wickedly. I always lent my house for them to put on the pastorals—even this year when I suspected something was up that would cause me trouble. That proves I wasn't an unbeliever. The only confirmations held on the plain, as far as I can remember, were held in my house. That was before the mob started running wild, and I remember I gave the bishop a meal, a tasty one, too, which he enjoyed very much, at least that was what he said in public. What I've always been opposed to, frankly, is people taking refuge in superstitions and customs as an excuse for laziness, cowardice, ignorance, and other vices, and confusing religion with witchcraft. This is one of the reasons why I didn't get on with Matiana, who was such a thorn in my flesh. I didn't wish her any harm but I used to curb her arrogance and her power, with which she did more harm than good. How different Teófila was! I won't deny that when I went to hear her talks and readings, and watched her at work, and saw her setting an example as a good Christian, I went chiefly because I liked her as a woman and wanted her for my wife. But she also inspired me with devotion—the Angel won't let me lie—and I was filled with respect as I watched her handle the children in her little school, and the grown-ups when she went over the catechism with them, and the girls when she taught them to sew. I liked this so much that I wanted Plácida to learn from her—not just sewing, but to be like her. Teófila was modest but Matiana is full of herself, she thinks she's the Lord's minister. The saint didn't go around creating false mysteries or lying to people or fooling them with magic. She was friendly towards everyone, her house was open to all, and she gave her advice and her services as a teacher freely. Why does Matiana shut herself up? What does she keep hidden in her room? Is she a miser, is she really a witch, or is she play-acting? I don't want to judge her, that isn't my business. What I'm trying to do is account for her ill will towards me, since she's the one who's chiefly responsible for my reputation as an unbeliever and a heretic. Come to think of it, who's the worse one? It's up to You to decide.

Now the body was laid out, dressed in the suit he wore on the rare occasions when he went to town on important business. His arms were folded; his feet, in their shoes, appeared huge, tied one over the other with purple ribbon; they had covered his face with a mauve handkerchief; the bed had been dragged into the middle of the room. Plácida did not want to have it taken into the parlor.

It was still raining gently. The sky was clearing. There were signs that the sun would come out again; it was still high. It would be a nice afternoon.

Gaunt, unmoved, dry-eyed, Plácida issued curt commands. Verónica was still thinking about the judgment; imagining it.

God, forgive me, I thought it was all a dream, that I was talking to myself, as I did in that vision I had on the Eve of All Souls, the vision that disturbed me. I'm dazzled by Your Presence. I can't see anything. I can't remember, I don't know if there was time for anyone to pray for me in that moment when You arrived and took me into Your Presence, if anyone remembered those prayers that I heard Your blessed Teófila use one day and that I now remember clearly, miraculously, although I'd forgotten them completely. "Remember not their old iniquities and sins committed in the fury and fervor of evil desires. Remember not the sins of their youth . . ." And of my old age. In the miracle of finding these words spring to mind, suddenly I see Your Divine Pity and I'm filled with joy. I can feel the Eye of Your Divine Providence, I have always worshipped it and looked after its Shrine. Forgive me for the sayings I repeated a little while ago. It's a habit of mine and I thought I was dreaming or speaking to myself. Yes, I was, I am, a great sinner. I can't see anything. But I feel I am in Your Presence, Lord God.

The end had been expected at any moment, but not in the form in which it came.

He had enjoyed his dinner although he had not eaten much. Since her return, Plácida had been inflexible in preventing her father from eating and drinking too much. The poor man scarcely grumbled and no longer grew angry because they would not let him have what he wanted. Plácida's return had given him new life. That morning he had taken a few steps along the terrace. He wanted to have his dinner in the kitchen. Although he had trouble with his speech he was in a good humor, showing signs of content at the omens of imminent rain. After dinner, he managed to get out the words and asked after Miguel Arcángel. Plácida helped him to walk towards the room to have his usual siesta. As they crossed the inner patio he looked at the sky, pointed out the formation of fleecy clouds, and sighed as though he wanted to cry. She left him sitting on the bed and went out, leaving the door ajar.

When the force of the wind and the smell of it announced the near approach of a heavy storm, Plácida went out to shut up the hens, to see that everything was secure in the yards (barnyards, poultry yard), and to bring in various things out of the rain. She was doing this when she heard the first clap of thunder. She hurried to the house to get to shelter before the rain began. Her first warning of the death came from the dogs. An owl flying away from the terrace removed any doubts. They were moaning and weeping in the house. She saw the women running. Andrea came to meet her: they had heard Amanda's frenzied cries; when they arrived the master was still twisting about, gasping; Amanda was sprinkling alcohol over his face and neck; she was lifting up his left arm, shaking it. "This is what's hurting him, this is what he's complaining about," she said. No, he was not complaining now.

Plácida flew across to them. Amanda kept on raising the master's left arm. Sensing Plácida near her, she muttered, "There is no escape from death and fate . . ." She let go of the arm, which dropped like a rag. Plácida grabbed her by the shoulders and shook her, asking her what had happened. She just managed to blurt out, "I heard him call out that he was dying, that a pain was running up . . ." An expression of intense grief came over her face. She moved her right hand up over her left arm to the armpit, clutched it with her fingers, and groaned: "That's the way it was, that's the way it was." Then she burst out sobbing and nobody could get any more sense out of her: "There is no escape from death and fate . . ." Plácida pushed her away and she fell to the floor. Several voices suggested that they keep trying to revive him: give him artificial respiration as they do to people rescued from the water, place burning coals on his chest near his heart, prick him with needles or pins, bleed him. Verónica took his pulse, laid her ear to his left side, looked into his eyes, passed a mirror in front of his mouth, decided that it was useless to make him suffer any longer, and said he should not be disturbed but allowed to render his account well. Plácida folded her arms. The dead man's face was constricted by an expression of pain and fright.

How could he end in this way, and not shot in a fight, or struck by lightning, or falling off a wild colt, or gored by a bull, he who was so vigorous, tireless, venturesome, and feared?

It was not long after Plácida and Verónica, having finished dressing the body, opened the doors—the rain still had not ended—when the event which sowed wonder and confusion occurred. Miguel Arcángel arrived at the Big House, followed by his children. They were soaked. Plácida, learning of their arrival, went out to meet them. Miguel Arcángel did not give her time to speak: he hastened to relate the strange way in which he had got the news.

"Matiana told me the moment it happened. I didn't doubt her. We were going through Betania, and since it was starting to rain we thought we'd take shelter somewhere. What God disposes . . . Matiana's house was the nearest. We were walking toward it, and just as we approached the courtyard, about to knock at the door, a flash of lightning blinded us and we were shaken by a clap of thunder at the same time. The lightning had struck there, on the house or the edge of it. I saw Matiana come out panic-stricken, frantic. I didn't even have time to think, 'If you're as brave as they say, how can you be so frightened by a bolt of lightning?' It was as though she'd just been waiting for me. 'Run!' she cried. 'Your father's just had a heart attack. You won't find him alive, but if you run you may get there, or your trying to get there may help him when the Creator asks him for a rendering of his accounts before the soul leaves the body. It will take a long time, certainly.' I didn't doubt her story for a moment. We didn't even get off our horses. We threw our cloaks over our shoulders. We've come racing through the storm and the barking of the dogs, this confirmed what Matiana told us . . ."

Forward in the name of the cross. Let the dead bury their dead. Go forth from this world Christian soul, in the name of God, in the name of the angels and archangels, in the name of the patriarchs and prophets, in the name of the holy apostles, and evangelists, martyrs, confessors, and virgins. And virgins . . . Although I am not worthy, I adjure you, infernal spirits, from Lucifer to the least important . . . On pain of penalties, curses, wrath and indignation, I notify and charge you all, without exception, to keep away from the dead man, not to dare to disturb, tempt, or trouble this dead man until he hands his soul into the keeping of his Redeemer; under pain of penalties growing heavier every moment, I forbid you to trouble, disturb, or tempt this dying man to any sin or fault that lies within your sphere of influence . . .

Miguel Arcángel and his children walked resolutely straight into the room where the corpse was. Plácida neither interfered nor broke out in accusations as she had intended to do.

At this moment the sun appeared, still high in the heavens. It was about four o'clock or half past four in the afternoon.

As the news spread from farm to farm, from house to house, it brought amazement, disappointment, and confusion. Compassion predominated. Throughout the plain the old insults were silenced. Some would think them but they kept them to themselves, choked them back behind their teeth or uttered them secretly among close friends.

Disappointment was great among those who had cherished the hope that Don Epifanio Trujillo's death would be more of a terrible punishment. They had thought he might die at the hands of his children, or in the prolonged suffering caused by a mysterious, horrible disease inflicted by Matiana's agency, or in an attack of rage in front of numerous witnesses. The disappointed included Matiana in their disappointment because she had not fulfilled her ancient ministry of celestial avenger: the flash of lightning nearly fell on her. The way Trujillo had met his death, in his bed, peacefully sleeping his siesta, was the last straw.

Their revenge will be to set it about that he was poisoned by Plácida, of course, or perhaps by Amanda, by some scheme of Jesusito's, Felipe's, or the King of Diamonds' himself. "How strange that no one can really give an account of how it happened, and no one was present when he died." Imagination unleashed, they will not stop short of naming Matiana as the author of the poisoning. "How strange that she should have known it. That's the way her miracles work!" Persistent rain of rumors. "They killed him, they let him die like a dog." Chatter in the kitchens, the fields, on the roads. "Plácida folded her arms."

The sun shone. It was a lovely afternoon.

"Tomorrow, if we're still alive, please God, if it's His will, we'll start sowing the seed, straight away, early in the morning, God helping us."

Part Five — DAMASCO AND GALILEA: THE COMING OF ELECTRICITY

Relics of the past

Relics of the past. Useless things. At one time they had attracted attention. Some of them had caused amazement like the gramophone that Don Epifanio Trujillo bought from some northerners. People made pilgrimages from distant farms to hear it. It was like a huge morning-glory or lily, sky blue with a gilt border, and from it you could hear the voice of Don Porfirio Díaz, as well as the bells and trumpets of April 2 in Puebla, songs of the region sung to the accompaniment of harps, corridos with mariachis, and the beautiful singing of a Sr. Caruso and other singers who trilled and warbled in a wonderful way. While being wound up one day, it gave a bang, jumped, and then refused to make a sound. It was moved around from one place to another, waiting until someone could be found to fix it, and got dented, and ended up in a corner of a barn, rusty and covered with dust. There are people who store in their memories extensive lists of strange and valuable things, together with the people they belong to and the place where they are now or where they were stored away: a barrel-organ that is or was in the López

House on the Tabor farm; a contrivance made of mesquite wood for binding books, which belonged to the Torres and remained among the junk in the chapel at Getsemaní; clocks in need of repair, some with alarms, others with chimes, and among them the clock that had belonged to Don Teódulo and that was a source of wonder because as the hour struck a little bird would come out and say "Cuckoo"; worn out musical instruments, bits of broken china, prints, big statues the worse for wear. It is a pleasant family pastime to call to mind and list those things that were their pride, that bring back the past to them: stories and faces, fallen gradually into complete oblivion. With his good memory Don Epifanio excelled at reminiscences of objects famous on the plain. Matiana is another of those who know, who best remember, and people enjoy hearing her talk about different old treasures on the farms, now relegated to the junk-heap by people and by time.

Some things have a shorter life in people's memories. They never find a way to emerge through the door of memory into conversations; they can find no memory wherein to lodge; and when, by chance, after a long time, they rise to the surface like ghosts appearing unexpectedly, they surprise the beholders. There is even some doubt as to whether they existed in fact or are inventions of the imagination—at least it is amazing how quickly they were forgotten and how quickly time passes. 'There is no cruelty like oblivion,' goes the saying.

It seems a hundred years since the machine was carried off and shots were fired at Matiana; since Herod, Caiaphas, and Nero were killed; since Plácida and Merced were attacked. Even more remote seems the business of the devil flying over the Tierra Santa and the events of the last pastoral competition in Belén. How quickly the commotion they aroused died away! The rains quenched it, and the labors of the seed-time.

I picked up the bones secretly, very early in the morning. That was all the buzzards, crows, and other carrion birds had left. I put them all in a wooden box, Herod, Caiaphas, Nero, and buried them in sight of the shrine, under the mesquite tree there. The Eye of Divine Providence can read my intentions, and seeing the remains of those innocent creatures so near all the time, it won't forget to see that justice is done and the machine, the source of so much trouble, returned to Merced.

The rainy season leaves no time for gossip. Each one is busy with his own affairs, there are no occasions to gather together. In the same way, a forest fire is kept under control by leaving open lanes. The houses are distant from one another; the muddy paths are soon full of weeds. Only used in cases of illness or to get some indispensable assistance from a neighbor.

Nevertheless, it was incredible that something so recent, so disturbing, as the death of the master of the Big House should be so soon forgotten. Sooner than the shooting at Matiana.

It was like the fire that cannot jump across the clearing and catch the trees and grass a few yards away. It was content to reduce its captive to ashes and burn itself out.

It died away in soliloquies, in boring repetition of the same thing among the same people in the house, at night, before going to bed, lulled by the rain, exhausted with weariness. Nothing new added or invented by idle curiosity to stimulate interest.

First, the rumor of his having been poisoned gradually died away for lack of evidence. Different images of the dead man struggled to persist, stored away in corners of the memory, now that the dislike and passions provoked by him in his lifetime had disappeared. They were now thoughts in the mind rather than words.

Even in front of me the shameless old man didn't stop repeating his sayings with their double meanings. 'Don't be frightened, little doves, I'm out looking for pigeons.' 'For the old donkey, a new harness.' 'He who is in love talks even to the stones.' 'What do I want with a hut if I have my jacket here?' 'No one will buy a pig in a poke.' Things like that. He just went on and on. He was worse than Rómulo, who always has a proverb on his lips, and the poor soul had such a good memory. When I discovered he was after Teófila, I'd pick up the knife whenever he came, just in case, and nothing would've stopped me from sticking it in him if he'd tried any of his tricks. When the girls didn't take to him he'd go to the parents and try to buy them, which he often did in the case of poor farmers who were in his debt or those he dazzled with his money. Now he's been judged by God and he's under the ground.

In the end, in spite of all the conjectures born of curiosity and ill-will, nothing worse happened. The expected quarrel between the step-brothers in front of their father's corpse did not take place.

Jesusito deliberately refused to take any risks. He did not mind facing Plácida's rage when she sent him a message to come so that she might tell him what she thought of him and kick him out; he was not afraid of an ambush or of meeting Felipe; he could have come well prepared for either contingency. What he was afraid of was that they might take advantage of his absence to seize his fortress and destroy it, thus cutting off his retreat. Jacob kept a constant watch on him, giving him no time to breathe. In his quarrel with Jacob, the latter had the advantage of him because, in addition to his cunning, power, and money, he had the government at his back, he himself was the government and could justify any persecution. As time went on, Jesusito was quite sure that if Plácida and Felipe had not already joined together against him, they would soon reach an agreement with the King of Diamonds. To put it plainly, the news that his father had died dispelled his hopes of getting back into his favor and persuading him to repudiate the Whirlwind and the Bully. His first impulse was to rush in and assume control of the situation by whatever means he could. But where would he be if he succeeded? The result would be doubtful and there was his father's body to be considered and the crowd there. Brute violence was not his strong point, and he did not consider himself capable of keeping it up, still less if the government, represented by Jacob, came down on him and took away the hiding-place where he was gathering together means to defend himself and, when the time came, to attack. He controlled himself, convinced that the best thing to do would be to watch the behavior of his enemies and find out the intentions they tried to hide or reveal in their actions regarding the dead man. It was a magnificent opportunity to remake his plans at a distance without compromising himself with actions and omissions at the funeral. Maybe this could help him to think of a way to sow discord, to start them quarreling, to form an alliance with one of them. He remembered the advice of his father: 'Even when you see you're winning, be careful.' 'He who leaves his house never finds it as he left it.' 'He who went away, lost, and the newcomer kicked him out.' 'Don't put all your eggs in one basket.' 'Sometimes the duck will swim, sometimes he won't even drink water.' 'To know your limitations is not to give up.' He sent his best spies to Belén.

From the moment the news arrived some time before sunset, Felipe spent the rest of the day and the whole night debating what to do. He had given a lot of thought to the inevitable happening and its consequences. Now that it was here, his doubts returned as to whether to go or not go to the wake and the funeral. He felt he ought to, more on account of what people might say than out of filial feeling or his responsibility as head of the family—rightly or wrongly, he was the eldest of the sons who bore the name. His father had regarded his as his first-born, with the right to succeed him in the Big House, until envy and trickery had intervened. On the other hand, he was afraid he would be driven to an act of violence by some hasty action of Plácida's or one of the busybodies. He was very sure he would be unable to meet the Sneak without laying hands on the criminal; his bile rose at the mere thought of seeing him again face to face. He would put up with anything except that. His stomach turned when he remembered the figure, the high-pitched voice, the mannerisms of Don Jesusito. But if he failed to go, people would say he was a coward or an ingrate, a bad son who was delighted at—who perhaps had wanted and waited for—the death of the old man. Also, he would be renouncing his rights to his heritage. The one wearing the pants there was Plácida, who had assumed command and was taking everything into her own hands. If he went, should he go alone? Or take a strong escort of his boldest men? 'He who owes nothing fears nothing.' Jesús was the guilty one. "I untied Plácida, and although I don't believe in gratitude, because there isn't any in this world, Plácida will at least acknowledge that."

It was almost dark when Felipe learned of the presence of Miguel Arcángel or Jacob in the Big House and the gossip about the miraculous way in which Matiana gave him the news. The Bully did not believe the story. "That old chatterbox, she's a tricky one," he remarked to the man who had told him and to those standing around. He was not afraid of Jacob's doing anything unexpected, either, for although he had stationed his policemen on guard, Jacob had sent him kind messages, wanting to win him over to his side. Felipe, of course, let himself be courted, but he avoided the snares set to catch him, biding his time. 'You're giving me lots of rope, but you won't catch me that way.' 'Time cures the sick man, not the ointment rubbed on him.' But it did not suit him, no, not at all, to expose himself to any violence, much as he liked a fight. Less so now that he needed to keep calm, to keep a firm hold on the pack and play his cards without making a mistake. 'In order to win you must first learn how to lose.' The bed creaked all night. Just as he was falling asleep, still half awake, half asleep, Felipe was startled by a sudden thought. He rose, though it was still dark, and ordered the animals to be fed and then saddled, ready to set out for Belén without delay. Only two trusted men went with him. It was a lovely fresh morning; everything looked as if it had just been washed.

Neither Rómulo nor Merced went to Belén. Nothing could induce them to. Nor Matiana.

Forgive us our debts, and lead us not into temptation. Why go where you're not wanted? I can still hear him and he hasn't finished yet. I don't pay people to like me, and I don't beg favors from my friends. As soon as I knew, I did what I could to help him, but I don't want to have my favors talked about, because a favor that's made public is no favor. These are his very words: 'Don't do a favor for a rich man, you won't get even a thank you.' 'Light the candle before the Saint who deserves it.' 'Not in the house of a rich man nor at the door of a poor man.' 'You'll always get worse than you give.' 'What I've never had, I never miss.' 'They give most who know least.' 'There is no worse misfortune than to serve the worthless.' 'Neither serve the man who was a servant nor command the man who commanded.' Although I don't want to go on listening to him, and I never approved of his shameless sayings. Lead us not into temptation. But he was right in saying, 'The house abandoned is unswept and unpaid for.' And I wouldn't accept even my health from this house, if I were dying. In Belén, 'He who does most is least thanked,' and 'He who has food forgets those who haven't.' Besides, 'I have enough for my needs when I have nothing.' Deliver us from evil. Why should I go, if 'The more I do the more I'll have to do,' and 'What is given without thought is accepted without gratitude.' Amen.

Miguel Arcángel was eager to take the body to the cemetery—that was the name he gave it—which he had just finished in Torres de San Miguel. Plácida flatly refused to hear of this. The burial would be, and was—if not there in the very patio of the Big House, then there on the slope in front of the terrace, where the construction of a graveyard would be begun tomorrow, with her father's grave in the center. Belén ought to have its own graveyard.

At night, late at night, the sharecroppers and farm laborers from the distant farms in the hills arrived at the Big House. They sang "Praised be to God" and an old, mournful hymn beginning: "From cruel death . . ." High, shrill voices alternated with the deep, rough voices of primitive farmhands.

Miguel Arcángel had a lot of cinnamon, coffee, and good aguardiente brought.

Well after midnight, Plácida went up to Miguel Arcángel, alias Jacob, alias the King of Diamonds, and said bluntly, " 'It's best to take the bull by the horns." She was not trying to pick a quarrel, she said, but he would find himself in trouble, worse trouble than Jesús and Felipe could give him, if, first, he did not leave her in peace and liberty to look to her own interests in her own way; second, if, as authority and friend, he did not punish Jesús for his outrageous crime, especially for the injury he had done her; and last, if he went on taking people away from her farms to give them a better salary at Torres de San Miguel. Jacob gave her a soft answer, he offered to work in harmony with her.

At the wake, as later at the funeral, there were more of the Gallos' people than the Trujillos'. There were not as many present, if only out of curiosity, as might have been expected. Neighbors sent excuses: that they had everything ready to start sowing that day, that they would come later to express their sympathy.

Don Felipe's arrival surprised nobody. Abruptly he went over to the corpse and stood looking at it for a long time; he did not cross himself, nor kneel down. He found a seat near the bed and stayed there for hours and hours without stirring, without talking to anyone or answering those who came up to him. It was obvious that every nerve was tensed, that his eyes were watchful; he was making an effort to control himself. From time to time he would get up, walk over to the body, drive off the flies, and return to his seat. Nearly the whole morning went by before Plácida or Jacob went near him.

Jacob took the initiative; he told him that they needed to decide the funeral details. Felipe followed him perforce. Plácida joined them and the three went into the parlor, where they remained with the door shut for ages. It was midday. The few people present at that time had huddled together in the kitchen. Those who tried to see what was going on gave no signs of getting excited about it.

The swarm of flies around the body increased in number.

At two o'clock they arrived with the coffin. The corpse was horribly swollen. It was difficult to get it in.

At three they took it up and carried it to the slope on the boundary. Again they sang "Praised be . . ." and "From cruel death . . ." There were no firecrackers, no drums, no pipes.

Neither Felipe nor Jacob returned to the Big House. As soon as the funeral was over they went straight back to their respective houses.

When they took the dead man out of his bed, and when, on their return from the improvised graveyard, they saw it empty, the mattress spoiled, useless, sagging, stained, left there in the middle of the room, there were many who thought of the time when that famous, wide brass bedstead in which Don Epifanio had slept, had begotten many of his children, and had finally died, would be taken to pieces and stored away; of the time when it would be thrown on the heap of useless things, gradually forgotten, lost.

Not forgotten for a single moment

Not forgotten for a single moment was the forecast made by Jacob of the day and even the hour when the first storm would break. That was one thing. Another—and this was even less likely to be forgotten because it was more miraculous—was Matiana's vision of the almost sudden death of Don Epifanio Trujillo. With every passing day the impression made on the region by these events grew deeper and each man added something from his own imagination.

Just the opposite happened in the case of the recent disturbances, which, appealing only to the farmers' desire for sensation, had been pushed rapidly into the background: the flying around of the devil— already a distant memory—that announced the arrival of the King of Diamonds; the theft of the machine; the killing of the dogs; the shots fired at Matiana; the quarrel of the bastards; the Towers of Babel, as the tall buildings Jacob was putting up on his farm began to be called—and this name stuck; the heart attack that brought death to Don Epifanio; his rendering of his account, and his wake and burial. Probably, when the rainy season is over, and this world of stories emerges again, story transformed into legend, the first dazzling glow of Matiana's vision and Jacob's prediction will lose their luster in the villagers' imagination, since this is what usually happens, though it seems hardly conceivable. The forecast of a good season was fulfilled more and more as time went on. People's amazement grew when they saw that the earth, carted with so much toil from the hill, was not washed away by the rain but was held in by the palings and abutments constructed so quickly by the Gallos. And by St. Anthony's day the ditches and canals were full, a sight never seen before, one which, like the towers, changed the face of the plain, now broken by big pools that shone like pieces of mirror strewn over the cornfields. Jacob at once set to making more water depositories. Another surprise, a big one, was the marvelous yield of the cornfields treated with fertilizer and sown with good seed compared with the chronic sickliness of the others; the former were so sturdy that they withstood the June hailstorms, which also seemed miraculous.

Surprise followed surprise. It was learned that a kind of huge needle reaching to the top of the highest silo was a lightning rod, the first this side of Cardos. And explanations were being offered about how and when this apparatus was used. And the word "Progress" was repeated, a word that had begun to be forgotten when the rains came, since if the earth does not always refuse to yield, memory does sometimes fail, with so much worry about what kind of a year it will be and whether it will bring good or bad luck.

Progress! Like when petroleum began to take the place of the sticks of pitch pine and the wax and tallow candles used on the farms for light. When this dirty, smelly liquid made its first appearance. When they brought lamps and wicks and other things that made the people afraid since they believed they were works of the devil. And that was just what they turned out to be, because there were so many fires and bad accidents, like what happened to the farm at La Canana where a drum of petroleum exploded and burned the house down, killing several people and injuring a lot of others. For years they couldn't talk about anything else, just as now they talk of the evils this electricity will bring, together with the lightning rods, the magnetic needles, the mills for grinding corn, and the other inventions. I was forgetting the famous airplanes and that instrument they say Miguel Arcángel has to predict rain, hail, and heat, if he really has it. I don't deny or confirm it and I forgot to ask him on one of the few times I saw him again. Although I'm inclined to think it's probably a kind of gift like that of a prophetess, something like mine when the thunderbolt hit and I knew for sure that Epifanio's days had ended. I didn't see him with my eyes, the way all the gossips in the plain declare. What they don't know they make up. And there wasn't any voice except that of the thunder to reveal it to me. Thunder and lightning at the same time, God help us! I was struck blind and dumb but I was absolutely certain that God, our Lord, was at that moment performing His function as Just Judge of the man who'd stirred up so much trouble—the old stallion with his clever use of sayings was answering the accusations of Satan in the presence of his Guardian Angel, who was there to help him or to make it worse with his testimony, who knows which? At that moment I sensed the arrival of Miguel Arcángel. I knew Providence had sent him so I could give him the news. As I did so, the whole mountain of resentment built up over the years against the old robber was swept away at a stroke, dissolved in a sea of pity that made me say all the prayers I've learned by heart for these occasions, as well as my most powerful prayers to ward off the infernal powers. That was all. Everything else they've made out of it is pure imagination, they just enjoy making up stories. Like all the gossip, like all this commotion about electricity. I've seen many people struck by lightning. Usually they're unrecognizable, shriveled up, burned to cinders. They're all agog to know what happens to me, and when they can't understand it they put it down to witchcraft when inspiration is a lot more common. That's all my magic is. To be able to feel far-off vibrations at the right time, and understand them and translate their meaning. To believe without wanting or having to see the invisible. To touch or hear the powers of the next world when they come and issue their commands. To respect them blindly and serve as their blind instrument. That's

As miserly as only she could be. There would not even have been water to drink at the wake if Miguel Arcángel had not brought the liquor. When the few people who came to Belén started arriving, Plácida hastily locked up everything she could. Of the dead man's clothes she did not give away—as is customary here—even the rags that would have been useful to the poor and to the farmhands. Not a scrap of anything. Not even to the women who helped her lay out the body did she give the most insignificant gift. She tried to bargain with the carpenter from Nazaret who made the coffin, and shouted insults at him because she thought the price was too high. The candles burning beside the body were brought by compassionate neighbors. What a heartless woman!

Once she was absolute mistress of the place, she cleared her throat and, as they say, stroked her moustache, tightened her belt, settled herself in the saddle, put her feet in the stirrups, tied her hat under her chin, gathered up the reins, raised her whip, dug in her spurs, gave a shout, and then, as they say, let herself go and was off like a shot. Who is brave enough to stand up to her? What a he-man of a woman!

Her first action was to send Doña Amandita away. "Go on, get out, go and find that son of yours. You can take your rags with you, but not another thing. Get them together right now and get out of my sight. Let's see if that scum'll receive you and look after you— and don't let me get started, you devil. Don't make me angry by pretending to be stupid, as though you couldn't hear or understand, just standing there like a stick." Verónica, Cleofas, Andrea, and Salomé intervened, trying to make the Whirlwind change her mind. They only succeeded in making her more bitter and provoking her further. She warned them not to meddle in what did not concern them unless they wanted to be driven away from the farm also. She yelled the same warning, with a string of insults, at those who begged her to leave the poor, inoffensive mistress of her father alone. Seeing that Plácida had turned into a scorpion, the pious women set about getting Doña Amandita's rags together, led her out of the Big House, and looked for some kind man to take her to Don Jesusito.

Like a lost soul, the faithful mistress let herself be led away, muttering between her teeth, as though it were an obsession: "There is no escape..." What an unfeeling woman!

The Whirlwind gathered together her younger stepbrothers, who had been hanging round the Big House, and put them in their place, told them where they stood, showed them the whip hand. From henceforth, they were told, she would be the one to hold the reins, to wield the whip. Anyone who did not like it could open the gate and get out before anything worse happened to him. She would not put up with lazy men or traitors. They knew her and knew that she never talked for the sake of talking; they knew what to expect from her. For those who behaved, bread; for the others, a stick. She was her father's sole heiress, by law.

By traitors she meant those who cast doubt on her right to succeed, or who joined or conspired with anyone in trying to dispute her rights. They should be particularly careful not to have anything whatsoever to do with the Sneak, so that they would not have to complain afterwards of any misfortune that might befall them. She would watch closely to see which were true Trujillos who deserved to receive a share of the inheritance, not by right but out of her gracious generosity. The first thing they had to do was to support their new mistress and help her rescue the lands that were in the power of trespassers who had no right whatsoever to them. Similar warnings had been directed to debtors, sharecroppers, farmhands, and neighbors all over the plain. Plácida had ordered them to be conveyed to all so that nobody afterwards might plead ignorance in making bargains with false pretenders, or in not breaking off all relations with the Sneak, his followers, accomplices, or abettors. The Whirlwind would not only keep a tight hold on her property but also make her hard hand felt by those who befriended her enemies and by those who did not recognize her immediately and give her her due as the only mistress of the domains that belonged to the late Epifanio. What a wildcat she was!

Naturally she abolished the old custom of inviting all those who passed the Big House to a meal. She would not give a taco or even a drink of water to those who came to the novena of rosaries for the deceased and those who came from far away to express their sympathy. With the rations drastically reduced, the servants at Belén went hungry. What a cruel, heartless woman!

And she never stopped from sunrise to sunset. She was like Don Epifanio in his active days. She kept an eye on everything, weighed and measured everything. Nothing escaped her notice, the badly milked cow, the hen badly placed on the nest, the furrows covered with weeds, broken tools. She went around giving out scoldings, curses, blows; making a fuss over trifles; inspiring fear as her eagle eye noted the smallest bit of carelessness. She forgave neither grownups nor children. She could not bear to see anyone doing nothing. She gave no one any rest. An unfeeling, cold-hearted woman!

I wonder where that shell can be, the one my grandfather used to keep on the suitcase by the bed where he slept. I wonder what could have happened to it. It was a big shell and looked as though it were made of marble, the inside pink, very soft to touch, like the flesh of those blond ladies must be, or to put it plainly, the flesh of those gringas that are talked about so much by those who've been in the north. I used to like to feel the inside of it, poking my fingers in when my grandfather wasn't looking so he wouldn't ask me why I was tempted to touch the inside of the shell so much. They used to say you could hear the roaring of the sea by holding the shell up to your ear. My grandfather would spend ages listening to it. Then he'd explain to me what the sea was. I could place the shell up to my ear without fear of a scolding. You could hear a noise just like the one you hear from the top of the bank when the river way below it is swollen in the rainy season, or like the wind inside the wells when there's a strong breeze. I don't know what madness would come over me, what strange fascination would make me tremble when I took it in my hands and put it up to my ear. I could feel it beating like my heart, or like a frightened animal, one of those we boys used to grab hold of: hares, squirrels, rabbits. My grandfather was very fond of his shell. It was really a curiosity rather rare in the Tierra Santa. I don't remember the story of how it came into my grandfather's hands. When he died I never saw the shell again. It looked like a big flower made of wax. I also thought it looked something like Florentina's ears. What thoughts you have when you're young! It must have been moved around until it got lost, until it was taken by one of the many people who wanted to have it. Nobody knows anything about it. I'd like to find it, to have it near my bed, to listen to it and feel it, trying to discover, to guess, all kinds of things, like the time I even wanted to break it and find what was inside it, in the heart of it, where my fingers couldn't reach, they'd slip no matter how hard I tried to get them in. What a pretty shell it was! I'd make up for my frustration by making Tocayo go around in spirals, although I couldn't find any connection between the dancing of my chestnut horse and the spiral shell that looked like flesh.

Plácida's nervous disorder got worse again because of her fanatical attitude toward sex.

During her father's lifetime this had been the source of great acrimony between them and a source of constant suffering for the girl. The old man took a delight in tormenting her with vulgar sayings and unbridled talk, not because he wanted to shock her, but because her exaggerated prudery, her sometimes really alarming reactions when confronted with natural processes, made him furious. He could not understand how any of his offspring could suffer from this kind of abnormality, and he proposed to cure the girl of it.

From her earliest infancy she had given evidence of an instinctive repugnance for anything to do with sex. She had to be raised on a diet of atole, because a few weeks after she was born she refused her mother's breast and there was no way of getting her to suck. She would cry, twist away, and shut her mouth, and when forced to swallow she would vomit and have diarrhea. The cruel streak in her nature manifested itself very early. The baby would claw and bite her mother, her brothers; when her father appeared the child would burst out crying and hit out at him with hands and feet. She actually kicked and scratched him when she got bigger. She could not bear to see her father touch her mother or to see a man and woman holding hands. After sobbing and shouting insults and threats with a stone or stick in her hand, she began to have hysterical fainting spells. Her frenzy at the sight of any kind of mating became obsessive. She took to killing flies when she saw them together; she would strike and often kill cocks with hens or dogs when they mounted the females; risking grave injury, she would attack goats, bulls, horses, donkeys in heat. It would drive her mad to see men's and women's clothing stretched out side by side in the sun to dry; in fits of rage she would tear them to pieces. She felt an uncontrollable urge to lash out at pregnant women and animals.

Epifanio Trujillo hastily took her to a foster mother. Moved from farm to farm, from foster mother to foster mother, Plácida merely got worse and worse. Trujillo thought of disowning her definitely as a daughter and even as a niece, but the strong, aggressive, tireless character of the girl won him over, the only flaw being her maniacal prudery, utterly out of place in the polygamist's environment. Even with her stepbrothers—supreme test of the patriarchal regime— Plácida was an efficient support except when she noticed signs of original sin in them. Then she would set upon them. Epifanio postponed for the time being either repudiating or giving formal baptism to his fanatical daughter.

The measures Trujillo took to cure Plácida's state of frenzy at the sight of real or apparent lust merely aggravated the situation. Advice, mockery, scolding, moving her to another house, forcing her to mix with other people, deliberate demonstrations of the processes of nature—all provoked greater crises. No, she would not agree that the force of amorous attraction was natural. This was not from spiritual purity, either: it was simple physical repugnance, a mysterious product of heredity.

Plácida was the daughter of Abigail, a very jealous, hot-blooded woman who kept Trujillo on a string, at one moment driving him mad, the next fulfilling his every wish. They goaded each other to fury. Abigail hated her daughter, but when Epifanio took her away she was beside herself with rage and stopped at nothing. Finally, seeing that she was getting nowhere, she left the plain and no one ever knew where she went, although there were rumors going around that she had taken to the life of the streets and had been seen in haunts of vice all along the gringo border—Tijuana, Mexicali, Ciudad Juárez—where she was famous for her outrageous behavior. Epifanio clung to his sayings: 'Don't try to retrieve a woman who leaves, or drive her away if she wants to stay.' 'As fast as one leaves another arrives.' 'Repay scorn with forgetfulness.' 'Better to love a dog than an ungrateful woman.' 'An unanswered letter and a runaway wife are best forgotten.' But the truth is that he still wanted her for a long time, the more so because rumors, true or false, of her conquests kept arriving. Perhaps on account of this secret desire, which grew to fever pitch, Epifanio never cast off Plácida, although for the same reason, thinking of her as her mother's daughter, he felt frantic impulses to crush her. Her frigid temperament, so different from that of her mother, protected her from her father's viciousness. Epifanio found that Plácida had inherited only her mother's tenacity in carrying out difficult tasks and her fury when she was jealous.

Plácida's puberty was late in coming and had an exceedingly disturbing effect on both her body and her mind. Her cruelty was accentuated on certain days. They even feared she had gone mad, stark, staring mad. She would destroy whatever she came across, or else shut herself in and refuse to see anyone or eat anything, complaining of intense, stabbing pains in her head and all over her body; she said horrible shapes danced in front of her eyes, which felt as if they were ready to pop out of her head; she had dreadful cramps in her stomach and kept getting sick and vomiting. Amanda, at whose house she was then living, helped her, managed to calm her in some of her attacks, showered her with household remedies based on herbs and suggestions, but was powerless to overcome the loathing Plácida felt for herself when she saw herself bleeding. The young girl actually did herself physical harm, scratching her face and arms, whipping herself with huisaches, beating her head against walls. The repetition of her period made her feel humiliated and her self-loathing increased. Believing that she was suffering from an illness that could not be cured and that she was nothing more than putrifying flesh, already putrescent, she wanted to die, to let herself die.

She broke out in a bilious fever; the whites of her eyes turned yellow and were covered with spots, as was her skin, which was ashen pale. She grew thinner and thinner. In spite of the fact that she had never put herself out to win people's good will, they came bringing her remedies from all the farms. Matiana, who had not yet broken completely with the Trujillos, brought her laxative pills and said she should drink water in which cornsilk had been steeped. ("That's a good joke," Epifanio would say. "They prescribe the same thing for her chastity as for my overindulgence, my chronic bladder trouble.") Matiana showered charms on her, and this confirmed the opinion of many that Plácida was bewitched.

Her fright at seeing the whites of her eyes yellow, her skin dry and itching all over, aroused in the girl a strong desire to live. This did not escape her father's notice and it relieved his anxiety, in spite of the fact that Plácida would not admit it and begged them to let her die. She recovered rapidly.

Epifanio had also noticed that his daughter enjoyed holding the whip and owning things; on the other hand, from his experience with his cattle he knew that certain diseases were cured by hard work, work that filled every minute. Plácida's symptoms were similar. He flattered her by making her absolute manager, and later owner, of the forest area he was working at the top of the Sierra de Cardos. Her enthusiasm and ambition, revealed by the glint in her eyes and the tightening of the muscles of her face, pleased her father, as did the bold alacrity with which she accepted the condition that it would mean going to live on the mountain, and the explanation that it would be rough work in which she herself would have to be both woodcutter and hunter, since there were many wild beasts there.

No sooner said than done. Barely recovered from her illness, the girl of fifteen marched off to try her fortune. Epifanio had calculated the beneficial effect on Plácida's disturbed spirit of the character and way of living of the people she would live with in her mountain exile: a serene, vigorous old man, Don Elías, and his three daughters, born and brought up in the mountain, old maids with no nonsense about them, even-tempered and hard-working.

Once he had taken her up there, he seemed to have forgotten her. He did not visit her for a year but was regularly informed that his plan was being carried out to the letter and that his absence and the absence of everything and everyone connected with the Trujillos were doing her good.

Then he decided to go one step further and take Felipe and Jesús up to the mountain with Plácida. He took them himself, and could see at once the vigorous simplicity and easy skill with which the girl assumed command over her stepbrothers, and how they, from the beginning, gave evidence of respecting her, submitting to her authority with good grace. The experiment was so satisfactory that he decided to have Plácida baptized and made legitimate immediately. This was done after the usual difficulties with the parish priest at Clamores, who always called down thunder and lightning on his head for his brazen lasciviousness, his licentious way of living, so un-Christian and so scandalous, more fitting for the worst of pagans; but especially for his wicked, unheard-of delay in bringing to be baptized the offspring of his unbridled lust. ("Ah, what a narrow-minded, fanatical priest!" the unrepentant sinner would mutter. "He just can't see things as they really are, as nature has made them. He hasn't got the slightest understanding of the meaning of crossing strains or grafting on new shoots to improve the stock. I say, 'Keep away from priests and the sun.' 'Hear them say Mass when you can, then leave them alone.' 'What do you want with angels when God is so great?' 'I never buy onions, so as not to have to carry the stalks.' 'Don't be like the salt that loses its savor.' 'If you do it at all, go the whole hog.' 'What are bells for if you're afraid of their pealing?' ")

The next step was to get somebody to propose to Plácida. Epifanio, of his own accord, was coming around to the opinion that this would not only provide the cure for the girl's emotional disorder—an opinion confirmed by the repeated advice of Amanda, Matiana, and many others worried about her abnormality—but would also be a means of testing her attachment to the family. His first choice was a strong young man, bold, half savage, who broke in the wild steers on the Galilea farms. Plácida rejected him scornfully, and when the young man persisted, she nearly split his head open with an axe, and he ran away in terror. When Epifanio heard this he could hardly stop laughing. That suitor was followed, weeks later, by a citified young man who had a shop and also acted as a barber in the town of Clamores. The string of insults Plácida hurled at him in her fury was enough for him. She had acted as though the devil in person had arrived to carry her off.

As a result, Epifanio installed her in the Big House with full domestic powers, and even he himself began to fall under the growing tyranny of his strong-minded daughter. He began to watch his words and actions in front of Plácida; but, on the other hand, he thought—as he had when she was a child—that the morbid suscepti- bility of his daughter would be lessened if she got used to his sayings. But he found that her hysterical prudishness, far from yielding to time or to the tonic of separation and work in the mountains, hardened her intolerance. Like the sternest mother or teacher in the face of obscenity, Plácida took harsh measures to repress the in- corrigible lasciviousness of her father. The suffering and disgust of the celibate girl grew to unbearable, tragic proportions when Epi- fanio made free with women or uttered lewd sayings from his in- exhaustible supply. 'Take a woman when you can, for if you don't you're not a man.' 'Give a woman what she wants—and you know what that is.' 'The best broth comes from the oldest hen.' Endless quarrels between father and daughter. Strained relations. Soon Epi- fanio began to act like a child caught red-handed; he would keep watch so as not to be seen or heard by Plácida; he avoided arguments with her.

Being mistress of the house completed the work of the mountains. This was when Jesusito got his own back by bestowing on her the nicknames the Whirlwind, the Bitch, the Sergeant Major, the Boss.

The worst, most unforgettable part of the outrage perpetrated by the Sneak was that the men hauled Plácida about and manhandled her in order to tie her up. Not for one second had the images and horrible sensations accompanying that indignity been blotted out of her mind. Plácida felt that her honor had been stained. The shock was worse than when she felt the onset of puberty. She would sooner have died; she could have killed her assailants. The horror of re- membering the affront, of not being able to forget it either awake or asleep, brought her back to the frenzy with which, axe in hand, she hardened her body in the mountains by cutting down trees and mutilating them. If only she could get revenge on the brutes whose coarse hands bruised her body, which had never before been touched by a male hand! Physical loathing of lust! Unconquerable aversion to sensuality!

Her revulsion against her father's nakedness when he died made Plácida leave to Verónica the undressing of the corpse and the putting on of the underwear and trousers he would be buried in. Plácida only helped put on his coat and shoes. Pretending to be busy with other tasks, she had hard work to control herself when, from the sounds, she could picture in her mind's eye the grim task Verónica was performing a few yards behind her. And what disturbed her most was the knowledge that at the sight of the naked body under her hands, Verónica was reconstructing the lusty story of the dead man's life; her sighs, her heavy breathing bore witness to it. Plácida had an impulse to turn around, leap at her, scratch her, hurl insults at her for her wicked memories. The bellowing of the stud bull and the braying of the stud burros, the rain pouring down from the sky and beating violently upon the earth to soak and fertilize it— these sounds re-echoed in her brain, making her head and stomach spin around and around until she was breathless. In her desperation and confusion, the vengeful thought entered her mind that she would have the corpse mutilated so that it might be buried free from its shame.

Chastity and cruelty possessed her, sweeping away any recognition of the joy of living life to the full, a joy which the death of the master had thrown into relief, and retaining only pictures of the unending debauchery which had been his life. The pitiless dismissal of Doña Amandita sprang from rancor against her son, but at bottom the most powerful motive was the store of memories of her prolonged amatory relationship, which had made Plácida suffer for years and years. It infuriated Plácida to remember the sayings her father would apply to his old concubine: 'She's just a bag of bones.' 'A royal road and an old love never stop rolling along.' What she had had to suffer from this indecency! Now she could get her own back by commanding chastity and suffering for those who had fallen into her power. She would watch for the first sign of desire in the eyes of men and women; she would dog their footsteps as they sought opportunities and sheltered places, at night, in the early morning, at midday, in corners, in ditches, behind walls, in the cornfields, by the springs and washing pools where the men waited for them; she would check pitilessly, cruelly, the birth of desire in children, its flaming in adolescents, its urgency in maturity, its flickering embers in the old. Neither relationship nor friendship, neither interest nor obligation, would prevent her from tearing out, extirpating from her domain, the vicious example of her father. She would impose the law of chastity whatever the cost.

She forbade the men and women, under pain of dismissal, to walk together outside of the houses; men were not to appear in white cotton pants, nor were women to go out without a rebozo; children were not to walk about naked; no one was to bathe in the stream. Married servants were sent away from the Big House and the bulls were separated from the cows. She chose unmated mares for her service. The law of chastity is the general law of work without rest until energy is exhausted, as she had learned from personal experience. Idleness, which allows time for wrong thoughts, is the mother of all vice. Work and whip. In this way there would not be so many wretched births, so much rebellion, so many debts.

Early in the morning she was up and out on her rounds, going into the houses, asking detailed questions, divining intentions, inspecting things, scolding, meting out threats, insults, blows. She never stopped all day long. And even at night she would pounce unexpectedly, here and there, catching them by surprise with her stubborn vigilance.

Oh, if only it would rain regularly the way it's doing now. Then the land would change and the nature of the men would surely change too, since they're bound to reflect the place where they live. Those here are unsociable, harsh, insensitive, inconsiderate toward the women, because that's the way of the land. And the land is like that because that's the nature of the sky above it: inconsiderate, fickle, barely dampening a few patches and then the rain stops. Or when it rains hard it just washes away the top layer of soil, leaving the bare clay and the huisaches, or hail destroys the cornfields. Or rather the men are like the sky and the women like the land. Oh, if the sky of the plain would change, it would bring a change to the men and the poor women of the plain here. The women are merely growing sadder and sadder, the way I am, like blighted cornfields when the drought comes early. I said this to Rómulo last night and he didn't like it. I said it because of the hopes raised by the season, who knows whether it's because of the death of that filthy old pig or because Miguel Arcángel has proved a good prophet. The fact is that by some miracle the season has been good up to now. It's a pleasure to look at the countryside and see the ears of corn forming in the cornfields, everything greener than it's been for years, the cattle fat, the cheese-racks in the houses filling with cheeses. Then in August the rain will probably stop and everything will go to the devil as it always does. In spite of the danger, I'm delighted with the change in the skies. I don't know what's happening to me at my age. It's as though a weight had dropped from my shoulders. I haven't done anything since the death of that pig toward getting the machine back, but my heart tells me I'll soon have it, I don't know how. I'm sure of it. I haven't told Rómulo this, so he won't say afterward that he knew. Poor Rómulo, so good and so helpless! Rómulo won't change even with the change in the skies, unless by a miracle of the machine when they give it back to us and by the intercessions of my daughter, Teófila. He's placing high hopes in the promises of Miguel Arcángel. Last night I said to him, "What's the use if you don't make an effort yourself?" He didn't like my saying that, either. He consoles himself with building castles in the air, poor man!

Stories began circulating that Don Epifanio Trujillo's soul was wandering around in torment, without rest, through the scenes of his misdeeds—the inevitable tales of his appearances, of his talking to this one and that one and the other, even of what they said he said to them. Those who believe that 'The sayings of the old are pearls of wisdom' are reminded as though subconsciously, of the saying 'To appear is not to come to life.'

In the damp evenings, when the cornfields can be heard growing, the song sounds:

> Doves flying and flying
> In the sky above,
> I will pay you for bringing
> News of my true love.

The rumor started that the machine of the late Teófila was working miracles. Vague at first, it began to gain weight and supporters. Proverbs were heard again, adapted to the situation: 'I think the furrow is ready for the seed.' 'I don't want God to give me things but to show me where I can get them.' 'I like black more than I fear the dead man.' 'Although what they're saying isn't true, it's enough that they say it.'

The song, "The clouds move across the sky, of that there is no doubt" is heard no more.

The news spread that by September 15, for sure, there will be electric lights and a mill for grinding corn, and that they will get water out of the wells by electricity in Jerusalén. The King of Diamonds and his boys are just finishing setting up some contraptions, enormous things, brought on muleback from the Capital. People are saying: 'He who wanders in the mountains will fall over the cliff.' 'The pitcher goes once too often to the well.'

At night the song is heard:

> Prison stairway,
> Some descending, some mounting,
> Step by step,
> To render their accounting . . .

The latest rumors are that it is true, yes, it is now known for a fact, that Jacob Gallo found the treasure that belonged to the Garabitos, and that is why he does so much for Rómulo and Merced. But the best thing is that Jacob has definitely found mines—how lucky he is!—and has already reported this to the authorties.

'Like the violin of Contla: sounding in season and out.' A falsetto voice, muffled by the rain:

> The cock is stirring,
> He is singing in the middle of the tree . . .

It was time to take the next step.

Some of the things were credible

Some of the things that they declared Trujillo's ghost said to them were credible, others were not.

The fact is that in spite of all the work to be done at the height of the rainy season, the master of the Big House, as if he had come to life again—which God forbid!—once more held sway over the people, instilling fear in all. In his time he was as clever and as insatiable as a coyote, and now, on the tongues of big and small, he again ranges through the length and breadth of the plain; there is no heart and no corner where he does not penetrate, with frightful lamentations, according to some, or with his typical shouts of laughter and ribald sayings, according to others. At night, in farmhouse after farmhouse, on the paths, on the roads, the people shudder at the dead man's lamentations and guffaws. And there is not a soul who can get up the courage after dark to pass near the hill where he lies buried. It is thought to have been converted into the site of a sinister witches' sabbath—hooting of owls, howling of coyotes, bellowing and braying from the other world; shadows, lights, terrors.

294

He haunts the Big House, too, however furious Plácida becomes; she foams at the mouth when anyone dares to ask her about it. Not one or two, but many, bear witness that they have seen the dead man walking about the terrace, peering into the window of the parlor, crossing the patio, sitting down by the fire in the kitchen.

People believe that Plácida has definitely seen him, although she pretends she has not, so as not to show signs of weakness or fear, which might make her lose people's respect. The general opinion is that it was the dead man who ordered her to put an end to every vestige of immorality, because until that is done his soul will continue to wander and find no rest, as a punishment for the great turmoil and scandals he caused in those lands. That is the reason for her fanatical sternness: her father's remorse, which she is attempting, cruelly, to assuage.

However, 'The dead to their tombs and the living to their fun.' How can Plácida dam up the stream of life? This year more girls have run off and fewer have got married. This year there are more people breaking out into song at night; more love songs are heard; guitars, violins, accordions, and other musical instruments have appeared again. This year there have been more dances, more drinking, gaming, and even willing women. The money coming from the Towers of Babel and the hopes of a good harvest have raised people's spirits. They are getting ready for magnificent rodeos and horse races, and they are all agog to go see the opening, on September 15, of the electric light plant they have heard so much about. The people leave their work to go and stare with curiosity as the machinery and wires that will make the contraption work are put in place, and they come back full of it all. They also talk of the ingenious system of canals—which many try to imitate on their farms—that avoids the waste of even a drop of water, carrying it all to a cistern that will give enough pure rain water all through the dry season; there will be no need to lug it up from the spring, and no fear that this will dry up. There will not even be any need for that hard trip to the ravine to wash clothes when the stream stops running. What a deep one the King of Diamonds is!

Nevertheless, when night falls and they are alone in the dark farmhouses, fear of the ghost of Don Epifanio descends on all. In case he should make his appearance, in case they should hear his lamentations or cackling laughter in the air, and in case he might want (they hoped he might!) to reveal the hiding place of some treasure that is on his conscience and that keeps him from resting, it has become the general custom to learn by heart the words indispensable for having any dealings with souls in trouble.

"In God's name I beg you, tell me whether you are of this world or the next."

Then they will cease to hear the lamentations and the dead man will reply.

Fellow Christian, as you value your life and for the sake of the Precious Blood of the Eye of Providence and the Powerful Hand, go to my daughter Plácida and tell her, urge her or any of my other sons or daughters, even the one who denied me, denied the blood-tie and forsook my name, the son I named Miguel Arcángel, which he changed to Jacob, as you know, tell them to hand over at once the machine that belonged to the blessed Teófila. Tell them that because of this I'm suffering countless torments, and for the same reason I'm without Teófila's intercessions, which would have helped me at the time of my death and now afterward. Tell them that God allows me to wander in torment on earth until they take pity on my suffering. Tell Plácida, as you value your life, that it's true that Miguel Arcángel or Jacob, whichever you find it easier to call him, gave me money to pay for giving back the machine, thinking I had it. And tell her not to be ungrateful, not to turn a deaf ear, not to refuse to listen. I've tried many times to talk to her, to tell her the things I've promised to do and the restitutions and amends she has to make so I can rest in peace. If she still won't listen, keep them in mind so you can repeat them to her later. She must go on foot to the Sanctuary of the Lord of Plateros; she must keep a lamp burning in the Shrine of the Eye of Providence, taking care that it never goes out; she must buy a gross of big wax candles for the Dolorosa of Clamores, and give the alms that are proper. Tell her not to be miserly, since after all that's why I left plenty of money and here it's just increasing my suffering. Don't forget these things. Also tell Plácida to come to terms with all those who had dealings with me— I cheated them all, even when I didn't rob them outright—so that my accounts can be settled by mutual agreement. Tell her, too, that driving away Amandita was an atrocious thing, and although I wasn't blamed for it and am not being punished for it, it has caused me great sorrow. Another day, if you carry out these commands, I'll come back and tell you other ways I want to make amends. Then I'll tell you the reward that will be given you for the favor you're doing me. All I can tell you now is that you won't be sorry for helping me, and if you don't, you'll regret it in this life and the next. Tell her, too, not to be cruel, that her cruelty makes my sufferings worse, that it doesn't do her any good, it does just the opposite, it's being written down against her, and her reckoning when her time comes will be terrible and just. You'll find out if you take care of this task that God has given me permission to entrust to you. But if you don't do it, look out for the consequences. I'm going now, my remorse drives me away, I wander and wander around what used to be mine, what I didn't know how to use properly. Oh, what a monstrous sinner I am, condemned to revisit the very scenes of my sins! Oh, how I wasted my life in false pleasures, in sheer folly! My time is up. I'm not allowed to speak any longer. Don't forget my requests. Remember my suffering. Go with God, fellow Christian!

It was Don Epifanio himself. There was no doubt in their minds. His very voice, although weaker. And he was more emaciated, his eyes sunken and tearful, his whole body wasting away as though it were made of turbid mist.

There was an outbreak of bilious colds.

Afraid to go to Plácida or the other Trujillos with the message, those who said they had received it went to Matiana to ask her advice, and begged her to charm away the dangerous errand as well as the presence of the ghost.

Madre Matiana invariably sent them off to carry out the commands, explaining to them that it was impossible to lay the ghosts of those in torment.

No, they had not been dreaming, they were awake when the ghost spoke to them.

Yet the mornings dawned radiantly clear, with all the glories of the rainy season. The sun with its face well-washed. The growing cornfields. The tiny hairs springing from the ears and shining golden in the summer light, with drops of water trembling on them from the rain during the night. Birds singing with all the force of lungs swollen with delight. Animals in heat, calves clinging to udders, hurrying ants. The joyful chorus of the birds, awake early: mockingbirds, woodpeckers, cardinals, thrushes, sparrows, pigeons, warblers, finches, quail, killdeer, doves, all joining their songs with the crowing of the cocks and the clucking of the hens, the bellowing of the cows, bulls, and calves, the strident braying, the joyful barking and neighing. Nevertheless, in the silence of the night, the ritual words came back to mind, just in case:

"In God's name I beg you, tell me whether you are of this world or the next."

Christian woman, know me by my raucous laughter. I am the late Epifanio Trujillo, who used to roar with laughter at the evil thoughts that came into my head all the time. God has given me leave to come and warn you that you and your family aren't walking in the straight and narrow path. You're like a twisted tree. Your husband—ah, this laughter!—repeats the same sayings I used to quote, like the one about the tastiest morsel being in someone else's house, and the other, 'Do you beat it as you stir it? What delicious chocolate!' Comparisons like 'The mare should have a belly like a maiden, breasts like a married woman, and haunches like a widow' have cost me dear. And remember that 'The mother who spoils her child is nursing a viper in her bosom.' You be careful, too, not so much for fear of Plácida and your husband, who have a pretty good idea of your goings on, as for fear of this other world, since 'All that glitters is not gold,' and 'Don't lend your wife for a dance or your horse for a bullfight'—this laughter!—it won't do you any good. Remind your husband, 'Hold on to the ears once you're on the mule.' Another thing I beg you earnestly is, go to my son Felipe and tell him to take back the machine without any further delay. I hope that when he's spoken to you and looked at you, he'll be cured of his desire to keep running after you now that you're married, and you'll be cured too from this hour and moment and won't let yourself be led astray by Felipe or anyone else. Don't imagine that I enjoy laughing the way I did before, when my whole body shook with mirth. Now I'm condemned to keep on laughing, when I'm not moaning. Now my hour has come, and you know—ah, this terrible laughter!—now you know what I had to say to you. Amen. This laughter!

One fine day Plácida went into the parlor at Belén and took down the pictures, respecting only the images of the saints. She carried the photographs of the dead, the pornographic postcards, the useless ornaments out to the patio. Wanting the quickest way to get rid of them, she set fire to them.

All the same, the people were more terrified of the ghost than ready to take advantage of the warnings attributed to him. Those who were supposed to take the messages did not dare to approach the Trujillos; they preferred to journey to the village and spend money on Masses for the dead man so that his soul might rest in peace. They thought that by doing this and by putting the case before the parish priest (since Matiana would have nothing to do with them), they would be relieved of further responsibility for delivering the dead man's message. But the parish priest also urged them to follow the dictates of their consciences.

But lust for life and hope in the future was undiminished. Because 'Hope dies last.' That is to say, it never dies while life lasts. The good season had given rise to a round of festivities unknown for many years on the plain, which had forgotten that the body needs its times of merrymaking, that life cannot be all sorrow.

Rodeos and horse races were held, and during them many weddings and elopements were planned. They also served to make the women, even the married ones, sigh deeply—the more unattainable the objects of their emotions, the deeper the sighs—at the sight of the straight-backed young men who, galloping at full speed, caught their beast by the tail and overthrew it in the space agreed upon; of those who endured the interminable kicks of enraged animals; of those who, riding bareback with chests thrust out, and holding on to the horns of the cows, proudly made them circle around and around; of those who won the races after exciting moments of suspense; of those who made no mistake when they twirled their lassos and stuck fast in the saddle when they broke in the bucking animals. Sighs, almost like the lamentations of women mastered by force. It was always like this in the old days, although melancholy almost put an end to the custom; it was dropped like dancing, also renewed now on this farm and the other, the people eager for some outlet.

Ultimately, the reason for all this exaltation is to give an answer to death, ghosts, poverty, and injustice.

"Let the Whirlwind rant and rave. She's just running around in circles. We're not her peons. Let Don Epifanio's soul go on wandering in torment. He brought it on himself."

Nevertheless, when the merrymaking was over, when people found themselves alone at night on the farms, the voice from beyond the grave was heard again.

Ah, fellow Christians, why won't you pay attention to me or even out of fear pass on the messages which, for your good and mine, God allows me to give you. Look out, there's fire here, don't get burned. Instead, you're trying to throttle your consciences in wild living, trying to forget my example. Each bird likes its own nest. Listen, open your ears, don't pretend not to hear, we won't say my lamentations or the raucous laughter to which I'm condemned, but other warnings as clear as the miracles that Teófila's machine worked, and which you want to silence with noise, and not see. There is Rómulo, her own father, wavering, going back on his word, deceiving himself with false hopes of profit from the mines his grandfather had been so opposed to. At least tell him not to be a fool, not to let himself be carried away by Palemón and the renegade. God will give him his reward for not coveting other people's property. And if you won't heed my complaints, be warned by the machine with its miracles. Get them to return it quickly. No bull is brave with two spears in its side. How long, how long shall I have to wander about without rest?

They swore that they felt currents of icy air and heard the noise of chains when the dead man appeared. Apart from the person he chose to appear to, no one else saw or heard him. There are many who have had to accompany others in the ordeal and be present during the conversation with the departed spirit; they describe how they had to hold on to the unfortunate victim, who trembled worse than a man with chills, and collapsed like a bit of rag, senseless, every drop of blood drained from his body. They could hear his words, but not the ghost's. Of the latter they glimpsed only a shadow, at most, whose features they were unable to make out. What they did feel were the waves of cold air. They boast that as much courage was needed for all this as to speak to the ghost.

But even though this direct testimony is so impressive, it is dissipated by the noise of merrymaking. It is the same when one seeks forgetfulness in drunkenness.

There is another very strong reason for their merrymaking, the discovery of mines on the plain, an event crowning the faith of many generations. The stones veined with gold and silver, and found very close to the surface of the earth, are on display at the Towers of Babel for all to see. The samples that Jacob sent to the capital to be tested have revealed a very high content of metal. The preliminary work to start the mine has begun. It will go ahead more rapidly once the rainy season is over. What a new edge it gives their merrymaking to see the arrival of the time so long awaited with a faith handed down from father to son!

"No, I don't deny it, and Jacob knows that you gave us the first indications. Too bad you didn't make up your mind right then to take part in the business, you'd be a joint owner now. But nothing is lost. I'm sure that Gallo will give you a chance as he says. Of course, not with the same position you'd have got in your own right if you'd made up your mind in time, the way I kept telling you." Palemón was speaking to Rómulo on the day he took him to the foothills of

Cardos, where he showed him the veined stones and the preliminary work being done on the mine.

"How clearly I remember my grandfather's words, the ones I quoted to you at that time: 'There's gold here and who knows what other metals, but I hope no one decides to work it, because he'll make these farms unhappy and start an endless train of disasters.' " Rómulo was talking as if to himself as he ran his tongue over the stones the way his grandfather used to do. He sighed deeply.

"What a pessimist you are, compadre! Fortune is calling to you and you're trying your best to stuff your ears with cotton and cover your eyes with cobwebs. You see progress coming and instead of running after it you stand still, looking backward like a stone statue."

"No, don't think I'm not impressed. And I feel bad about all the opportunities slipping through my fingers. I'd like with all my heart to go ahead at full speed, but there's something broken inside me."

Excitement. Excitement everywhere.

Nevertheless, the real or exaggerated warnings of the soul in torment are heard again at night in the conscience, along with his threats to those who do not carry out his commands. Of all those who say he has spoken to them, not one dares to go to Plácida or any other of the children and pass on to them the dead man's urgent entreaties.

"Why should we? We'd actually be risking our lives, these wicked people don't stop at anything and wouldn't believe us anyhow. We'd better keep quiet and wait."

In view of the general cowardice, Matiana took upon herself, once again, the responsibilities of others.

Early one morning she left her house on foot. All alone she took the road to Belén.

"Forward in the name of the cross . . ."

Eyes flashing, voice thundering, implacable, hieratic, Matiana confronted Plácida.

"In the name of God . . ."

God's will be done. Good night

"God's will be done. Good night," said Madre Matiana, the blood streaming down over her horribly disfigured face. The crowd that had gathered did not want to leave her alone. Nor did it want to believe in such a disaster, the news of which was spreading like wildfire over the plain.

"They've put out Madre Matiana's eyes! Both eyes!"

No one, even for a moment, believed the cryptic explanation of the victim:

"It was a mad cat."

She would give no further information.

"Go home. There's nothing to do but accept God's will."

It was midnight but nobody went. People kept arriving.

The crime must have been committed at dusk, under cover of the heavy downpour falling at that time; but howling and bellowing could be heard above the noise of the storm, and this aroused the neighbors. Each house felt as if the lightning must strike it and set it on fire. The first to hear Matiana's cries was Rómulo, and he rushed to her through the rainstorm and lightning. There was no candle lit in the house, but the lightning revealed Matiana's face. Rómulo was horrified. He spent ages asking anxiously what had happened without getting any reply. Matiana, soaked with blood and rain, kept on shrieking inarticulately like a wounded animal; she groped about, groped along the walls, in despair. Rómulo stood as if turned to stone, not knowing what to do. It did not even occur to him to strike a light. He managed to hear Matiana saying: "I can see. I'm not blind. Get me some cobwebs." Shortly afterward, Doña Merced arrived. She was no less horrified, but she threw her arms round Matiana and pushed her toward the room. It was locked. She finally managed to get Matiana to take out the key. "I can see, I can see, I'm not blind." Merced lit candles and could see the sightless eyes hanging out of their sockets like shapeless fetuses. She hastily got Matiana to bed, asked what she should do for her, and, without waiting for a reply, sent Rómulo to put water on to boil. Matiana's groaning grew quieter.

"Send someone to tell the commissary at once," Merced told Rómulo.

"No, no, I don't want him to do that. Not for anything in the world. Just help me to wash and put some compresses on. I'll tell you what to put and where to find them. That will be better than cobwebs. But not the police, not for anything in the world, do you hear me? As you value your life." All covered in blood as she was, Matiana was sitting up in bed, supporting herself on her arms, trying to stand up. Merced calmed her and shouted to Rómulo to hurry up with boiling the water and to bring it to her quickly. Following Matiana's directions she found and set out the medicaments; she tried to staunch the blood, which was still flowing, then she washed her face. The pain made the patient flinch; she pressed her lips together, making an effort to keep back her moans.

"Until I can cut them, put on some compresses with arnica, as hot as I can bear. Then cover the wound with the ointment in this jar. Soak a big wad of cotton in this flask and put it on my eyes, and tie them up firmly with the new handkerchief I have there between the sheets. Boil some quassia in water, drop a piece of cane in it and a few drops of valerian, it's in that black bottle. I can't hear Rómulo. As you value your life, don't tell anyone, least of all Miguel, not for anything in the world."

Voices were heard, neighbors began to arrive. Matiana was shaking with anger as well as pain.

"How can you keep this hidden" Merced asked, "if heaven has spread the news with thunder and lightning?"

The storm was over, but the thunder sounded very near and there still were flashes of lightning.

"God's will be done. Forward in the name of the cross. At least keep people out of here. You can do that."

The poor woman touched and smelled the jars of medicine to make sure they were the right ones.

"If only my hand was firm at this moment, I'd cut that hanging flesh as if it were an umbilical cord," she said while Merced applied the hot compresses. "The truth is, I'm beginning a new life, without eyes."

The cattle had stopped bellowing, but the restless barking of the dogs filled the dark night.

Rómulo came back. Merced charged him to keep out, at all costs, the many people who were arriving from the distant farms, their voices rising, consternation on their faces, unable to give any very clear account of how or from whom they had learned the news. They were anxious to know exactly what had happened. If Matiana was still alive. If there was any hope of saving her life, helping her, avenging her. If a miracle by the machine, performed at Teófila's intercession, would do her any good. Who was or were the culprits. What was going to be done. The steadily growing crowd was getting more and more impatient. They kept demanding to see Matiana, to see for themselves that she was still alive. Rómulo could no longer keep them back. To appease them, he let one of the most insistent women go in. She came out at once, weeping. The belief spread: "We must go and get the machine, at any price, to see if it will perform the miracle of restoring her sight."

The suggestion had the effect of a stone dropped into a well, the ripples spreading in ever-widening circles, reaching farther and farther. The people gathered in the shadows, speaking urgently in low tones.

"The machine! There's nothing else we can do for the poor soul."

Those who did not gather in groups with a conspiratory air began to reckon up the miracles attributed to the blessed machine, and went over again the number of circumstances: the children of such and such neighbors were at their last gasp, and everybody had given them up for death when their parents invoked it, and the illness left them as though a hand had taken it away; so and so had had a cataract for years and years, so and so had suffered from leprosy and his flesh was falling off in pieces, and so and so suffered sharp attacks, still another neighbor couldn't even move with hydropsy, and all of them were cured by touching the machine of the Blessed Teófila. These names were well known. Many other recent cures of people with consumption, gall stones, paralysis, all hopeless cases, were added.

"The worst of it is that Don Felipe is delighted with the business, so in spite of having agreed with Don Jacob to give it back on the day his father was buried, there he is, making excuse after excuse, doing a nice business with the Holy Relic, charging people for touching it, even for permission to see it and pray to it."

This remark was another stone falling with great effect upon the darkened spirits of those who filled Matiana's patio.

The list of miracles ended. The conversations drew to an uneasy close, giving free reign to secret thoughts and deliberations.

The newcomers started off the conversations again, the hubbub increased, they were impatient to see Matiana.

Now they were knocking at the door, trying to force an entry, talking loudly, thoughtlessly. Neither the pleading and sharp rebukes of Merced, nor the compassionate gestures of Rómulo, nor the arguments of the understanding neighbors could restrain them. Only the presence of the Healer could persuade them to withdraw.

Finally it was announced that Matiana would come out.

A long time passed, during which impatience flared.

Finally Matiana appeared in the doorway of the Mysteries. They brought the pitch pine torches nearer to see her better. There was a shout of horror. Her head was bandaged, but the blood was seeping through the cotton and running down her face, which was drawn with pain. A frightful mask made more impressive by the flickering light of the torches. Her hands, always so determined, were trembling. In a voice which she tried to make calm, she said:

"God's will be done. We can only accept God's will. Go home. Goodnight." The effort was too much for her, and she fainted. Merced, Rómulo, and some of the bystanders lifted her up and carried her to her bed. Mingled voices:

"The Machine!"

"The cat! Let's kill it!"

"Justice!"

"Put an end to all of them!"

No one would go home.

It was after midnight.

Jacob arrived with a troop of horsemen. He went straight into the room and remained alone with Matiana. Silence reigned in the crowd. Time passed. A word was heard, indistinctly, then repeated clearly, and rapidly taken up by everyone:

"Justice!"

The flashlights, brought by those who had come with Jacob, flickered over heads and walls. The noise continued. Jacob appeared in the doorway and raised his hand to ask for silence. He advanced into the middle of the patio, the people gathered around him.

"Justice will be done. Have no doubt about that. The criminals will not escape. They will be made an example of, without mercy. I took the necessary measures before coming here. It is fitting that you all act as correctly as I tried to act, even though I risked losing your respect. I wanted to allow time for them to think things over and observe the law of their own free will. As long as they did nothing worse, some abuses could be borne. From now on it's going to be different. Stern punishment, even for misdemeanors, whoever commits them. Apparently that's the only way authority will be understood; with a stick in its hand. There's no reason for you to be here. Go to your homes, at once."

"Teófila's Machine!" The words could still be heard.

wealth. With a family you can be happy though poor and it gave him strength. He suffered great want, which made him compassionate and at the same time made him see that not everything in the world is good and that each man must live so as to be sufficient unto himself. This idea made him proud, but not vain or cruel. He could understand other people's weaknesses. He tried to correct them and could pardon them. He taught his family happiness with personal dignity, reserve, and silence, without too many or too few words. We didn't follow his example, we worried too much about the future and didn't learn to keep what he left us or be content with what we had, but that's another matter. This has been the misfortune not only of the Garabitos but of all the people of the Tierra Santa. Full of envy and without any pity. My grandfather knew fear and discouragement, but it never made him bitter. He never nursed a grudge against anyone. Life's harshness never bred hatred in him, only faithfulness and tenacity in fulfilling his obligations. And success never turned his head. On the contrary, he was humble with the poorest, keeping his pride for his equals or for people richer than he was. He never tried to revenge himself on others for his own faults, or for faults that weren't theirs, or for misfortunes that couldn't be helped, like natural disasters. I never heard him lie or take shelter behind false pretenses. He ordered his actions by the law of honor, as was the general custom in the Tierra Santa, from Cardos to La Tapona, from El Tabor to the ravine. How far we are, farther with each passing day, from that way of understanding life! When were there ever any crimes? At most, crimes of passion, but very rarely. Never for gain or to settle disputes. We might have known: 'A crouching cat is sure to pounce.' This is what I kept telling them but they wouldn't listen to me, not even Jacob. He trusted in his soldiers, but when the time came they couldn't defend Don Felipe from the crowd that was roused to fury by what had happened to Matiana and the Machine, and couldn't protect the Big House either. What I say is, "What do they gain by it?" Matiana's eyes won't be given back to her, or grow again. And there wasn't any need to go so far as to dig up the dead man. That will bring more calamities. But still less will be gained by arresting so many people just like that and blaming them for what happened. That's just shutting the barn door after the horse is stolen. Jacob wants to recover his authority through fear. If he'd acted in time he wouldn't have lost it, as I told him at the time of the robbery of the Machine and the shooting at Matiana. How many evils he would have avoided if he had listened to me. Now that it's all over, thank God, we're all sorry—even I am, and I didn't take part in it. We're chiefly sorry for having dug up the dead man God had already judged and sentenced. That wasn't the way to avenge our wrongs— and who was more wronged than me and my family?—or to stop his appearing to people. Matiana's the first to defend Plácida, saying she's in no way to blame, as was thought at first on account of the visit she paid her to give her a scolding. Neither was Don Felipe. Apparently it was all the work of Jesús and he's the only one who's escaped, at least up to the present. My poor dogs! I remember and I get angry again at the runaway. He should have been the one they hanged, although Don Felipe wasn't any angel. I think his dreadful death was a punishment for having kept and exploited the Machine. That's what Merced thinks and she's even said that the destruction of the Trujillos is the greatest miracle performed by Teófila's Holy Relic. I tried to scold her for these words and she nearly hit me with a piece of wood. I had to drop the subject and start thinking of other things. I wonder, for instance, if it can be true that they discovered my grandfather's treasure, and what has happened—I haven't had time to ask Palemón about it—concerning what I told him one time. It was the same day that we were talking about the mine, and I told him about the caves in La Tapona and the sloping banks upstream. My grandfather examined them carefully, talking of making a reservoir there. Surely they've explored those places and all the others I unwillingly told them about, remembering my wanderings with my grandfather. I feel tempted. And I'm angry, too, at having made rich men richer while I still haven't got a penny to bless myself with. But I won't say anything. I'll put up with it. Oh, if only the Machine would perform a miracle for me, for me, Teófila's father. I sacrificed myself in order to give her pleasure and buy her the Machine that—who would have thought it?—was to become Mithe people have been leaving her alone. A faithful few—Rómulo among the number—still visit her but less frequently. Left to herself, Matiana tries out her apprenticeship at living by touch. It doesn't seem to be any more difficult for her, illuminated as she is by her inner light.

On that ill-omened night, Jacob had no sooner made sure that the news was true than he sent messengers to bring doctors from Clamores and Jerez. Acting on the suspicions he had about the culprits, he immediately ordered certain steps to be taken. Not until then did he set off on horseback for Matiana's house, a distance which he covered in half an hour. He firmly opposed Matiana's determination to cut the strings hanging from her eye-sockets as soon as her pulse became stronger.

Closely questioned, Matiana confirmed the suspicions of the commissary. Some strangers whom Matiana could not describe had attacked her as she was crossing the courtyard, without giving her time to get a look at them; they had hurled themselves straight at her eyes; it was all premeditated, carried out rapidly, in complete silence, in complete darkness; she was aware of them jumping over the wall hurriedly; they were not on horseback; they must have gone along the bed of the stream. "Plácida's wicked work," was Jacob's opinion. Matiana had violently rejected that suggestion from the beginning. She was sure it was not Plácida; she had reasons for swearing this. News of the outrages began to arrive with the rescued Machine. Jacob sent fresh orders to stop the rioting. He himself went off to the farms where the outrages had taken place.

The reserve corps at Damasco had been powerless to restrain the fury of the attackers or to save Don Felipe. They had been ordered to arrest him but the mob took them by surprise and set fire to various places on the farm. Felipe had offered little resistance, merely firing a few shots; terror made him lose his self-control and this precipitated his ruin; other shots by the corps only infuriated the people further, and they besieged and immobilized the eight policemen there present.

While some returned to Betania with the rescued Machine, others advanced insolently on Belén. They discovered that the guards had seized Plácida and were taking her to Torres de San Miguel. An attack was hastily organized with the manifest intention of seizing the prisoner and lynching her. After a violent skirmish that left two attackers dead and many wounded, the police dispersed the attackers and went on, with Plácida safe and sound. The mob reorganized, and, learning from experience, did not follow the police but attacked the Big House, sacked and burned it, and finally vented its anger by digging up the body of Don Epifanio; no one could check its unbridled frenzy. On his arrival an hour later, Jacob succeeded in arresting some of those furiously engaged in the task of destruction.

Alarming news came from Galilea. Jesusito's resistance was fierce; several times he had driven back the forces of authority that besieged him, inflicting losses on them. Jacob marched off with reinforcements. The shooting lasted all night. Jacob, at the head of his force, succeeded in taking possession of the fortress, inside of which he found two individuals who had kept up the firing to cover the Sneak's retreat. Three more men had been captured before the attack began, when they had tried to run to the farm; they turned out to be those who were actually guilty of the attack on Matiana; their terror at being arrested betrayed them, as did the spots of blood on their clothes and hands; they ended by confessing it publicly.

Following up the trail of the Sneak brought no result. It went on, fruitlessly, for weeks.

The doctors were there when Jacob got back in the middle of the morning. They reached a decision and set to work, admiring the stoicism of the patient. At the entreaties of the commissary the doctor from Clamores stayed for two days. Her fever went down rapidly and she gained strength. Jacob came around to see her every day. He had sent some of his servants to look after the sick woman, but she began to beg them to leave her alone. Her request became a demand. Her visitors, except for a few faithful friends, were quite ready to take her at her word; either they found nothing new to look at, or they were tired of the blind old woman's mute suffering. Matiana kept opening the doors for the fickle, who went off happily in search of something different.

It was obviously important to let people know what those actually guilty of the injury to Matiana had confessed. It was arranged that the most important villagers should meet and talk to them. They were not men of the plain but some of the ruffians hired by Jesusito to make war on his brothers. The plot was revealed. The idea was to terrify the people by the pitiless mutilation of Matiana, which would immediately be laid at Plácida's door, and Jacob would be blamed for his inaction. Once indignation was aroused, Don Jesusito would advance directly to destroy Torres de San Miguel, where he had accomplices whose job it was to see that Jacob did not escape. When he was liquidated, it would be easy to fall upon Plácida, Felipe, and the other Trujillos who stood in the way.

It was quite true that Don Jesusito had spies and armed men in Jacob's territory. It was easy to catch them before they fled. They were made to confess their guilt publicly.

Amid great commotion it was noised abroad that troops would come to take away the prisoners. Soldiers had never been seen in the Tierra Santa, or else the oldest villagers had forgotten them. It caused a general sensation when the picket of horsemen crossed the Sierra de Cardos, passed along by Getsemaní, camped in Jerusalén, and rode around by Damasco, Betania, and Belén with a display of force. The uniforms, the kepis, the long weapons, the gleaming bayonets, the leather straps, the well-matched horses and their saddles, the shape of the bugle and the way they blew on it, the words of command and the order of the movements, the captain's unsheathed sword and the sumptuous difference of his uniform, the regulation stiffness of each movement—these things shook the region.

The display of force culminated in the ley fuga. The first to fall, in the vicinity of Galilea—they say they took them there to check some facts—were the spies caught inside Torres de San Miguel. A few days later they were followed by those who had put out Matiana's eyes. The bodies, tied on a mule's back, were taken around the farms, stopping wherever there were groups of villagers. The idea seemed to be to exhibit them as a warning, although the soldiers tried to pretend that it was an accident of the journey.

The other men arrested, and their families, became frightened.

Jacob waited till he was asked to free those mixed up in the death of Felipe, the digging up of Don Epifanio, and the damage done at Damasco and Belén. He pretended to be inflexible. He managed to get as many people as possible involved in the requests, including the most important villagers. He went around raising hopes, bargaining and earning gratitude so that the whole neighborhood would feel itself under an obligation to him for the favor of his indulgence. Unwillingly, he started setting the prisoners free. But these and their families had already struck a bargain with the miraculous Machine, and they attributed to a miracle of the Machine the favor of their liberty. (Later, the ex-votos exaggerated the event, showing the giver fleeing under a rain of bullets which the troop of soldiers aimed at him, or facing a firing squad, or about to be hanged on a tree.)

There were no more rumors of any further appearances of Don Epifanio. The Sacred Machine added this relief to the list of its miracles.

Rómulo's faith was absolute when he affirmed that the greatest miracle of the Relic was that granted to Doña Merced. She was so busy worshipping the Machine and attending to all the many tasks involved in its cult that her bad temper disappeared; she became kinder to her husband again. There are some who are not quite ready to admit this, blaming Doña Merced's bitterness on the wickedness of Don Epifanio, who had sown trouble between Rómulo and his wife. "But after all," thought Rómulo, "wasn't it the Machine that came and made everything all right? Why beat around the bush?"

How true it is that everything has its good side, and that Our Lord turns evil into good. All the power, the money, the shrewdness of Miguel Arcángel were not enough. Poor Matiana's sacrifice was necessary for the Machine to work the Miracle of setting the blood of the men on fire, they seemed to have nothing but water in their veins before, and also to arouse their sense of dignity, hurling them against those who stood with their feet on their necks and lost no opportunity to humiliate them. I tried and failed. No one would follow me. Matiana, with her sacrifice, moved the Machine to have pity, and to fill the men with the courage to go straight off and take it by force from the wicked hands that kept it, and to restore it to the place where the blessed hands of Teófila had consecrated it. What long months of human authority had failed to do was done in a short space of time. And in the process the Machine also removed the scourges of the plain, reduced to ashes the seat of their abominations, brought to dust the last ramparts of their injustices. Compared with this punishment, the visitation of God's wrath, the poor men who were killed by bullets, hunted from behind like hares, seem innocent, however guilty they actually may have been. As it says in the proverb, 'The man who gives the command is the guilty party.' Miguel Arcángel knows what he's doing. The worst of it is that the soldiers have found their way here now, and we'll never get rid of them. Now that we're free from one lot of oppressors, another lot of worse ones will take their place. Yes, certainly worse, because the new ones bring what they call Progress, and as far as I can see this is a series of tricks very well worked out and practiced, in addition to better weapons and ready money. But anyhow it's very human to want changes, even though we know the new is worse than the old, since when all is said and done 'No evil can last forever.' I can't understand how the land managed to put up with the Trujillos for so many years, the way they ground us underfoot to their hearts' content. They seemed to be immortal. A breath from the Machine swept them out of our way and put an end to their plans for maintaining their rule. It was even a good thing they stole it, they didn't know it would bring about their destruction. And I consider it was worth all the anguish and suffering that seemed as if it would never end, the pain I felt at seeing them take Teófila's body out to the graveyard. And Matiana's blindness was not in vain if by it the destruction of the wicked and the triumph of the Holy Relic could be brought about. When I kneel before it I don't feel time passing. I seem to be dreaming happily. Then I recall the horrors of that night when the Miraculous Machine returned in triumph, the horror of seeing Matiana trying to put her eyes back in place, all bloody, and then feeling around for cobwebs to place in

"I may be misjudging him, I hate him so much. You're a thousand times worse than he is. There's no comparison."

"At least I'm not capable of planning a crime and sheltering behind the fact that you'll be accused of it immediately and given no time to prove your innocence. I tell you this, not to excuse myself, but to make you understand, not so much the past as what I suggest you do of your own free will: go far away until the commotion is over and people's feelings quiet down with the passing of time."

"You clown! Why don't you have me hanged once and for all? They must have told you they refused to let me spare you the trouble."

The struggle went on for several days on two fronts: to prevent Plácida from attempting to commit suicide again and to convince her of the danger she ran by remaining on the plain. Trembling with indignation, she refused in the vilest language to take the money Jacob offered her for the journey. She rejected the suggestion that she should spend some time on the farm up in the mountains where she had lived for so long. In a rage she rejected the suggestion that for her protection she should stay at Torres de San Miguel.

"I've told you a thousand times, I'll either stay in my own house or die. Why does it take you so long to decide which you want me to do? You'd rather argue. A lot it matters to you what happens to me, you play-actor!"

One day, she burst out:

"I've decided you aren't such a clown as I thought. The fact is, you're afraid of me, because of what may happen to you if I stay on my own property. As my father used to say, 'When the muleteer sells his mule it's sure to be because the saddle has galled him,' and the one about 'A man who's setting off skyrockets can't see the one in front of him,' and 'When the shop is put in order, the flies come around.' On the other hand, you won't risk killing me, you'd prefer others to do that, the same as with Felipe, my brother. But they know your game now and the marked cards you use."

"You stubborn fool! Do as you please. Anyhow, the worst is over."

"Yes, you set up a reign of terror by shooting unarmed men in the back and letting the soldiers carry them off, by throwing the stone and hiding, then washing your hands, you pig! And you'll still play cat and mouse, you've come out of it very nicely, you got a good price for your generosity toward the criminals who killed Felipe, and the dirty brutes who profaned my father's body—though after all, even if it seems incredible and you've denied him, he was also your father. It was for your own convenience you let them go, making them beg for their freedom. You clown, you figure that the only one with a grudge is in your hands and can't demand justice from the law because you're the law. A nice joke that is! Yes, you're a thousand times worse than the man who made a laughingstock out of you when you tried to destroy him. 'Shame past is soon forgot but the advantage gained remains.' That's your motto. And another is, 'Stolen goods don't become the thief but they enrich him'."

"What you should do is get married, to see if that will cure your madness and make you gentler, you stubborn blockhead."

These words enraged her further.

Jacob let her go as she wished, unable to make her accept clothes or money or anything at all.

Plácida set off, daring them to kill her. Starting at Rómulo's, she went around to the houses of all those she considered her enemies and guilty of taking her property. She heaped insults on them; she dared them to hang her as they had hanged her brother; she said she had brought nothing to defend herself with, that at least they could stone her or she would stone them. No one accepted her challenge. The children, once they had got over their fright at sight of her, laughed at her, shouted after her, "Madwoman! Madwoman!" Plácida ran after them, throwing stones. She spent some days among the ruins of Damasco. She walked as far as Galilea. Finally she took refuge in what was left of the Big House.

Disheveled, haggard, covered in rags, she came to Matiana one afternoon, threw herself at her feet, flung her arms around her knees. "Take me in. I've come to serve you on my knees, in penitence for the evil those of my family have done you, and to beg you to forgive us and calm down the wrath against them. I know you defended me. That's what I'm relying on, and the fact that you can

fear and pain. It still writhes and groans and sweats at the mere
announcement that God is coming to make use of it. And it suffers
even at the thought of aiding a desperate neighbor, a thought that
fills the spirit with pleasure. I managed to hope, after enduring the
last terrible suffering, that the burden would be lighter for the spirit,
and that now, without eyes, the flesh would make rapid progress.
But here, with this poor creature, it rears itself up again like a young
untamed mare, just as in those long months that wore down my
spirit, inducing it to rebel, after I knew the sentence Justice would
pass on the unhappy family and the price I would pay for others.
"It's unjust!" the flesh cried in terror, and the spirit, forced along by
the fearful flesh, seconded it. Therefore, since my full consent was
necessary for the sacrifice, Justice couldn't be done on that day when
Jesús missed, because of the lack of harmony between my weaknesses and the Design of the Invisible Powers. They had to wait long
enough for the spirit to take command and, when the time came,
endure the suffering, worse than death or birth and perhaps more
despairing. My worst imaginings paled at the hour of suffering, so
that I couldn't keep back the howls of pain and the terror, and the
spirit couldn't regain control until a long time afterwards, until the
flesh felt the company of Rómulo and Merced. Even then, with my
eyes hanging out, I cherished the illusion that I wouldn't be blind,
because I could see lightning flashes and other lights dancing about
in my brain. This is what happens when the eyes are plucked out,
a terrible and interminable dancing of lights hammering in your
head. That's why, when Rómulo came, I cried out, "I can see, I'm
not blind," and although I was well aware it was only a hopeless
illusion, my hands tried to put back the eyes that had been torn out.
Now the body is insubordinate again, crying out: "The Whirlwind
is guilty of the horrors you suffered. It's unfair for her to try to
impose herself upon you by hypocrisy. She's a savage woman, and
mad, too, absolutely mad. At any minute she'll fly into a rage, she'll
tear out your hair and end up by strangling you. With her family
you never know to what lengths they'll go. The least she'll do is spy
out your secrets, mix up your cures, sap your strength. Are you
going to let her in blindly to the room of Mysteries, let her end up

—and she will—by throwing you out the way she did with Amanda? No, she doesn't come here with good intentions. I assure you of that. How can you believe this horrible woman wants to serve you? On the contrary, she's coming here to order you around, to overthrow you, to avenge herself, to humiliate you. You're not a child who can't understand. Just remember the kind of person she's been and how she behaved toward her father. Now she'll be worse, seeing she's insane. It isn't fair for her to be able to wheedle you into taking pity on her." My old flesh seems like a young filly off the lead. Yes, Plácida seems to have gone mad. Since this is a consequence of the price demanded above, a price I should pay, to a certain degree I'm to blame for her madness and must make reparation. To tell the truth I never really knew what the Justice of God meant, or the kind of sacrifice that would be required of me. I only knew the Will, the Plan, but not the details. How astonished the people are, and some have said so, how astonished I didn't foresee what would happen, so as to be prepared, as though it were easy to face the Powers on High and make them change their course, especially when I had agreed beforehand to suffer whatever came, and when I was expecting it without knowing the day or the hour or the kind of torment they had in store for me. The worst of it is that Miguel Arcángel allowed himself to be lead astray, ignoring my warnings and forgetting the saying, 'With what measure ye mete, it shall be meted out to you again, and he who kills in error . . .' Worse, bringing soldiers. From now on he'll only be able to keep his position by force of arms, by terror, just building on sand the way the Trujillos did. All his money, all his cunning won't help. Life is like this, no one learns from his own experience. One evil goes and another comes. After the Trujillos, the Gallos. Poor Miguel Arcángel! He's not a bad man, but he took the downward road and strayed from the straight and narrow path. God in Three Persons, guide me so that I may know what to do with this pitiful child!

Underneath their admiration and fear, the people felt resentment against the King of Diamonds, however much some of them paid lip service to his determination, his speed of action, his magnanimity.

What they could not forgive him was the drastic display of authority and his making them feel that he was above them all, lord and master of lives and estates, discarding the mask of being just another neighbor or at most a distinguished villager because of his wealth and his experience. The office of commissary was understood to be a title to display, not a justification for unsheathing his sword, at least not the way he did.

On the other hand, in their heart of hearts the people felt a certain unwillingness to accept in one and the same person the commissary in command of armed forces and the investor with a large income. Endless proverbs were constantly on the lips of the dissatisfied: 'You can't have your cake and eat it too, or ring the bells and walk in the procession, or make soup from tortillas, or toast your tortillas and make tacos of them as well, or mix enchiladas with chilaquiles, or serve two masters, or dance in calzoneras, or down a drink at one gulp, or chew everything in one mouthful, since the important thing is not to eat but to digest your food and the pot is in no position to call the kettle black.'

Jacob allowed more than enough time for the clouds to disperse and the inauguration of electricity to produce the anticipated effect.

The worst part of the dogdays intervened, July and August.

The dread month of August, calamitous, bringing stillness, the baleful moon, diseases to plants, people, and cattle, and death to old people and children. Month of anguish, a time that brings toppling down the highest hopes. The most promising cornfields are blighted and burn up in the drought; the fattest cattle grow thin and fall prey to the diseases brought by the heat; the healthiest children die off in a twinkling with diarrhea and fevers; looking at this moon makes one blind; any sore becomes infected, any illness gets worse suddenly and cannot be cured; water, fruit, food go bad, are rapidly infested with worms; the strings of insects are deadly; the air is full of death-bearing germs; the ponds are poisonous. Death and the devil lie in wait everywhere, with their train of calamities. The devil flies around at the end of the dogdays, at the end of dread August.

This was when the plain expected that Plácida would strangle

Matiana—all kept a watchful eye open—or do away with her in some other fashion. They kept telling Matiana this, in all kinds of ways, but Matiana seemed to be deaf as well as blind.

The dread day of St. Bartholomew drew near, came, and went. Day when the devil and his vassals have a free hand. The days immediately following it went by, September came. Matiana was still alive, still following her tranquil ways.

Plácida maintained her docile desire to be the slave and daughter of the thaumaturgist; she also continued in her other, stranger form of madness, that of giving away the property of the Trujillos—lands, animals, tools—to those who had been laborers and sharecroppers on her family's estates.

Then the people on the farms raised their voices, glorifying in this the greatest miracle of the Blessed Machine, which had tamed the wild beast of Belén, kept her at peace, stirred her heart and moved it to pity.

Differences of opinion and heated discussions were inevitable: that Matiana had Plácida bewitched, or that Jacob had given her a drug that turned her wits, or that the madness had come upon her as a result of the outrages of the soldiers. Nor was there a lack of jokes at her expense.

"What a pity," Palemón said, "what a pity that friend Merced burned the new sewing machine Jacob brought to Belén at Epiphany, and that Jesusito took it away from Plácida so cruelly. Otherwise, at the rate the Whirlwind is moving toward sainthood, we'd soon have two miracle-working machines in this blessed land." Rómulo and several villagers were disgusted at this joke, which they considered blasphemous.

The drought was brief and benign. There were fewer illnesses, deaths, and other misfortunes than in previous years. St. Bartholomew's Day passed peacefully and the dogdays came and went. Whether because of this or whether because she had fallen into discredit as a healer and had been replaced by the Machine of the Blessed Teófila, the fact was that Matiana had few calls, when in other years she could not keep up with the demands made on her to heal, to help at deathbeds, to put the dead in their shrouds, to exorcise, to purify people, cattle, and lands. So Matiana need not have hastened to train Plácida to help her in these tasks or to perform them herself. For the first time she acted as the healer's successor, an office Matiana had decided to confer on her, provided that when she had demonstrated her capacity and merit, the Unseen Powers gave their consent, since according to Matiana there is One above who takes, gives, and assigns. It was not long before the tongues of Palemón and others wagged maliciously.

"She certainly let go of a bird in the hand for two in the bush. She refused to inherit a good fortune to come and be the successor of a bundle of mysteries. A fine exchange!"

The passing of the dogdays, the good, corn-producing rain that September brought in its train, and even the gossip and jokes, favored Jacob's plans. He had managed to keep out of sight from the time he went off with the soldiers at the end of July.

Persistent rumors circulated around the farms regarding the great fiestas being prepared at Torres de San Miguel to celebrate the Fifteenth and Sixteenth of September* with the inauguration of electricity, and these rumors were preparing the ground. At the beginning of the month the more important farmers began to receive formal invitations with the program of events. The Sunday before the Fifteenth, a group with pipes and firecrackers went around the farms, giving out colored programs with photographs of the national heroes.

Memories stirred. How many years was it since the national birthday had been celebrated anywhere on the plain! So many that the custom had been forgotten; the day passed unnoticed by the majority, and fewer and fewer villagers took the trouble to go to the town for the Fifteenth.

The King of Diamonds had flags and tricolor ribbons distributed free to every house. They caught the people's fancy and were very popular. They pleased chiefly because they were a gift.

Things were going like clockwork. Even worry about the whereabouts and the flight from justice of Don Jesusito were forgotten.

---

* The days when Mexico's independence from Spain is celebrated.

Jacob had managed to have him captured and brought to trial in the capital, where he fled and tried to stir up trouble to obtain justice. Gallo redoubled his care to keep the rebel's capture a secret; it only got out as a rumor which Jacob denied.

Heaven was on the side of the victor. The rains, which had kept up, stopped on the eve of the celebrations; the fourteenth dawned clear, bringing Indian summer.

People started arriving on the morning of the Fifteenth. First came peddlers and curiosity-mongers, the former to get a good place to set out their wares, the latter to get a good look at the machine that would produce electricity and to watch the last preparations for the event. But they had to work for the privilege. The King of Diamonds and his helpers, jokingly and in earnest, set them to work, since there was work for all: sweeping, watering, carrying planks, putting up posts, making festoons and bunches of sweet-scented marigolds, hanging them up, helping the carpenters to put up fixtures.

Rómulo was one of those helping to see that the jobs were done quickly.

In the afternoon the crowd increased. Neither the pastorals at Belén nor the dances at Getsemaní in their best years had attracted such a multitude. Most of the people were prepared to spend the night at Torres de San Miguel, for although the greatest attraction consisted in seeing the electricity and remembering or being disillusioned concerning the famous Grito,* they were also as interested in watching the Great Historical and Allegorical Procession, announced for the morning of the Sixteenth, and the Great Battle of the Flowers with the Sensational Rodeo that would take up the whole afternoon. A Band Concert and Fireworks with castles and squibs completed the program, which would also include Queens and Other Great Amusing and Thrilling Surprises.

The first surprise was the presence of Jacob's wife and his mother, who had arrived on the fourteenth at dusk, after so long an absence that they seemed almost legendary figures.

* The "shout" or call to arms with which Padre Hidalgo launched the war of independence.

Sara Gallo was older, but still vigorous and active, and retained her air of resolution and integrity. 'A good vessel does not lose its value even when old.' For Florentina time had stood still and work and years had merely served to round out her figure and enhance her charms. Rómulo and other old men could not believe in this miracle. (Ah, Florentina!)

The two women set to work together the moment they arrived. They were the first to undertake and direct the tasks that still remained to be done. They were anxious to give food not only to those who were taking part in the celebrations of the Fifteenth but also to all those who came to the house. They did this with country simplicity, which at once earned them the devotion of the country-people. Both of them had amazing memories; they addressed people by their names and recognized young people by family resemblances; they recalled incidents, important and trivial, that flattered those concerned, and asked questions about debts and interests. It seemed as though they had just returned from a short trip. Even those who had not known them before and those who had not even heard of them followed them about, flocked around them, would not leave them, hanging on their words and watching them. Doña Merced came to pay them a hasty visit, but her concern for the worship of the Blessed Machine would not let her stay for the merrymaking and she hurried back to Betania.

As dusk fell, the electric plant was set going, while the people crowded together with fearful expectation, jostling each other, trying not to miss a single thrilling detail of the operation, expecting at any moment some diabolical surprise. And this seemed imminent from the formidable noise produced by the machine, the vibration and giddy gyrations of the pulleys, the rapid whirring of the band, the dirty faces of the mechanics who went to and fro inspecting again and again as though possessed by some anxiety or fear. Most of those standng around withdrew as the noise started. But curiosity prevailed and they watched from a distance. They waited. Their ears were deafened. No sign of anything supernatural. They got tired and started moving off. The arrival of the music carried off the last curiosity-mongers.

The crowd collected around the platform where Jacob was going to inaugurate the power plant. The same band of musicians that he took to Belén, now reinforced, played gay melodies, drowning unpleasant memories and cares.

Night had fallen. The darkness was lit, as it had been for centuries in the countryside, by pitch pine torches, only now there were more of them, to celebrate a festival and commemorate the passing from one era to another. Expectation mounted, kept less and less in check by the heroic efforts of the musicians. There were impatient murmurings, whistles, thumping, catcalls.

Finally the King of Diamonds appeared with his following of distinguished villagers; the police honor guard heard the order, "Attention!"

Just as the magistrate was about to set foot on the first step of the ceremonial platform, two dark shapes placed themselves resolutely in his path. Jacob, taken by surprise, stopped short. In the shadows he recognized Plácida, who was leading Matiana, both of them illuminated by the dramatic chiaroscuro of the torches and the smoke. The fresh breeze of an unexpected storm was blowing. Amazement was reflected in the first row of spectators.

Plácida stood there, firm, mute, her eyes gleaming, holding on to Matiana with one arm. There was a sudden clap of thunder. Matiana moved forward, raised one arm—the flickering light from the torches made it now longer, now shorter—and lifted up her head. Her face was gaunt, as though carved, the empty eye sockets filled with reddish gleams. She raised her voice:

"Take it, Miguel Arcángel, take this that I never accepted from you, that you have always refused to take back. I have made this journey with great sacrifice to hand it back to you, and to remind you that the higher you rise the greater your fall will be. There are no short cuts in the straight and narrow path."

Since no hand received the package she held out, Matiana let it fall. It was the gold coins that Jacob had begged her to take that night on his return to the plain. The clink of metal was drowned by a second, louder clap of thunder.

"God's will be done. Good night." Pulling Plácida after her, Matiana rapidly withdrew, without giving Jacob time to answer or to put into action his intention to detain her.

Just as the people hiss when the fireworks displays fail to start on time, or when the fireworks fail to catch, so those at the back, unaware of the presence of Matiana and Plácida, or of the incident which had occurred, burst out in displays of impatience.

Jacob and those with him climbed hastily onto the platform, and the current was turned on at once. As the strings of bulbs lit up, the exclamation of surprise was unanimous, delaying the reaction of applause mingled with fanfares and the explosion of firecrackers. One by one the torches were put out. The King of Diamonds held up his hand for silence; without waiting for complete quiet, he started his speech:

"I like to do things on a big scale . . ."

Another flash of lightning shone, followed by a furious clap of thunder. One by one, big and heavy, the first drops of rain began to fall.